Niramaya

A Female Medic's War Journey

Niramaya

A Female Medic's
War Journey

SEAN C WARD

Troubador Publishing Ltd
Unit E2 Airfield Business Park,
Harrison Road, Market Harborough,
Leicestershire LE16 7UL
Tel: 0116 279 2299
Email: books@troubador.co.uk
Web: www.troubador.co.uk

ISBN 978 1 83628 256 3

British Library Cataloguing in Publication Data.
A catalogue record for this book is available from the British Library.

The manufacturer's authorised representative in the EU for product safety is
Authorised Rep Compliance Ltd, 71 Lower Baggot Street, Dublin D02 P593
Ireland (www.arccompliance.com).

Printed and bound in Great Britain by 4edge Limited
Typeset in 11pt Minion Pro by Troubador Publishing Ltd, Leicester, UK

This book is dedicated to war medics.

নিরাময়

Nirāmaẏa means 'healing' in the Bengali language.

Author's Note

Niramaya: A Female Medic's War Journey is a work of fiction set in the first two weeks of December 1971, when East Pakistan became Bangladesh following the Bangladesh War of Liberation. The Bengali people occupy a large proportion of the northeast of the Indian subcontinent in the People's Republic of Bangladesh and the state of West Bengal in India. Sunni Islam is the religion of most people in Bangladesh, followed by Hinduism, and smaller numbers practice Buddhism and Christianity, among others. Religious harmony in Bangladesh, like in every other country, is a work in progress, and the toleration depicted between various ethnic and religious groups in this book may seem fanciful to experienced observers of society in Bangladesh.

Bangladesh, for the most part, is located on the delta plain of the world's greatest rivers, including the Ganges (Padma) and Brahmaputra (Jamuna). The country is frequently subjected to cyclones, flooding, and storm surges. The country has beautiful mountains, but the seemingly endless alluvial plains are among the most alluring features of the country. Events in this book take place in areas only a few metres above sea level, but it was hard not to mention mountains for dramatic effect in some of the scenes.

Of course, the characters are fictitious. The women featured in the story are composites of some extraordinary women encountered while doing voluntary development work in northern areas of the Indian subcontinent. Their stories are real. The stories of the suffering experienced by people, mainly women, in the Bangladesh War of Liberation are real. The timely intervention by the Indian Army in the final months of 1971 brought an end to the atrocities. It resulted in independence for Bangladesh, now a thriving country.

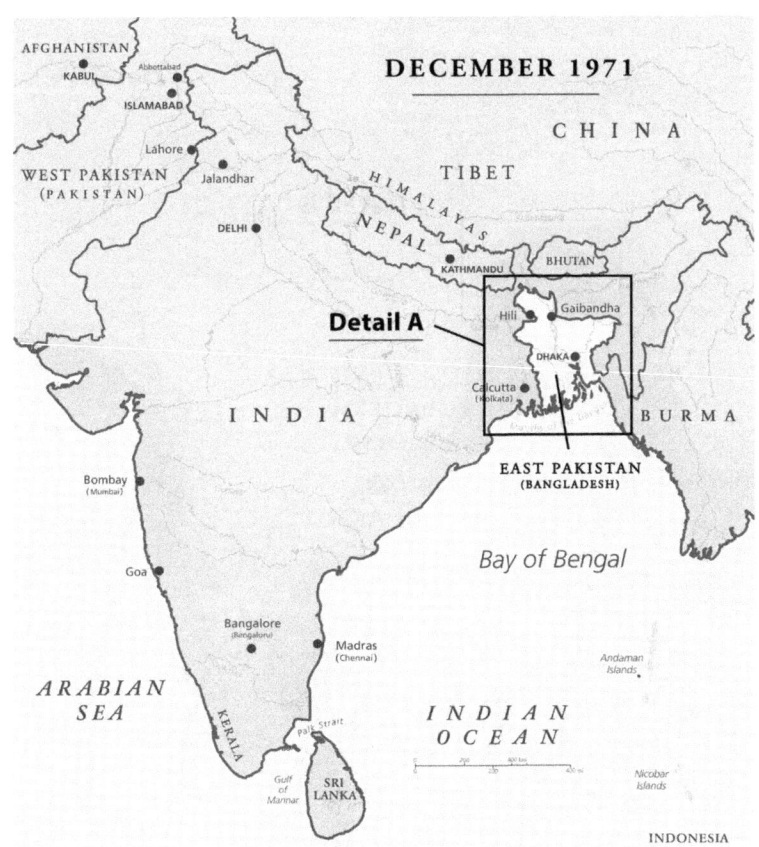

The Indian Subcontinent

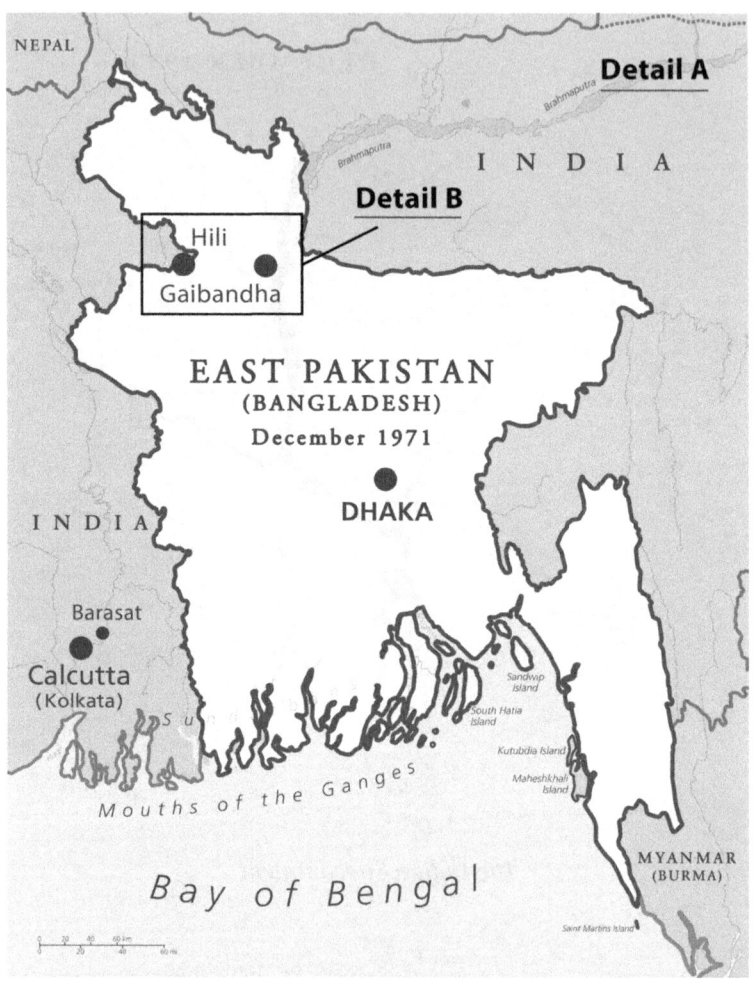

Detail A: East Pakistan (Bangladesh)

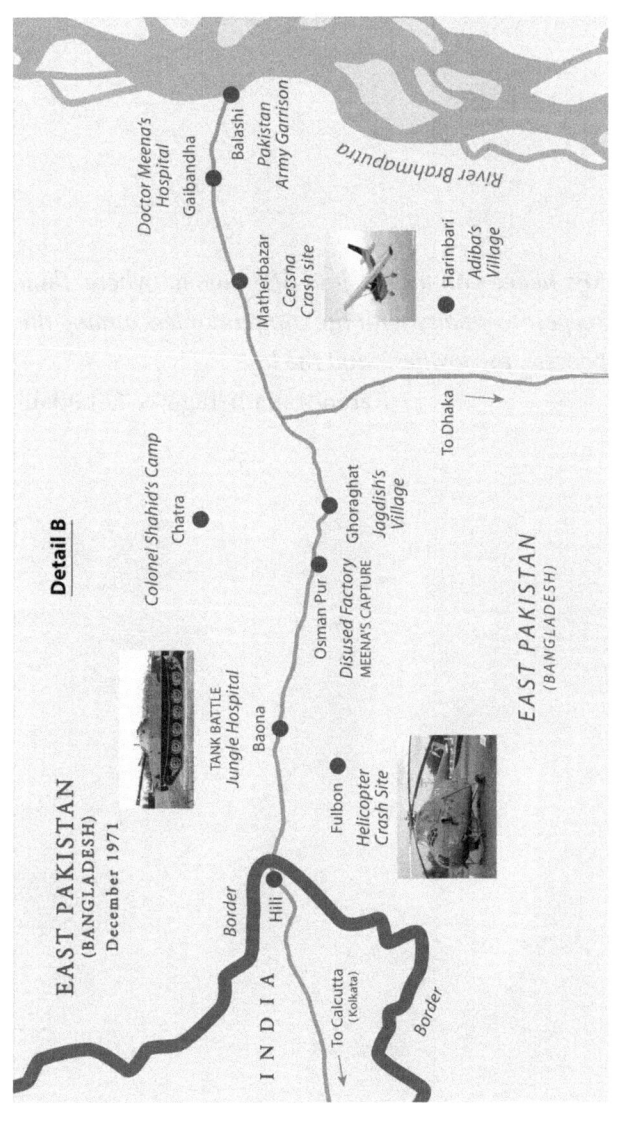

Detail B: East Pakistan (Bangladesh)

xi

My heart can never find its way to where thou keepest company with the companionless among the poorest, the lowliest, and the lost.

Rabindranath Tagore, 'Gitanjali'

Chapter 1

Arrivals Hall, Calcutta Airport, December 1971.

A bead of sweat ran down his back, and worse, an annoying little rivulet trickled around his groin. The urge to scratch was overwhelming, but Shane had to maintain decorum because of the crowd watching him as he emerged from the customs area. What was so interesting about foreigners that made these people stare so intensely at him? It was as if they knew the cause of his discomfort and could not wait for him to scratch. He would not give in, even though the stares of the multitude were neutralised by the stunning smile of one particular individual in their midst. He was to be met by a lady doctor and expected to find a stern-looking, no-nonsense medic, but the sudden bond with the lady in the crowd overwhelmed him. His heart skipped a beat when she beckoned him over to join her at the barrier separating them.

***

The December humidity was intense as Meena and her driver, Lal, drove through the congested streets of Calcutta to make the airport on time. Surrounded by taxis, rickshaws, buses, and pedestrians, they rounded the figure of a white cow sitting in the middle of the road, chewing the cud and oblivious to its surroundings. The man driving the vehicle following them kept pace but at a discreet distance. Meena was on a nodding acquaintance with him by now. Her father's man, no doubt. After all, her father had hinted that he would know her every move on entering India from East Pakistan. They had reached the final month of 1971 and once again, the tensions were mounting on the border since the recent shelling of an Indian Army forward lookout post by the Pakistani military, frustrated by Indian collusion with insurgents in the area.

Meena had crossed the border in a convoy of the Red Cross, whose many stations in the troubled region were an ominous sign of things to come. She was loosely associated with them as a doctor and radiologist. Her mission was to collect a European technician from Calcutta Airport and, more importantly, the accompanying equipment, including vital parts for her X-ray machine. How she was to get the technician and equipment to her hospital in Gaibandha in East Pakistan, she did not know since the technician had been given a permit to enter the border area on the strict understanding that both he and his equipment remain on the Indian side of the border.

The press of people was agonising when she finally reached the airport arrivals hall. As on previous occasions, she was aware that only some of these people were meeting arriving passengers; the rest were there for various reasons, mainly to exploit the many foreigners who chose this city as a starting point in their quest for answers to life's many questions. The Indian culture usually subsumed these foreigners, and they would suffer upon returning to their homes while trying to reconcile their vivid experiences on the subcontinent with the relative dullness of life in their home countries.

The sliding doors opened again, and another group of bewildered-looking foreigners was disgorged from the customs hall. Meena scanned the newcomers as the people around her jostled for a better position in the crowd, which would give them access to the foreigners and the business opportunities they presented. Fighting her way to the front, Meena instinctively recognised the person she was there to meet.

Meena beckoned the man to join her. The foreigner had that look in his eyes, a strange mixture of puzzlement and adoration. Meena was used to this but smiled, nonetheless. She immediately felt that she could control this encounter. However, she needed to be careful because her mission was so important that she would have to cultivate a strong bond with this man to retain him as an ally in what she had planned. She was conscious that, in the past, her looks had served her well but at a price, and the look in this man's eyes urged caution. In her mind, men usually fell into two categories: those who followed basic instincts with obvious consequences and those who were attracted to her as a challenge because she had an air of confidence about her that seemed threatening.

She was good at hiding her weaknesses but always feared the breaching of her defenses and what form it might take. The close calls in the past concerned her physical attraction to people, but she was determined not to succumb to this in the future. She convinced herself that she would fully control any such encounter. But this encounter was proving to be intense, and she could not control the feelings coursing through her body, so she endeavored to strengthen her defenses somewhat, while simultaneously considering how easy those defenses were to breach.

Usually, when meeting people for the first time, she had the ability to know which traits of her personality would interact best with the new acquaintance. Looking at this man should have initiated this process, but fear and panic rose in her when she realised that no strategy was forthcoming. The smile on his face told her he had her at a disadvantage. Mentally, she retreated and resorted to formal. Formal was more appropriate in this instance, she convinced herself. Usually, she dominated first encounters with men, intellectually or by force of beauty. Subconsciously, she was aware of the usefulness of using both to advance her cause. Realistically, there would always be a time when all emotional gamesmanship proved ineffective, and total honesty needed to form the basis of a first encounter with strangers. She gave a brief greeting in German as she welcomed the man to India in an attempt to neutralize his stare. "We can converse in German if you wish, but I only know about six words of that language, so that would leave me at a disadvantage," Shane said with a smile.

She considered this development. The voice was softer than she had anticipated, but his sense of humour was evident. "Oh, I'm sorry, I expected somebody from Germany since the equipment originated there. And anyway, you look German," Meena said snootily, and immediately regretted it. He seemed to realise this and decided not to press the issue on how a German looked. Instead, he smiled while rubbing his chin. They both readjusted mentally, and their smiles and eye contact indicated a truce; they would take each other more seriously from now on.

Neither knew where this sudden bonding would take them in the future, but the immediate priority was work, and the arrival of two porters struggling with a heavy trolley diverted their attention from each other. "This is the equipment then," Shane said. "I had to pay a fortune in excess baggage because some of the assembly contains lead. I considered discarding the wooden crate, but the X-ray component is also quite delicate. Do you know what happened to the original damaged parts of your X-ray machine? It would be helpful to have them if we need to use some of the components during assembly."

Meena had to think of a credible answer without revealing that the damaged X-ray machine was actually in her hospital in East Pakistan. That particular revelation could come later when she got to know this man better. "I'm sure they were stolen," she said, "and are currently being meticulously copied by some entrepreneur in a remote factory. Indians are world leaders at replicating complex technology, and I would not be surprised if dozens of these items become available in the market within a few months." She did not wish to discourage him by disclosing the fact that Pakistani soldiers had invaded her hospital in search of insurgents who had been active near her hospital. When they eventually departed, she discovered a bullet hole in the X-ray tube inside the protective housing of the machine, rendering it useless. Several calls through the Red Cross eventually secured the replacement part and the services of a technician to carry out the repairs. "I'm Dr Meena, by the way," she said, to change the subject. Exchanging names always brought an air of expectancy. She felt that revealing a name opened another window into a person's character. It was as if the name carried the force of one's personality. She hoped he would have a strong name.

"Shane Ryan, and I'm Irish," he said. She wasn't disappointed. Some names had a nice enigmatic quality, and she tried to ascribe character traits to this new acquaintance. He seemed aloof and distant. Shy, maybe, but with a commanding physical presence. "I'm wondering why you couldn't wait until they become available, because this seems like a lot of trouble."

Shane didn't want to give the impression that he had no interest in this project, but the trauma he had suffered in his own life over the past few months still rode heavily on his shoulders. The massive effort he had made recently to drag himself from the depths of despair had culminated in this trip organised by Maria, his sister-in-law. The aid agency for which she worked responded to the Red Cross request for help and was only too happy to source the vital spare parts and use Shane's engineering skills.

He knew that Maria also saw this journey as an essential part of his mental recovery process. She felt that the burden he had to bear must be intolerable at times, and it was, but his apparent strength had also acted as a crutch for her after the tragedy their family had suffered. Shane was glad that Maria would arrive soon. She would organise the distribution of medical supplies with her agency in war-torn East Pakistan as soon as the necessary permits had been secured. Until then, he must cope with his anguish alone and use this project as a distraction from the recent events he was determined to suppress. He remembered the times when Maria had wanted to get closer to him and always had designs on him, but when her twin sister Amy had a chance meeting with him, everyone knew he and Amy were right for each other. In the end, Maria was delighted with her sister's happiness. Who could have imagined the tragedy that would eventually overtake their whole family, and Shane in particular?

Meena was acutely sensitive to the pain of others, and she didn't need to see the tears welling up in his eyes to realise that he had mentally left her company and visited somewhere very dark and painful indeed. *Tread carefully, Meena dear, a story here needs to be told,* she warned herself. Her instincts demanded that it be heard, but not just yet. "We don't have the luxury of waiting. Our X-ray machine is a vital piece of equipment in our hospital. Sadly, tuberculosis is beginning to take hold in our area, and this equipment will help us diagnose the early onset of this and other illnesses sooner, especially in children," she replied.

This was true, but in addition to this, her supposed allegiance was to the insurgents entrusted to her care. Their casualties had been increasing lately because of frequent clashes with the Pakistani Army. War injuries among the civilian population were also a concern; they always seemed to suffer the most during the conflict. Atrocities were on the increase, and her hospital near Gaibandha in East Pakistan just happened to be in a strategically important area exposed to constant fighting.

These insurgents, or freedom fighters, the Mukti Bahini, tolerated her hospital in their stronghold, provided she treated their wounded. She had no choice since these men were not very disciplined. East Pakistan was part of Bengal and comprised much of the northeastern Indian subcontinent. Local Bengali officers, native to the area, who had deserted the Pakistani Army to fight for independence, did not always curb the excesses of other nationalist-minded groups with their own agendas. Appeasing all these diverse groups was all Meena could do at present, since another all-out war between India and Pakistan was a distinct possibility. The Bengali insurgents hoped that a new country, Bangladesh, would be born from the dying embers of East Pakistan. There was only so much a population could tolerate after the Pakistani Army martial law administrator turned the army on the people. Meena's worst fear was that the inevitable civilian casualties would include children. Mothers and fathers she had helped through the trauma of childbirth, hunger, and various natural disasters were turning up in increasing numbers at her hospital with war wounds, just as they were recovering from the devastation caused by the recent cyclone that swept in from the Bay of Bengal and inundated their low-lying country with catastrophic flooding the previous year.

Meena's absolute commitment to these people could not be overestimated. The people entrusted to her care valued her efforts and enthusiastically responded to her many projects to enhance the health system in the region where they lived. She was determined to ensure that their collective initiatives should not be in vain, so every effort needed to be made to ensure that any impending war would not lead to the disintegration of her community. A brief spell as a newly qualified doctor during the war in Vietnam in the recent past brought forward images of broken, wounded children, a sight she did not wish to see repeated. And she prayed there would be no landmines. Her expertise was in amputations, a skill learnt in a most painful way by having to salvage or remove the remnants of tiny, mangled limbs blown apart by landmines.

The villages where she worked at present were vulnerable because of their proximity to the main road between India and East Pakistan. The war would bring not only death and destruction, but also a mass exodus of refugees to neighboring India. As she had witnessed on their journey from her hospital in East Pakistan, this process had intensified recently. The ensuing chaos of people fleeing the war would undo the structures she had so painstakingly put in place with the help of her villagers.

"Doctor, I have read about the fighting in East Pakistan. I understand that our work will be conducted on the Indian side of the border, but will the conflict affect us in any way?" Shane said.

Meena felt guilty at the innocence of his question and felt obliged to give him an overview of the politics of the area where their journey would take them. She took Shane aside to give him the brief history of events she usually gave to visiting foreigners. "Please call me Meena, Shane. The politics in this region are complex, but I'll give you a very brief overview of what's happening. We don't have much time, so I'll update you when we're on the road. So, the Pakistani Army declared martial law in East Pakistan months ago. Since then, their soldiers and local collaborators have committed atrocities against the civilian population, including murdering teachers, intellectuals, and even high-ranking officers and soldiers in their own army, who just happened to be Bengalis from East Pakistan. Assaults on women in particular are a feature of this oppression and are being used as an instrument of control. I am certain that very soon, the Indian Army will invade to help the local freedom fighters, called the Mukti Bahini, overthrow the present government, and create a new country, which will be called Bangladesh, which translates as 'the country of Bengal'.

"The predominantly Muslim population of East Pakistan consider themselves Bengali, since the cultural region of Bengal comprises a large portion of the northeast of the Indian subcontinent. Hili, the place we're travelling to, is in India and very close to the border with East Pakistan. As you will see, the Indian Army is ready to invade to stop the ongoing violence against the civilian population. Most of the Pakistani Army in East Pakistan is comprised of soldiers from West Pakistan and, culturally, they could not be more different from the Bengalis of East Pakistan. The only thing they have in common is their Muslim religion.

"Now, let's keep moving. Your eyes are beginning to glaze over. I will explain the situation in more detail on the journey."

Shane had actually been listening but decided not to object and followed in Meena's wake towards the exit. It was into this cauldron of aggression that Meena must now return. Indeed, she had heard that a government-in-exile, residing in India, had declared independence for Bangladesh. Their chosen leader had been under arrest over a thousand miles away in West Pakistan since the beginning of hostilities. Sheik Mujib's influence still motivated the insurgents, and the clashes between his supporters and the Pakistani Army had become more frequent and vicious. Meena did not wish to reveal too much to Shane and overwhelm him with thoughts of encountering conflict on their journey.

Chapter 2

With all these complex thoughts and concerns on her mind, Meena led the way through the crowd towards the exit, while Shane seemed struck by the good humour of the people. She wanted to keep moving but was intrigued as she observed him interacting with the people in the arrivals hall. Most had a smile on their faces as they followed him, and he responded with a friendly greeting. It did not matter that they found every foreigner a novelty.

"Doctor, I'm surprised at the number of men with bloodstains on their teeth. You are correct about the high incidence of tuberculosis in the population." When she laughed, honestly not seeing the joke, he wondered at another aspect of her beauty as her cheekbones became more pronounced and her eyes watered over.

"These people don't have TB, Shane," she revealed between laughs. "The red between their teeth is not blood but the residue from chewing *paan*, which is a drug that induces a high, slightly more potent than tobacco. It is derived from betel nut, mixed with spices and some lime powder."

Just then, a man brushed past them and spat a huge amount

of red liquid into a corner container filled with sand, obviously there for that purpose.

"When we go to the villages, the men will offer it to you, and it is considered impolite to refuse." She observed the look of horror on Shane's face and could not control another fit of laughter. She was undertaking a serious mission and had been unprepared for a morning of humour. She was intrigued by this European, whom she had prejudged as someone who would focus only on the job and keep communications to the bare minimum required to repair her X-ray equipment. Sudden eye contact with Shane assured her of some very interesting days ahead. She inwardly rejoiced that they seemed to be on the same wavelength. The adrenaline flow increased with thoughts of what lay ahead as she reached a state of readiness for the journey.

They exited the cool airport terminal into bright sunshine. "Doctor, I'm surprised that it's not unbearably hot, as I expected, but it is very humid," Shane said as he pulled his sweat-soaked shirt from his back and took in the interesting cocktail of smells assaulting his senses. Not all were unpleasant due to the abundance of vegetation, lit up by spectacular displays of different-colored bougainvillea.

The arrival of quite a decent vehicle surprised Shane as he observed the well-maintained, white, long-wheelbase Land Rover pulling up beside them. He noticed the insignia of the Red Cross organisation prominently displayed on a placard inside the windscreen and the standard ambulance red cross emblems painted on either side of the vehicle. The porters loaded his equipment in its wooden crate on to the roof rack with some difficulty as he and their driver, Lal, helped them. Meena passed the porters some rupees, and they seemed more than happy as they touched their foreheads in a respectful salute.

They were soon underway when the Land Rover was loaded with the rest of the luggage and equipment.

"Shane, I can't understand how you can survive on the

contents of just one small backpack," said Meena as she pointed to his bag, which took up hardly any space.

"You might be more surprised when I tell you that the bag also contains the tools I will need to repair your X-ray equipment," Shane replied.

The smile never left her face as she observed Shane in the front seat with his foot on the dashboard as Lal negotiated the road packed with pedestrians and traffic. The smell of cow dung was familiar to him, but he was still amused that the jeep had to swerve around several cows, oblivious to the chaotic traffic around them as they scavenged among the discarded vegetation piled high in several places on either side of the road.

"Holy," said Lal.

Shane turned to Meena for an explanation.

"Cows are revered in the Hindu religion. If we hit one, a crowd would soon gather, and we'd be in trouble," said Meena from the back seat, where she sat behind Lal. Shane tried not to stare as a few loose strands of her hair blew in the cool breeze from the open windows. The beige-colored saree she wore was a modest garment but still enhanced her fine figure. Each time he addressed her, he had to consciously control where his eyes automatically tended to wander. This gave testament to the unfounded assertion of many men that a woman's peripheral vision was just as acute as a full-on stare; the slight smile as she looked out of the window confirmed this.

He remembered teasing his wife, Amy, about this supposed ability in women, and about their equally acute hearing; they could not only hear the conversations taking place at the five tables surrounding them in a restaurant, but also comment on the various topics being discussed, as well as the outfits worn by the other women. Nights out with Amy were never dull. His shoulders sagged as the memories of Amy once again overwhelmed him.

Empathy, another great quality possessed by some people,

surfaced as Meena noticed this and reached forward to touch Shane's shoulder, causing him to turn suddenly and meet her concerned stare while wondering how she seemed to be aware of his sudden descent into despair. He briefly touched her hand in acknowledgement that he had recovered and felt the tingling in his shoulder and hand long after she had withdrawn her hand.

A steady stream of refugees had filled the road from East Pakistan since martial law had been declared. People were dying at the hands of the military units of the Pakistani Army in their aggressive attempt to isolate insurgents from among the population, causing the people to flee to neighboring India. More than once, Shane felt sure that someone would be struck by their vehicle, and the visible tension on his face did not abate until they entered their first port of call at the Missionaries of Charity in Barasat, on the road north towards the border.

"We work with the sisters here on occasion, Shane, and always call when we are on the road home," said Meena. "This beautiful and tranquil place is home to patients with ailments so severe that were they to remain in their home communities, they would surely die or, at the very least, lead a miserable existence. The combination of old age, senility, and frightening physical and mental handicap may be distressing for you to observe."

The thoughts that engulfed him earlier were planted firmly in the back of his mind as his attention was now totally concentrated on the harrowing sights before him.

Meena said, "This is a shock tactic I use to introduce people to the conditions they will likely encounter when working with me. Most foreign volunteers stay and immerse themselves in this thankless but extremely rewarding work. Some, however, seek refuge on the next available flight home."

Shane felt somehow at home here. The people before his eyes, who had terribly deformed limbs, would have appalled him had they not been so well looked after in such a beautiful setting. All around were trellises covered in the ever-present pink, red, and amber bougainvillea. Trees with dense foliage towered over the buildings, providing shelter from the sun's heat, and lowering the facility's temperature and humidity by a few degrees. He was thankful that it was early December; he could only imagine the discomfort of living here during the summer months. Young women from the kitchen and dispensary were drawing water from a well, and their laughing and joking added to the tranquil nature of the surroundings. He felt self-conscious, his face red from the heat and his shirt soaked with sweat.

Just then, a young girl with a radiant smile emerged from one of the buildings and offered them cold drinks from a tray she was carrying. He had never tasted anything so refreshing. Meena explained that it was *nimbu-pani*, or water with fresh limes, which he could see growing on several trees in the compound. *Pani* was water, and this was a word he felt sure he would use frequently in the coming weeks. Shane gratefully gulped down the contents of the glass but noticed that Meena and Lal merely sipped theirs. He was sweating profusely, but they looked cool and dry. Drinking a lot meant sweating a lot. He was learning by the minute and quickly adapted to the locals' ways while sipping a second glass of the refreshing liquid, signaling to Meena with a smile that he was indeed a fast learner.

Meena was greeted by Sister Angela, an American who had once taught philosophy at Harvard but was now a comforter to the sick and dying in this haven for the unwanted and unloved, one of the many run by this order of nuns. Sister Angela had a list of patients for Meena to see. Usually, Meena needed to prescribe the proper medication to offer relief from the discomfort of twisted and deformed limbs.

The sisters also ran programs to help them detect and treat diseases like leprosy. Meena was delighted to see that Shane was beginning to explore, and the look of concern on his face told her that he would be flexible to her needs, and that maybe he would be a partner in the plan she had for him rather than an unwilling accomplice. Sister Angela went to walk with him while Meena went to work in the dispensary. The place Shane was drawn to most was the area where children with mental and physical disabilities were being looked after by several foreign volunteers. Sister Angela explained that most of these children were waiting for families to come and collect them and provide respite care for varying lengths of time in their homes, ensuring a future life full of affection.

As Meena finished her consultations and evening fell, they settled down for the overnight stay in this beautiful place, intending to resume their journey early the following morning. Meena wanted to avoid travelling during the night. It would take them ten hours to reach their destination, Hili, just inside the Indian side of the border with East Pakistan. As far as the Indian government was concerned, this was the final destination for their medical equipment. As far as Shane was concerned, this would also be his final destination. His permit stated that the medical centre in Hili, run by the Red Cross, was to be his sole area of operation and that he was not to go within one kilometre of the border with East Pakistan.

What he did not know was the extent to which Meena had gone to deceive the authorities. Her request to the aid agency in Ireland, authenticated by the Red Cross, ensured the procurement of the equipment and technician for a worthy cause, albeit in a location totally different from the one sanctioned by the authorities. She hoped that the paperwork and red tape would take months to catch up with her and that the equipment would be safely installed in her hospital in Gaibandha in East Pakistan by then. All that remained now was to convince Shane. She could proceed straight across the border covertly, but she did not wish to expose him to danger unless he was first made aware of the risks.

Meena prepared to spend the night with the sisters as Shane and Lal shared a room in a gatehouse where a night watchman kept vigil over the compound. Meena and one of the young women from the kitchen brought them food as the sun set. Meena left while the men ate their food, explaining that it was a convent after all, and strict rules were in place.

Shane had never tasted such food. He had expected it to be hot and spicy, but the rice and *dal* made from lentils tasted wonderful. The vegetables were flavored with aromatic spices and cooked to perfection. He had been quite hungry and finished the meal before noticing the absence of meat, which he didn't miss.

He soon felt very sleepy with the jetlag catching up on him. Sleeping on folded blankets on the hard floor didn't bother him, and soon, he fell into a deep sleep. The following morning, he awoke feeling totally refreshed as a sunbeam crept across the floor to shine on his face. He was aware that his vivid dream had been of his wife, Amy, and recounted one of the more pleasant experiences they had shared with their baby Rory as he took his first steps. Before he could lose himself in this moment of recollection, Meena arrived with tea and bread on a tray. They went to sit outside near a flowerbed, in sight of the night watchman and Lal, who were watering the plants. Meena was still conscious of her surroundings and the need to respect the convent's rules.

Shane could not have imagined a more beautiful setting, with well-tended plants of many varieties growing beside them as they sat on the grass drinking tea and eating freshly baked chapatis.

"Shane, the aid agency I contacted in Ireland arranged for this equipment to be sourced and for you to deliver and install it. Do you know the lady I was talking to who worked so hard to assist me? Her name is Maria," said Meena, observing Shane as the hand holding his cup stopped in mid-air.

"I think you were talking to my sister-in-law," he replied.

"Well, that's a coincidence—" said Meena, but she was cut off in mid-sentence as Shane suddenly got to his feet and retreated to the gatehouse. Meena sat stunned for a few minutes before collecting the tray and returning to the kitchen, feeling that, for some reason, she had ruined her chances of persuading Shane to cross the border with her.

Chapter 3

"I apologise, Doctor, I'm really sorry. Family issues suddenly overwhelmed me when you mentioned my sister-in-law, Maria. Nothing sinister, I can assure you. I love Maria, and I can tell you now that she saved my life by arranging for me to do this assignment. I find it hard to talk about all the issues, so do you mind if we avoid family discussions, please?"

Meena was so glad that Shane had at least explained that there were unexplained issues concerning his family. She would not intrude. Not yet. However, she did need to know. Feminine curiosity was a factor for sure, but his state of mind would be critical in the coming days, and she needed to be certain that she could rely on him.

"Sure. It is me who should apologise. And call me Meena, please," she replied as they loaded the jeep again.

Sister Angela passed a cloth bundle containing bread and water for the journey to Meena through the rear window. She held Meena's hands as they shared an intense prayer for a safe journey. The compound gates swung open, and the jeep turned towards the border as the sun cleared the trees. Ominously, they passed the constant trickle of refugees heading in the opposite direction towards Calcutta. They were a pitiful sight as they pushed makeshift carts with all their worldly belongings. Shane didn't appreciate the significance of what they were seeing, but Meena and Lal certainly did as they proceeded with a growing sense of foreboding.

The only good thing was that Shane's humour had returned, and his conversation lifted the mood in the vehicle as Meena translated Shane's anecdotes into Bengali for Lal. She explained that her knowledge of Bengali was not great. Shane looked enquiringly at her, and she felt obliged to explain her origins.

"My mother is from New York; my father was born in Goa. They are separated. Sort of. They have a powerful marital bond but choose to live thousands of miles apart."

Shane stared, intrigued, and noticed Lal straining to understand every word as she continued.

"My father is a high-ranking officer in Pakistani military intelligence. My parents met at the United Nations in New York, where they both worked for their respective governments. Their superiors tolerated the liaison due to the special relationship between Pakistan and the United States. Cynics might allude to the billions of dollars in arms sales from the US to Pakistan, and the reciprocal access grudgingly granted to US intelligence agencies to sensitive areas in Northern Pakistan, close to the border with Afghanistan.

"My father's presence is tolerated in many volatile countries for reasons best known to intelligence communities worldwide. I was born in Abbottabad, Pakistan. My father taught at the officer training academy, so I am fluent in Hindko, our local dialect, and Urdu. I have a good working knowledge of Punjabi and Pashto. I did, of course, attend an English-medium school for girls run by nuns. Most of the girls in my class were Muslim, many of whom were my best friends. The fact that my family was Christian did not matter one little bit to any of my school friends, and our boisterous reunions still raise eyebrows among locals.

"My mother would travel to the United States Embassy in Islamabad twice weekly for work. It was really funny, because both my parents had their own security guards outside our house. I attended school there until I was twelve years old, and then my mother whisked me off to attend high school in New York and exposed me to Western influences. What a culture shock that was! But I endured and finally ended up in Harvard Medical School."

Shane didn't realise that he was staring over his shoulder at her with his mouth agape until she reached forward and gently closed his mouth by pushing his chin up. He smiled at the humorous gesture and said nothing but turned and observed the road ahead in contented silence as he digested all this fascinating information, and eagerly awaited the next instalment. When not reflecting on her surprising origins, he contented himself by thinking about her extraordinary green eyes.

The journey to the border area was tense and very tiring. The Indian Army was moving men and equipment forward to secure the frontier. The fighting in progress in East Pakistan led to increasing tensions with India on both sides of the subcontinent. The Indian Government ensured full readiness by maintaining a strategic military presence at their borders while preparing for any eventuality.

The Land Rover was soon slotted in between two low loaders carrying tanks. It was unnerving driving behind the trailer in front with the main gun of its tank pointing at their windscreen. The two soldiers sitting astride the main turret saw the humour of this and carried a smile on their faces, which was not reciprocated.

There were, however, advantages to being part of a military convoy: security checkpoints on the route never had the chance to quiz them or detain them until the necessary bribe had been paid. Stopping them meant delaying the military convoy, which was unthinkable in the circumstances. The Indian Army, one of the largest in the world, was a force to be reckoned with. They were humiliated by a Chinese invasion in 1962 and vowed after that debacle never to be caught unprepared again. During that encounter, young soldiers were sent to fight in the high passes of the Himalayas using clothing and equipment meant for the tropics. Thankfully, for no apparent reason, the Chinese suddenly retreated and spared the blushes of the Indian Army. As a result of that humiliation, the Indian Army was now very well equipped, to such an extent that their soldiers were considered the spoiled children of India.

The turn-off for Hili, their destination for today, was soon upon them, and they waved goodbye to the soldiers in the military vehicles, which continued their journey to the border on the main road. During their stops for sustenance, the officer in charge never revealed their destination since it was classified. Captain Singh seemed too young to be in charge of anything. Maybe his Sikh headdress disguised his age because he had served two tours of duty with the United Nations in Africa and was a veteran of the previous war with Pakistan in 1965. He informed Shane that he had also worked in Southern Congo with United Nations peacekeeping troops from Ireland.

Meena was glad that Shane was out of earshot when Captain Singh informed her that he knew of the purpose of her mission and that she should not be surprised if they met again soon. He knew she would eventually cross the border into East Pakistan, and she concluded that, ultimately, the Indian Army units, of which he was a part, would soon follow. This ominous development made her realise that time was running out and that she must cross the border as soon as possible. It was not her intention to be caught up in the invasion when it did happen. She needed to get to her hospital in Gaibandha and confront the developing political situation near her hospital. She felt compromised by events but didn't seem to have a choice. She desperately needed the goodwill of any military units operating near her hospital. They would not tolerate her activities were it not for the fact that her hospital provided a valuable service. She also knew that some of the more militant factions on either side of the conflict would have no hesitation in eliminating her and the people travelling with her when they eventually crossed the border, regardless of her status as a doctor.

Before he departed, Captain Singh once again assured her that he would meet her again. She knew he would be reporting contact with her to his commanders. Meena hoped that this liaison would prove helpful, not least because her association with the Indian military would ensure a reliable source of medical supplies. But it would come at a price, and she wondered what favors Captain Singh's superiors would expect of her in return. The conflict between insurgents and the Pakistani military had already undermined her ability to function normally in her hospital. Her involvement with so many military groups would compromise her even further. She would need to have a conference with Shane before nightfall to fully explain her position and precisely what she had in mind for him, while not fooling herself into thinking that getting her X-ray machine fixed was her main priority.

They finally reached Hili late in the evening. They met with local Red Cross officials, who provided sleeping space for them in their many tents, making up a hastily assembled tented village beside the local hospital. This facility was the first point of contact in India for refugees fleeing the fighting in East Pakistan as they crossed the border. They were encouraged to keep moving further into India to avoid the facility being overwhelmed. The people were given a meal and water for their onward journey and were treated for any medical emergencies that arose. The more severe cases were transferred to better-equipped hospitals in Calcutta. Doctors were in short supply, and no permanent surgeons or specialists were available, the Indian Army providing specialist consultants as needed. This shortage was not a very satisfactory situation, so the local medics were always happy to greet Meena. She was also relieved to meet her nurses, Monica and Esther, who had been dropped off the previous day to collect medical supplies in the trailer of their jeep, ready for the onward journey.

They settled in for the night, and Shane went in search of food. Meena stared after him, smiling as he tried to isolate the smell of food from all the other challenging smells assailing his nostrils. She felt they were now allies trying to confront the substantial humanitarian emergency unfolding in the area. When he didn't return immediately, she searched for him, conscious that he was among the few foreigners in the complex.

Meena found Shane standing in the centre of the Red Cross warehouse, staring at thousands of sacks of wheat and rice donated by several aid agencies from around the world. These agencies had set up camps outside the Red Cross compound, and Hili was also a base for an Indian Army reconnaissance unit with a small airfield attached. He was impressed by the Red Cross's efforts and admired how they did their work and kept a very low profile. They avoided media attention and never sought to publicise their efforts. The other agencies, however, were seldom out of the media spotlight. Portraying their badges and emblems in the most prominent places seemed necessary, and they actively courted the media. Meena admitted to being wary of these non-governmental agencies. However, she admired most individuals who worked for them and used their nurses and facilities when needed.

The non-governmental voluntary agencies were invaluable in rebuilding in the aftermath of the cyclone that had recently hit East Pakistan. However, that was last year, and their work was still ongoing. Sensing a new conflict was in the offing, and with the advent of martial law in East Pakistan, they stayed and pleaded with the martial law administrator for complete access to the country. This was refused, mainly because they would give the world media a biased account of military activities.

Therefore, all foreigners were strictly banned from the interior of East Pakistan.

The prospect of any foreigner being arrested as a spy was also very real. Indeed, Meena's role was unclear politically; she used politics to advance any cause that would benefit the poor and marginalised. Her motivations could be misinterpreted as favoring one faction over another, which was the risk she took every day. It was a dangerous balancing act and a volatile political climate into which they would soon venture.

After discussing the politics of aid with Shane for ten minutes, Meena broached the subject of the assignment she had planned for him. She whispered a prayer and began by invading his body space and capturing his stare. He did not step back. She saw this as a positive sign, so she proceeded. His overlapping presence certainly made her feel that anything was possible. His intense, benevolent stare contrasted with the physical power of his muscular forearms and broad shoulders. She steeled herself for the conversation ahead.

"Shane, I know this is supposed to be your final destination and that your permit does not allow you to go any further. However, I need your expertise to install my equipment, which is not here in India but in my hospital in East Pakistan. I have deceived your agency, the Indian Government, and the Red Cross, and I am sorry to say that I have deceived you. Please come to East Pakistan with me by illegal means and risk being shot by both the Indian and Pakistani Armies, as well as by uncompromising insurgents along the way, who represent many factions. There will be no reward whatsoever for you.

"On returning to India, you may be thrown in jail for violating the terms of your visa, suffer widespread notoriety in your own country, and possibly be the cause of an international incident involving Pakistan, India, and Ireland. The Red Cross and the United Nations may be vilified for breaching international agreements and protocols. But I can only ask you to trust me when I say your efforts will make a difference. I will leave you now to reflect on what I have said. Please don't chastise me for my actions and deception. If you wish, my driver, Lal, will take you back to Calcutta. Otherwise, please come and see me at the hospital."

She walked slowly to the warehouse door and felt his eyes on her back. She had registered the look on his face during her monologue and could not see surprise, only resignation. She thought this man did not seem to care what happened to him. From what was he running that made him so distraught? Maybe she was wrong to expect him to decide in his present mental state. She felt sure that he was about to reveal the cause of his hurt and would use it as a reason for going home. Could he possibly use it as a reason for staying? Please, Lord, make him stay. Please.

"Wait, Meena, please." He noticed the tension increase in her shoulders. She slowly turned around to face him. A sunbeam from the setting sun caught her in profile and shone through the dust from the warehouse, enveloping her in an aura, and it was then that he realised the extent to which any man, and indeed woman, might come under her spell.

He initially considered defying her before succumbing to her delicate yet powerful presence. He noticed once again how the wheaten-coloured saree she wore accentuated the beautiful lines of her body. There was something very special about this woman. In the short time he had known her, this fact had been made clear to him. The urge to learn more was overwhelming, and he was determined to see where this remarkable journey might lead. He was fully aware that she did not need rescue; she would complete her mission, no matter what.

He walked towards her and was sad to see a look of apprehension in her eyes. On reaching where she stood, he got so close that he could see his reflection in her eyes. He held up his hand as if in salute. She instinctively stepped forward and slowly raised her hand until it came in gentle contact with his. They lingered there for an indeterminate time and just let the energy flow between them. It was an extraordinarily intimate moment; no words needed to be spoken. Eventually, a smile slowly lit up his face, and she inwardly relaxed. *Thank you, Lord, thank you!*

Chapter 4

An idea was slowly formulating in Meena's mind. When a course of action presented itself as a solution to her problems, she would analyze it until a realistic solution presented itself based on her logical reasoning. There was real danger now, however, so she was extra cautious. A simple error of judgment would be catastrophic. So absorbed was she in this thought process that she was unaware of a burning pain in her hands. When she became conscious of it, she realised that her deathlike grip on the chain-link fence was the cause.

The reason for the distraction lay on the other side of the fence, and her eyes never left the object until she could imagine it fulfilling all her requirements. The Cessna aircraft belonged to an Italian priest named Father Francesco, whom she knew well. He was an old friend of hers but he was now in hiding in the jungle, since the Indian authorities had served him with a deportation order due to his work in sensitive tribal areas, primarily due to the rising tensions and the threat of war. He was pretty forthright in his views on the area's politics, and after a few failed attempts at his arrest, he decided to relocate to the safety of a remote tribal village. In response, the Indian Army had commandeered his aircraft, which in the past he had so generously put at the disposal of local hospitals for emergency medical evacuations by air.

The Cessna was ideally suited to negotiating the jungle airstrips hastily prepared by villagers in several locations on both sides of the border. The thoughts in her head were radical, and she needed one more day to bring her plan to fruition. Tiredness was ever present, so Meena decided to rest for a while and wait for a new day, hopefully one full of solutions. She would need to consult with the officer in charge of the nearby Indian Army reconnaissance unit to devise a plan.

Shane relaxed on the verandah of the medical centre in the approaching darkness. There was a beautiful smell from the nearby vegetation. He gestured a smelling motion awkwardly to one of the nurses to enquire the name of the plant. She observed his peculiar behavior until she could no longer hide the laughter.

"The smell is from a jasmine plant and is more pronounced in the evening and nighttime. That is why it's known locally as Raat Rani, or Queen of the Night. The flowers are used for making garlands and for many religious ceremonies," the nurse explained.

Indeed, this was one of the smells of India, although since he'd arrived, he had been introduced to other memorable smells, good and bad, which were etched in his mind, and not only smells but also a sensation at the back of his nose, a strange combination of smell and memory that manifested itself when he recalled past events, especially if they were traumatic or significant. The memory of the moment would be forever associated with the dominant smell present during the event.

"My name is Esther, and I'm a nurse in Dr Meena's hospital," the nurse said. "We have been told that you've come to repair our X-ray machine after the damage done to it by the soldiers."

She was called away before he could ask her to clarify what she had just said about soldiers damaging the X-ray machine.

Maybe he had misheard. He decided to forget about it for the moment.

For over an hour now, Shane had been observing Meena standing at the fence, staring into the darkness at the outline of the army aircraft. She chatted briefly with an Indian Army sentry and then resumed her silent vigil. Her reverie was eventually interrupted by a commotion at the gates to the compound. Esther came running, shouting her name and urging her to come quickly. Meena invited Shane to accompany her as she conversed in Bengali with Esther. It seemed that a man had arrived with a severe injury and needed attention.

Just then, the electrical power failed, and the place was plunged into darkness, apart from the distant glow of lights from the nearby military compound. Apparently, this load-shedding by the local electricity supply company was common, and several oil lamps were produced. Meena asked Shane to go with Lal and start the standby generator while she proceeded to find out the nature of the medical emergency. She certainly inspired confidence with her calmness while others ran around excitedly.

Two men in a group of six carried their brother on a makeshift stretcher and placed him on a table for Meena to examine. She knew by the smell that this would be a long night. Meanwhile, Shane and Lal had the generator running, and some of the compound was now dimly lit, so Shane went to see what the commotion was about. He was about to enter the medical centre when the sound of distressed machinery came from the generator shed. The lights went out again, and he observed the smell of hot metal on reaching the generator. A puddle of oil was visible under the engine, and from the look on Lal's face, this was serious. The engine had seized due to all the oil leaking out.

Shane grabbed the torch from Lal's hand and ran to the medical centre to inform Meena. He rushed into the dimly lit room, where several nurses and Meena attended to the patient on a table. He took one breath and immediately felt nauseous. This smell was the worst he had ever experienced and one he would never forget. He gathered himself and accepted a glass of water from Monica, the nurse assisting Meena as she removed the dressing. After telling Meena the bad news concerning the generator, she beckoned him forward with his torch, the brightest light source in the room. She shouted for Lal to bring more batteries for later.

Shane was mentally begging to be relieved as torchbearer, but Meena only directed him to hold the light steady on the most horrific injury he had ever seen. How could this be a part of a human being? The bones in the lower leg were exposed, and what was left of the surrounding flesh did not look healthy. The shock of what he was observing kept him from being sick, although the remainder of the rice and *dal* he had eaten earlier was battling to stay in his stomach. The patient sang quietly to himself as if in a trance and seemed oblivious to his predicament. Shane observed an intravenous drip that the nurses had attached to the back of the man's hand, and he hoped that the fluid draining into his system would provide relief from the traumatic pain of the wound in his lower leg.

As Meena administered the general anesthetic, she identified Jagdish, the man on the table, as a man known to her. He came from a village she had attended frequently in East Pakistan. Along with his brothers, Kamal and Birender, he had been returning through the jungle from the market early on the previous day when a black bear confronted them. Efforts to frighten the bear off proved unsuccessful; it seemed determined to relieve Jagdish of the two kilos of sugar he had bought in the market. He struck the bear with his bamboo staff, which enraged the bear even further. When the bear closed in on Jagdish, he had no option but to run and climb a tree, hoping his brothers would frighten the bear away.

While climbing the tree, the bear caught his trailing leg with a swipe of his powerful claws, and Jagdish fell to the ground in agony. The bear seemed only interested in Jagdish's sack, which contained the sugar. With encouragement from Birender and Kamal, it retreated from the injured man and fled to the jungle with its prize of sugar. They ran to aid Jagdish, who lay in agony on the ground. There was a fearful wound on the calf of his right leg, where the bear had struck, and the men were aware that this was far worse than any farm accident they had previously witnessed. They could only comfort their brother, who was in severe pain, with local remedies made up from herbs traditionally gathered from the jungle.

On reaching home, though, his injury worsened, and they knew his only chance of survival was the missionary hospital over the border in India, usually a day's walk away. Jagdish's wife, Sujata, had heard from a village woman that the lady doctor was due to arrive from Calcutta that evening. They wasted no time and made a more robust stretcher using lightweight bamboo poles, which would carry the unfortunate Jagdish. They plied him with plenty of beer made from Mahua tree flowers to numb the pain. It would be a race against time to get help before the wound became infected. These farmers knew about the dangers of infection in even the most minor wounds. It frightened them to even gaze at this injury, while at the same time they reassured the patient that all would be well.

They bound the wound as best they could, and Sujata gave them antibiotics and aspirin tablets for the journey, which they had collected from all the people in the village. Sujata and most women in their village had attended the hospital, which the men hoped to reach as soon as possible. Sujata remembered the journey well, having made the same journey three times in the later stages of pregnancy. She whispered encouragement to Jagdish, telling him that his brothers would get him to Dr Meena while remembering the difficult terrain they must negotiate to save her husband. She prayed at the shrines in her house to her deities, Lakshmi and Ganesh, that Dr Meena would be at the hospital when they reached it. Her three children, sensing the tension of the occasion, gathered around her as the smell of burning incense sticks intensified her prayers.

Several men from the village insisted on accompanying them on their long journey to the hospital. Two of the men had recently deserted the Pakistani Army after they had witnessed atrocities being committed on civilians. They were fit and well organised and used their army training well. This was a Hindu village in a predominantly Muslim country. Still, the neighboring villages in the area worked together for the good of all, so sharing the burden in times of need came as second nature to these farmers. The six men took turns being stretcher-bearers, one on each corner, and set a fast pace while chanting to maintain a good rhythm. This shared effort resulted in them covering the distance in a remarkable ten hours. Their journey was helped by friendly villagers who willingly took turns carrying the stretcher. Everyone knew the value of cooperation among the villages in the jungle. This extraordinary effort was rewarded when their journey ended in the late evening, having negotiated the border crossing at a location known only to locals, whose disdain for borders was well known. Their spirits lifted when they were informed that Dr Meena was indeed available, and they were directed to the hospital.

The men retired, exhausted, to the kitchen for food and rest, safe in the knowledge that Jagdish's best chance of survival lay with the doctor who had delivered their children. Dr Meena's hospital in East Pakistan was unavailable to them because of Pakistani Army activity in the area. Still, they were also aware that Dr Meena regularly attended clinics at the hospital in Hili on the Indian side of the border. This and Sujata's assurance reinforced their decision to risk a border crossing to save their brother. A volatile military, suspicious of insurgency, was best avoided. The soldiers may choose to view Jagdish's injury as a war wound, so they took the chance of finding the doctor in Hili. Transiting the border was a regular occurrence for them, even in normal times, and they were well acquainted with the jungle pathways that avoided border posts as they availed themselves of markets to sell their produce. The advent of borders was only a recent occurrence that made life more difficult for people who had lived without them for hundreds of years.

Shane held the torch as steady as he could, but the odd twitch betrayed his unease. Occasionally, he caught Meena's eye and was subjected to a wordless lecture, which seemed to assure him of similar crises if he remained with her. The apparent master-disciple feeling unnerved him, and he fought, with little success, to dispel the notion that he was not the master. This did not bother him greatly since he knew he was observing something special. He also knew that, occasionally, history threw up extraordinary characters, and he felt sure he was in the presence of one now. *But let's not get carried away!* he thought. This was, after all, a woman in need of his expertise. Never mind the fact that her reliance was ill-founded to a large degree. Sure, he was a very good technician, but the crash course on assembling the X-ray machine he had received in Frankfurt did not fill him with confidence in his ability to impress this woman; he knew he would have to run to keep up with her. That was the thing about great people; they managed to inspire the people around them to achieve goals far beyond their usual capabilities.

He was in the process of trying to ascribe negative attributes to her when Monica, the nurse, retrieved a stainless-steel saw from the sterilizer and placed it in Meena's hands. She had made an incision above the knee of Jagdish's wounded leg and put several clamps on blood vessels. The infected wound was too close to the joint to allow Meena to save the leg below the knee. This injury was life-altering for this man, and Shane wondered about his future prospects. The saw was then placed on the bone, and Meena began a sawing motion on the exposed femur. This development was Shane's cue to clock out, and he was unaware when the nurses retrieved him from the floor and placed him in a nearby cubicle.

Shane awoke as usual to bright sunlight permeating the room and felt a tremendous sense of wellbeing. What had they given him? He was unsure of his surroundings and looked around to see if his wife, Amy, would emerge from the sunlight of the patio doors carrying fresh fruit and orange juice, as she did most mornings when they were on holiday in Spain. He was almost floating with feelings of love and contentment, so secure in knowing her absolute love for him. The smell of disinfectant confused him, and he abruptly realised that the beach house in Spain was but a vision, a faint abiding memory of paradise in the arms of a very special woman. He was reflecting on the unfairness of it all when a rustling sound came from outside the curtained door through which the morning sun was shining.

A vision of beauty did appear from the sunlight, carrying a bowl of freshly brewed tea that smelled wonderful. Meena knew how to make an entrance. It was as if she had tapped into his subconscious and presented him with what his mind craved. She was once again framed by a backdrop provided by the dazzling sunlight.

"Good morning, Shane," she said in a voice that belied the fact that she had just come through such an eventful night. "It is eleven o'clock, and you have slept for eight hours, no doubt due to the jetlag catching up with you. We leave soon, and we must discuss our plan of action. There are a few surprises in store, and I must ask for your cooperation if we are to be successful. Firstly, though, we must be straight with each other, and I was hoping you could lay your soul bare for me now and tell me your story. If I am to ask you to undertake this journey, then I must be sure that the mental anguish you carry with you will not affect your ability to give this venture your undivided attention." Shane lay on the bed, propped up by pillows, with the tea bowl resting on his chest. This was the first time anyone dared to broach this subject with him, and his sense of euphoria in this new, intimate friendship almost caught him off guard. His initial enthusiasm for a full-blown heart-to-heart faded quickly when he felt the depression welling up inside. He searched for a reaction from Meena. She waited, looking at him but keeping her distance, arms folded and leaning on a makeshift partition that divided the hospital cubicles. A serious air pervaded the space between them as she waited for an answer. He vainly fought for any excuse not to give one. Neither of them was willing to concede in this contest of wills, and just as Shane felt obliged to say something, the partition gave way, and Meena tumbled backwards, head over heels to the ground. The apparent exalted status to which she was accustomed as a surgeon evaporated, and her usual gravitas dissolved with the outburst of laughter from all in the medical centre. Birender and Kamal rushed to her aid, and amid the nurses' laughter, she gathered her composure and calmly acted as if nothing had happened. A howl of pain emitted from the next cubicle, and everyone turned to see Jagdish doubled up laughing; the more he laughed, the more intense the phantom pain from his missing limb. He reached down to soothe the pain in a limb that was no longer there.

Nobody present in the area could resist further laughter at this strange run of events, so each hastily exited. Jagdish's bed was wheeled outside with drips attached. Only Meena remained, and Shane observed the tinge of red on the beautiful olive skin of her face. She may have been embarrassed by this incident, but she still looked at Shane and waited for an answer. *No escape then,* Shane thought to himself. As Birender replaced the partition, she slowly sat on the bed, and Shane knew resistance was futile. Her weight on the bed beside him caused the sheet to tighten around his chest, trapping him in the bed under her expectant stare. He wasn't going anywhere, and this lady wasn't moving until he revealed all.

Chapter 5

Meanwhile, Meena's father found himself trapped in his hotel in Dhaka, the capital of East Pakistan. DaSilva stared out from the hotel's top floor over the tension-filled streets. The Continental Hotel was now home to the many foreign journalists covering the volatile situation provoked by the increasingly insistent demands of the people for independence. A state of civil war now existed, and refugees were flooding into neighboring India. Gunfire could be heard around the city, and the unit of the Pakistani Army detailed for the protection of the foreign journalists nervously surveyed the approaches to the hotel as insurgents were striking at will in several vital areas of the city. The military commanders were keen to portray to the international community the notion of a benevolent martial law administration, conscious of the will of the people, and with a willingness to tolerate dissent and deal with it amicably. The journalists were unconvinced and made this clear by attempting to communicate with the insurgents. This brought an angry response from the Pakistani Army officer in charge of security at the hotel, who threatened to shoot any journalist who defied the curfew.

DaSilva knew that his mission was a hopeless one. The government in Pakistan, and the president, entrusted him with the task of retrieving the situation by whatever means possible. He was given ultimate authority in all behind-the-scenes activity concerning East Pakistan. He was answerable only to the president, a former army general based in West Pakistan. DaSilva's name never appeared on official documentation. He was confident, as was the president, that East Pakistan would gain independence and become Bangladesh. Their main aim was to convince the new leaders to remain within a federation of Muslim states on the Indian subcontinent.

DaSilva knew he was too late. Once the army disarmed their local Bengali units and antagonized the civil administration, it was a foregone conclusion that the groundswell of public opinion would be for an independent Bangladesh, and any notion of retaining this new country within a federation would be thwarted. The Pakistani officers from the west became suspicious of their eastern comrades, whose Bengali origins made them potential mutineers. Indeed, many Bengali officers had already deserted and were now fighting with the insurgents in rural areas. They were becoming well organised, and their familiarity with the terrain and the local language ensured effective opposition to the Army of Occupation, which the local population now called the Pakistani Army. This ensured a collapse of all the civil structures, the normal functioning of which ensured stability. This further provoked the army into repressive measures, and atrocities were becoming commonplace.

DaSilva needed to make every effort since the president wanted a new two-country alliance to maintain a vice-like grip on the common enemy, India. Distracting India in the east might enable Pakistan to bring other disputed territories in the west under Pakistani control. DaSilva laughed at this notion; he was only too aware of the consequences of war with India. The last time the two countries engaged in battle was in 1965; it had resulted in an uneasy ceasefire. Since then, he had become one of the top behind-the-scenes facilitators. Because he was a Christian, he was seen as less of a threat to both Hindus and Muslims. He was well known in the United States and Russia and could easily move between India and Pakistan. He commanded the respect of top diplomats and military personnel from all countries in the region. Indeed, his dream was for India, Nepal, Sri Lanka, and Pakistan to be united in a federation of states on the subcontinent. A forlorn hope, maybe, but this was his ultimate goal. He admitted to himself that this was getting less likely by the minute. His only hope of contacting the insurgent leadership now was through his daughter, Meena, since their leadership had relocated across the border to India, from where, months previously, they had declared independence for Bangladesh.

Intelligence reports revealed that Meena was in constant contact with the leaders of the insurgents through the medical assistance she provided to their wounded. DaSilva also knew that she was in contact with Indian Army Intelligence. She was the only one who could get a message to Colonel Shahid, who emerged as one of the leaders of the military arm of the uprising and represented the recently established Bangladesh government-in-exile. Although not the only military leader, he was the most important. Shahid coordinated the activities of the insurgents in remote jungle areas. If intelligence reports were correct, he was also influential among senior officers from the military who had recently deserted the Pakistani Army to fight with the insurgents. This provided DaSilva with an opportunity to influence the situation. He knew Shahid from their time together in the military training college in Abbottabad in West Pakistan, where their families had been quartered. He hoped Meena could at least maintain a line of communication with Shahid and make him receptive to future meetings with him. His man had lost Meena in Calcutta but had eventually caught up with her again in the town of Hili on the Indian side of the border. He had arranged for her to be given a package prepared by him to be passed on to Shahid. She would guess the package's origin, which was now in the hands of the Indian Army Director of Intelligence, who was based in the Hili area from where Meena would eventually cross the border into East Pakistan.

During a recent trip to Delhi, DaSilva had convinced the Indian Government to allow Meena and her fellow travellers a free run into East Pakistan. That way, all the warring parties could maintain a line of communication. The Indian Government did not have any territorial ambitions in the developing conflict; it was content to see a stable, democratic state of Bangladesh being created, and if that caused Pakistan a headache in the process, then that would be fine with them. India delighted in the discomfort of its neighbor, while not wishing to antagonise them too much because of their alignment with other, more powerful countries. India's allies advised caution since they were unwilling to see another Vietnam created. A stable Indian subcontinent suited each superpower in world politics, and none wished to see this balance upset.

Meena could not know the extent to which her father was relying on her. He knew she would focus on the needs of her people, and he had to ensure her goals and his at least ran parallel. DaSilva knew Shahid would trust Meena without question. Relying on old family friends did not bother him; he was sure Shahid would at least try to persuade the supporters of their leader, Sheik Mujib, that an eventual meeting with DaSilva would benefit both sides. The problem was that so many unstable factions in the Pakistani Army and among the rebel insurgents would put Meena in great danger. Meena's mother was foremost in DaSilva's thoughts as he formulated his strategy. If her mother had known of Meena's predicament, she would not have been pleased with her husband's actions. He convinced himself that Meena would be making this journey in any event, so he could only try to ensure her safety. He could not, however, predict the actions of groups in the conflict that were a law unto themselves.

He knew Meena would be aware of his role in this conflict's political intrigue. DaSilva had talked with Meena's mother, Antoinette, that morning, and assured her he was looking after Meena and that he knew of their daughter's every move. Antoinette had not been convinced as their conversation ended, and with good reason, as he observed the smoke rising from several burning buildings in the capital city. This conflict intensified by the hour, and he felt a growing urgency to be on the frontline, where he would be in familiar territory, trying to influence the leaders of the most powerful groups emerging as future leaders in this fledgling state. He knew he could do nothing to change things while confined in this increasingly claustrophobic hotel.

Chapter 6

Amy stepped from the aircraft, struggling under the weight of the two flight bags. She didn't mind so much having to carry the bags; it was, after all, traditional for the first officer to carry them. What bothered her was all the people in the viewing lounge watching her. They could not possibly understand the hierarchy among airline pilots. The fact that this duty usually fell to the male or female co-pilot would be lost on them, and all they would see was a subservient-looking woman doing the bidding of a male co-worker. That co-worker was Roy, the captain, who walked with a swagger beside her under the weight of a tiny briefcase and a duty-free bag containing bottles that rattled noisily with every carefree step he took. She noticed the smile on his face and felt Roy knew what she was thinking. He gleefully started playing to the audience of onlookers.

Roy did look dashing, she had to admit. The men in uniform seemed to attract more attention than the women. His cap was at a rakish angle, and the four gold bars on each sleeve caught the sun beautifully. She wore no cap and no tie and always seemed to look like a laundry bundle beside Roy, and the three gold bars on her uniform jacket always seemed so dull, and that stupid cravat-like scarf she had to wear around her neck made her feel so claustrophobic. She smiled at Roy all the same because she really loved working with him. He was a superb pilot and a training captain on the Boeing aircraft, which they regularly flew together. When it came to the serious business of flying, he was absorbed in delivering the flight safely to its destination. He demanded a professional approach from all the crew and emphasised the need for safety awareness at all times. He didn't have to say much but people still got the message, although he was not without humour and conveyed it more through his expressions and demeanour than through constant demands and instructions.

Roy had agreed to a game of squash with Amy even though he knew she would beat him again. He respected her as a superb athlete and marveled at her figure as the mother of a two-year-old boy, Rory. After fifteen years of marriage, he was glad he was in a happy relationship, with a wife, Caroline, who induced butterflies in his stomach each time he saw her and their four wonderful children. Caroline was a tower of strength in their marriage. She knew Amy well. They were like sisters, and she had counselled Amy during pregnancy. She introduced her to Shane, and now they too were in a great marriage. Amy had clung desperately to this extended family ever since losing her mother and father in quick succession recently. When her father died of a stroke a year ago, Amy knew that her mother would not wish to live for long without him and passed away in her sleep a few months later. The intense love that had bound them together in life united them again in death. Amy and her twin sister, Maria, missed them terribly.

Roy's strategy did not pay off. The extra three duty-free bottles he had placed in the flight bags that Amy had to carry did not affect her game. After carrying the bags, he thought her arms would be like jelly, but she ran him ragged around the squash court. Another player was waiting for her to subject him to the same punishment. Amy ran to phone the childminder to tell her she would be home soon, and that Shane would be home before her. Roy retreated, sweating, to the changing room as Amy's next victim took to the court to warm up.

Earlier, upon discovering the three extra bottles of Roy's whiskey in her flight bags, Amy had given them to the crew control staff before Roy could retrieve them. He dared not protest. This girl had subtle ways of getting even with him. Even Caroline took Amy's side, and both would gang up on Roy if he were in danger of winning an argument that cast men in a more favorable light. Roy and Caroline were Rory's godparents, a duty they took very seriously. Joint family celebrations were chaotic when all the children were together. Their two boys and two girls were all under ten, and their youngest was four. They all doted on Rory, and when their neighbors' children joined them, the ensuing chaos was hard to contain.

Amy entered the house and threw her keys on the hall table. Rory ran to meet her as she came through the front door. He nearly fell over before she caught him. Shane had just arrived home and was cooking. The smell invited her into the kitchen, where she observed a table laid for two with tablecloth, napkins, and candles. She hadn't thought he would be here to celebrate her twenty-third birthday since his work involved so much travel.

Lately, he had mentioned working full-time from home, enabling her to pursue her career. This was unheard of even though it was now 1970. He assured her he could do most of his engineering work from home, and when the need arose, they could have Lucy, their childminder, come and stay with Rory. This would give Amy the chance to concentrate on her career unhindered. She was one of the first female commercial airline pilots for her airline, and Shane knew how important flying was to her. She needed flying in the same way she needed sport, and as he observed her beautiful face touching Rory's, he realised the extent to which he needed her and loved her, knowing she would return that love tenfold.

The look in her eyes confirmed this, and the sudden thought of not having her in his life gave him an inner panic attack. Nevertheless, he warmly embraced her and relieved her of Rory to allow her to change out of her uniform. She had the next few days off, so she could totally unwind at home. After changing, she eased herself onto the sofa, and he poured her a glass of red wine and watched her as she made the most of this moment. He placed Rory between them as he joined her on the sofa, and from behind a cushion, Shane produced a small jewelry box, which he opened in front of her face. She could not contain her shock and happiness as she observed the beautiful earrings, but straight away started to scold him for having spent so much, although she stopped mid-sentence as she slipped them through the piercings on each ear. One of the most endearing things about her was the way she tilted her head while doing so, the look on her face, and the way her eyes latched onto his. The earrings looked perfect. She looked perfect. Everything was perfect; this moment would be etched forever in his mind.

They could not stop talking and shared thoughts on everything that had happened during the day. Rory was soon asleep on the sofa between them, and an hour later, the oven timer announced that the casserole was cooked. Amy took Rory in her arms and placed him in his cot after preparing him for bed. He slept immediately, so she didn't need to read him a story. Over dinner, Amy mentioned that she would go shopping the following morning and take Rory with her as she would not be flying for a couple of days. She suggested Shane could hitch a ride and meet them for lunch. Rory was growing so quickly, and it was time to look for clothes for a fast-growing, nearly three-year-old boy. Amy loved the chores of motherhood and was happiest looking after her little boy. She could not bear being away from him for too long.

She couldn't believe her luck when she'd been presented with a beautiful baby boy. The pregnancy had gone very smoothly; it was as if she had an agreement with her unborn baby never to cause each other pain. She waved at all the other bemused mothers in the maternity ward as she left for home, sooner than was expected, eating an apple, with a nurse in tow carrying her newborn. A beleaguered-looking husband brought up the rear, carrying all the bags, and he seemed so rattled that they were tempted to put Shane in the empty wheelchair intended for the use of the exhausted new mother.

Amy was the type of woman who wouldn't even have stretch marks after the delivery and would return her figure to normal by performing a few sit-ups each day. When Amy held Rory while bathing in the bath with him or dressing him, she rejoiced at the beautiful structure of his body and the beauty of his face. Whenever she held his little body, she marveled at the intricacies of the organs within his ribcage and tiny, delicate head. Each functioning organ in his body worked to produce the amazing biological marvel that was their son. All their efforts were directed at ensuring Rory would be content and healthy in childhood, and these efforts seemed to bear fruit since his demeanour was always happy and topped off with an enchanting little smile.

His smiling eyes during breastfeeding mesmerized Amy, making the scratches from his little fingernails while feeding more bearable. She bore these marks on her breasts and arms like trophies while Shane insisted on cutting Rory's nails; his only mission was to preserve her perfection, especially when she wore low-cut tops on evenings out. She smiled at his ulterior motive for maintaining her unblemished skin without his knowing the efforts she would make to look good beside his well-toned physique. *How did he maintain such a fitness level from jogging a few miles daily?* She was sure he was a secretive member of the local gym. She didn't care once they were all fit and healthy.

They retired before midnight, both slightly drunk on the bottle of wine they had just consumed between them. Rory had been asleep for hours, and they knew he would not wake until five o'clock, ready for action and shouting for their attention. Neither minded attending to him during the stillness of the night. It seemed to them that this was an essential moment for bonding, and both of them usually ended up sitting together, observing the contented little bundle consuming the contents of his bottle when he was smaller, or these days, watching him as he scrutinised each of the characters in whatever storybook he was reading.

Shane never missed an opportunity to observe Amy and Rory as they played, marveling at Rory's physical and psychological development. He smiled at how alike Amy and Rory were in looks and temperament. As he looked at Amy, he was transfixed by the extraordinary transformation of her body during pregnancy and after the birth. How the body could change so radically was beyond comprehension. The growth of their newborn baby further enhanced this fascination, and he hoped to witness this process again soon as they contemplated extending their little family in the near future. They wanted their children to be of similar ages and grow up as companions, without too much of an age gap between them.

Shane was stuck to the pillow the following morning, vaguely aware that Amy was leaving for her usual morning run. His promise of the night before to rise when she did was conveniently forgotten. She slapped him playfully when he suggested that maybe at twenty-three, she was too old for the exertions of a morning run. He heard the front door closing as she took to the street. Barney, their postman, mentioned once that seeing her run was the highlight of his day. More than one early morning driver was dangerously distracted at the sight of her passing on the pavement.

Amy had a smile for everyone and inwardly thanked God for

good health and a wonderful family. She was religious and felt sure that a powerful being was controlling events in the world to a certain extent, but that this being and nature sometimes conspired to create often cruel and inexplicable events. She felt in control of her destiny, though, and without tweaking the tail of fate, she was determined to pursue her dreams relentlessly.

She remembered once watching a column of ants crossing the road, observing many being killed by each passing car, but they continued regardless of the fate of their comrades. They persisted in whatever goal nature pressed them to achieve. In the same way, it was hard to rationalise the deaths of innocent humans or those plucked from this life into oblivion by the hand of fate. With these thoughts, she felt a chill in her spine and immediately whispered a prayer, asking God to protect her and her family from all evil and danger. She tried to prevent the negative thoughts from taking hold and forced herself to think of Rory, but she was overcome by the fear that the good things in their lives would somehow be balanced out by tragedy. It was an irrational but unusually pervasive thought, she concluded while continuing her run on such a beautiful sunny morning.

These thoughts remained as she entered the house, and, having showered, she sat down to the breakfast Shane had prepared. He noticed the troubled look on her face. She eventually discussed the negative thoughts she had experienced earlier. He assured her that this was just a defense mechanism in the brain that allowed her to confront the possibility of future events that could threaten to dismantle their happiness. At times like these, he was aware of her vulnerable side and he watched with concern as she protected Rory in her arms. This moment soon passed, and she bounced back, laughing and joking once again.

Shane knew they had no control over events, and quite often, they discussed what they would be like in old age with grandchildren and a peaceful retirement. He noticed her usually fertile imagination deserting her when planning too far ahead. She would just stare at the flickering flames of their fire during winter evenings and listen as his imagination ran riot. His happiness was infectious, she had to admit, and she felt comforted by his absolute commitment to carving out a secure and happy future for their family. She was a most willing participant in this process. The affirmation came in the form of the three smiling faces in the recently taken family photo, framed on the kitchen wall near the door, forcing them to observe it every time they left the house.

Shane strapped Rory securely into the baby seat in the back of Amy's car. The seat was positioned so Amy could see him in the rear-view mirror. The summer morning sunshine and the smell of cut grass enhanced Shane's optimism. They hugged as usual, but he was shocked by the intensity of her embrace. He had never been so immersed in such a sensual moment with her as he was now, so he was forced to reassure her once more that everything would be all right. She was still experiencing residual negative thoughts from her run earlier. Their eyes met, and suddenly, there was only serenity and peacefulness between them as he tore himself away, and soon, they were gone. He felt only all-consuming love and retreated to the house, oblivious to his surroundings.

They'd had these moments before, especially when she returned from a particularly turbulent flight. He would sometimes scan the frequencies of his air band radio, searching for her voice, especially during storms. When he did hear her, he was always amazed at the air of calmness in her voice, even though both she and Roy would be struggling to get the Boeing aircraft onto the ground, often in atrocious weather. When she eventually arrived home, he would hold her tightly. Amy always made light of the seriousness of flying in such weather. He could, however, feel her sweat-soaked shirt, and he knew she had been at the limits of her capability. Adrenaline would still be coursing through her system for hours after the flight, and it took a decent-sized glass of wine to get her down from the highs of those challenging moments.

Nevertheless, this girl wallowed in the challenges that life threw at her from day to day, but what he feared most were the outside forces over which she had no control. How many times had Amy compared the dangers of driving to statistically less dangerous flying? And anyway, she explained, why should only men continue to lead the way in technically challenging and potentially hazardous ventures? She convinced him there was no point worrying about things they had no control over, since risk management was a part of everyone's life. "If we were to stop and overthink the dangers we expose ourselves to daily, our movements would be significantly curtailed," she would say. She was not one to sit back and let events dominate her approach to the day; she charted a course around trouble. Some people were observers in life, and others were motivators and partakers who made things happen around them. He often wondered how she would be as an observer. Finally, he admitted to himself that the spark in their relationship was provided by the tension of her choosing the unorthodox, riskier approaches to life.

The traditional urge to cosset and protect was denied him since she was so independent. But occasionally she displayed a vulnerability, which swept over her like a waterfall. Thankfully, this did not happen too often, and he usually had total confidence in her to control the events she encountered, but with some help from friends when she needed it. These thoughts reassured him somewhat, but he still had a nagging doubt about her state of mind this morning as he watched her car disappear at the top of the road. He trusted her instincts without question. When she worried, he would always reassure her but inwardly panic until the ensuing events proved that her fears and precautions were baseless. On occasion, though, her intuition had proved dramatically correct.

The time they went island-hopping while on honeymoon in the Caribbean involved several short flights on fifty-seater twin-engine propeller aircraft. Amy had refused to board the plane on the final leg, feigning sickness. Bemused passengers and aircrew bypassed them in the terminal building, and he resigned himself to going on the ferry as he observed her with her head resting on her arms. Shane could not help but smile because he was getting to know her strategies for dealing with events that forced her out of her comfort zone. He was so relaxed just being with her that he didn't care about events they encountered as long as they were faced together. Having decided not to board the aircraft, and realising that Shane was indifferent to their predicament, she suddenly perked up and displayed no symptoms of illness. He was too busy loving her to be angry with her as they stood waiting for the bus to the ferry in the shelter, surrounded by lush tropical vegetation. She drank from her water bottle as he relaxed in the beautiful surroundings.

As the aircraft began its take-off roll, she went to watch at the chain-link fence that ran parallel to the runway. He watched with increasing tension as her hands clutched the wire tightly. He noticed the intense look in her eyes as she observed the aircraft accelerating down the runway. He was about to ask her what was wrong when the nose wheel of the aircraft collapsed suddenly, and with a loud screech and a torrent of sparks, it slid to a halt in the scrub beside the runway adjacent to where they were standing in a cloud of dust. Shane nearly collapsed with fright at this dramatic turn of events. It took some time for the airport's antiquated fire engine to roll towards the stricken aircraft. By the time it reached it, the passengers and crew were calmly exiting at the plane's front door, which was now level with the ground. The passengers were sauntering through groups of banana trees on their way back to the terminal. One lady was even taking photographs of her husband standing in front of the collapsed nose of the aircraft, with the captain trying to coax them away from the danger area. Thankfully, nobody was hurt, and all the passengers eventually joined them on the bus to the ferry. This drama was the most exciting thing that had happened to the passengers during their holiday, they all declared, but they regarded Amy with great suspicion and gave her a wide berth. She spent the journey on the ferry staring at the dolphins racing in front of the boat, and Shane was wise enough to let her be and not intrude on her innermost thoughts. This event was more than intuition; a premonition had just occurred. Never once had she boasted about the extent of her prescience, and never once after that had they discussed the event. During subsequent flights, though, he would observe her out of the corner of his eye as they boarded. Her smile acknowledged that she knew she was being observed and why.

While thinking about this incident, Shane found himself staring down the road. Since there had been other incidents, they all flashed through his mind. He couldn't manage this relationship if he overreacted each time Amy felt uncomfortable with a thought or feeling. No, he would take his own advice and calmly review the events that gave rise to these extraordinary insights each time they were sprung on him. Her thoughts often seemed isolated and without foundation, so his mind refused to consider anything other than a rational explanation, resulting in his evaluation of each event becoming entwined in fear and doubt. His spine tingled now, and he found himself sweating. The postman, Barney, jolted him back to reality and enquired about the worried look on Shane's face. Shane instinctively, and for no apparent reason, dragged him to his van and begged him to follow, as quickly as possible, the route Amy had just taken minutes earlier. Barney complied without question and hastily drove towards town while observing the white knuckles of the young man sitting beside him as he gripped the dashboard. To relieve the tension, he mentioned that he had seen his young wife earlier during her run when he was delivering mail at the start of his route. Shane nodded, but his eyes remained transfixed on the road ahead.

Meanwhile, Amy easily negotiated the country roads while maintaining eye contact with Rory in the rear-view mirror. He smiled at nothing in particular, and it made her heart lift. She needed to cuddle him and contemplated pulling into a picnic area up ahead to do just that. But instead, she reassuringly spoke with him as she usually did on these journeys. Like so many parents, she longed to strap him in beside her in the front passenger seat to enable her to physically interact with him directly as she drove, while at the same time acknowledging the dangers of doing so.

Amy smiled when she considered the dangers of constantly staring at him in her rear-view mirror. She contented herself by diverting her thoughts to the beauty of the surrounding countryside in the mid-morning sunshine. She was always aware of slightly negative feelings associated with thoughts of wellbeing. Still, she was accustomed to this and always dismissed these negative feelings as an innate warning system, bred into humans to warn against dropping their guard. She imagined ancient cave dwellers enjoying eating summer fruits in a lush meadow while at the same time watching the nearby forest for signs of predators. This morning's dominant feeling was of summer smells wafting through the car's open windows as the warm breeze ruffled Rory's hair.

The road narrowed into a single lane due to roadworks, and a line of traffic formed ahead of her as she came to a stop. She looked in her mirror and noticed several other cars gently stopping behind her. She applied the handbrake while constantly checking the mirror to ensure drivers approaching from behind would know of the hold-up and stop in good time without rear-ending cars behind her. The line of vehicles ahead came together on a steep incline on the outskirts of a picturesque local village. Amy looked across the fields at the river in the valley below, winding its way towards the village. The morning mist held the sunlight and cast a beautiful translucent sheen across the valley. She was overwhelmed by an overpowering sense of wellbeing that stood in stark contrast to her feelings of early morning, which were now firmly banished as she faced the day with renewed vigor. The lows of life were indeed worth it if feelings such as these were the end result, she convinced herself.

The line of traffic showed no sign of moving as usual, and Amy turned around to check that Rory's restraints were secure. Her friend Moira was a doctor in a busy casualty department, and she convinced Amy of the need to restrain young children in vehicles. Moira had seen too often the horrific injuries needlessly inflicted on children whose parents refused to install special child seats with restraints. The resultant catastrophic injuries when children went airborne in a crash convinced Moira of the need to advocate for child restraints in cars. Amy simply complied with Moira's advice without question. Moira insisted that these restraints would soon be mandatory for adults and small children. The advice was not lost on Amy, who, as a pilot, knew the forces a human body could be subjected to in sudden deceleration, such as a head-on collision.

With these thoughts in mind, she turned on the radio and searched for money to buy a newspaper from a vendor, who sold from car to car at this spot each morning. He had just completed a sale to the driver of the vehicle ahead of her, and she smiled as he laughed at whatever banter the driver shared with him. He was still smiling as he recognised Amy and approached her with a newspaper. She knew he would chat with her for a while as usual, and she needed to have all her usual answers ready in response to his usual good-natured flirting. He would always reach in and tickle Rory and make him laugh and wind him up terribly. Consequently, it would take her ages to settle him.

The newspaper vendor looked at her mischievously, and she

was bracing herself for the onslaught when she noticed the smile disappear from his face and being replaced by a look of sheer terror as he dropped the bundle of newspapers. She observed him staring back up the hill behind her, so she turned and followed his gaze to see what was bothering him. What she saw made her blood run cold. An enormous, fully laden truck was hurtling out of control down the steep slope, and the driver was gesticulating wildly from the cab window for them to get clear. She could hear him screaming, "Brakes failed, brakes failed." She needed no prompting, and her finely honed skills in the event of an emergency took over.

She was out of the car in no time. She roared at the newspaper man to run ahead and evacuate the passengers from the vehicles in front to avoid them being caught in the inevitable pile-up, which was only seconds away. She then turned her attention to freeing Rory as she opened the car's rear door and calmly got to work, untying the straps Shane had so diligently tightened just minutes beforehand to safeguard Rory from a collision from the front. She plucked him from the seat as the seatbelts fought to keep him there and glanced out of the rear window, only to see the driver jumping from the truck a hundred metres away as his truck tore into the line of vehicles that had formed behind her. There was no time to consider the plight of the occupants of those cars.

She now had Rory in her arms and started to run forward. There was no other way but forward as roadworks barriers blocked every other route. She noticed that the people in front were fleeing, and she could see the terror in their eyes as they looked back up the hill at the destruction unfolding behind them as they ran. Amy felt sure she would make it as she heard the thunderous impacts behind her. Just fifty metres from her abandoned car, the brakes of the truck suddenly applied, but rather than bringing the fast-moving, out-of-control vehicle to a halt, instead, it jack-knifed and skidded sideways, overturning, and hurtling its load of heavy machinery through the air towards the line of cars in front.

Amy could not resist the urge to look back. She knew safety lay ahead only metres away, but the deafening noise from behind had to be investigated. Clutching Rory tightly, she turned, and what she saw defied logic. The truck was sliding on its side down the hill while tearing into parked cars, including hers, which rose toy-like and rode over the vehicles in front. The energy of the movement was frightening, and the speed at which this mayhem advanced towards her took her breath away as she held on to her child. She agonised as she thought of the people who didn't have time to evacuate their cars.

She felt sure that this fierce energy would dissipate before it reached her, and that the danger would be averted with inches to spare, like in the movies. Her mind calculated the movement of the cars piling up as non-threatening, and if she ran a few more metres, she would be safe. However, the trajectory of another unrecognisable object puzzled her and didn't make sense. Because it was airborne, its movement was not restricted by the cars, which absorbed the enormous energy of the impact of the truck and gradually dissipated this energy. Instead, the huge object sailed through the air with only gravity and momentum affecting it, pulling it towards her in an arc. It looked like a lathe from a machinery workshop, and she knew that these machines didn't defy gravity and inertia easily. She thought the object must have been dislodged from the back of the truck on impact when it overturned and felt that she could afford the luxury of working out the physics of the situation since the danger was now averted. She took one last glance over her shoulder and saw the machine bounce off the roof of a car. She could only look on helplessly as the trajectory changed dramatically and sent it directly at her. It could not be avoided, and so she instinctively ducked into a fetal position on the road with Rory tucked inside her as she braced herself.

Thoughts of how she would relate this extraordinary event to Shane were foremost in her mind. She was so close to Rory that she felt his heartbeat against her rib cage. He would need a change when this ordeal was over. But her baby bag was in the car. That nice newspaper vendor could retrieve it for her. People were very helpful after disasters such as this, and she felt sure that someone would be there to bring her home. She hoped the car insurance covered this event. She resolved to give that truck driver a good telling-off when this was over.

Shane would surely laugh at the predicaments she created for herself. The smiling faces of her departed parents, Shane, and everyone she loved flashed before her eyes. Feelings of absolute love overwhelmed her. For an instant, she felt a crushing sensation, which reminded her of being under a pile of bodies once during a mixed rugby match in college. The discomfort she felt then could be tolerated when she realised the ruck of bodies would soon disengage. Where did that thought come from? She observed dark liquid flowing on the road surface away from her body. The heavy machine continued into the ditch, obliterating the barriers as it rolled unchecked. *They sure will have a hard time retrieving it,* she thought. *Dad could help them since his company has cranes. But he's no longer with us.* Confusion clouded her thoughts as she struggled to command her mental processes. The pool of dark fluid was spreading.

Daddy! I knew you would come to help the men retrieve their machine from the ditch. They're going to have such a job cleaning the road after this. Did I pay you for the newspaper? Please ask my dad to take Rory for a walk. Oh, and get my baby bag from the car. Things are getting very blurred, and I can't see too well. Is that Rory with Daddy? But he's walking so well! He looks so beautiful and grown up! Wait until Shane sees him!

"Oh, there you are, darling. Please go with Rory and Daddy and tell them I will be along shortly. Just help me up because my arms are very stiff from carrying Rory. We can all go home and have a nice salad for lunch! Shane, all I want is for us to be happy forever, and you know that my happiness depends on you being happy. Why is my arm twisted like that? I'll never be able to play squash with an arm like that. How did you get here, anyway? Why are you crying? Come, lie beside me, darling, and hold my face in your hands. I need you to massage my back like you usually do when I've had a bad day. I'm just going for a walk with Rory and Daddy. You wait here and clean up this mess; I'll not be long. Tell Roy that I need a few days off to sort myself out. This feeling is so good that I want it to go on forever. Shane, why are you so far away? Please come closer; we can walk together. Rory and Daddy are waiting for us. Come with us, darling, please."

***

Shane clutched the postman's arm as the scene of devastation unfolded in front of them, and they skidded to a halt. They both sensed death in the air. Shane's instinct was to rush to the centre of the carnage, but a burly man with blood running from his arm and forehead tried to restrain him. He broke free and slowly ventured forward, unsure where to go. No, the car wasn't amongst the debris. It was hard to distinguish makes and models, and there seemed to be more than one red car like Amy's in the pile-up. Maybe she had taken another route. But he knew this was the only route, so he scanned the faces advancing towards him from the bottom of the hill. He recognised nobody. The smell of burning rubber and spilt fuel was sickening as the dust from the impact settled. Just then, he noticed a familiar number plate poking out from between two unrecognisable chunks of metal, and his heart sank. Surely they couldn't be trapped in the mass of tangled metal before him. People were emerging from the wreckage of cars and going to assist those less fortunate, whose cries were becoming louder as the shock of the impact wore off and the realisation of their predicament and injuries became clearer.

The postman had related to the truck driver that his companion was concerned for the safety of his wife and baby son. Barney knew from the look on the driver's face that he had just witnessed something horrible. He was gently coaxed into revealing what had happened as they both observed Shane starting to claw in vain at the wreckage. They guided him towards what appeared to be a bundle of clothing a few metres away, just beyond a hole in the road gouged out by some unknown force. The truck driver, nursing what appeared to be a broken arm, revealed that he remembered one of the machines from his truck dislodging and becoming airborne before crashing onto the road and rolling over a girl running with a baby in her arms. Shane was not listening but instead was totally focused on a shoe, which he recognised as Amy's.

He felt the futility of trying to convince himself that his family had survived this. He was soon on his knees beside Amy and Rory; hearing her speak was the only thing preventing him from going into shock. How was this possible from a body so broken? He was soon beside her, kneeling in the blood that flowed from the two bodies he had so regularly loved and caressed. He could tell from her eyes that she was not in pain yet. He knew she was dying and that the twisted little body beside her was already dead, so he smiled at her and listened intently to what she was saying. He held her face when she asked him to and wished so very much to accompany her, as she requested, on whatever journey she was about to take. Her eyes soon clouded over, and he felt the life fading from her face. He closed his eyes in desperation and suddenly realised that a cloud had descended on his life, and only darkness reigned.

Chapter 7

Shane opened his eyes and saw Meena. She was so close and holding his two hands in hers. The sense of a bond with her was as intense as his bond with Amy had been. He felt so at ease with her. It was as though a mighty force had, all of a sudden, worked to dispel his grief. She had not said one word during the time it had taken him to unravel his painful past. Only then did he realise the true nature of one with the gift of mental and physical healing. He visualised all the implements and medicines associated with healing, the use of which she was so adept at. Still, there was something else, something in the realm of the spiritual, a spark, the source of which he could not fathom but simply acknowledge. They had been there for two hours. Meena got up and slowly walked away. He showered and felt a whole lot better, having offloaded issues that were previously taboo.

Before now, nobody had dared broach the subject of his lost family. He had to admit that this had been a mistake and unfair on their relatives, who were suffering just as much from the loss of such a significant figure in their lives. He looked forward to meeting with them for a collective therapy session, from which they could all move forward as a close-knit, supportive family.

Once again, he followed his nose to the source of cooking and eventually arrived outside the hospital kitchen, where he was greeted by Esther, who gave him a meal of rice and the usual tasty vegetables, okra and aubergine, which he had never tasted before. He watched as the cooks prepared meals for all the medics. Meals for the transiting refugees were being prepared in a separate area, where the contents of huge pots bubbled away. He was determined to find out what spices they used to enhance the taste of simple vegetables in these rural areas. He felt refreshed and warm as he stepped outside onto the verandah and smelled the early afternoon air, which promised rain. The monsoon was over, but he was told that this area was often subjected to sudden storms from the northwest, which brought a mass of cool air and welcome rain, turning the dusty roads to mud and making any journey difficult until all the groundwater evaporated.

He searched for Meena and eventually found her in discussion with who appeared to be very senior Indian Army officers outside the tented compound that served as their command centre. They seemed deferential towards her, which was unusual, and not for the first time, he got the impression that she commanded a lot of respect from figures in authority. He remained at a respectful distance and waited for them to finish their discussions. Their conference soon ended, and Meena walked towards him with a smile on her face.

The assembled officers couldn't help but look at her retreating figure. She knew their eyes were following her every move, and her smile told him that their interest in her graceful movements and figure only reinforced her ability to get what she wanted. He smiled at their weakness at the hands of this woman and smugly felt himself a part of her winning team. Precisely what their team had won was beyond him. His smile disappeared, though, when he realised from the look on her face that he was the focus of her next onslaught. He knew that she had shattered the convention of male superiority with the Indian officers just now, but he was determined to confront her on equal terms. With this in mind, he stretched to his full height and thrust his chest forward to show her he would not relent in the face of such tactics.

"We leave early tomorrow morning on a journey that will eventually take us to an area near our hospital in East Pakistan. We will be going in that aircraft over there." She pointed towards the Cessna aircraft she had been observing earlier. "An Indian Air Force flight lieutenant will be our pilot, and we will take your equipment with us. Lal will drive Monica and Esther with Jagdish in our jeep. I need to monitor his recovery in our hospital. We should reach there long before they arrive in the jeep," she said.

"Yes, Meena," replied Shane meekly, while observing her as she continued her march towards the medical centre. Shane's shoulders sagged and he looked deflated. He looked over at the group of officers, and as one, they raised their teacups to him in homage to another victory over a subservient woman. Shane once again drew himself up to his full height and retreated in Meena's footsteps to regain some dignity. Their laughter conveyed the fact that he was failing miserably.

That evening, Lal and Shane struggled to position the equipment in the confined space in front of the rear seats in the Cessna. It rested against the back of the pilot's seat on the left side of the cabin. They had removed the equipment from its heavy crate and discarded all the insulation and timber. They then constructed a protective layer around it into a more manageable package, with some of the wood from the crate. The box now weighed much less, but still weighed as much as Shane. He ran over to Meena and expressed his concern about the aircraft's ability to get airborne with such a load. She was confident it would manage and assured him there wouldn't be a problem. Shane could not be convinced, so Meena relented, and to put his mind at ease, she searched for their pilot for the journey across the border.

Shane returned to the aircraft to finish loading and stood back to take a good look at the plane, which he hoped would keep them safely aloft over hostile territory for the one-hour flight. He could feel the adrenaline coursing through his system and tried to figure out a way of telling Meena this journey was not for him and that maybe he would be better going with Lal by road and allowing Monica to take his place on the flight. He knew this was a weak suggestion since the road journey involved possible encounters with border control officers and police who could detain him for violating the terms of his visa. When war threatened, the civil powers in any area were undermined by army commanders. This caused resentment and led to petty officials being less than cooperative. Shane was aware of all these factors but still struggled desperately to find a way out of this flying venture without losing face.

Monica had come to load food and water into the aircraft for the journey. This was the first time he had seen her without operating theatre scrubs and facemasks. She was not only beautiful but exuded an air of gentleness and calm. She tried to reassure Shane that the aircraft was in good shape and capable of taking the load safely. She would take the jeep with Lal to their hospital in East Pakistan and meet them there. She explained that taking the X-ray equipment and him by road would be too risky because of possible encounters with the Pakistani military and groups of insurgents. She and Esther would travel in the jeep with the medical supplies in their trailer. Monica mentioned that she had flown on this aircraft often with Meena while evacuating seriously ill patients to Calcutta. Shane never bothered to ask who the pilot was on those occasions.

He was asking her about the size of the engine and its capability when a voice from behind interrupted. "The engine is a 230-horsepower Continental with a three-blade propeller, as you can see. The engine and propeller, like the aircraft, are manufactured in the United States, and the whole aircraft has been overhauled recently by Indian Air Force engineers. The reason it looks so disheveled is because of the special camouflage, which is common to all our military aircraft."

Shane's mouth dropped open when he observed the source of this brief lecture. Meena stood behind what appeared to be a sixteen-year-old boy in flight overalls, which boasted wings on the left breast and bars on the shoulders, identifying him as a flight lieutenant. He proffered his hand, and Shane meekly shook it. The handshake was firm and full of confidence.

"Adam Keeler at your service. I will be honoured to transport you and your equipment to your destination." Shane was speechless, and the sight of Meena standing behind the young pilot with a smirk on her face didn't help.

Keeler led Shane to the engine compartment, where he opened the cowling hatch to check the oil level. Sure enough, the engine gleamed and looked in top condition. "I have absolute confidence in this aircraft; otherwise, I would not fly it," said the young lieutenant. "I am, however, very concerned about the nature of the mission. We cannot fly too high, or we will be exposed to radar from within East Pakistan. As we are not at war with that country, at least not officially, we are technically violating the sovereign airspace of a foreign country. They can legitimately scramble units of their air force and shoot us down. We cannot depend on aircraft from our own air force to give us air cover, as we do not yet enjoy air superiority in the area.

"Should we fall into the hands of the Pakistani Army, we will almost certainly be shot as spies after public humiliation in front of the world's press. It would confirm to the world that India is directly involved in undermining the Government of Pakistan. And you are worried about the airworthiness of this fine aircraft?"

Shane mumbled a reply of sorts, but Keeler was not finished.

"So, we must fly very low to avoid radar. This, however, will expose us to small-arms fire from every armed individual on the ground who decides to take a potshot at us, and – who knows? – they may be lucky and score a direct hit on some vital component on the aircraft, or indeed the pilot and occupants."

Shane looked at the ground and was extremely uncomfortable as Keeler smiled at Meena.

"But that is nothing compared to the damage a heavy machine gun can do, or if we are unfortunate enough to encounter an anti-aircraft battery. And as for surface-to-air missiles…"

"Okay, okay," Shane said in a tone of resignation as Meena and Keeler laughed at his discomfort.

Keeler apologised, put his arm around Shane's shoulder, and invited them for tea in a ramshackle hut, which served as the officers' mess. "Seriously though, Mr. Shane, I have flown several missions to the same destination, and I'm confident we can avoid trouble. We must first fly north about fifty kilometres to a jungle airstrip, which is controlled by the Mukti Bahini, who are made up of Bengali elements of the Pakistani Army who have deserted and local people who have armed themselves in their struggle for independence."

He looked at Meena, who took up the briefing while they drank tea, which had the necessary calming effect on Shane. He certainly needed it as he caught Meena's eye. She looked uncomfortable.

"Shane, I have had to compromise my principles in undertaking the first part of this journey. I have not told you before now of my motivation for agreeing to this expedition. My father is a high-ranking officer in Pakistani military intelligence. I know he is involved in conflict resolution and has been involved in peace negotiations between Pakistan and India.

"Flight Lieutenant Keeler's commanding officer informed me earlier that my father asked them to request me to deliver this package to Colonel Shahid, who seems to be one of the senior military leaders of the insurgents, or at least the ones in contact with the outside world, including the Indian Government. He is also an old family friend, and he and my father served in the Pakistani military. I know the package contains an offer of peace talks with the 'Rebels', as he calls them, and is a last-ditch attempt to maintain the union between East and West Pakistan. This offer is being made without the knowledge of the Pakistani Army or the Martial Law Administrator in East Pakistan. Their army only wishes to oppress the people and rule by force, but my father wishes to at least try to maintain the links with those elements of the military who have deserted. He feels that it is a long shot but one worth trying. It was hard for him to admit that the army had committed too many atrocities on the people they were supposed to protect, but he was willing to attempt to redeem the situation by covert means. If the offer came from the Martial Law Administrator, it would not inspire confidence among the insurgents as he is seen to have the blood of his people on his hands.

"I promised to undertake this task against my better judgment, but it will have been worth it if it helps bring peace and stability to the area. The package also contains brief details of Indian Army plans for this area in the event of an invasion."

"Meena, why can't your father undertake this mission himself if it is so important?" Shane was perplexed by this turn of events and the intrigue that went with it. He felt that Meena was betraying the whole purpose of her work, and he reminded her of this fact, saying, "You are compromising your safety and the lives of all the people you work with who will be affected if the Pakistani military captures you with such incriminating material in your possession."

She averted her eyes and said, "I am finding it difficult to defend my actions, but I must trust my father's judgment. He is seldom wrong in these matters. He admitted to Indian Army Intelligence that should this initiative fail, then the Indian Government would certainly commit troops across the border to confront the Pakistani Army and prevent more atrocities from taking place. The Indian Government intends to pave the way for independence by helping an interim government maintain regional stability. Having done that, they fully intend to withdraw and return to India as soon as possible. My conversation with senior officers earlier confirmed this. Their main concern is that peace should be established in the region. They know the Chinese are watching closely to see whether India tries to annex the disputed territory. If India does this, then you can be sure they will threaten to invade as they did in 1962; only this time, they will remain.

"The Indian Government is in a precarious situation. They seem to have pulled a lot of troops down from the border with China to strengthen their hand in this impending conflict. Did you notice the Alpine gear carried by soldiers in convoys arriving today? They have come from the high border passes in the Himalayas, north of here. They have been at over ten thousand feet, and now they are being asked to fight in tropical conditions at sea level. The whole region is under threat, and I fear we are in the midst of a very volatile situation.

"Shane, if there is any chance that our actions could shorten this conflict, then we must involve ourselves. My father cannot be here to do this because he must be contactable by all the parties involved to ensure no misunderstandings occur. I will relay any information to him through our Indian Army contacts here. He will not respond to anyone else for fear of being compromised. Also, me delivering the package will legitimise the operation as Colonel Shahid knows me and will take what I have to say seriously."

Later in the evening, Keeler and Shane chatted near the army compound. They observed Meena walking arm in arm with Monica and Esther in the fading light. "A formidable group of ladies," noted Keeler.

Shane agreed and asked Keeler about the different garments worn by the women.

"Well," said Keeler, "I am no expert, but the nurses are wearing a shalwar kameez, which is basically a long dress or shirt worn over loose-fitting pyjamas. Many working women usually wear this garment. As for the good lady doctor, she is wearing a saree, which has many regional styles. It is the most versatile of garments and is universally recognised in every country on the subcontinent. It can transform instantly from the most revealing garment into the most modest garment and will be worn in rice fields or boardrooms. I have to say that the doctor is a good exponent of the virtues of the saree.

"My mother and sisters wear sarees in the Delhi style when shopping. As my name suggests, our family has British ancestors who married local people. Our community likes to refer to themselves as Anglo-Indian, but to be precise, we are Eurasian or mixed-race, as I suppose you would call it. Now, it's time for sleep; we have a busy day ahead of us tomorrow."

The officers and Shane retired to their respective tents for the night after a feed of Indian Army rations. Shane slept well, mainly because of the shots of whiskey from military stocks. Meena had politely declined the alcohol as she left earlier, conscious that she was the only lady in the company of officers.

An early breakfast preceded their departure, during which Shane confronted Meena and sought further assurance that all this intrigue was a good idea. Meena once again brought Shane to the operations tent to meet with Keeler. Shane apologised for being persistent as they walked together in the early morning sunshine.

"I will not even try to understand the politics, Meena, but I'm certain you are sincere in your efforts. The only reason you need to convince me is that our work at your hospital seems to be secondary in importance."

Meena replied, "I can assure you that it's not. Anything I can do to prevent the deaths of innocent people in this conflict will have been worth it. I don't know which direction this conflict will take, but when it is over, I will be sure that we at least facilitated the best possible outcome. I truly believe this, Shane."

Having observed their debate, Keeler got up from the table and stretched. "We had better be on our way then, ladies and gentlemen," he said.

He unfolded his chart on the table and pointed out their route. "The moment we take off, I will communicate very briefly by radio with our contact at the destination. Ten miles from the destination airstrip near the town of Chatra, we must look for a white flare at a pre-arranged location. They usually send up the flare when they hear our engine in the distance. This flare signifies that the landing area is safe and not threatened by elements of the Pakistani Army. We must keep radio transmissions to a minimum. The flare should go up approximately fifty minutes after we take off from here. The people on the ground can then prepare for our arrival at the improvised landing strip, which I know from previous missions. And Doctor, I believe you know the terrain. Of course, we cannot fly directly to our destination; instead, we must follow a circuitous route planned precisely to steer clear of roads, railways, and rivers on which gunboats are currently active.

"As a precaution, I will not use the radio during the flight, but we can hear transmissions. This will be useful if we must abort our mission for any reason. Should we become separated on the ground, you must proceed to your hospital in Gaibandha by any means. If any other armed elements intercept you, you are on legitimate Red Cross business and are returning to your hospital. The package, which must be given directly to Colonel Shahid, is on the aircraft. I understand, Doctor, that your presence will convince Shahid of the authenticity of the material we deliver. In addition to your father's material, it contains vital information and military charts detailing the movements of Indian troops in this sector, should war break out. This will enable Colonel Shahid to coordinate his fighters with advancing units of the Indian Army in the event of an invasion.

"If I am incapacitated for any reason and should anyone other than Colonel Shahid try to relieve you of this bag, then there is an incendiary device, which can be activated by pulling the red loop visible on one corner of the bag. Don't worry, Mr. Shane. I fully intend to be there when we give this to Shahid, and the presence of Dr Meena is critical to convince the colonel that our information has come from a legitimate source. This is only one set of plans for a relatively small sector, so if the plans are destroyed, then I'm sure the guerilla fighters on the ground will get the information through other channels. However, we need to ensure that this package doesn't get into the hands of the Pakistani military. With respect, Doctor, I am surprised that we are involving the daughter of a high-ranking officer in Pakistani military intelligence. But that is only a personal opinion. I must defer to the wisdom of our intelligence services in involving you and your father in this process."

Meena and Shane looked at each other. The package seemed to contain more compromising material than was first revealed to them. This intrigue was getting out of hand, and Meena's eyes betrayed some discomfort. Shane picked up on this. He smiled at her, and she was somewhat reassured. She met with Monica and Lal and instructed them to proceed by road to their hospital as planned and to place the Red Cross placard prominently on the windscreen of the Land Rover. They had already loaded Jagdish's stretcher. Meena checked that he was comfortable. Jagdish held her hands in his, and this wordless exchange was all they needed.

Monica seemed uneasy as she embraced Meena and seemed reluctant to let her go. Meena spoke some comforting words to her, which Shane didn't understand, as she kissed Monica on both cheeks and wiped away her tears. Both women seemed to get a boost from this encounter, and each set about their tasks in preparation for the journey. Meena urged Monica and Esther to be careful and to return here if they encountered any sign of danger on the journey. She marked on their map several missionary schools and churches on the way, should they need help. As Shane and their driver, Lal, looked on, the ladies joined hands to pray for a safe journey. Meena then collected her medical bag and proceeded to the aircraft.

Keeler checked all the exterior surfaces of the aircraft before climbing aboard and strapping in. Shane strapped himself into the back seat and checked the restraints on the wooden crate and Meena's medical bag beside him. Their other luggage was in the rear compartment behind Shane's seat. His earlier doubts about the aircraft's ability to lift all this equipment and people were soon dispelled when the powerful six-cylinder engine roared to life. The noise was reduced by the headsets each of them wore.

Keeler sat in the left-hand seat and deftly manipulated the engine controls. Meena looked on and waved to Monica and Esther from the right-hand front seat. She looked comfortable and very much at home as Keeler taxied past rows of army vehicles parked at intervals amid jungle trees and vegetation. It was amazing how the jungle wrapped itself around such a large force. The only vehicle they saw moving was their white jeep and trailer on its way to the main road to the border in a cloud of dust. Luckily, the rain had bypassed their camp, making progress for the jeep easier as it left the dirt track and turned onto the tarmac road to the border.

The aircraft taxied towards the far end of the jungle clearing and bounced and weaved over the uneven terrain. It turned into the wind and stopped. Keeler said, "I must do power checks to ensure that the engine will perform correctly during the take-off and in flight." He applied the brakes and eased the throttle lever forward, and the engine roared as oil pressure and temperature were observed. He manipulated the flight controls, and Shane noticed surfaces moving at the tips of the wings when the control column was turned left and right. Then, as he pulled the column rearwards, Keeler looked behind him to check the movement of controls on the surfaces at the aircraft's tail.

"Those are the ailerons on the wingtips; they cause the aircraft to turn," Meena explained. "The movement of the elevator at the back causes the aircraft to climb and descend. And now the flaps will extend at the back of the wings. They will ensure extra lift on our take-off roll." Shane assumed Meena had picked up this knowledge during the frequent medical evacuation flights Monica had mentioned earlier.

A motor whirred, and the flaps extended at the rear of the wings. "Okay, everything is in working order," said Keeler. "Make sure your seatbelts are tightly fastened and hold on as the runway is quite bumpy." He lined the Cessna up, and after a quick check of the instruments and engine power, he pushed the throttle lever forward, and the aircraft accelerated down the runway. Shane was shoved back into his seat as he observed the vegetation becoming a blur on either side. The ride was bumpy, but Keeler soon pulled back on the control column, and they were suddenly airborne. They banked sharply to the left in a climbing turn, which brought them back over the airfield as Meena reached forward to move a lever that retracted the flaps.

"Thank you, Doctor," said Keeler. "I'm glad you are familiar with this aircraft." It was incredible. There wasn't a single sign of the mighty military force camouflaged on the ground below as they levelled out and took up a course that would bring them across the border into hostile territory and towards their destination. After levelling off at a thousand feet, Keeler started a stopwatch and settled down to study his chart. "We will be in East Pakistan in ten minutes. I hope to climb to three thousand feet in an area we know has no radar coverage, and this should keep us safe from small-arms fire. We will still be in the range of anti-aircraft batteries or fifty-calibre machine guns, so please keep your eyes peeled; if you see anything you think is unusual, then I need to know. Okay?" Both nodded in agreement, and Shane started to scan the terrain and as much of the sky as he could see around the overhead wing of the Cessna. Keeler made the quick radio transmission he had talked about and was answered with a curt reply of "Acknowledged."

Chapter 8

Shane could only think about one thing, and that was of bullets rising from the jungle and piercing the fragile structure of the Cessna. He sat on his hands for a while in the belief that they would protect his most vital organs from ground fire. When he noticed Meena looking at him and smiling, he quickly folded his arms and assumed a more relaxed pose. He wondered if there was any thought safe from her.

"Shane, I can assure you that bullets will not stop at the organs you choose to protect but will most likely continue up through your body and probably exit from the top of your head. So relax; if it does happen, you won't even be aware of it."

He still looked uncomfortable and said, "As a woman, you cannot even begin to understand the attachment we men have to our lower appendages, and the sheer terror we experience when some external force threatens to cause us to part company." They all laughed and settled down more as they passed over the beautiful terrain not far below.

Keeler tweaked the instruments frequently and consulted the chart to ensure its content matched the contours and ground features below. True to his word, he avoided rivers, railways, and roads, but always kept sight of them in the distance. The mostly flat landscape and many rivers confirmed this area as the delta of the mighty Ganges and Brahmaputra rivers and their tributaries as they flowed majestically towards the Bay of Bengal. The people below would be accustomed to the seasonal rise and fall of the freshwater from the rivers and seawater from the ocean, and their devastating effect on low-lying areas. No borders were visible from above, and there was no hint of the impact of violence on the population below. From their aerial vantage point, everything seemed so normal.

On several occasions, Shane drew Keeler's attention to craft on rivers in the distance, which looked like gunboats. Keeler explained that the people below depended greatly on the rivers that traversed the country for transporting goods. He was satisfied that Shane had seen fishing vessels or river barges. The rivers, which offered a livelihood to much of the population, could also be a source of death and destruction when cyclones and hurricanes struck from the Bay of Bengal, causing severe flooding and massive loss of life. Hadn't they enough to deal with, keeping the excesses of nature at bay, without the ongoing political upheavals?

However, a new nation was possibly emerging, and birth pains would be inevitable, Shane reasoned. But how many innocent people must die to facilitate the birth of a country? Shane was in the middle of these thoughts when suddenly Meena drew their attention to the flare a few miles ahead and slightly to their right. The stopwatch showed fifty minutes.

"Near enough perfect timing. I will begin our approach now, so make sure your seatbelts are secure. Shane, please ensure that your equipment is also secure. I don't want that crate dislodging and coming in on top of me during landing."

Shane did as Keeler asked, glad Keeler had dropped the formal 'Mister' from his name. "Yeah, everything is secure," Shane responded as he braced for the landing.

They were getting very close to the ground now, and looking ahead, Shane could only see trees with patches of reddish-brown clearings in between. Barely visible was a strip of land, which seemed as thin as a pencil. Surely, he wasn't heading for that. He noticed the sound of an electric motor as the flaps extended at the rear of the wings once more on either side of the aircraft. Keeler had asked Meena to extend the flaps, and she reached forward and operated the lever. Shane once again dismissed her evident familiarity with the required procedures for landing based on her having paid attention during previous flights.

The aircraft was lined up on the narrow strip in the jungle, and Shane felt an adrenaline rush as trees became visible on either side. The sudden thump heralded their arrival in a blinding cloud of dust. Visibility was only a few metres beyond the windshield and zero to either side as the aircraft braked hard and taxied to a halt. Keeler cut the engine.

"We usually taxi using engine power, but I'm anxious to avoid the engine noise being heard," said Keeler.

The sudden silence was unnerving. He slid his seat back to the stop, as did Meena, and he let go of the controls as he turned off several switches while consulting a checklist. Several figures materialised out of the swirl of dust on either side, and one man with a rifle slung on his shoulder attached a tow bar to the nose wheel of the Cessna and then commanded loudly for the rest to push. Four men were pushing the wing strut on either side and moving quickly over the ground.

The dust had now settled as they were pulled towards the jungle. They could make out the outlines of several vehicles in the undergrowth. Suddenly, the aircraft was swallowed up by the jungle. Freshly cut banana tree branches were placed methodically over every inch, and chocks were placed on the wheels to prevent it from rolling. This process all seemed like a familiar routine to these men.

"They are very efficient, are they not?" asked Keeler in his usual clipped military tone as they alighted from the Cessna, now hidden under a canopy of greenery that blended in completely with the surrounding jungle. There was no way it could be spotted from the air, or indeed, from the ground. The man shouting orders earlier stepped forward, business-like, shook Keeler's hand, and motioned for them to follow him to the vehicles. Shane felt that the man gave the impression of tolerating the visitors as a means to an end. The other men were a rough-looking bunch who all eyed the newcomers suspiciously. Their leader delegated two men to stay with the aircraft as he handed one of them a field radio and issued instructions in Bengali. Each of the men nodded submissively. Meena held on to the package and asked Shane to bring her medical bag with them on the short journey to meet with Colonel Shahid. They made their way to the vehicles, one with a heavy machine gun mounted on the back. The blotted-out star and crescent insignia of the Pakistani armed forces was just visible on the doors of all the vehicles, leaving no doubt as to the origins of their transport.

As they mounted a jeep, they noticed one of the men left behind climbing onto the top of the aircraft's wing. Another man handed him a hosepipe from a barrel on the back of another truck, barely visible beside the plane.

Keeler explained that they were refueling with aviation gasoline and preparing the aircraft for the next leg of their journey. "They are under strict instructions to destroy the aircraft completely should any army units threaten to overrun the improvised airstrip," he said.

"But what about our X-ray equipment?" said Shane in alarm.

"It would then become a casualty of war, I'm afraid," said Keeler. "Don't worry. The army has been very slow to venture so far into the jungle lately. These men and their comrades have been inflicting heavy casualties on the Pakistani military in ambushes and attacks on army patrols, as you can see from these captured vehicles. Let's go now and meet Colonel Shahid.

His headquarters moves occasionally, but it should be no more than a thirty-minute drive from here. I have flown several missions into this airstrip, but it will be my first time meeting the colonel. Again, for security reasons, we must follow a circuitous route in case military agents observe us. Many people are still sympathetic to the army, so we must be careful."

There was no humour on the faces of those fighters who accompanied them as they faced each other in the back of their jeep. Their leader, Hassan, seemed to impose his serious demeanour on the rest. Keeler said, "Hassan was a leader in a prosperous village nearby, which experienced the excesses of the military in a search for militants. He told me previously that some locals were falsely accused of collaborating with the insurgents. This was not the case, as the villagers were only concerned with farming and the welfare of their families. They had a school and a welfare centre and had successfully developed disease-resistant crops with the help of the United Nations after last year's devastating cyclone.

"They could not convince the soldiers of their innocence, and without warning, they set about making an example of their village to discourage collaboration with rebels in the area. They systematically burned every building to the ground and destroyed all the crops. Men were taken into custody and never seen again. Women were violated, and in some cases brutally murdered. Hassan returned to his village from a trip to Dhaka, where he was buying seed, and as you can imagine, he is still traumatised by the destruction that greeted him. He is now an uncompromising enemy of the authorities and will not cease fighting until a just and peaceful government is installed in their country. If this means independence, then he will have no problem with that. His immediate priority is to avenge the destruction of his village and its people." Hassan looked at them and nodded slowly with a determined look. He only understood a few words of English, but he knew precisely what Keeler had told them. Meena gently placed a hand on Hassan's shoulder, and he visibly relaxed. Hassan announced in Bengali, while Meena translated, that he was coming to terms with losing his village and trying to create a future for his family as best he could. Thankfully, his family had been spared, and he was very supportive of his wife, who had experienced unspeakable terror in the attack.

Meena said, "Contrary to what people in developed countries think, women who are raped are seldom shunned and ostracised by their communities and families, but the damage occurs mainly when the women withdraw into a world of shame and self-loathing, and the condition can be so destructive, causing the inevitable breakdown of relationships.

"The fact that Hassan's wife is a trained nurse helped," she explained, as Hassan revealed more. "She busied herself with rebuilding the community to regain what had been taken from them. She is acutely aware of the effects tension and stress are having on the children in the villages, so her primary aim is to implement programs aimed at relieving their trauma. Hassan takes immense pride in her efforts and their two young children, who seem unaffected by the recent events. He feels it's time for everyone to partake in building a new country. The current conflict is only a small part of that process, and Hassan is confident of ridding the country of their oppressors and banishing them back to West Pakistan, where they belong."

"His wife sounds like you," said Shane. Meena hid her blushes with her hands. Shane was getting a first-hand account of the consequences of war on these people. It made his decision to join Meena on her journey seem more worthwhile. He was forced once again to consider the notion of a hierarchy of suffering, and he wondered how his family tragedy compared to the suffering of these people. Hassan seemed confident that these strangers were allies and worthy of trust. On making this assessment, he and his comrades started to smile and joke among themselves.

Chapter 9

The small convoy moved slowly along the jungle path. Villagers on the route offered food and tea, and the passengers soon realised the extent of the villagers' support for the freedom fighters, or Mukti Bahini, as they were known locally. It would be challenging for the army to subdue these villagers, so they confined their activities to the bigger towns and highways more and more. Ironically, the civil service still tried to function as best it could, and all the government institutions feigned normality. The rivers were vital arteries in supplying essential food and materials to inland areas. So, the army confiscated most vessels for their own use, and they were now a target for the Mukti Bahini forces, which attacked and looted them whenever possible.

However, to try to overthrow the Pakistani Army with such meagre resources would take a very long time, and they realised early on in the struggle that assistance from their Indian neighbours would be an essential component in any victory over their oppressors. Encouraging close ties with the Indian Government would not have been their first choice. Still, they couldn't rely on help from the international community or the

United Nations because of adverse reactions from the Russians and Americans. The Chinese were also watching events very closely. India was their only ally for the present, and they felt they should exploit this relationship fully and hope that once independence was achieved, the Indian forces would only stay for the length of time it took to form a stable government. In the meantime, the troops massing on the Indian side of the border would soon be coming, and the Mukti Bahini would assist them in trying to overthrow the Pakistani government and its collaborators, and gamble on a swift Indian withdrawal once independence had been assured. This strategy betrayed their suspicions of any motivation the Indian government may have for invading, but any help they could get in freeing themselves from tyranny would be gratefully accepted.

***

Colonel Shahid surveyed the terrain before him. Always conscious of the need to occupy an area that could be easily defended in an attack, he expressed satisfaction with the defensive positions hastily arranged for his meeting with the visitors, whose convoy would join him soon from their improvised airfield. According to reports on the radio, they were fifteen minutes away, and he decided that once the meeting was over, his units would again disperse and relocate elsewhere. This would ensure that they could remain one step ahead of the army, which was, no doubt, kept aware of their movements through their network of informants.

Shahid was confident that his closest advisors were to be fully trusted. Some elements of the Pakistani military had only recently defected to his guerilla army. The field equipment they brought with them included radios that could be used to transmit their location to units of the Pakistani Army operating in the area. He was uneasy, therefore, since his visitors were unaware of the importance of the items entrusted to their care. The outline of the planned invasion by Indian Army units in this sector was part of the consignment. This also contained strategic rendezvous points, where the advancing Indian troops could gain a foothold and control communications routes, such as railway junctions and bridges at river crossings. These were the actual plans. He knew that the Pakistani military now possessed the more elaborate fakes, which were leaked to known collaborators. He questioned the use of the doctor as a courier but agreed that should she be captured, then her contacts in the Pakistani Government, including her father, would ensure her release. He hoped his old friend DaSilva would never suspect the true nature of his daughter's involvement. Shahid knew that DaSilva's hope for a federation of states on the subcontinent was futile, at least in the short term. No, independence for East Pakistan was the only way forward, and whatever alliances needed to be forged in the future would be the new government's job. The formation of Bangladesh was Shahid's priority, and as a soldier, he felt it was his job to facilitate this process by whatever means he could.

Shahid moved down the hill to his jeep and proceeded to his temporary headquarters. He prepared the new package for onward delivery and hoped they would not object to this change of plan. He had no choice. Their aircraft was the ideal means of delivery. He knew his allies to the south must be made aware of the plans to coordinate their movements and assign objectives during the invasion. The package for onward delivery contained codes and names of vital contacts in areas of importance who could impart crucial local knowledge of the terrain to Indian Army units as they advanced further into the country on their way to the capital, Dhaka. The delivery by air was an inspired decision, and it avoided the many possibilities of interception if it was delivered by any other means. Too many times in the past, their operations had been compromised by intercepted phone and radio communications.

He listened to the sound of vehicles approaching and went to meet them. He smiled as the young woman alighted from the first vehicle and came to greet him. She certainly had her mother's good looks and carried herself as proudly as her father. He was suddenly racked with guilt for putting her in danger and felt the weight of betrayal on his shoulders. He resolved there and then to reveal everything to her. The decision to help him would then be hers; he would not force her to do his bidding.

"What's the matter, Uncle? You don't look too pleased to see me?"

He realised that his smile had turned into a look of concern, and he grinned sheepishly. How could the little girl he once knew while teaching in the military training college in West Pakistan have become such a beautiful woman in so few years? "Forgive me, child, you have surprised an old man with a vision of beauty in a sea of ugliness. These days, I am so used to seeing the devastation of battle that you overwhelm me. Surely, your dear mother is present when I look into your eyes."

They embraced warmly, and he motioned for them to follow him to the buildings, a former headquarters of a brave police force that had been the first line of defense against the Pakistani Army as they tried to enforce martial law on the population. Many courageous police officers now formed a critical component of his guerilla army, providing arms and vital local knowledge.

His training as an officer in the Army of Pakistan ensured an unwavering devotion to etiquette and good manners. This quality was tainted, he believed, by the fact that he and his colleagues were deserters from an army to which he was once lovingly devoted. It pained him to witness his erstwhile comrades falling in battle before his eyes. He needed to remind himself daily of the need for this war and hoped it would not be prolonged and vicious. It made him question his motives, seeing fellow Muslims being overwhelmed by ambushes orchestrated by him, and with the intervention of his old enemy, India. How ironic! Only a few years ago, he had commanded an artillery unit in a war with India near their border with West Pakistan. Now, as he prepared to meet them as allies, he felt the old certainties drain from his usual assertive demeanour. He trusted the Indian Army officers without question but was deeply suspicious of their political superiors in Delhi. Indeed, there were contingency plans to evict the Indian Army should they overstay their welcome in the new Bangladesh.

Shahid turned to Meena and gestured to the foreigner waiting at a respectful distance.

"Don't worry, Uncle, he is a European technician who has come to repair my X-ray equipment."

He eyed the European curiously. "I believe you, Meena, dear, but forgive this old man's suspicious nature. I cannot believe in coincidences in these troubled times. I am so conscious that the Americans and Russians would do anything to infiltrate our units, for whatever reason. You can rely on me being courteous, but please forgive me if I refuse to share information with you in his presence."

For the first time, Meena realised the extent to which she had entrusted herself to Shane, and suddenly, a dark cloud of doubt crossed her mind. She recovered sufficiently to defend her good judgment. "If he is representing some foreign power, then I am certain that it is a benevolent intervention, and I can be certain of his loyalty and discretion. Please trust me on this, Uncle. Now, let me introduce you to him and our Indian pilot."

Shane looked about him at the collection of heavily armed men as he stood waiting beside the vehicles. There were disciplined, smartly dressed soldiers, but among them were villagers in bare feet carrying an array of weapons from mortars to heavy machine guns. They eyed him suspiciously. His eyes refused to meet theirs, and he sought out the haven of security surrounding Meena and a distinguished-looking man in a uniform similar to the soldiers he had seen, none of which contained insignia or headgear portraying previous rank. The man had grey hair and a kindly face, at least from a distance, and Shane slowly headed in their direction. The man observed Shane, and his neutral expression changed to one of polite concern as Meena whispered in the man's ear and smiled. Shane relaxed and held his hand out to this influential figure while looking to Meena for support. Once again, she seemed to be reveling in his discomfort.

"Colonel Shahid at your service, sir. Welcome to our camp, Mister...?"

Meena was soon at his shoulder. "Shane," she said.

Shane gripped Shahid's hand and did indeed feel the warmth. "Ah yes, Mr. Shane, please follow me and let us drink some tea. I hear that you had an uneventful journey on the aircraft. I am so glad, since Pakistani Army units are operating in this area and one could be unlucky enough to encounter anti-aircraft fire. Not the best introduction to our beautiful country."

Shahid then greeted Flight Lieutenant Keeler more solemnly, recognising the need for formality since Keeler seemed to be the first member of the Indian armed forces to set foot on the emerging new nation of Bangladesh. Keeler knew differently, having inserted and extracted by air several Indian Special Forces undercover reconnaissance patrols sent to survey strategically important bridges that would be used for river crossings in the event of an invasion by the Indian Army. The significance of the moment was not lost on them.

"Keeler, you say. Not a very Indian name. I presume that you hail from the Anglo-Indian community. Did you have a brother serving in the West in '65? I seem to remember an Indian fighter pilot named Keeler being shot down in that war."

Keeler seemed astonished that this man knew his elder brother. "Why, yes! How...?" Keeler trailed off the enquiry and was suddenly conscious of the need to keep information to himself.

Shahid smiled and informed them all that his unit had captured a Flight Lieutenant Keeler, whose fighter jet had been shot down during hostilities in the last Indo-Pakistan War. "I often wondered what became of him when we handed him over to our intelligence people after capture."

Keeler's eyes dropped, and he reverted to a polite silence. Shahid was immediately aware that things had not gone so well for the pilot, who he assumed was Keeler's brother, and the shame he felt was evident. He had been aware of the mistreatment of prisoners in earlier conflicts and knew that neither side was blameless.

"I understand, Lieutenant. I would, however, be glad to know that he is well and safely back with his family."

Keeler assured him that he was and immediately sought to change the subject. Shahid did not need to know that Keeler's brother was now retired on grounds of disability, but seconded to Indian Air Force Operations to help formulate the Indian Air Force strategy in the event of an all-out conflict between the two countries.

In recent weeks, Keeler had made several flights to jungle airstrips in this region, including where they had just landed. Still, he did not feel the need to share these experiences with Shahid, to avoid compromising his country's involvement in sensitive operations. Previous flights had dropped off people who had been involved in intelligence gathering. Keeler knew better than to converse with those people during the covert flights, or even to remember their faces. He was acutely aware of the dangers of being shot down and falling into the hands of Pakistani Army Intelligence. Shahid seemed to understand Keeler's reticence and moved the conversation forward.

Shahid continued his briefing during tea and concluded that their efforts on his behalf could reduce casualties in their sector. The package they had delivered was passed to his assistants and taken away. He counselled Meena that the villages

86

in the area of her hospital may be strategically important but also assured her that the presence of the hospital should offer a degree of protection from military operations. "Please convey a message to my good friend DaSilva that when this conflict ends, and we have achieved independence, I will implore the new government to consider an alliance with West Pakistan for the overall good of the region. Like him, I dream of a federation of states on the Indian subcontinent that will end conflicts and create a powerful alliance against all superpower interference in our politics. I do not think it is achievable soon, but this conflict is a good opportunity to lay the groundwork for such an idea. Let us get you on your way again; for us to remain in this place for too long could invite attack from the air if our position is divulged."

Meena embraced him fondly. "Yes, Uncle, I will convey the message. Please look after yourself and all these young men. Should you need urgent medical assistance, please send transport to collect me. Do everything in your power to prevent either side from using landmines and ask your men not to leave munitions lying around where children can find them when the war is over."

All those present who understood English pondered this as nothing more than a lofty aspiration but politely nodded in the affirmative.

Meena was shocked when Shahid produced another package to deliver to his comrades near her hospital. She did not hide her look of dismay but reluctantly accepted the package for onward delivery. *This is the nature of relationships in times of war,* she reasoned with herself, unconvinced. If Shahid was embarrassed, then he certainly didn't show it. He had assured them that their onward flight progress would be monitored, and when they landed at their next destination near her hospital, they would be met by people who would relieve them of the package. Keeler confirmed that he intended to drop them and their equipment while leaving the aircraft engine running and then depart immediately back to his base in India.

Meena concurred and mentioned that this was also her wish. "We can only do our best, Uncle. May I ask you for some morphine, please, before we depart?"

Shahid passed the request on to one of his officers, and as they walked to their vehicle, a medic appeared and presented Meena with a military satchel with a red cross on it. "Courtesy of our friends in the Pakistani Army, captured recently. I think you will find all you need, including field dressings and morphine."

Meena was delighted and appreciated the significance of receiving essential medical supplies from these soldiers, knowing they were leaving themselves short. "Thank you so much, Uncle. I will not forget your kindness."

Chapter 10

Having reviewed their instructions, they proceeded back to their vehicle. Shahid left them in no doubt that his troops were only a small part of the many groups aligned against the Pakistani Army. It would be a while before all their forces could be unified. Some were just bandits, out to take advantage of the conflict and make as much as possible from the suffering of a displaced population. Meena knew this and had promised Shahid that they would be careful to avoid such groups and the Pakistani Army.

"Is he really your uncle?" asked Shane when they were departing.

Meena smiled. "No, it is simply a term of endearment used for older family friends. I also call his wife 'aunty'. She is a good friend of my mother. I am sure all our families will have a reunion when all this fighting is over. I hope Shahid survives the conflict; the new country will need good men like him. However, he was being polite when he agreed with my father's dream of a federation of countries on this subcontinent. This is simply diplomatic hyperbole. There is no way these people will countenance any future relationship with Pakistan, due to the level of pain inflicted on them by that nation."

The return journey to the airstrip was uneventful, but the villagers looked on in anticipation as they passed. Meena knew they craved stability in their country and to be left alone to cultivate their crops and raise their children free from fear and violence. The threats from nature in the form of cyclones and flooding were more than enough to contend with. War was something they did not need. Besides, the political situation never affected yields in their harvest. Stability would bring prosperity, and peace to worship at their mosque and go about their daily lives. This was all threatened by talk of an escalation in the war, and Meena could see that these people were on the verge of taking to the road as refugees to avoid the fighting. This would lead to a vast humanitarian crisis, for which the aid agencies were unprepared since the present government refused to allow foreign groups into the country's interior.

The inability to help people in their home areas meant they would need to walk long distances to avail of aid facilities in neighboring India. The potential for disaster was very real, and Meena panicked inwardly when she considered the implications for the welfare of these vulnerable people in the event of such an escalation. She decided to concentrate on her area and prepare for every eventuality. They had enough food stocks and medicines to last for one month at least. After that, she would need to abandon her beloved hospital and take to the road with the people. It would be foolhardy to expect the war to be over quickly. She could only make short-term plans as circumstances may overtake her. She observed Shane and Keeler and prayed that God would keep them safe. She also worried about the progress Monica was making in their jeep. Sending her and Esther on the journey was not a very smart move when she considered the frequent reports of rape and violence against women in this lawless society.

Hassan stopped the jeep at his village and requested that Meena accompany him to one of the buildings. Several villagers needed their wounds examined. Luckily, none were infected, and she noticed they had been dressed by medics from Shahid's makeshift army. She was happy to provide them with some of her supply of antibiotics before they left. She was briefly introduced to Hassan's wife, Zainab, and they immediately bonded. Meena knew she would be working with this woman in future and asked Hassan to accompany Zainab to her hospital soon to include the village in their various health programs. Hassan's demeanour changed considerably, and he thanked her. Such a significant return for even the smallest act of kindness. Meena figured that this was the reason Hassan had asked her to visit his village and recognised the actions of a genuinely effective village leader.

With this thought still in her mind, after only a short drive, Meena saw that they had entered the jungle clearing and noticed the propeller of their Cessna poking out through the greenery. Ten men suddenly descended on the plane, and in no time, it was stripped of its camouflage and rolled out into the open. Keeler checked the oil level under the engine cowling and climbed onto the struts on either side of the aircraft to lift the fuel caps and check the fuel quantity. He knew the men had meticulously prepared the plane for the journey, but he was only following procedure by sticking to his checklist. The aircraft technicians looking on understood this. Keeler realised that the men were ex-Pakistani Air Force people, and he asked Hassan's permission to interview them, as they must have had vital information on the strength and deployment of Pakistani Air Force units where they had been stationed. He also wanted to know about anti-aircraft batteries along the route they must now travel

It turned out that the technicians had been stationed at Chittagong Airfield and had serviced Sabre fighter aircraft of the Pakistani Air Force. Even though they had deserted their units, they were still unwilling to betray their former comrades by divulging vital information to this Indian Air Force officer who, until recently, had been their sworn enemy. Keeler appreciated this and so did not press the issue. He saluted them and shook their hands.

He approached Meena and Shane and requested that they load their gear onto the aircraft again and climb aboard. He finished his inspection of all the outside control surfaces of the plane and climbed aboard himself. He was very businesslike and proceeded to read aloud his checklist as the men on each side pushed the aircraft forward and positioned it on the runway, clear of the trees. Keeler looked to one of the technicians for a thumbs-up signal and got clearance to start the engine. They were engulfed in a cloud of red dust as it roared to life. He immediately began to taxi and backtracked to the end of the runway. On reaching the end, he had already completed his pre-departure and power checks while taxiing, so he immediately applied full power when they lined up on the runway stretching before them. They accelerated down the clearing, and as they passed the group of men on the ground, Keeler eased the control column back. They were airborne again, the powerful aircraft climbing into a clear blue sky.

"We will soon reach a railway line, which we will follow for twenty minutes before turning southeast towards our destination, which is ten miles from your hospital and surrounding villages. It is too close to our destination to fly higher than fifteen hundred feet, so we must keep our eyes peeled for military units because any troops on the ground will fire on us. Both sides will view us as the enemy and a noisy, relatively slow-moving target in the air, which is too tempting for any armed man to resist."

Shane immediately turned his attention to the ground below and systematically scanned the tracks and roadways through the jungle for movement. He tried not to think of the consequences of encountering gunfire from below.

As the aircraft levelled off and he was happy with the flight's progress, Keeler said, "Pardon my coolness during our conversation with Colonel Shahid, but my brother's experience at the hands of his fellow officers in the Pakistani Army is still fresh in my mind. Interrogation methods in use these days never consider the long-lasting psychological trauma that remains with the victim. Thankfully, my brother is a strong individual, and he currently advises aircrew on what to expect should they fall into enemy hands. Oh, and I do not share Shahid's optimism that your area will remain free from conflict."

Meena's heart sank.

"Just north of your hospital is a low plateau. The terrain near your local villages slopes down to the Brahmaputra River, along a valley through which a railway runs parallel to a road, which makes it an ideal location to place artillery units that can control troop movements on both road and railway. So, I am certain both sides have recognised this fact and intend to occupy your hospital's surrounding area. Of course, you are also aware of the Pakistani Army garrison at Balashi on the river, a few miles from your hospital."

Meena turned to Shane, and they both looked worried. Meena felt sure that Shahid's package contained plans to counteract the scenario just outlined by Keeler. The thought occurred to her to throw the package out of the window. Just then, Keeler banked to the right and began climbing. Shane saw the slightly higher ground ahead, and Keeler pointed it out on the map. Beyond it, the ground sloped away towards the river below.

"When we cross this higher ground, we will slowly descend towards our destination. Again, our clearance to land will be a white flare ten miles from our destination. They have been instructed to send up the flare only when they hear the sound of our engine. "Radio communication is too dangerous in this area. Please keep a good lookout and inform me of anything suspicious looking, no matter what."

They approached slightly higher ground covered in trees when Shane noticed something not quite right in a clearing ahead. He was in the back seat on the right side of the aircraft behind Meena, looking ahead. Keeler looked left as he maintained the descent as they neared their destination.

"Lieutenant Keeler, I just noticed a reflection off something on the side of that hill."

Keeler banked the aircraft to the right but used the rudder to maintain the heading. He rummaged in his flight bag and pulled out a small pair of binoculars. As soon as he had focused on the hill, looking past Meena and observing the area in question, he immediately dropped the binoculars and applied full power by ramming the throttle full forward as far as it would go. At the same time, he banked sharply to the left. "Jesus, I'm sure that's a Pakistani anti-aircraft position, and I think I also saw a heavy machine gun located there. Start praying and tighten your seat be—"

Just then, an almighty bang shook the Cessna, and a whoosh of air and debris filled the cabin. Shane was paralyzed with fear and clung to the seatbelt mount to try to make sense of what was happening. The ceiling was suddenly red, as was Meena's left arm and face. He looked at his knees and noticed blood everywhere. *This can't be,* he thought. His heart sank further when he noticed Keeler slumped forward over the control column. *Oh God, please don't let him be dead.* This he felt more out of self-preservation than out of concern for Keeler. He regained his senses somewhat as he noticed Meena recover from the shock. She immediately took her head in her hands to examine for injuries.

"I'm okay, Shane; this is all Keeler's blood."

The plane was on a slow descent, and Shane noticed a big hole in the floor beside him and two in the ceiling, one directly above Keeler. The tie-downs on the crate to his left were mainly shredded, and when he moved to check on Keeler, the crate's weight caused the remaining strands of rope to snap. The crate suddenly broke loose, ramming Keeler's seat forwards and pushing his body into the control column. This caused the plane to enter a dive at an alarming rate of descent. Shane looked through the blood-spattered front window and noticed the ground rushing up to meet them, with only jungle showing in the windshield.

Meena reacted immediately and shouted, "Shane, release your seatbelt and climb into the luggage compartment behind your seat. Pull the ropes of the crate rearwards, towards you, as hard as you can. Do it now, or we will soon die."

The words were said calmly, but Shane got the message loud and clear. The word 'die' had the desired effect, and he released his seatbelt and immediately fell forwards onto the back of Meena's seat, which thankfully held. He could nearly stand on the back of her seat and reach behind the partition that divided the luggage compartment from the cabin. He pulled himself over the back of the rear seat into the compartment, wasting no time in turning and catching hold of the crate ropes. He pulled for all his worth. He noticed the greenery in the front window and glanced at Meena, whose eyes were riveted on his. The look told him that death was not an option. He heaved with all his strength, and suddenly the heavy crate eased towards him.

Meena wasted no time. She pushed Keeler back, and without force acting on his control column, she now gently pulled her control column back towards her. Shane could not believe it when the Cessna slowly recovered to level flight, and soon, the forward window looked out onto clouds once more. She then eased the throttle back, and as the engine's roar ceased, things became a little calmer.

"Now, Shane, stay there and tie the crate securely with the seatbelts. When that's done, come forward and help me with Keeler. She reached down to the floor in front of Keeler and wound his seat back fully. "This plane has a very simple autopilot. I can engage it for now, and it will automatically maintain altitude and heading on its own. Also, push my bag forward so I can reach into it, and please open the medical kit Shahid gave us."

Shane secured the crate and retrieved the medical kit. He opened Meena's bag to enable her to reach back and extract a drip and some heavy bandages. She hung the drip from the sun visor, expertly inserted a needle into the back of Keeler's hand and placed a piece of tape over it. Using her stethoscope, she listened to his heart and then proceeded to examine what appeared to be a severe wound to his right thigh.

"He is still with us, but we must land as soon as possible. Here, come forward and place these bandages on the wound. Bind them firmly but not too tightly. Thankfully, the projectile seems to have missed the femoral blood vessels, but he has lost a lot of blood, and the femur is shattered. We are about twenty miles from my hospital, so I am going to land on a nearby road, regardless of which armed groups we meet."

Shane looked at her and tried to comprehend exactly what she had just said. "What do you mean, *you* are going to land? We should try to revive him so he can do it. I don't know how you managed to get us out of that dive but don't push your luck, Meena. Please give him something to make him conscious."

"Shane, I am happy that his vital signs are stable, but even though he is stable, there is no way he could fly this aircraft with such an injury."

The look on Shane's face indicated many emotions. He was concerned for Keeler and truly afraid for his own safety but wrapped around those emotions was the feeling of disbelief as this woman calmly assumed responsibility for her patient and the control of this complex machine. She seemed to have no concept of their precarious situation, and he sought words to express his outrage.

"Meena, get on that radio right now, and to hell with the radio silence. Make a mayday call and tell anyone who will listen that we are neutral in this conflict and urgently require assistance to land. Surely they will direct us to a proper airport."

Meena glanced back at him and listened to Keeler's chest

again with her stethoscope. Shane looked past her through the windshield and swallowed deeply. The rising ground ahead looked dangerously close. Meena followed his stare, immediately pulled her seat forward, and flicked a switch on the instrument panel in front of her. The aircraft lurched for a moment as the autopilot disengaged, and Shane struggled to control his bowels. Meena expertly set the Cessna up in a gentle left turn and levelled off on a heading that brought them clear of the hill. She engaged the autopilot again and turned to face him once again.

Shane had settled himself between the front seats and now had a vice-like grip on each of the blood-stained seatbacks. He held her stare. He was losing patience with this woman and was close to breaking point. She took hold of his hands, caressed them gently, and slowly began to ease the tension from his body. He felt a mild, pleasing sensation course through his system and soon felt calm. He realised his predicament and suddenly pulled away in embarrassment and quickly folded his arms. She maintained the stare, and he returned it like a scolded child confronting their mother. He resigned himself to the situation and abandoned any further attempt at confrontation. He glanced out of the side window and began to sink into the comfort zone of the past he craved so deeply.

Meena realised this and knew of the dangers of this type of regression. She knew that she must not let him go there. One physical casualty was enough to bear, without having to cope with a mental case as well. "Shane, listen to me. Please listen right now. I don't wish to be alone with what lies ahead. I need you to be with me. Help me, please."

He glanced at her with contempt, or was it just plain anger? "Meena, please be serious and try to see the trouble we are in. I could cope with you as an extraordinary doctor, but now I see you fly this plane and wonder who or what you are. I felt we had an understanding that there would be no more secrets between us. I laid my soul bare before you, and you now return the favor with intrigue and deception. I'm unsure whether you are working for some government and you're using me to give your mission credibility. However, I'm here by choice, and given my present circumstances, I don't care too much about the future. You did warn me of possible danger, but the intrigue bothers me. I feel honesty is not important to you and that your precious mission is blinding you to the needs of others. You seem to have a hierarchy of needy people around you. The neediest seem to distract you from the needs of others. I only crave honesty and truth. Now, please call for help on the radio before we die."

Meena turned away, but he had noticed tears welling up in her eyes. He feared that he had said too much. He was about to speak again when she interrupted.

"Please fasten your seatbelt as tightly as possible, Shane. We are close to our destination. I never noticed a flare, so it would be dangerous to proceed to the airstrip. That anti-aircraft battery will have reported our heading by now, so the army will be looking for us. I know a straight section of road about ten miles from our hospital, near the village of Matherbazar, which could take this plane provided it is free of traffic. We need to land immediately. Keeler is very ill, and I have no more drips and only six ampules of morphine in my bag, and hopefully a few more in the army medical kit. So, we urgently need to get him to my hospital before he regains consciousness."

Shane said nothing; instead, he leant forward, secured Keeler's restraints, and rechecked his bandages. Meena banked the aircraft to the right and rolled out on a heading, which brought them into a valley with dense foliage on either side. Shane could make out the form of a road meandering through the jungle. Meena consulted Keeler's blood-stained chart and immediately began a descent. *No doubt she has a plan,* he thought to himself, and he let some unkind thoughts about her have free rein. He never realised that he had laughed out loud until Meena turned and gave him a stare that would dissect iron. He shrugged as she turned her attention to the task at hand.

"Shane, I'm going to land on that road ahead." He looked into the haze ahead but saw nothing, and fear again took hold of his nether regions. "I can see some civilian trucks, so I hope the drivers understand what's happening just before we touch down. We will only get one chance," she warned.

Just then, something snapping caused them to focus on the hole in the floor beside Shane's feet. Several flight control cables were visible, and on one of them, all but a few strands were broken. They protruded from the hole in the floor, through which Shane could see the ground below. The aircraft began to roll, and Meena corrected the movement with the control column. "I think that cable is the one that controls the rudder. There is no way I can control the aircraft easily without the rudder if the remaining strands on that control cable break. I'll be landing straight ahead no matter what, and hopefully, I will keep rudder movement to a minimum to prevent stress on that damaged cable. Thankfully, the road is dead ahead, so hold on tight and see if you can also hold Keeler."

Shane could see the trucks on the road ahead a few hundred feet below. They all seemed to be travelling in the direction they were landing. As Meena struggled with the control column and the engine throttle lever, he could see the road stretch unobstructed in front of one truck for at least a half mile. The aircraft stabilised somewhat when she extended the flaps, and as she reduced power, it plummeted suddenly towards the road. She made some final adjustments to the control column and took a final anxious look at the damaged rudder cable, visible through the hole in the floor.

Trees were now visible on either side, and Shane caught a glimpse of a truck as they passed overhead with only inches to spare. The trees and some telegraph poles were dangerously close to the wingtips, and as the wheels touched the ground, the cable in the floor snapped, and the Cessna suddenly veered off the road and into the vegetation. It just missed the trees and gradually slowed as Meena controlled the braking. The engine noise reduced as she closed the throttle, and the aircraft came to a stop. Their seatbelts held, as did Shane's grip on Keeler.

Meena was jolted forward even with the seat harness restraining her, but her arms instinctively came up to protect her face and arrest her impact on the glare shield above the instrument panels. She had the presence of mind to turn off the necessary switches during the shutdown. The sudden silence was so welcome. She immediately turned her attention to Keeler. "You can let go now, Shane; we are safely down. Let's get him out of here quickly."

It was hard work extracting themselves from the aircraft, which was still remarkably intact but surrounded by vegetation. Two truck drivers descended the embankment from the road and gently removed Keeler from his seat, under Meena's guidance, as she supported his injured leg. Keeler surprised them all by suddenly regaining consciousness and letting out a string of curses in protest at the severe pain that the movement was causing.

Meena smiled at Shane, and he realised that this was good news. "He is a very strong and fit young man, and his system is bearing up well to the injury. Let's lay him down, and I'll give him another injection for the pain."

She asked bystanders to organise some pieces of wood to make a splint for Keeler's injured leg and retrieved a bandage roll from her bag to tie the splint and immobilise the leg. Two men produced tree branches suitable for the job as a crowd gathered to investigate this strange event and render assistance in whatever way they could. Meena spotted no uniforms in the crowd, but it would not be long before military units arrived. She noticed the identification tags around Keeler's neck, identifying him as Indian military. She reversed them so that they hung down his back instead. He glanced at her and smiled through the pain.

"Madam, I don't know how we are alive, and on the ground, but I am glad someone has taken control of this mission. Should the military arrive on the scene, please leave me in their care, proceed to your hospital and await contact from Shahid's men. I don't think I can remain conscious for much longer." He relaxed as the morphine took effect.

"Yes, Lieutenant. I plan to ask one of these truck drivers to drop us near our hospital, and we can improvise a stretcher to walk the remainder of the journey, which is less than a mile from this road. By now, the nearby Matherbazar villagers will have learnt of our arrival, since news of dramatic events travels quickly in the jungle. Thankfully, they are very loyal and will endure serious danger to themselves to help us. I am also certain that Shahid's people are observing us right now, so we should have a degree of protection from the Pakistani Army."

Keeler dozed off, and Meena once again checked his blood pressure and the dressing.

Shane was trying to communicate with the people, and one college student who happened to be passing introduced himself in English as Hossain and volunteered to travel with them. Together, they secured the services of a truck and prepared an area in the back where Keeler could travel comfortably on their makeshift stretcher.

Hossain said, "I was in my final year studying medicine at university. I have experience as an intern at Dhaka University College Hospital. Towards the end of March, our studies were suspended after martial law was declared. All medical students were helping at the various medical facilities around the capital. I accompanied two doctors to Dhaka University's campus during curfew when the army attacked strongholds of rebellion.

"As the students on the campus were known leaders of the agitation against the authorities, they were targeted, and the campus became the focus of a savage onslaught from mortars and heavy machine-gun fire. I witnessed terrible atrocities at the hands of the soldiers, and my two colleagues were killed while assisting the many wounded civilians who had sought shelter in the university. At one stage, I was in hiding as soldiers rampaged through the residential blocks, killing indiscriminately."

Shane noticed that he wore the look of a man old beyond his years, who had seen unspeakable acts of violence.

Hossain continued, "Madam, one of the first victims of war is truth, as you know, but I do not lie when I say these things happened. I fled for my life and fully intend to help rid our country of those responsible for such acts. I instructed the villagers to move the aircraft to a safe place where the army would not find it. Rest assured, the army will not know you landed here, so you should evade capture. I have been on the run for nine months now and frequently return to Dhaka to procure medicines for our fighters in the rural areas."

Meena ensured that Keeler was settled comfortably and informed Shane and Hossain that they should get moving if they were to reach her hospital before nightfall. She glanced back at the aircraft, which had been pushed back onto the road by at least twenty willing locals, towards a junction and up a dirt track. These people were resourceful and had fashioned a length of wood fitted to the nosewheel to steer the aircraft. The last thing she saw of their Cessna was the tail disappearing and being swallowed up by the dense vegetation at the side of the road.

Meena initially eyed Hossain with suspicion but dismissed her concerns and accepted their need for his help. Her intuition cautioned that they would need to be on their guard against people suddenly inserting themselves into their company. Her guard was up as she surveyed all the people around them, but she shelved her suspicions for now because of the need to get moving as far away as possible from this drama scene that had attracted so many curious onlookers. She could not blame them when she took a moment to review the extraordinary spectacle of an aircraft landing on the road beside where they lived. Such events would indeed enter the realms of folklore in the area.

The truck moved off; Shane and Hossain sat on sacks of rice and wheat in the back, and Meena sat beside Keeler. He looked comfortable enough, mainly due to the effects of the morphine she had given him, but he needed blood urgently. Hopefully her equipment would still be intact at the hospital, and the fridge with her blood supplies in working order. She checked Keeler's blood group on the discs around his neck and felt confident that she had at least one bag of his O-negative group in her fridge. Shane had removed the replacement X-ray equipment from the aircraft, which rested securely beside them in the back of the truck.

The army called to Meena's hospital quite often these days and usually raided her stocks. She relied entirely on the supplies provided by the insurgents and the Red Cross convoys, which were becoming less frequent due to looting and the danger of being caught up in the fighting. She would be glad when this journey ended, and she could concentrate on her work as a doctor and leave all this political intrigue behind. She could not afford to be a political figure, but the way the villagers regarded her lately ensured that she would be associated with the freedom struggle, which did not sit well with her status as a doctor. Politics was not the reason for her being here; she would consciously try to avoid being a part of it.

She would ensure that the local commander took possession of the package given to her by Colonel Shahid, which would end her involvement once and for all. She looked back at Shane and observed him clutching the package as if his life depended on it. The contents would undoubtedly bring death and destruction to many, she thought once again. The point of no return had been reached; the only way casualties could be kept to a minimum was if the war ended soon. She inwardly prayed for this, and for the safety of her villagers and the children in particular. She could not countenance a repeat of her experiences in Vietnam and the devastation resulting from delicate little bodies being close to airborne, hot and angry shrapnel from exploding ordnance and anti-personnel landmines. A forlorn hope, she thought, as she checked the blood-soaked bandage on Keeler's leg.

Chapter 11

The Cessna was back! The radio message was garbled and unclear, but Major Ali Khan rejoiced when he heard the message. It had evaded them several times, but this time, he knew they had it. The aircraft, almost certainly Indian Air Force, was heading in the direction it took on at least two occasions previously. The only difference was that this time, the anti-aircraft battery had been in place on its route. If the reports were correct, the battery commander was sure that they had hit the Cessna, causing it to descend rapidly before they lost sight of it. He reported its last known heading and was confident they had inflicted severe enough damage to force it to land. The major immediately called for transport and assembled a force of three armoured personnel carriers, each carrying ten men, to accompany him. Hopefully, he could arrange for helicopter support, and with some luck, they could capture this spy plane that had been violating their airspace at will in recent weeks.

The major knew that war with India had not been declared, but border skirmishes were ongoing, and he would make sure his sector was secure. Capturing the Cessna and pilot would improve his standing with his superiors, and maybe even a promotion to colonel would soon follow. He also wanted, by all means, to be posted with his family to West Pakistan and away from the turmoil of this area of their country. It annoyed him that this campaign was already a lost cause; too many mistakes had been made. The Bengalis would have been content with a degree of autonomy, having won a majority of the votes in the recent election. This did not please the ruling elite in West Pakistan, and they sought to assert their authority by clamping down on the emerging Bengali rulers and their parties.

He agreed with the recent imposition of martial law, which was needed to maintain law and order, and curb civil unrest. He fought the Japanese in Burma with the Martial Law Administrator, General Niazi, when both were junior officers. Indeed, Niazi persuaded him to remain in the newly formed Pakistani Army after the British partitioned the subcontinent in 1947. That partition had been a disastrous compromise and resulted in continuous conflict between India and Pakistan. War with India was once again a distinct possibility as their troops massed on the Indian side of the border. He had been ordered to disarm and detain the Bengali officers and men in his command. Still, before he could carry out the order, they had fled to the jungle with their weapons, and he now knew he would possibly encounter these former comrades in battle as he set off in search of the Cessna.

Most of his senior officers were from West Pakistan, and they showed absolutely no understanding of the local Bengali culture in East Pakistan, resulting in shocking errors in judgment. He was determined to make the most of a bad situation and hopefully distinguish himself in combat. This was the only way he could hope for recognition as an outsider in his army, given that his birthplace was Bihar in India. For military officers born in West Pakistan to tolerate colleagues born in India would be unusual. Accepting someone from Bihar into their ranks would be intolerable, so the major, as a Bihari, was under no illusion as to the difficulties he would continue to face in gaining acceptance among officers in West Pakistan. The irony was that he was never fully accepted in East Pakistan either, where the Bengali population also showed intolerance to their fellow Bihari citizens. Progressing in East or West Pakistan would be equally challenging for him. However, he saw this mission as a personal challenge and was prepared to be judged on its outcome.

Venturing into the countryside with such a small force and no backup would be risky. He calculated that he could reach the garrison at Balashi on the River Brahmaputra before nightfall. Balashi was a strategic town at the junction of river, road, and railway, and the forces there had been reinforced recently by gunboats, which had secured the river in the area from attacks on commercial vessels by insurgents. These vessels provided the vital link for supplies from towns on the coast, and the military relied heavily on them. From Balashi, they could count on support from other units that would be more familiar with the terrain.

The small force made steady progress through mostly deserted villages unhindered. He observed the surrounding countryside from his command vehicle at the head of the convoy. They eventually reached Balashi at dusk and settled in for the night. During his briefing with the local commander, Lieutenant Shah, a radio message confirmed that a Cessna aircraft had definitely been hit and was last seen descending towards the main Dhaka highway near Matherbazar, an hour's drive from the Balashi garrison. Major Ali Khan rejoiced at the news. He informed the commander that they would start early the next day and hunt down the Cessna's occupants.

Lieutenant Shah revealed that he had a source in Matherbazar who would know of any incident involving an aircraft. If there were survivors of the crash, then he would know about it. He also had suspicions concerning the activities of a lady doctor at the local missionary hospital in the nearby town of Gaibandha, who was a frequent visitor to India. Intelligence reports suggested that she might be providing medical assistance to rebels, in addition to spying for India. Requesting further information on her from military intelligence was met with silence. The suspicion among his officer colleagues in Dhaka related to her origins in West Pakistan and the fact that she had an American mother. When they sought information on her father, they were threatened with severe consequences from superiors.

The major was intrigued by this information and confirmed they could use this lady's hospital as their starting point the next day. After all, her hospital was in the same area, just off the main road, near a cluster of villages he considered hostile, and therefore worth investigating. Lieutenant Shah also reported that the lady doctor's driver was a reliable source of information and had been in contact with an officer at a security checkpoint near the Indian border. He revealed that the lady doctor and a foreigner had recently departed India in a light aircraft. The major dismissed this information as unreliable; he knew informants would say anything to protect their regular payments from the military.

The garrison had, however, been placed on high alert; the Indian military may be about to invade, after all, and this aircraft was probably scouting for their advance units, which could already be in the area. Both officers would ensure their sector was secure and not get caught off guard. Major Ali Khan phoned superiors in Dhaka and requested a helicopter to assist them in their mission the next day. He knew this was a vain request but made it, nonetheless. The helicopter would give them a great advantage and help discourage an ambush on the road they would travel on tomorrow. Though very useful, the helicopter was also very vulnerable to fire from the ground, but the risk would be worth it if they did discover the Cessna. Their presence on the ground and in the air would surely discourage the enemy from engaging his convoy in battle. The daily patrol on the river by two gunboats in support would be an added advantage. He felt sure that all contingencies were covered, and that security would be tight, with minimal risk.

Both officers retired for the night, safe in the knowledge that the following day would be eventful and sure to provide a clearer picture of the Cessna's location. The major's suspicions had been aroused for no apparent reason by the mention of this lady doctor. His last thoughts before sleep related to some event in the past, but he could not make a connection.

Chapter 12

Thankfully, the truck finally came to a halt, and Meena negotiated the extraction of Keeler's stretcher with the help of Hossain and the driver. Shane was helping to unload the spare part for the X-ray machine. Several locals materialised from the jungle nearby, and their loud greetings acknowledged the arrival of Dr Meena. They eagerly set about relieving her of the makeshift stretcher carrying Keeler. She was obviously among friends here, and children clung to her eagerly as they set off on a track that meandered through the vegetation. They sent the truck on its way, and far from seeking payment, the driver presented them with two sacks of rice for the sick people in the hospital.

Meena was touched by this gesture by the driver, a Hindu from Calcutta. Indeed, the truck's cab was a mini temple to the goddess Kali, to whom the Bengali Hindus had a particular devotion. This was the great irony of the Indian subcontinent: the tolerance shown by the ordinary people for each other's religion in everyday life, only to be undermined by those intent on creating disharmony and confrontation between otherwise stable communities. The disharmony between Hindu and

Muslim communities was a fact of life in this country, but occasionally, a shining light of tolerance and cooperation shone brightly and shattered the usual suspicions and distrust among people.

Keeler was awake again and being borne aloft by four strong men. He sought out Meena, who looked at him with some concern. He was very quiet, and surely the pain could not have abated that much. She was desperately afraid that he would go into shock and that septicemia would threaten his survival.

"Only another half mile to the dispensary," she assured him, and he smiled briefly, which reassured her greatly. She marveled at the strength of the young man. During the journey in the truck, he begged her to save his leg from amputation as he had many more years as a fast bowler in cricket ahead of him. She could not conceal her worry but nevertheless convinced him that he would indeed play cricket again.

Just then, she remembered the orthopedic braces left by Russian doctors who had visited her hospital recently. Based on a system developed by Gavril Ilizarov, an orthopedic surgeon, the system used strong wires inserted through the bones on either side of the fracture. The wires were then supported by external frames to form a rigid structure to promote healing of the fracture. In time, the fractured bones grew back together, and the wires were removed to leave a healthy and robust joint. She had limited experience using the technique but felt sure it was her only option with Keeler's injury. His femur had been shattered by one of the bullets that had penetrated the airframe of the Cessna.

Thankfully, some of the energy had been expended by the time it reached his leg, and it seemed like a clean enough break with few fragments and had miraculously avoided severing major blood vessels. With this in mind, she picked up the pace and marched determinedly, and the others were forced to keep pace with her. Shane was bringing up the rear with four women carrying the X-ray equipment and all the other supplies on their heads. The lady carrying the X-ray part did not seem to be aware that she was carrying over sixty kilograms on her head. Each sack of rice was nearly as heavy, and he marveled that they could still move so gracefully. Hossain explained that carrying such loads was second nature to them and that their daily chores consisted of carrying water from the river and huge bundles of firewood from the jungle. They gracefully negotiated the uneven surface and smiled as they exchanged banter. He had no idea what they were saying but felt sure that he was the subject of their conversation. Suddenly, quite a substantial building of European design loomed ahead, and he saw Meena disappear inside. They had arrived at her hospital.

Shane took in the surroundings and was impressed by the beautiful vegetation surrounding the hospital, which was a very impressive building, situated in a place where mud houses were the norm. A generator hummed in the background, and he realised that electricity was not available in the nearby villages, which put everything in perspective. Only then did he remember the package given to them by Colonel Shahid, and he noticed Hossain holding it in the company of some of the villagers as they disappeared into an area behind the hospital. He presumed Hossain would keep the package safe. He was suddenly distracted by an elderly nun directing the new arrivals. He entered the building in search of Meena, and one of the first rooms he passed contained the X-ray machine. He closely examined it and discovered the outer casing opened, revealing what seemed to be a bullet hole in the vital component for which he had the replacement. He retrieved his tool kit and the new component with the intention of starting work immediately.

He was greeted by the elderly nun, who was European and spoke with a definite German accent. She took Shane's hand and led him to their refectory for refreshments. She produced the usual jug of lime juice from the fridge, and he gratefully drank the cool liquid.

"I am Sister Gertrude. You must be tired after such an eventful journey. The villagers told me of your ordeal and how lucky you are to be here in one piece. Some of the younger ones had run ahead, and they could not contain their excitement while telling us that Sister Meena was coming and bringing a flying machine with her! They have very fertile imaginations at that age. Come, let us see how the young man is doing. He is under the care of an excellent doctor. Sister Meena is a very experienced surgeon, so he stands an excellent chance of recovering fully from his injuries."

She led him in the direction of the operating room. Shane stopped suddenly and looked enquiringly at her. "Sorry, Sister Gertrude, did you just say *Sister* Meena…?"

Just then, Meena emerged from a room in search of them, and Shane noticed a plain brass cross on a chain partially covered by the folds of her saree. The cross had not been there during their journey; he was sure of it. He stared incredulously at it, and Meena, noticing the object of his attention, placed her hand over the cross between her breasts and moved towards him. "Shane, please, let me explain…" But he had turned away, bewildered, and walked slowly to the exit. She stared after him in dismay and then suddenly shook off the incident and turned to Sister Gertrude. "Come, Sister, we have work to do."

The night was very still and so peaceful as Shane sat alone on the edge of the road leading to the nearest village. It was late, and the stars were at their most beautiful in the near-total darkness. Nevertheless, people still moved about, and he observed them setting up campfires and settling down for the night. The lady doctor was back. People came from all the villages for treatment. Armed men were also to be seen but kept on the move and always seemed to be glancing anxiously towards the track leading to the main road. He could only assume that they expected the army to descend on the hospital because of their dramatic arrival earlier. Surely, everyone must know by now, no matter how hard the locals tried to keep it quiet. If the soldiers were to attack now, they would most likely come from the direction of the main road. Shane felt a little uneasy at the prospect but felt sure that no military force would be stupid enough to venture this way until daytime.

Earlier, he had observed Hossain giving their package to a group of armed men, and they suddenly disappeared into the jungle. He wanted to confront Hossain to find out what was happening but was intimidated by the weapons they carried. He was perplexed when Hossain joined the men and even seemed to command them. He decided to consult with Meena about what they should do about the package, even though he knew she would be busy treating Keeler. He briefly interrupted Meena as she was scrubbing up before operating on Keeler. Both she and Sister Gertrude had apparently spent a lot of time preparing the operating room for the surgery. He noticed an array of mechanical devices and surgical implements aligned on trays adjacent to the trolley where Keeler lay unconscious, attached to the usual drip and monitoring equipment.

When he told her about Hossain and Colonel Shahid's package, she stared at him for a while before responding. It seemed to her that her earlier suspicions concerning Hossain had been accurate. At least the worry of being caught with such incriminating material was gone and only Keeler remained to link them with the Indian military aircraft. He stubbornly refused to give up his identification tags and insisted on continuing to wear his flight overalls, which identified him as an Indian airman. Meena respected his wishes. There was a certain logic to his concerns; he was anxious not to be regarded as a spy in the event of being taken prisoner by the Pakistani Army.

"Thank you, Shane. There is nothing we can do about it for now. Hopefully, the package ends up with the local commander. Maybe Hossain is part of the local insurgency group. In a way, I'm glad to be rid of that package, and to be honest, I was very uncomfortable when that man Hossain suddenly appeared in our company. Now, I must go to operate on Keeler. Please make yourself comfortable and I'll call you if I need your help in the operating theatre." He noticed her smiling just before pulling up her surgical mask. *Fine,* thought Shane. *At least her sense of humour is intact.*

Shane went to sit on the hospital verandah and continued to observe the people as they cooked on open fires. He knew Meena would have difficulty trying to explain the presence of a wounded foreign airman in her hospital. So, he searched in his bag for his passport and the papers that identified him as a Red Cross worker. He hoped this would ensure his safety in the event of dealings with the military. He was deluded, thinking they wouldn't notice the stipulation that he remain on the Indian side of the border. He knew he would be in trouble and decided to settle on the excuse that he was simply here to repair hospital equipment while understanding that the presence of a foreigner would in itself mean trouble.

Later in the night, he completed fitting the part to the machine, and his work was done. The training he had been given in Germany had been excellent and everything made sense as he expertly navigated the complex internal workings of the machine. It was difficult for him to imagine what would motivate anyone to damage such a critical piece of medical equipment. He carried out all the tests required from the maintenance manual and all that remained was for Meena to test the machine on one of her patients. The generator had been started earlier for Meena's operation, which enabled him to do the tests, and on completion, one of the nurses had gone in search of Meena to inform her that her X-ray machine was ready for use.

Meena came running and excitedly surveyed all the power lights working as normal, and without a thought enveloped Shane in an intense embrace that made everything worthwhile for him: the journey, the flight, the deceit, even. She ran to get Keeler, issuing instructions to her nurses as she went.

Shane now viewed Meena using the machine on Keeler through the window of the X-ray suite. He stared as she examined the pre-operative X-ray images and could not take his eyes off her as she worked. The severe fracture showed dramatically in the developed images she had placed on the light box and Shane wondered if the leg could ever be repaired and work normally again.

He had witnessed one amputation already and could not conceive of a situation where Keeler would have to wake up to such a devastating outcome. He had forgotten all the lies and deceit and realised that this woman would do anything for her patients; they were her primary concern, and he was grateful that Keeler would come under this envelope of intense care. Even the shock of discovering the bullet hole in the machine registered with him now and he understood the deception, reasoning quite rightly that he may not have undertaken the journey had she told him what had caused the damage to the machine.

Shane finally accepted the fact that nothing could deflect her from putting maximum effort into keeping this facility running, against all the odds. This was her life and sole motivation for living. He slowly began to realise the extent of her commitment and if he managed to take his attraction to her and her beauty out of the equation and stop them clouding his judgment, then everything began to make sense. How shallow it seemed for him to consider such a beautiful woman and talented doctor so out of place in this environment. His mind could only see her in a richer, urban setting, and rather than share her with a multitude of poor and needy people, he could only envisage her as being more at home in the sterile, clinical, and more affluent environment of a big city.

***

Sister Gertrude woke him at about two in the morning; Meena needed him in the operating theatre. He had eaten earlier and eagerly retired to his room to shower and had fallen into a deep sleep just as he was reviewing the last few days and the drama of the flight. He was suddenly awake and after throwing on his clothes, he immediately followed her and brought his tools as she suggested. Meena was bent over Keeler's leg, and he noticed the wound on his thigh and felt like retreating. She asked him to place his wire cutters and medium-sized screwdriver in the sterilizer, and to put on a gown and mask. Sister Gertrude showed him the sink and gave him soap to wash his hands. When he finished, he gloved up and approached the table. Meena asked him to cut steel wires on the table to a certain length and she then placed clamps on each strand, which in turn held wires leading towards circular steel frames around the thigh on either side of the wound.

The stainless-steel wires went through the skin and bones in several places and were attached to two steel frames above and below the entry and exit wounds. Meena had obviously drilled through the bones earlier on either side of the break and inserted the steel wires, which now protruded from the skin in several places on Keeler's thigh. The individual segments of two circular steel frames were then secured to the wires with his screwdriver. She asked Shane to cut all the excess length from the steel wires and make them flush with the outside of the frames to complete the operation. The whole thing, to Shane's amusement, now looked like a running frame in a hamster's cage surrounding Keeler's thigh. She noticed the smile in his eyes above the face mask before they all, once again, headed for the X-ray machine with the trolley. Keeler was still unconscious under the general anesthetic. The images, taken from several angles, showed an amazing array of steel wires and frames holding the broken bones of the femur in place.

She seemed happy with the outcome and adjusted the frame slightly to perfectly align the bones. They returned to the operating theatre to close the wounds and she then covered the whole area in iodine and instructed the nurses to bandage the leg and put a cast on the knee to prevent movement and immobilise the leg. They then went for tea and Shane noticed the time. It was four in the morning. Meena was on a high and elated. She didn't think that the operation would have been such a success. Shane was caught up in the moment and embraced her. She kissed his cheek and smiled, then retreated suddenly, leaving the room for bed. He stared after her longingly and felt sorry that the moment was so brief. Tiredness overtook him once again, and he suddenly felt very weary. He too headed for bed. Sister Gertrude brought him tea and suggested that he sleep in the cool of the verandah of the medical centre.

He took her advice and rolled out a mat. He pulled the sheet around his shoulders and dozed off at around five in the morning. When he had enquired about Keeler before sleeping, Sister Gertrude informed him that the young pilot was comfortable.

"He was lucky to be here with Sister Meena," she'd said. "Just last year, a visiting Russian surgeon had taught Meena that technique and his surgical team had left several spare assemblies from which the special braces could be manufactured. Had this not been the case, then that young man may have lost his leg. There is a divine spark guiding that young woman in her surgical work. She is a gifted surgeon and, by all accounts, a gifted pilot."

Sister Gertrude left him and retired to the hospital, as energetic now as when he had first met her when they arrived earlier, leaving Shane to reflect on her wise words.

Chapter 13

People were awakening as the sun came up and Shane could smell wood burning from their fires nearby as they prepared their morning meal. The first meal of the day was their most substantial and he noticed vast quantities of rice being consumed in addition to the usual vegetables, which smelled delicious, and he realised that he had not eaten a full meal in nearly twenty-four hours. This caused him to review those event-filled hours through which he had lived, and it dawned on him just how lucky they had been. His thoughts focused on Meena, and he decided that from now on he would just accept her for what she was and not pass any remarks on her actions. She seemed totally devoted to her work with these people, and apparently, she was prepared to go to any lengths to ensure their survival in this wonderful oasis of healing and caring in a country torn apart by conflict.

"Good morning, Shane!"

She appeared from around the corner of the building, and he turned to greet her. The sun was rising behind her, and he could not see her face but her outline in silhouette caused him to stare. Once again, she had him at a disadvantage. Slowly, her smile materialised from the glare. She carried a small kettle, from which she poured the usual beautifully aromatic tea into a cup and offered it to him. He sipped it gratefully and smiled inanely at her from under the sheet, his head resting on his rucksack. He was unshaven and smelled awful, but she smelled wonderfully fresh, and he could not believe she had just completed a five-hour operation only hours previously.

"Keeler is awake and in good spirits and asking about you. Maybe after breakfast, you could go and see him. He is rather anxious about being captured, but I'm trying to keep him here for at least a week before arranging for him to return to the border." She sat cross-legged in front of him and regarded him with a playful smile.

"Meena, I surrender! I will ask no more questions and shall not speculate on what motivates you. I realise that a powerful force is working inside you and that it must be given free rein. I am humbled in your presence when I witness the extraordinary events happening around you. I now know that you are inspired, but I don't know the source of your inspiration. This trip is a revelation for me and has revived my spirits enormously. I can now face life once more and cope with whatever comes my way. Life is fragile and I know now not to expect too much from it. So please be assured that I will, from now on, just go with the flow, and not be surprised even if you levitate and turn this tea into whiskey, I promise."

The smile was still there, and she regarded him for some moments before laughing, but without humour. Then she suddenly turned serious, and her shoulders hunched forward as if a tremendous weight had been placed on them. She sought out his hands for comfort and he gladly offered them. The intensity of the grip surprised him.

"I know, Shane, that you see my actions in an extraordinary light, but I can assure you that I am all too human in so many ways. When duty calls, I fight so hard to avoid it and face a constant battle to overcome my fears. When I find myself in the depths of despair, there appears from within me a force, which seems to guide my every move during times of trouble. Sister Gertrude refers to it as the Holy Spirit guiding me from within along a path of greatness. She says that history throws up people with such influence just when they are needed most, and that these people will be protected in every way until their work or influence is no longer needed.

"Can you imagine how this makes me feel, especially when we survived an incident like that aircraft journey? Yes, Shane, I sometimes do feel inspired, and I genuinely do feel my prayers are heard. I do believe in God, and I am certain my actions are guided in some way. I find that when my actions are selfless, then things seem to work out better. It is as if working for others for no reward elicits a reaction from a divine source that more than compensates for the lack of material gain. Also, the sense of achievement and personal gratification is multiplied when I successfully complete a task that is of benefit to others, while never losing sight of the fact that pride usually comes before a fall.

"When I was studying medicine in the United States, I learnt to fly. I have flown that aircraft to Calcutta many times for medical supplies, and occasionally to our hospitals in India with patients who have needed specialist care. The Indian military commandeered it from an Italian mission located just across the border in India. The priest in charge is also a pilot and we work together. He lends us the aircraft and we, in turn, help out in his dispensary, where he looks after mostly tribal people, whose villages straddle the border as if the border didn't exist. They have inhabited those areas for centuries and have nothing but contempt for an imaginary line drawn on a map by foreigners. I will ask Keeler to have his Indian Air Force colleagues retrieve the aircraft for repair as it is vital to our operation here. Hopefully, we will be able to continue to use it when this conflict is over. Also, you saw exactly how important our X-ray machine is to the successful operation of our hospital. So please accept my sincere thanks for restoring this vital piece of equipment for our use."

Shane noticed that her serious face had turned to a smile as she reminisced. He was beginning to get the measure of this woman and felt sure that her apparent weakened state was just a ploy to lead him on once again, forcing him to reveal more about himself. He resigned himself to a stubborn silence and was determined to maintain it. Once again though, she surprised him and caught him off guard. Her gaze became more introspective and intense.

"Shane, I told you earlier that I have an American mother, and she is living in her hometown in New York State. Also, as you can see, I am a member of a religious order and Sister Gertrude is responsible for that." She extracted the cross from the folds of her saree and held it up to reinforce the point. "I met her in Harvard just after I finished my medical studies. She is my mentor and inspiration. She even managed to convince my mother that life as a doctor among the poor would be the most fulfilling career for me.

"My mother is still in shock from the encounter, and to this day she can't understand how her precious daughter was whisked away from under her nose. She is from an extremely wealthy family, and it is through her fundraising efforts that this hospital continues to operate. Please do not broadcast the fact that she is a very influential member of the intelligence community in the United States. I have to be honest with you, she relies on reports from me to give her organisation up-to-date and accurate information of what is happening in this country. It may seem subversive, but this accurate information enables them to formulate the most effective policy when dealing with government officials in this country, who tend to embellish their accounts of the dire situation that exists here. There is someone else in this area who feeds her information. I'm not sure who, but I have my suspicions.

"My father is, as I mentioned previously, working for the Pakistani Government, and if my intuition is correct then he will be found in the thick of the politics surrounding this conflict. My parents met when he was in Washington as a military attaché in the Pakistani Embassy there and in the United Nations in New York. During that time, he cultivated contacts in many different embassies, contacts he exploits shamelessly to this day. That is why he can move between countries with impunity during times of conflict. He is part of a sub-species group of intelligence operatives made up of similar diplomats from every country. It seems to me that they are the ones who decide the real policies that govern events all over the world. I try not to ask him too many questions regarding his work whenever we meet. I'm conscious that he is watching over me and that my safety is his priority. My mother would have it no other way, and even though he is motivated by overwhelming love for me, that love is reinforced ten-fold by my mother's scrutiny of his every move concerning my whereabouts and activities. He loves her dearly and we both laugh at his subservience to both of us. Our family reunions are amazing. Someday you will join us, I'm sure of it.

"I spent my early teenage years in Abbottabad in Pakistan. During that time, my mother returned home to New York after an amicable split with my father. She always referred to herself as a widow due to his constant absence from our home. They are such good friends though, and still have the highest regard for each other. When my father visits the United States, they have a good time together – discussing me, no doubt," she said with a smile.

"She dotes on him and worries about his work and the intrigue that surrounds it. I am concerned for him too. He enjoys such a status amongst all the shady characters in so many governments. He gets treated like royalty by secret services the world over, to such an extent that I wonder whether it is these agencies, and not governments, which are the real power behind the conflicts everywhere.

"He is the product of his Portuguese ancestry and his Catholic upbringing in Goa. I feel that being neither Muslim nor Hindu isolates him somewhat from factional politics on this subcontinent. I understand that he holds a very high rank in the Pakistani military, but he is loath to speak of the exact nature of his work. My mother's Baptist upbringing imparted a love of sacred scripture in me that I found inspiring, and this sustained me through my medical studies at Harvard, to such an extent that I felt compelled to consider religious life. Meeting Sister Gertrude sealed my fate and her extraordinary influence on me has never waned, even to this day.

"You cannot believe the pressure my father put on me to return to live with my mother and lead what he terms 'a normal life'. When I defied them both to become a religious sister in this order, I thought they would disown me completely, but instead, they both offered me encouragement and support, thinking it was just a phase I was going through. They could foresee my future from an early age and knew that my life would be far from ordinary. They both believe in predestination, or karma, you see, and they saw the futility of resisting my desires and aspirations. They worry terribly for me but know that the drama that is my life must be played out to the final act. Well, I too feel divine forces at work every day and can only go with the flow, and hope that my actions will be for the greater good, even though my methods may sometimes seem illogical and insensitive. I feel sorry for the people around me, though, as I am a hard taskmaster and feel so cruel at times. You know I am fond of you, and I'm attracted to you, but I know where my future lies, and your recent loss may cloud your judgment. So let us be simply close friends and enjoy each other until we eventually part."

Shane felt a warm sensation course through his body and

also felt elated by her words and revelations. He knew that what she was saying was true and that he only had a fool's hope for a future with her. For any man to spend his future with this woman would mean risking living the life of rolling dice, not knowing which face would present itself from day to day. At least she had clarified her position and, far from feeling rejected, he felt allied to her in her ambitions for the future. "Meena, I understand perfectly what you're saying and I'm grateful that you clarified where you stand. I know you would be unhappy in any other walk of life. Your judgment can, however, be clouded by your devotion to these people. All I ask is that you consider your welfare more often and try to yield to the wishes of those around you, who see things that you may be blind to. When you venture forth on your various missions, please recognise others' anguish for your safety and keep their needs and worries in focus at all times."

Meena was nodding in agreement, but he felt sure that her mind was elsewhere. He wasn't wrong.

"I can hear our jeep, Shane!" she shouted suddenly. She nearly frightened him to death as she jumped up, spilling his now-cold tea on his chest as she did so. Armed men were taking up positions as they too heard the roar of the Land Rover's engine in the distance. They were expecting an assault from the military, but Meena was in full flight as fast as her legs could carry her towards the improvised road. She was shouting at the men in broken Bengali to put away their weapons. They complied but took up defensive positions, nonetheless. The sound of the jeep got closer, and Shane could make out the roar of the engine as Lal negotiated the rough terrain with the four-wheel-drive engaged. Meena had disappeared around the bend in the path leading to the main road, followed by all the village children, who were intent on catching her.

Soon the vehicle appeared, and the children were perched precariously on the trailer with Meena sharing the front seat in an embrace with Monica, who looked ecstatic and relieved at the end of the journey. Esther's arms were draped over Meena's shoulders from the rear. He realised the close bond among these people and appreciated the love and concern they had for each other. The sense of community was very strong and heartening to see. It became evident to him that this bond was one of the things Meena had succeeded in creating, and he perfectly understood her absolute commitment to maintaining it, no matter what.

Chapter 14

The jeep rolled to a halt outside the hospital and Lal cut the engine. Meena hugged Esther as she alighted from the rear of the jeep. A deafening roar from the children replaced the engine noise. People who had been camping in the nearby jungle now started to emerge as they realised that a fresh supply of medicines had arrived at last. Meena helped lift the children off the trailer and escorted Monica and Esther into the dispensary after welcoming Lal and asking him not to bother unloading the jeep, but instead, to go to his family in the village. Shane noticed Lal talking with some of the armed men and the way they eyed the trailer left him in no doubt that they intended to avail of the supplies at the earliest opportunity. The men returned to the shelter of the jungle and Lal left in the direction of the village.

"Where's Jagdish?" Shane asked. He was puzzled when Lal turned away and avoided eye contact with him. He had enjoyed good relations with the driver since his arrival in the country days previously. Lal didn't seem all that comfortable in the presence of the armed men either and looked relieved to be away from them. Shane shrugged off the incident and followed the ladies to the dispensary. The day was warming up fast as the people lined up in the shade of the trees and waited patiently for the doctor to start receiving them in the day clinic. He would ask Monica about Jagdish. He assumed that they had dropped him off close to his home village on the journey from the border.

The dining room was alive with chatter as Esther and Monica shared their experiences of the previous twenty-four hours in Bengali and English. Sister Gertrude translated for him, and he was surprised to find out that the jeep had had to divert around fighting only thirty miles from their present position. Some commando unit of the Indian Army had been surrounded in a village near a ground-based radar installation. They had failed in their bid to destroy the radar and suffered several casualties in the process. A helicopter that had tried to evacuate them had been targeted by anti-aircraft fire and was forced to retreat, empty and trailing smoke, to the border. The surviving Indian soldiers, when captured, had been wearing civilian clothes and spoke Bengali, and had insisted that they were simply locals and part of the insurgency.

The area had been in chaos with the Pakistani military reinforcing local units with heavy armour and anti-aircraft weapons. Apparently, they were expecting the area to be bombed, and they were taking no chances. When stopped at a checkpoint, Lal had taken an officer aside and explained that they were part of a medical mission. After a call on the radio and a wait of three hours, the officer allowed them to proceed. Monica was relating the fact that Lal had saved them from arrest and detention. It was then she mentioned that after the encounter with the army, Jagdish and Lal started arguing in a dialect that neither Esther nor Monica understood and soon after, Jagdish demanded that they drop him at the next small town, which was just a few miles from his village. He thanked Monica when she tried to dissuade him due to the seriousness of his medical condition, but they could only look on as he left them. Their last sight of him was as he made his way unsteadily on his new crutches towards a shop, where he seemed to know the owner.

During the rest of the journey, Monica could not convince Lal to explain his altercation with Jagdish. Meena looked towards Shane as if he should have Lal with him. When he shrugged his shoulders, she immediately went to look for him and Shane followed. Meena questioned some of the locals and they informed her that Lal was last seen departing his village by cycle and seemed to be in quite a hurry. They were puzzled by this, and Meena looked anxiously towards the road.

"I fear the worst, Shane. In the past, some of the local fighters have already suspected Lal of being an informant. It would be hard to convince them that the jeep and those in it had negotiated an army checkpoint and come through unscathed. Perhaps Lal was the reason they let them through. It would make sense if they wanted him to continue sending intelligence reports to the military. There's no way the army would allow a jeep fully laden with medical supplies to proceed without taking some of the medicines for their own use."

The worried look on her face caused him to wonder what all these developments meant. It didn't take her long to make a decision. Shane was now fully determined to trust her judgment and help in whatever way he could.

"We must have Keeler moved soon, Shane. I want you to unhitch the trailer from the jeep and drive him to an insurgents' field hospital in the jungle near Baona, which is closer to the Indian border. Hopefully, the insurgents can arrange to have him evacuated from there. Driving the jeep directly to the border is far too dangerous now that the army is on high alert. We have to trust the insurgents in that jungle hospital to get him across the border by whatever means. I simply don't trust the local fighters now that Hossain seems to be controlling them. I'll send Monica with you, as Keeler will need constant nursing and medication. It's far too soon to move him but we have no choice because the military will soon be here in strength if I'm right about Lal. We could hide Keeler in one of the nearby villages but it's impossible to know who's watching our movements."

Shane felt apprehensive about the plan but said nothing. Meena explained that Monica would know the way and that they'd be taking a route through the jungle that was not frequented by the military, and for the most part was in the hands of the insurgents. She hoped to get help from a man in the village who once drove a truck for a quarry company.

"It's too late in the day for the military to advance as far as here without quite a large force, so if you leave soon then it should be safe enough. I will send word to the local commander of the insurgents and request a meeting. He may assist us as the arrival of our medical supplies will be of value to them, and getting Keeler back into Indian hands will surely help their cause because of his knowledge of the local terrain. I'm also anxious about that man, Hossain. He seems to be controlling the armed men around the hospital. I feel that he's a leader of one of the radical factions not aligned with the official freedom fighters, the Mukti Bahini."

Shane mentioned that he had seen Hossain leaving earlier with Shahid's package, and also about Lal's encounter with the armed men from the jungle.

"Shane, I don't care about that package. If we're caught with such incriminating material, then we could be in serious trouble. We have to assume that Lal is an informant. His hasty departure without even meeting with his family is suspicious, so we need to be very careful. I fully expect the military to be here soon. It would be wise for us to abandon the hospital and hide in a remote village, but we can't all leave and there's no way I can desert my people here and let them face danger without me. But you and Keeler cannot be found here when they come." She briefly embraced him and hurried away to meet with Monica.

Shane set about his task and as soon as the trailer was

unhitched, he filled the jeep with diesel from the tank that supplied their generator. He checked the oil and water and made sure the jeep was prepared to take a stretcher. The engine was still warm from the previous journey, and he made sure the spare wheel mounted on the rear door was inflated. Some of the local men helped him and he noticed them keeping their weapons close by. They laughed and joked but he didn't understand what they were saying. Hossain appeared suddenly and Shane noticed the men stiffen and respond to his commands. Shane innocently informed him of their planned evacuation of Keeler and immediately regretted revealing the information. Noticing the look on his face, Hossain smiled and took him aside.

"Mr. Shane, we don't know who's who these days in this war. The local commander may be here soon, and he will assist you on your journey. He will send men ahead to inform the other leaders of your coming. I feel that you can accommodate maybe two of my men in the jeep, for your safety."

Just then a group of men appeared from the jungle and the one leading them approached Hossain. He seemed to be subordinate in the way he responded to Hossain's conversation – or was it orders? A map was produced and laid out on the ground. The men huddled around it and after some discussion, they departed towards the jungle again. Two men were left behind and immediately took up positions facing the road.

"Don't worry about all that, Mr. Shane. We were just considering the best possible route for you to take to avoid roadblocks on the way. My friends assure me that there is nothing to concern you. I shall accompany you, of course, so you can be assured of an uneventful journey. We must ensure the safe delivery of Lieutenant Keeler back to the border, you see." He smiled, put his arm around Shane, and led him towards the hospital. "You know, it is a marvel and a wonder to consider the strange circumstances in life that bring us all together, is it not?"

Shane seemed unsure of what to make of the situation. "Hossain, I feel that you are much more than a medical student and it is no coincidence that you suddenly arrived here just as this drama is unfolding."

Hossain's face suddenly turned serious, and he fixed Shane with a look that bordered on hostility. "This driver, Lal, has been under suspicion for a while now and we are sure he is passing on information to a brother of his in Dhaka, who works as a clerk in a government department. Our people have overheard their conversations recently and he seemed to be imparting information that could compromise our security. I have restrained my people up to now and given him the benefit of the doubt because of the good doctor's influence. It's a mystery to us how they managed to pass that checkpoint on their journey from the border when other locals have been subjected to beatings, and even execution on one occasion, when they tried to negotiate the same checkpoint. We feel that this man, Lal, poses a serious threat to us."

The real implication of what Hossain was saying suddenly dawned on Shane and he said, "So, you are the commander in this area, Hossain? Let's be honest here. After all, I did see you taking possession of the package we were supposed to deliver to the local commander."

Five loud bursts of rifle fire came from the direction of the village and the men suddenly crouched low, as did Shane, who seemed unsure of what to expect in the next few minutes. He looked towards the dispensary as Meena burst through the doors. She stood on the top step and looked in the direction of the village. She then turned to Hossain, and they held each other's stare. The hostility was overwhelming, and Shane struggled to comprehend the meaning of the encounter as Hossain looked away and Shane could only see the look of guilt on his face. Meena's fists came up to the side of her face and she suddenly let out a despairing scream that frightened Shane much more than any gunfire.

"No..." she screamed. She then seemed to recover her composure and, with one hand holding up the folds of her saree, she sprinted in the direction of the village. Monica and the other nurses followed, and Shane hesitated before accompanying them, while looking back at Hossain, who only walked purposefully behind them. Meena was sprinting hard, and nobody could catch her as he saw her disappearing into the jungle on a track that seemed to be a shortcut to the village from where the gunfire came.

Shane was breathless as he emerged into the clearing, around which mud-bricked houses were dotted in a haphazard but neat layout. He stopped and scanned the unfamiliar surroundings until he came across a crowd walking slowly towards a well at the centre of the village. He was confused by what he saw and needed time to interpret the scene before him. Meena seemed to be moving as if in slow motion towards a few individuals, big and small, who were lying on the ground about the curved slope that formed the boundary of the well, and on which stood three men with weapons pointed towards the individuals on the ground. Shane could smell the smoke from the discharge of weapons. Meena slowed and fell to her knees and lifted the smallest individual in her arms. On reaching, Shane could see the child's small head resting in the crook of Meena's left arm. The look on Meena's face alternated between despair and that of a medic looking desperately for vital life signs from the bodies lying around her. It had not exactly registered with Shane yet what lay before him, but the nature of the terrible vista materializing before his eyes slowly dawned on him.

The blood flowing over Meena's arm was dark and full, and left Shane in no doubt that the child's life had been drained away from her little body. The villagers slowly inched towards the scene of devastation and eyed the huddle of bodies apprehensively. They wanted to do as Meena was doing but eyed the gunmen warily. Hossain shouted an order from behind Shane and the three men suddenly ran back towards the jungle and took up a position behind Hossain, with their weapons pointed at the advancing villagers. It was the first time Shane had seen Meena cry and the look of distress on her face drew him to her side. He gently took the child from her arms. She forced herself to give the child up and, with no small effort, turned her attention to the little boy lying prone beside the body of a young woman, who was obviously the mother of the two children. The boy's face had been obliterated by the force of the bullet as it passed through him, and on exiting it had taken a portion of his skull with it. Meena did not need to check for life and instead took a cloth from one of the villagers to wrap around the tiny face and contain the contents of the child's shattered head. As Meena moved to the mother, relatives started to make themselves known. As the wailing started, Shane could see the men of the village turning their attention to Hossain, who stood with his arms folded a short distance away.

Shane felt his arm being gripped as he lowered the child and noticed Monica standing close behind him for protection. Meena was tending to the mother, who seemed so young and didn't seem wounded in any way until she turned her over and the abundant blood staining her back between her shoulders was evidence that she had indeed been shot. Meena turned her again, laid her on the ground, and gave her into the care of some women. She stood up and walked back in the direction of the hospital. She stopped in front of Hossain and stared at him but said nothing. Eventually, he succumbed to the intensity of the judgmental stare and meekly tried to offer an excuse for the traumatic event that had just taken place. Meena still said nothing but held him in her gaze until he turned his attention to the villagers and tried to address them as subordinates.

The hostility evident on their faces made him back away until his comrades used their weapons to halt the slowly advancing crowd. Hossain had one last, defiant message for the villagers before departing. "Let this be a warning to collaborators. Assisting the occupying power will not be tolerated." The armed men guarded his path into the jungle and soon they were gone, but the atmosphere still held an air of menace and tension.

As the bodies were removed by the villagers, Shane and Monica followed Meena as she walked dejectedly ahead of them. Monica was telling him that she and Meena had delivered these children, and that the young woman had sometimes worked at the dispensary. Shane still didn't understand, and so Monica stopped and faced him.

"The young woman was Lal's wife, and the children were his son and youngest daughter. Their other daughter is at present with Lal's brother in Dhaka, the capital. This is in reprisal for Lal's treachery, according to Hossain. He had previously warned the villagers that such acts would, in the future, lead to reprisals such as this. The villagers were having none of it though and made that clear to him. He was lucky to have his friends there to save him.

"These people just wish to be left alone, away from the effects of the fighting. There is enough death from disease and hunger without armed men threatening them. I think Hossain got the message, but eventually, it will be he and his kind who will run this country."

Shane took one last look behind him and saw the group of people disappearing from sight among the mud buildings, carrying the bodies of the children and their young mother. He wondered whether those children had been in the crowd that met the jeep on its arrival less than an hour ago. Whatever Lal had done, Shane thought, there was no justification for this barbarity.

Shane was becoming hardened to the death of children in his life, and he was not comfortable with that fact as it threatened to plunge him once again into the depths of despair.

All he could do was support Meena and hope that her resolve and determination would somehow inspire him and navigate a path for everyone through this very challenging time. He was anxious about undertaking the journey with Keeler but resolved to dig deep and try to portray the leadership qualities that had deserted him after the tragedy of losing his own family.

Chapter 15

DaSilva anxiously paced up and down in the hotel room. He stopped in front of the window and surveyed the city streets below. The tension was rising, and killings had increased as the army came under pressure from insurgents who had infiltrated from the countryside and now held various key areas of the city. DaSilva made his feelings known as he could see all his plans coming to nothing as each day passed. The two other men in the room looked at each other. They seemed resigned to listening to the tirade and kept quiet. Eventually, DaSilva calmed down and sat near the window, against the advice of the hotel staff, as gunfire had been directed at the hotel regularly in the last twenty-four hours. Most of the journalists had been evacuated and only the most dedicated now remained. Both men with DaSilva had only arrived hours before and had to be admitted through a rear entrance disguised as laundry workers. They also had documents declaring themselves as journalists, as had DaSilva, but one man was from Indian Army Intelligence and the other represented the newly established Bangladesh government-in-exile.

"General DaSilva, we must accept the fact that no solution

exists to this situation that could retain links with West Pakistan." It was the man from Indian Army Intelligence who spoke, and DaSilva was inclined to agree with him. Captain Sinha was well-versed in the politics of Pakistan and could see the eventual outcome of this conflict in every detail. He explained that since Sheik Mujib, the leader of the government-in-exile, had been arrested and flown to West Pakistan, a martyr was created who inspired all Bengali people to embark on a struggle that could only lead to independence. The other man, Mister Abdullah, had been on Sheik Mujib's staff at the time of his arrest and had himself only narrowly escaped capture. He knew exactly the intentions of Sheik Mujib and the representatives of his government.

He now addressed DaSilva. "It is with a heavy heart, General, that we must resort to such violence in our quest for independence, but please remember that the army, since March of this year, has killed many, many thousands of my people, and displaced possibly millions, so they must pay the price for these war crimes."

DaSilva turned to the two men and after a moment's silence, he stood up. "It is so tragic that everything got out of hand so quickly. Had events been handled properly in the beginning then Sheik Mujib would now be leading the government of all Pakistan. But the ruling elite in West Pakistan could not accept a Bengali leader from East Pakistan, nor could they see the danger of denying these people autonomy. I've therefore decided to abandon my mission. I can only inform the government that any further intervention is futile. I foresee a reluctance on the part of the local Pakistani Army commanders to accept defeat so easily, so an invasion by the Indian Army is inevitable. I can only hope that the resulting war will be brief.

"My job now is to try to fashion an alliance on the subcontinent that will keep us all secure from intervention from any superpower, and hopefully, the international community will take us seriously in the future. I can only ask both of you to convey these wishes to your superiors. On another matter, Captain Sinha, do you have any word on the aircraft and its whereabouts?" Captain Sinha took a deep breath; he had been avoiding the subject up to now. DaSilva had been briefed about Meena's mission on behalf of the Indian Army earlier and was anxious to know more. He found it hard to understand the need for such a dangerous mission and now his patience had been exhausted. Sinha removed his jacket and detached the inside lining, exposing a military map of an area of East Pakistan bordering India.

"The aircraft has not returned, I'm sorry to say. We intercepted Pakistani radio messages that seemed to confirm a light aircraft had been hit by an anti-aircraft unit located in this area."

He pointed towards a hilly area quite a distance inside East Pakistan, which would make it nearly impossible for a crippled aircraft to reach India. DaSilva's worst fears had been realised. He already rehearsed in his mind breaking the news to Meena's mother. He knew, however, that Meena had the luck of the devil – or, as she would say, *'It's in God's hands.'* He banked on her being alive, but it was a vain hope in the circumstances. Why had they involved her in this futile exercise? Why had she agreed? He was not entirely sure that the Americans were not behind her decision to involve herself. Her knowledge of the languages and culture of Pakistan would certainly have attracted the attention of American intelligence people among students and academics during her studies in the United States. He tried to dismiss his suspicions that Meena's mother could somehow be involved due to her close links with the American State Department. Maybe she thought that linking Meena with these agencies would provide her with another layer of protection because of her suspicion that DaSilva himself could not adequately look after their daughter.

Sinha concealed the map in his jacket and moved towards the door. Abdullah followed him but seemed to remember something. "General, we have a man in our local headquarters who keeps insisting that he has information about events in that area. Maybe you should accompany me now and we can determine if what he says is true. I don't wish to get your hopes up, but he mentioned reports of an aircraft landing on a busy road. This could simply be helicopters from the Pakistani military conducting operations in that area. I'm afraid that quite often, these reports have been embellished by the time they reach our intelligence people."

It was the chance DaSilva had been waiting for and, regardless of the outcome, he was keen to get out of this hotel. They all left the room together and headed towards the basement and the back entrance to the hotel.

At the rear of the hotel, the three men were directed by staff towards a linen storage area. Abdullah's men were waiting and hurriedly requested that all three should conceal their clothes with laundry workers' clothes. When they had finished, they were positioned on either side of a handcart that contained several huge bundles of hotel linen, which had to be taken outside of the hotel grounds to a nearby laundry. Three other men assisted as the handcart was slowly wheeled to the exit. These handcarts were a common sight on the streets of the capital and unlikely to draw attention from the military.

DaSilva was at the rear and watched the gate closely for soldiers. His pulse raced as two soldiers clad in battle dress turned their attention to the approaching cart. One of the men from the cart moved to meet the soldiers and jokingly held out his arms as if they were friends, reunited after years apart. The soldiers looked disinterested and instead shouldered their arms, pulled the man aside and held him against the wall. The cart kept moving though, and DaSilva took a peek at what was happening behind them. He saw the man lower his hands and produce a bundle of notes from beneath his clothing. The soldiers turned in a huddle to count and share their illicit bribe and forgot about the man who now ran towards the cart and cursed at all the others to put their backs into it and heave that cart as fast as they could away from the hotel. DaSilva, like most West Pakistanis, understood very few words of Bengali, the language of East Pakistan, but he needed no encouragement or translation to push with all his might as the cart picked up speed towards the safety of the side streets surrounding the hotel.

Several armed men appeared from doorways as they passed and took charge of the cart as Abdullah barked orders at them. DaSilva watched passively and was astonished when suddenly, two people, a man and a woman, emerged from the bundles of laundry on the cart. Both were foreign and carried cameras and were soon whisked away to the safety of a nearby house. Abdullah explained that it was essential that the foreign media be given a chance to see and record the true extent of damage and killing from the perspective of the freedom fighters. He intended to allow the journalists access to as many areas of conflict as he could and then try evacuating them to India, to hopefully give a true picture of events both in the capital and in the interior.

"General, you must be very careful in their company, even though your intentions are indeed honourable. I do not wish for their reports to reflect any confusion regarding our intentions."

DaSilva was so surprised at the presence of journalists in the first place that he raised his hands in a gesture of compliance. "Mr. Abdullah, please be assured, I have only one concern now and that is the safety of my daughter. Surely, I will be involved in whatever solution arises at the end of this conflict, but for now I am at your service and offer myself as a mediator, should the need arise. And please, call me DaSilva from now on; those journalists need not know my identity." Only half-jokingly, he added, "I will manipulate the media in my own good time."

Abdullah smiled and inwardly acknowledged the power of the media in the world of conflict. They were moving towards the outskirts of the city, and he noticed the two journalists now dressed as locals, wearing appropriate headgear with their camera equipment hidden from view. The way ahead was cleared for them by their armed escort and in several areas, they needed to enter buildings and emerge on the other side, thereby bypassing roadblocks. Only once was fire exchanged with the military in an area regarded as the frontline in the conflict. After this, it was a straight run to the jungle, where finally they could relax, away from the threat of the army.

Abdullah seemed pleased and more at ease now that they were safe. "We are reasonably safe now and in territory held by our people. The military is wise enough not to move on our positions as we have several heavy machine guns and grenade launchers. We are preparing ourselves for an all-out assault on their positions in the near future. Hopefully, we can negotiate a peaceful settlement in the meantime, but unfortunately, I do not see the Pakistani Army conceding anything to what they see as groups of anarchists."

Sinha prepared to leave them but before he departed, he took DaSilva aside. "Sir, I do not doubt the outcome of this conflict. I feel sure that a new government will be installed soon, and the sooner, the better. The only thing I'm not sure of is the number of people who will die in the process. You are aware that an Indian Army invasion is imminent. We predict relatively rapid air superiority over East Pakistan when the invasion commences, and hopefully, the Pakistani Air Force will be neutralised shortly thereafter, if my intelligence reports are correct. They pose a credible short-term threat but ultimately, they lack the resources for a sustained aerial campaign. I am sure that as soon as a stable regime is established in the capital, the Indian Army will depart. My government would like to see a strong, independent Bangladesh emerge. The hope is that a partnership with other countries on the subcontinent could form a formidable alliance in the region. I know that there are people in Pakistan of the same view, and we can only hope that they emerge as rulers in the future. There has to be a better way than constantly being in a state of war with each other."

DaSilva was impressed by the sincerity of the man. "I too hope this vision of yours is realised, but I am older and know too well the suspicions of each other, which seem to dominate the volatile relationship between India and Pakistan. However, I will do my best to encourage acceptance in West Pakistan of the democratic will of the people in East Pakistan. I am not yet ready to abandon the East to unstable forces but hope for a quick resolution to the conflict and a return to stable government. Before you depart, can I ask you to advise the advance units of your military to at least be aware of the missing Cessna and those on board."

Sinha agreed to get a message to his local army commanders on the border to have a helicopter stand by for a rescue mission in the event of them receiving any communication from the pilot of the Cessna. He shook DaSilva's hand and departed with several fighters through the jungle.

DaSilva was torn between going with Captain Sinha and staying with Abdullah. He chose the latter, based on his assumption that Abdullah would be better equipped to get him to the area where the Cessna was last seen. Looking for Meena would not be Abdullah's main concern. DaSilva understood this and just how fluid the situation could be during battle, so he decided to simply get to the interior of the country under the protection of people who knew the area. Cultivating a close bond with Abdullah was his primary concern for the moment. He knew that Abdullah was aware of DaSilva's position in Pakistani intelligence but like any good leader, he tolerated this unusual relationship with his enemy's man on the ground in the hope of exploiting DaSilva's high-level contacts as the volatile political situation evolved. DaSilva knew this and was also happy to go along with the arrangement. The strategy was well known to him. He smiled to himself as he thought of the ancient quote: 'Keep your friends close but keep your enemies closer.' Both he and Abdullah would proceed on this basis when dealing with each other in the future.

The journalists asked many questions and were glad to have been chosen to represent the international media in the interior. Both were freelance and the woman seemed English, and the man had a New York accent. The woman, Alicia, kept eyeing DaSilva as if she knew he was an influential figure and was not put off by his polite but firm refusal to engage in conversation. She relented for the present, but he knew she would persist in her efforts. The other journalist, Brad, latched himself onto Abdullah, who seemed flattered by all the attention. Nevertheless, Abdullah was in no way deflected from his mission and he resolutely set about organising their journey inland.

He had somehow procured a truck from the docks, complete with a driver and a full tank of diesel, and they set off, the journalists secreted in the forward section of the covered trailer, just behind the driver's compartment. DaSilva spotted a telephoto lens poking out through a slit in the timbers that made up the trailer. He moved to do something about this security risk but thought better of it. He was, after all, here as a guest of Abdullah and did not wish to strain that relationship, even though his natural tendency to lead was hard to suppress at times. Instead, he satisfied himself by curling up on top of sacks of wheat and peering out at the passing countryside from the security of cover among the various other items stacked in the back of the covered trailer. The truck and its occupants looked harmless and similar to other trucks on the road, but DaSilva knew it would not stand proper scrutiny from determined searches by the military.

As the truck made its way along the road, they crossed several bridges that showed signs of conflict. Pakistani soldiers were well dug in and looked nervous, and with good reason, since these bridges would provide vital control should the Indian Army invade. The resistance fighters in each area made their presence felt and frequent pressure was kept on the military to test their morale. DaSilva didn't quite know how Abdullah had secured the permits necessary to negotiate the many checkpoints on the journey. Abdullah simply said that the food they were carrying was for a forward military garrison at Balashi. At one point they were even requested to carry military mail to this garrison. Apparently, the unit responsible for delivering mail didn't have the stomach for running the gauntlet of a road fraught with danger so that a few homesick soldiers could receive mail from their families in West Pakistan. This provided Abdullah with another lever to use while negotiating any further checkpoints.

Military mail carriers seemed immune from suspicion and the grin on Abdullah's face broadened more and more as his confidence grew at each encounter with the army he was fighting. On seeing the green mailbags with the military insignia of the Army of Pakistan, they simply waved them through. You could be sure that this strategy would be used by Abdullah in the future. DaSilva smiled at the audacity of the man and his admiration grew the more time he spent with him. He may have had the appearance and demeanour of a shopkeeper, but it was no mistake that Abdullah would be in the inner circle of the future leader of this country, Sheik Mujib, and therefore he felt it was a relationship worth cultivating.

The serious side of the conflict became apparent as they proceeded, and the site of upturned, burnt-out military vehicles became a common sight. The road had been mined in places and DaSilva stared ahead at the surface of the road with increasing concern. Abdullah seemed relaxed enough and relied heavily on information passed on to him from villagers along the route. On a few occasions, armed villagers accompanied them and guided them around areas of the road where mines had been laid. Abdullah was formulating a plan in his mind, and he shared it with DaSilva.

"The mail given to us for delivery is destined for the garrison in Balashi. This is the army's strongest force in the area and one we have tried to take over on two occasions in the past. We have lost a lot of good people to this venture and our local commanders have been demanding heavier weaponry to give them a chance against a well-equipped army garrison that frequently sends patrols out to terrorise the surrounding villagers. This cargo of mail gives us legitimacy and I am sure their people have radioed ahead to announce our arrival. It would be a tremendous chance to gain intelligence and see the internal layout of the barracks. This information would be very useful in the event of a future assault."

It seemed like a good plan, but both DaSilva and the journalists would need to be dropped off a few kilometres short of the garrison. Abdullah dealt with the protests from the journalists in a very polite manner.

DaSilva needed to evaluate the risks posed to the garrison by his inaction. He was, after all, a fellow countryman of the officers and men in the garrison and he would need to play out his strategy very carefully in the coming days if he were to have any chance of achieving his overall objectives. These objectives were becoming less clear by the minute as he interacted with men like Abdullah, an East Pakistani Bengali who was typical of an educated class wronged by a careless government in West Pakistan, oblivious to the needs and rights of their citizens in the East. Technically, Abdullah and his fighters were Pakistani and subject to the same laws and privileges enjoyed by those in the West. However, since the foundation of the state, it was evident that the central government in West Pakistan saw those in the East as second-class citizens. The advent of martial law negated their rights even further, and giving the military control of a volatile population would, in his view, prove catastrophic to any plan to maintain a form of union between the eastern and western parts of the country.

DaSilva would also do anything to discover Meena's whereabouts, by whatever means available to him. He must try to cultivate his links with all sides in the conflict, including the Indians, to ensure his influence with the eventual victors. His instincts told him that the Indian Army would indeed invade soon and with the help of people like Abdullah, eventually overthrow the military power and establish an independent state of Bangladesh. He could not see anything but an ignominious defeat for the Pakistani Army in any future fighting. How they were to extract themselves from such a volatile situation was the question, and he set about formulating a strategy that could help them in the event of their defeat. It pained him to see these once-proud regiments being used by their government in such a callous fashion. It would be hard for them to retain any credibility, given the scale of mischief perpetrated by them since the establishment of martial law.

Surely there would be officers who would eventually realise this and embark on a process that would resolve the situation with the least amount of bloodletting. The locals, however, may not be too well disposed to letting the aggressor get away with the evil deeds perpetrated against a mostly innocent population. The key to negotiating an equitable settlement lay with the Indian Army, and he would need to also cultivate relations with them. Meena, with her contacts and knowledge of the rural areas, provided the best chance of this. He would need to find her soon. He prayed she was still alive.

His mind was preoccupied with thoughts of her growing up and her incessant thirst for knowledge. Thankfully, Meena's mother could provide all the answers to the many questions the little girl asked. Quite early on in her life, he realised that she and her mother were hewn from the same stone, as both were intent on assimilating as much knowledge each day as they possibly could. The thing that startled him most was their power of retention, and Meena's ability to regurgitate copious amounts of information on any subject at will. He had always been careful asking questions in their household, the often long-winded and detailed responses threatening to overwhelm him. Keeping quiet was sometimes the best option.

Chapter 16

Monica stood behind Meena and gently massaged her neck and shoulders as she sat at the refectory table in the convent. Meena's eyes were closed, and her arms folded as her mind dwelled on recent events. She should be hardened against such barbarity by now, having dealt with it so many times in the past, but she couldn't help agonising over the deaths of children in particular. Their tiny bodies had sustained the joys of life and hope for the future and a barely contained excitement that each moment in the day promised a new adventure and new experiences. When they ran into her arms each time she visited their homes, she marveled at the miracle of life contained within their delicate heads, and as her hands enveloped their tiny chests, the awesomeness of the racing heartbeats always threatened to overwhelm her. These were the joys and wonders of everyday life for a doctor. The spark in nature that made this life force possible was such a mystery. That it could be taken away so suddenly and in such a cruel fashion made her inconsolable. She knew, however, that her inner strength would eventually rescue her, and she set about conditioning her mind to move on and confront the situation. She also knew that people would now look to her for leadership and instruction. She opened her eyes and observed the group of people sitting around the table. Shane had his face cupped in his hands and held her stare. She knew she could depend on him, and her eyes smiled in affirmation. This was a time to dig deep into the mental reserves that she knew existed and set her apart in some special way. It was as if she had been chosen and had a divine spark burning from within. The recent events were a trigger, enabling her to avail of these reserves, but it also reminded her that she was working at the absolute limit of these reserves. She shuddered to think about what challenges lay ahead and wondered if she would cope. The people around her reassured her in a strangely comforting way and her inner strength was bolstered by their presence. She knew she would need to rely on them in the coming days since one thing was certain: things were going to get far worse, and she had a real sense of foreboding. The fighting would surely escalate, and she felt they were in the eye of a storm, with all the forces of war about to be unleashed on their country.

She leant back in the chair and Monica rested her hands on Meena's shoulders as she turned and smiled at her and held her hand in reassurance. Monica withdrew and sat beside Meena, drawing comfort from her closeness. Sister Gertrude sat passively, eyes closed and praying. Meena took a deep breath, and they all waited expectantly.

"Okay, this is how we will proceed. The jeep will depart immediately towards the border and hopefully rendezvous with units of the Indian Army. Shane, you will drive, and Monica will accompany you." She sensed Monica tensing beside her but continued, nonetheless. "Lieutenant Keeler must be reunited with his people so that he may receive immediate medical treatment. His condition is stable, but he needs to be in a proper hospital. If he stays here much longer then I fear for his life, not only medically, but simply because he could fall into the hands of the Pakistani Army, and this would have disastrous consequences, not only for him but for all of us."

Shane was uneasy and during the silence that followed her announcement, he took the opportunity to voice his concerns. "What will you do while we are away? Surely it would be better if we all attempted to reach the safety of India. Nobody could have foreseen the events that led to Keeler's devastating injury."

Meena stood and looked at each of them in turn. They could see the strain she was experiencing. "My movements are being closely watched by both sides, Shane. The Pakistani Army still has agents in the area and that man, Hossain, will insist that I stay to look after their wounded. He is a very dangerous man and certainly not a part of the mainstream resistance movement. I could be wrong, but I think he is part of a small but very violent group, which wants to see an independent Islamic state being created in this region. By all means, I am determined that neither he nor any of his men will accompany you on the journey to India. I only need you to do as I say and trust that it is the best option."

Monica took her hand and held it tightly between hers, and Meena tried to reassure her that it was not only the best option but their only option. Monica spoke in Bengali and seemed to be pleading with Meena. Meena said a few words and Monica reluctantly withdrew and walked slowly to the door. She was met by Sister Anna, one of the other nuns, who reassuringly put her arm around Monica's shoulders and led her away.

There were tears in Meena's eyes, and she began to explain her reasons for insisting that they should go. "Monica is not happy because she is sure she would not survive another dangerous journey. Her trip from India with Lal and Esther was very frightening and she feels that they would have been killed at any one of the many checkpoints encountered had it not been for Lal. She doesn't feel up to another equally dangerous journey. I need a nurse to accompany Keeler, and she is the only one experienced enough to look after him.

"Shane, please prepare Keeler for the move to the jeep. I have sent word to Prem Das, an elderly man from the village who was once a truck driver and who is familiar with the road to the border. He will accompany you. He should be here by now. You can rely on him to navigate all the best possible routes to avoid trouble. If you leave soon, then you should reach India before nightfall. On the way, if you encounter trouble then you can visit a temporary hospital in the jungle near Baona run by the insurgents, and they will help you get Keeler across the border to safety. I hope Keeler will stay conscious and liaise with the Indian Army when you cross the border. There is no way that man Hossain's men will be going with you. If needed, at the appropriate time I will distract them by asking them to come to the kitchen to collect food for the journey, and you can simply depart without them."

She knew Shane was unhappy with the plan, but hoped he would understand. He got up and headed for the door but looked back and caught her eye. "I will look after Keeler, so don't worry, but Monica will be happier here with you. Just show me how to inject the morphine and tend to the wound if it starts to bleed. Oh, and be certain that as soon as we deliver him to the Indian Army, I will return. There is no way that I will desert you."

Meena seemed deflated as she sat down. "Shane, you cannot remain here. You will be caught up in the fighting and neither side will see you as friendly, since you only have a permit to be in India. Please don't make this difficult for me." She looked at Sister Gertrude, who had remained silent up to now, willing her to support her plan.

"Mr. Shane is correct," she said. Meena's eyes widened. "He must be shown how to treat Flight Lieutenant Keeler in case he and Monica get separated."

Shane laughed as he walked to the door and when he was out of sight, Meena seemed to visibly weaken. Her reliance on him at that very moment revealed itself as something more and she was shocked by the intensity of the feeling.

She got up and started to follow him but pulled up short. Once more, the leader in her took hold and made her realise that the chosen course of action was the right one, and she set about putting the plan into action.

"Yes, child, the burden of leadership can at times be overwhelming, but I'm sure you're doing the right thing. We simply must not be found with that young Indian pilot in our midst."

Meena simply squeezed the elderly nun's hand as they both walked arm in arm from the room.

Chapter 17

Abdullah heaved himself up into the cab of the truck and secreted a machine pistol under the driver's seat. DaSilva noticed at least half a dozen grenades in the compartment also and started to have misgivings about the plan they had agreed on. Abdullah could see the concerned look on his face.

"Mr. DaSilva, don't worry, please. This is only a reconnaissance mission. There will be no fighting, I can assure you. The mail we are carrying gives us legitimacy. I intend to spend as little time as possible in the garrison. They may offer us refreshments and during that time I will simply try to ascertain the location of their munitions store and how their defensive positions are organised. I expect them to be in high spirits once they realise we are delivering letters from their loved ones in West Pakistan. It is surprising how loose the tongue of a happy person becomes, and I will merely exploit this and lend an ear to their discussions in as polite a way as possible. These weapons are only insurance in case our conversation become a little heated. I'm sure you understand. My men here in the jungle have been instructed to mount an attack at the first sign of trouble."

DaSilva noticed the smirk on his face and realised, not for

the first time, that Abdullah's almost comical exterior disguised a shrewd and capable leader. He could only stand idly by and deal with events as they arose. He was in no doubt that Abdullah would not think twice about killing anyone who crossed him.

The engine of the truck roared to life and three men jumped up on the rear and positioned themselves comfortably on the sacks of wheat, rice, and flour. They too had grenades hidden in their clothing, and beneath the planks on the floor of the trailer was a selection of small arms ready for use in a hurry, should they need them. DaSilva could only watch helplessly as the truck headed down the slight incline towards the Balashi garrison in a cloud of dust as the sun glistened off the mighty Brahmaputra River to the rear of the fortified military installation.

He positioned himself with the two journalists on an embankment from which they had an excellent view of the garrison. Abdullah had relented and allowed them to advance with him to this forward position. It would, after all, ensure a photographic record of unfolding events. What Abdullah didn't tell them was the instruction he had given to his men, that in the event of the battle not going their way, all used films from their cameras were to be destroyed. Oblivious to this command, both journalists pointed their telephoto lenses in the direction of the truck as it made its way downhill. They noticed several soldiers at the main gate of the garrison priming their weapons and taking cover when they heard the sound of the approaching truck. In particular, DaSilva focused intensely on the actions of the men on the heavy machine guns surrounded by sandbags on either side of the gate. He did not need to reflect on his combat experience in the past to realise the damage they could inflict on any attacking force. The tension mounted and the three of them could hardly contain the fear they felt about the outcome of events in the next few minutes.

**

"*Nice timing,*" Abdullah thought to himself as he gestured to the driver to slow things down a little. He could see the soldiers in the distance taking cover behind sandbags and priming their weapons, including the machine guns that had decimated his brave men in previously unsuccessful attacks. The sun shone behind the truck and into the faces of the guards so all they could see was the outline of a truck in a cloud of dust approaching them through an intense, dusty glare. It gave the advantage to Abdullah, but his one fear was that an inexperienced soldier would fire on them in panic, so he made the driver slow down even more as he slowly ran his gaze from one end of the camp to the other, taking in as much detail as he possibly could. At about one hundred metres from the gate, his attention was drawn to inert figures lying in a gully just off the road. It did not take him long to realise that these were several dead bodies in various stages of decay. This had a devastating effect on him, and he started to sweat profusely.

The driver observed Abdullah and shouted at him to regain concentration on the job at hand. "Sir, please don't let those bodies distract you. They are fallen comrades from previous attempts to take the garrison. When the people came to reclaim the bodies of their dead, the soldiers simply opened fire on them also. Now, you can see in the distance that two officers are running from a building at the rear of the garrison. I am certain that the building to the right of the officers' mess is where they store their ammunition and food supplies. I will try to park as close to those buildings as I can."

Abdullah had seen many casualties, but he could never get accustomed to taking them for granted as mere fodder of war. He was only too aware of the grieving families left behind. He knew this weakened him as a leader and he struggled to avert his gaze to concentrate on the layout of the garrison. The bodies lying there could at least have been afforded the right to burial in the Islamic tradition, and the fact that they had not hardened his resolve to capture this garrison. Still, he began to have second thoughts about the venture when he noticed at least a hundred soldiers assembling at the perimeter of the garrison when the approach of the truck provoked a general alert. There was no going back now, however, and so he steeled himself and outwardly portrayed the confident buffoon that had served him so well in the past. As they neared the main gate, they were surely the only focus of attention, and the potential target of the many weapons pointed at them.

***

Major Ali Khan and Lieutenant Shah ran from the officers' mess and tried to ascertain the reason for the alarm being raised. The major was not happy with this further complication. They had been ready to depart at sunrise on their mission when the unexpected arrival of the helicopter delayed them. He was surprised and delighted when it landed on the parade ground in a cloud of dust. On closer inspection though, he noticed only the two pilots and a two-man maintenance crew; there were no armaments on board, only two drums of aviation fuel. The crew of the Russian-built helicopter explained that they functioned merely as a transport for general staff and government VIPs and that they had no combat experience. They informed him that they had also done evacuations of wounded on a couple of occasions.

There was no time to express his dismay at this revelation, so he set about getting his men to install a gun platform on the special mounts designed for it at the door on the left side of the aircraft. The major instructed them to mount a fifty-calibre machine gun on to these mounts. The pilots seemed nervous about this development and let their feelings be known. They were under instruction to return for other duties that evening and they had in no way envisaged undertaking a combat mission. The major paid no heed; he took them to the officer's mess and gave them a briefing.

"The mission is simple. All I need you to do is provide a security blanket for my motorised column on the road. Keep us in sight at all times and if there is any sign of activity on the road ahead which looks threatening, then open fire on them immediately and inform me by radio. Is that clear?"

They both nodded but the major could see that they were unsure about entering a combat zone. He tried to reassure them and felt that coercion would be counterproductive. "Look here, I really need you boys to help me out here. We have reports of an Indian spy plane being downed in this area. Our anti-aircraft units reported a hit, and they were sure the aircraft had been disabled and descended towards the jungle. Consider the impact on your careers if we could manage to locate the crew of this aircraft and return them to Dhaka as prisoners. It would be a major coup for us and the world press would focus on you as the captors of Indian military personnel who directly violated our sovereign airspace when we are not even at war with them. I can assure you that our superiors would look very favorably on your achievement. And don't worry, my most experienced sergeant will be on board with you to man the machine gun."

The pilots looked at each other and he could tell that they were won over. That was the point at which the alarm sounded, and the major ran from the building, readying his sidearm as he went. Lieutenant Shah, the garrison commander, joined him to see what the commotion was at the main gate. The lieutenant had been annoyed when the major and his convoy arrived, all business-like, upsetting the routine of his garrison. He had hoped that the major was here to relieve him and permit him to return to the relative safety of headquarters in Dhaka. He felt deflated when the major started talking of a search mission to find an enemy aircraft. He had hoped to be excluded from the dangers posed by venturing out from the relative security of the garrison.

They had beaten off two attacks already and he felt secure in the knowledge that the rebel fighters and army mutineers had learnt their lesson and would avoid another bloody encounter. The sooner the major took himself and his convoy off, the better. He had already persuaded the commanders of two gunboats that their presence at his garrison was not needed and he was glad to see them depart upriver earlier. There was no point in presenting themselves as high-value targets for the rebel leaders, he reasoned.

Chapter 18

The jeep was ready for departure, and as Shane helped Monica fashion a hook to hold an intravenous drip for Keeler on the exposed metal structure on the ceiling, he remembered her last journey with Jagdish and realised just how experienced she was in carrying out medical missions such as this. She seemed capable and had obviously performed mobile nursing duties on many occasions. He took comfort from this but worried that she did seem preoccupied. She noticed the look of concern on his face.

"Mr. Shane, I am very worried about Dr Meena and I'm fearful about this journey. Please don't concern yourself about me. I too wish to return here as soon as we deliver our patient to safety in India. I will not desert the doctor for longer than is necessary. It is important to reach the border in as short a time as possible due to the lieutenant's serious condition. The brace on his leg will prevent him from moving about too much, but if needed, he may be able to walk with the help of crutches. Hopefully he will not need to move on his own, but my biggest fear is being separated from him on our way to the border."

Shane was surprised at the intensity with which Monica

spoke. He simply nodded and left to fetch blankets and water for the journey. He turned after a few steps and noticed the tears coursing down Monica's cheeks. Was it tension or was it simply deserting Meena again that made her so fearful? He could not say, but he became aware of the close bond between her and Meena. They had been through a lot together. He could see the extent to which a person could command such loyalty; he was, after all, smitten by Meena too, and he was aware of the possibility that others may be affected by her in the same way. Meena's apparent aura permeated the lives of so many.

Monica finished loading her medical supplies and walked dejectedly towards the nurses' quarters located behind the hospital. She caught Shane's gaze, and her face resumed its composure. "Love really does hurt, Mr. Shane, as I am sure you are aware."

She turned and walked away, and he was left to ponder her words. Had Meena shared his family story with Monica? He felt confused but snapped out of his thoughts and set about ensuring the vehicle was ready for the journey. Some of the men in the compound would help him load the jeep. He did a thorough check of the tires again, including a second spare wheel stored on the roof, and secured two large containers of drinking water behind the driver's seat. Earlier, on Meena's instruction, they had emptied the trailer of all the medicines and hospital supplies in less than ten minutes and now they were under lock and key in a secure storeroom. Meena didn't need to explain that her motivation was to deprive Hossain of access to these supplies. Her mind was made up about him and she wanted him to be aware that battle lines were drawn and that he could expect nothing from her, regardless of the consequences. Shane agreed but kept a wary eye on the jungle in case Hossain and his men should reappear.

Shane returned to the hospital and found that Keeler was conscious, but he seemed full of drugs and smiled when Shane arrived with two men to help carry him to the jeep. Esther tied a sheet around Keeler to secure him to the stretcher and detached the drip from the bedpost. While she held it aloft, they maneuvered him through the door towards the compound. Meena appeared and directed operations. She seemed happy with Keeler's condition and reassured him that he would soon be in an Indian Army field hospital. He thanked her and warned her to be careful as Pakistani forces would almost certainly be searching for him. "I'll inform my people about this place and will do my level best to ensure that your good works will be recognised. I feel that things will get much worse in this country very soon, so you must prepare your people for any eventuality. Indian forces will inevitably involve themselves soon, and hopefully, their efforts will result in the installation of a new regime in this country which will not be hostile to the population. I pray for this and the continued success of your work."

Meena walked beside the stretcher and said, "Nurse Monica and Shane will look after you, Lieutenant. They have limited morphine but there should be enough for the journey. Tell your medics that the leg is doing well, with no sign of infection. I am confident that it will heal well, and time will tell as to whether you will play cricket again. There will be a lot of physiotherapy needed. So, good luck and hopefully we will meet again when this horrible conflict is over."

He was placed in the jeep and Esther secured the stretcher and hung the drip from the roof. She returned to the dispensary with Meena, and Shane was left to acquaint himself with his guide, Prem Das, who was a Hindu from just across the border. He revealed that he worked as a truck driver and also as a foreman in a quarry in the hills. His English was quite good and, like so many others, he too was indebted to Meena. She had saved his life after he had been crushed by a falling boulder in the quarry where he worked. He limped, but only slightly: another miracle of healing. Shane was glad of his company, for he knew that this would be a difficult journey. Prem Das assured him that he had good knowledge of the alternate route they must take to the border as he had travelled it many times. Monica was taking her time, and Shane went looking for her. He ran to the nurses' quarters behind the hospital and was just climbing the steps to the verandah when he felt the need to hesitate and stopped. He was sure he had crossed a boundary by even thinking about entering the nurses' quarters and was just about to retreat when he heard Meena speaking in Bengali in tones that suggested that she was comforting someone. The conversation stopped and as he was turning to leave, he glanced through an open window and observed Meena and Monica in an embrace. Meena then held Monica's face in her hands and wiped her tears with her thumbs. During a final embrace, Meena viewed Shane through the window. Shane was hugely embarrassed, but Meena just held his stare and spoke gentle words of encouragement to Monica. It was as if he weren't there. He turned and left and felt the need to drive away without having to confront Meena yet again. He neutralised his thoughts and forced himself to concentrate on the journey ahead.

The two ladies finally came around the corner and Monica, oblivious to the fact that he had been privy to their interaction, climbed into the back of the jeep, and set about making Keeler comfortable for the journey. Shane didn't wish to make eye contact with Meena, but her overwhelming presence forced his averted gaze around until his eyes locked on to hers and he stopped the engine and walked towards her as if hypnotised. He felt weak at the knees and swallowed hard as his mind searched for the appropriate words.

He need not have worried as she only smiled and disarmed him completely. She spoke softly, out of earshot of the others. "Shane, Monica loves me dearly and I love her. Mine is a caring, tender love similar to the love I have for you."

His heart seemed to lift with the intensity of her words. He began to speak but thought better of it. Whatever he said could only seem hollow, after all. She was not finished speaking and he held her stare, wallowing in the depths of her eyes.

"When Monica was fifteen, she was forced to leave her village on the eve of her marriage because she confided to her parents that she was in love with a lady teacher who taught her in school. Even as a fifteen-year-old she knew it was irregular, but she felt sure her parents would understand the goodness of any feelings of love for another person. But they didn't. They were scandalised to such an extent that her father and uncle beat her mercilessly and insisted that no more should be said on the matter, and forcefully instructed that she would marry the next day and that would be the end of it. Well, she ran away that night and after two days of wandering, she ended up here, having nowhere else to go. She was so distraught that she had not realised she had walked thirty miles from her village during the day and night without food. We assured her that she could stay for as long as she wished. She was fearful of telling us her name because it would link her to a religion, so we asked her to think about a name for herself. She couldn't decide, so Sister Gertrude called her Monica. Thus began the career of one of the best medics I have ever worked with.

"We enrolled her in our nurse training program, where she surprised everyone with her ability to excel at every subject. So, if her happiness depends on me showing her affection, then that is what I will do. If you think I do it only to retain the services of a wonderful nurse, then you would be correct. But to be honest, I enjoy her loving me and it is comforting to know that she would give her life for me. And so, I return the love and feel no remorse. Now, please look after her for me and if you feel the need to return here then I will be glad to have you. It is your choice to be here even though you know war is imminent. Hossain must have had second thoughts about sending his men with you, so please go now just in case they appear. Drive safely and listen to Prem Das. He is a good friend, and he knows the border area very well. And Shane, please try not to get shot."

She walked away and he turned and set about preparing everyone yet again for the journey. He looked at Monica in the rear-view mirror. She was once again the efficient nurse, and no hint of her anxiety showed. *What an extraordinary girl,* he thought as he guided the jeep out of the compound and up the jungle path towards the road to the border. He wanted to think about Meena and what she had just said but he was preoccupied with the job at hand. He suddenly realised the magnitude of what he had undertaken, and the dangers of being intercepted by the Pakistani military, especially while transporting an Indian airman.

He looked at the people lining the road and wondered who among them could be an agent for the military or government. Maybe he should worry more about Hossain's people; they had, after all, proven how ruthless they could be. No wonder the number of people on the road heading for the Indian border was increasing. They were fearful of groups such as Hossain's and their tendency to get what they wanted through violence and intimidation. He glanced at the reassuring figure of Prem Das sitting beside him. The man was a picture of tranquility in his traditional clothing and headgear. Shane could smell the *paan*, much loved by the locals, and he remembered his first introduction to the substance at Calcutta Airport. Sure enough, when Prem Das smiled his teeth were bright red, and he rolled down his window and spat an enormous mouthful of red liquid in the direction of the ditch before settling down for the journey. Monica smiled as their eyes met in the rear-view mirror.

The true nature of terror had been alarmingly evident these past few days. The future was so uncertain for families with children, and despite Meena's best efforts, people were running to the relative safety of India. Shane wondered whether the agencies from abroad would be able to cope with the sheer number of refugees embarking on such a journey and worried about their safety.

"Mr. Shane, please don't look so worried." It was Keeler, who was suddenly awake. He sounded remarkably well, and Shane was forced to turn around and look at Monica to find out the source of his newfound strength. She simply nodded towards her medical bag, and he could make out the syringe and several ampoules of morphine in it. Keeler had a look on his face that suggested he was ready to party. "Nurse Monica, please give me my flying tunic from under the stretcher." Monica extracted the flying overalls and handed the garment to Keeler.

The tunic had been washed thoroughly by some local women in the hospital, but the right leg was missing, severed mostly by the force of the projectile entering his thigh and exiting out through the roof of the aircraft after causing major damage to his leg. Shane could only imagine the pain Keeler must have suffered initially and how lucky he was to have passed out immediately, and to have such a skilled surgeon on hand to deal with the horrific injury. Monica passed her scissors to Keeler, as requested. He proceeded to cut the stitching inside the back of the tunic and eventually extracted a very flat plastic folder, from which he produced a map. Shane and Monica were intrigued as they looked on. Amazingly, it also contained several items which made up a basic survival kit. There were three oddly shaped plastic objects, and he assembled these into what could only be a radio of some description.

The piping around the waist of the tunic was ripped further and a wire antenna was extracted, which he attached to the radio. He was sweating profusely, an indication of the superhuman effort his body was making in conjunction with morphine to overcome the pain.

"There we are; now we should be able to contact my people to organise an evacuation. With some luck, I should be home before nightfall. Forgive me for not discussing this option earlier but there were too many ears listening and the dangers of this information being passed to the military was too great. After all, loyalties change dramatically during times of conflict." He collapsed onto the stretcher and Monica immediately set about taking his pulse and blood pressure. She exchanged a glance with Shane, and he knew from the look in her eyes that Keeler had reverted to the comfort of unconsciousness. She was happy that his vital signs were all normal and began making him as comfortable as possible.

Shane sped up and in a swirl of dust, the jeep negotiated the twisting jungle path until they reached the major highway that would eventually lead them to India. Prem Das surprised him when he spoke very clearly in English. He was concerned earlier about not revealing his proficiency in English due to the possibility of being labelled. He was happy to be considered an uneducated manual worker to blend in with others like him. He preferred to be respected as a skilled quarry worker and driver rather than as an intellectual. It suited him to be respected for his wise counsel and his knowledge of historical events. He explained that he had worked with the British Ordnance Survey as a driver during the 1930s. He knew every boundary and roadway in the northeast of the subcontinent, having helped to survey them before and after the time of the British. Shane looked forward to hearing more of his stories in the future. Prem Das revealed that if they kept to this road then they should reach the border before dark. "But sir, there is not a possibility of remaining on this road because I am aware of army troops at several junctions, so we must divert at certain places to avoid them."

He took Keeler's map and pointed out the first detour less than twenty miles ahead. Prem Das marveled at the map's accuracy and recognised that he had been involved in its production with British surveyors before a border divided the two countries. Those people had insisted he converse in English with them, not due to the imposition of some warped colonial convention but out of concern for his ability to retain the knowledge of cartography and surveying. They were obviously aware that the British days in India were numbered and were anxious that the knowledge should be passed on as accurately as possible. Prem Das realised this and ensured he was in a position to do the same for subsequent generations. Shane now understood Meena's decision to retain the services of such a skilled navigator for their journey.

Shane noticed several locations on the map marked with a red circle alongside map coordinates. Prem Das suggested that they could be the pick-up or drop-off points alluded to by Keeler. The Lieutenant groaned and was suddenly awake again. He saw Prem Das holding the map for him to read and he simply pointed weakly to one of the red circles, which was about fifteen miles from the border. Prem Das knew the location well as he had camped not far from there at a junction where road, railway and river intersected, an obvious point of reference for surveyors and so easy to distinguish from the air. Keeler was fumbling with the radio, and it suddenly burst to life with static noise, and they could hear Morse code on the airwaves. It went silent as the correct frequency was selected and Keeler uttered an unintelligible sequence of phrases a few times and waited.

Having tried this several times, he turned the radio off and crashed once more into the stretcher. "We need to preserve the battery and get closer to the border; maybe another twenty miles and we will try once more. This radio is not very powerful. Now, Monica, would you kindly help me into my one-legged uniform? There is no way I'm going to be captured while wearing a hospital gown." With great difficulty, Monica managed to help him put on the flight suit while delicately negotiating the external support frame and plaster cast on his leg. He then drifted into a fitful sleep but not before ensuring his identification discs were prominently displayed on his chest as they settled down for the journey ahead. Shane had a sense of unease and wondered if Keeler was succumbing to the inevitability of capture. They drove on in silence as he kept his thoughts to himself.

Shane wasn't too concerned for Keeler – Monica seemed happy with his condition – but they both knew that the journey must proceed without a hitch if he were to survive. He was grateful to have Prem Das and Monica with him and felt rather confident now that they were making progress. He thought of Meena and knew Monica had the same thoughts as he viewed her in the mirror. Was there no room in this society for this beautiful, capable girl? He was saddened by the intolerance of her family but felt that her situation would be no different even in 1970s Europe. He was ashamed to think of what the attitude of his people would be to Monica's situation. Up until the time he became aware of her plight, he too had an ambivalent attitude to such relationships and was now forced to modify his thinking. Monica caught his stare and smiled back at him. He felt butterflies in his stomach and was sure she could read his thoughts. But the smile said much, much more. She seemed at ease with him now and he felt the burden of her complete trust in him. He smiled back, of course, and he hoped she didn't see the uncertainty in his eyes.

"Monica, please call me Shane."

Her smile broadened and transformed her beautiful face. "Sure," she replied.

Prem Das signaled that he should take a left turn at the next junction, and as the jeep left the road once more, Shane was surprised to find a decent track through the jungle heading in the general direction of the border. Their journey took them past mostly deserted villages and soon they had travelled another twenty miles. It was then that he caught the glint of the sun from an object in the sky, forcing him to bring the jeep to an abrupt stop.

Chapter 19

Major Ali Khan was at the point of ordering his men to open fire on the approaching truck when his radio operator came running towards him from the building housing their communications equipment. The major held his hand in the air as he tried to calculate the threat posed by the truck approaching slowly towards the main gate. His men were crouched low behind layers of sandbags and his sergeant eyed him expectantly, waiting for the signal to open fire. The radio man held a signal sheet aloft while also eyeing the truck with suspicion. The major took the paper and read it while keeping his arm held high. The message stated that they should soon expect a truck delivering mail to his garrison. He barked an order to stand down and requested the sergeant to take some men and confirm the intentions of the occupants of the vehicle, which had finally come to a stop just short of the gate, now slightly open and with every weapon in the garrison trained on the truck's windscreen.

There was a tense standoff as the sergeant went outside to interrogate the driver and another individual who alighted from the vehicle. Both he and the sergeant exchanged a few words and then they started walking towards the compound. The major noticed the soldiers relaxing as they saw the smile on the sergeant's face. When they reached the major, the sergeant gave a smart salute and informed him that the man accompanying him was simply delivering mail to the garrison. The major eyed the newcomer cautiously but before he could say anything, Abdullah introduced himself.

"Sir, may I say what an honour it is to provide this esteemed establishment with such a vital service, and to humbly play our part in assisting your excellency in your efforts at restoring peace to our beloved country. Abdullah Iqbal at your service."

The major was not in the least impressed with this charade and made his feelings known. "Enough of your lunacy. I have a good mind to string you up on the nearest tree to reward your insolence in a fitting manner. What else is in the truck? Lie to me and suffer the consequences."

Abdullah did not need to feign fear as he succumbed to the verbal onslaught from this officer. Major Ali Khan's reputation was well known, and mercy and kindness were not the most obvious traits of his character. But Abdullah also knew that any new regime that emerged from this war would need officers such as this man, unpalatable though it may seem. Any future government would have security in the new nation as its primary concern and they would need to depend on men like this major to deal with the many violent factions that would try to assert themselves and threaten the secular democracy favored by most people for their new state.

This issue would need addressing soon but he put it to the back of his mind as he confronted the tension-filled situation before him. "Sir, we are simply transporting wheat, flour, and rice to the market in Gaibandha but felt humbled to be requested to divert to Balashi garrison to provide this mail service to our boys at the forefront of the fight against terrorism in this area." Major Ali Khan simply ordered Lieutenant Shah to commandeer the entire contents of the truck for the needs of the garrison and left

Abdullah pleading with them to be allowed to keep his precious cargo. Within minutes the driver of the truck was being ordered at gunpoint to reverse the truck towards a small warehouse at the rear of the garrison, where the compound bordered the river on which they had observed the departure upriver of two gunboats earlier in the day.

Abdullah was left pleading as he saw the soldiers eagerly unload the sack of mail. They were all so distracted that only one soldier reluctantly supervised Abdullah's men unloading the various sacks from the truck. The soldier never noticed when only two of the three men doing the unloading exited from the warehouse as he locked the door. Abdullah pleaded once more to Lieutenant Shah for the return of his produce, or he would be left penniless. The lieutenant was concentrating on the distribution of the mail and dismissed him gruffly, threatening to have him shot if he didn't get himself and his truck out of the compound immediately. Abdullah complied and shed tears and seemed genuinely distraught at the injustice of it all.

The truck moved slowly in the direction of the gate and each occupant scanned a different part of the compound as they had on first entering so that the vital areas of the garrison and headcount of the soldiers would be recorded in their memories. Abdullah eyed the helicopter with suspicion and feared the consequences of their enemies having access to an aerial gun platform, which could wreak havoc on his men during their assault on this compound later in the day. He thought briefly about throwing grenades through the open side door as they passed the large aircraft but dismissed the notion as suicidal. At least he had a man on the inside now. He smiled to himself at the thought of the major trying to defend against an attack from outside the garrison as his man on the inside fired from the storeroom. They also had an option of sabotaging the garrison's munitions, which were contained in the storeroom, if the attack failed.

He had chosen Ali Hassan for this perilous duty because of his experience with explosives in a quarry in the hills. His roadside bombs had deterred the enemy from using the roads in anything other than armoured vehicles. As soon as Ali Hassan became aware of their attack, he was to prime his explosives and try to get to safety as best he could by using a smaller explosive charge to blow a hole in the wall bordering the river. The detonators and timer had been hidden deep in one of the sacks of rice, and a few sticks of dynamite in another, having correctly calculated that the soldiers would not be able to resist stealing their precious cargo. He had stressed to Ali Hassan to blow up the munitions and weapons only if he observed their attack on the compound failing. Their main priority was to preserve the munitions for their own use. Abdullah desperately hoped their assault would succeed as the cache of arms and munitions included mortars and a huge stock of assorted small arms and assault rifles, which would replenish his own dwindling supplies.

***

Inside the storeroom, as soon as Ali Hassan completed preparing the explosives, he armed himself with a rifle and spare magazines taken from the garrison's plentiful stock, intending to assist his comrades during the assault with fire from the only window that opened out onto the compound. He had been shocked when they first entered the storeroom carrying the sacks to see so many racks of weapons, including assault rifles, mortars and handguns, with enough ammunition for each weapon to repel prolonged assaults on the garrison. His primary target when the assault started would be the soldiers manning the machine guns on either side of the main gate, through which the main attack would take place. The defenders would not be expecting fire from inside the compound and hopefully, this would reduce the murderous crossfire on his comrades during the main gate frontal assault.

He would prime the explosives timer to go off ten minutes after the first shots in the assault began, ensuring the destruction of the munitions in the event of him being killed. He nervously kept the main explosive timer and battery close by, should he need to rapidly disarm the device. A simple switch from the battery to the other smaller explosive charge at the wall bordering the river was placed on the window ledge looking out over the compound. He planned to blow the hole in the wall as soon as the assault began. He knew the army issue rifle was a very reliable weapon and he also had plenty of spare magazines within easy reach. All he could do now was sit and wait and trust in Allah and pray for Abdullah's good judgment and success in the coming battle. Resisting the urge to blow the hole in the wall and simply run would be difficult, but he trusted Abdullah and knew their leader would get them through this.

***

Nobody was expendable in the eyes of Abdullah. Unlike other commanders, he treasured the lives of each of his men. He wished for each one to return safely to their families as soon as the hostilities were over. The irony of Abdullah viewing himself as a pacifist was not lost on him. He was aware of his past successes and the number of men who had died on both sides of the conflict due to the decisions he had made. Each combatant was some mother's son, and he silently exhorted Allah to limit the suffering of families with loved ones in the conflict. He then turned his mind to his present situation. He couldn't believe they were finally exiting through the gate and heading for safety. They had only to wait now and choose the most opportune time to strike.

The armoured vehicles would soon depart from the garrison.

That is, if the major did as they predicted. Abdullah had been informed by locals that the major was intent on capturing the crew of an Indian spy plane recently shot down in the area. Maybe this would present them with the opportunity they so badly needed. He cautioned the driver to slow down and not seem too eager to be away from this place, where many of their comrades had fallen in the recent attempts to take the garrison. He willed the cover of the nearby trees to come quickly, and he didn't relax until they were safely in the jungle and reunited with their friends.

DaSilva and the journalists were waiting for him to reveal what had happened but Abdullah needed time alone with a cup of hot, sweet tea in an attempt to overcome the nausea he felt over the fallen comrades he had seen on the road, the verbal assault from the major and from leaving Ali Hassan alone with a huge task to perform. DaSilva recognised the condition and left Abdullah to the peace and quiet he so obviously needed and exhorted the journalists to do the same. They all needed to step back from the tension of the past hour and relax before steeling themselves for the inevitable assault that was to take place, the outcome of which was far from certain.

Chapter 20

Meena noticed a void since the departure of the jeep. She feared for its passengers' safety and tried to convince herself that all would be well, and that Prem Das would guide them safely around any trouble spots. Were they to be caught by the Pakistani Army then it would prove very difficult for Shane as a foreigner, and also because of his association with Keeler. They would refuse to believe any story he told and would see only foreign interference and intrigue in his presence in their country, for which he did not even have a valid visa. Spies were not tolerated, and as foreigners, both he and Keeler could be in serious trouble. She chided herself for not thinking this possibility through in her eagerness to get Keeler and Shane to safety across the border. She rationalised her actions by trying to play down the seriousness of them being captured and paraded before the world press. At least, she reasoned, they would be alive and their subsequent treatment open to the scrutiny of a multitude of committed foreign journalists. She also agonised over sending Monica with them, but she'd had no choice. She knew that Monica would normally do anything she asked without question, and she therefore felt real guilt as Monica had voiced her anxieties before they departed, and Meena had not really evaluated what she had to say. Taking advantage of Monica's loyalty and love for her had been heartless, she felt.

There was nothing she could do for the present and so she set about organising help for the villagers with the cremation ceremony for Lal's family, one of the few Hindu families in the village. Their Muslim neighbors were devastated at the pointless deaths, but sadly, they were well versed in the funeral rituals of all the religions in this diverse community. Before going to Lal's village, because so many things crowded her mind, Meena was forced to seek solitude in their small chapel. She sat cross-legged on the floor and regarded the plain wooden cross on the wall behind the altar. Slowly the tears and keening began to subside as one by one, each problem faded into the background and her mind started to focus on solutions for the unfolding events, without fully suppressing thoughts of the traumatic events of the past few days.

This, for her, was the nature of prayer in any religion: an intense interaction with the deity, while at the same time laying bare all the problems of the day. The slaughter of innocents could not be explained in the context of a loving deity, and she didn't need it to be. Human intervention influenced the outcome of events. Evil was always present, and it would triumph if not for the actions of good people, regardless of their beliefs. The difficulty lay in determining the extent to which good people had become so exposed to evil events that their consciences were desensitized and no longer able to make a clear distinction between good and evil, especially in a war setting. Condoning evil activities could be presented as the safest option and so their society progressively descended into chaos as more and more good people passively looked on while evil triumphed. Individuals sought the security of the rabble, and any dissenters were ostracised, ridiculed and, frequently, violently subdued.

She knew too that history also produced extraordinary

people to confront evil and recondition populations to displace malevolent forces, and this is what she prayed for most. Her prayer also asked that her villagers would remain immune from this process. The hatred in their hearts for the people who had butchered Lal's young family would surely manifest itself in some way and she felt duty bound to minimize their exposure to the dangers of retribution. She had to confront her hatred for Hossain as the perpetrator of the crime, while at the same time realising that he had the potential to inflict far greater damage. So, for now, her primary mission was to counsel the villagers against actions that could so easily escalate an already fraught situation. She went to seek the counsel of Sister Gertrude, as she usually did in difficult situations. The elderly nun always had an answer and words of wisdom to sustain Meena, no matter what problems they faced. She found her washing the floor in one of their operating theatres and once again she had to listen to her mentor's story of how Florence Nightingale had reduced deaths from infection in the Crimean War by simply following strict rules of hygiene. Meena never disputed this and now she simply stood at the door to the operating theatre with her arms folded.

"Come child, let's go to the refectory and have some tea," Sister Gertrude said as they made their way to their living area beside the hospital. Meena made the tea and they both sat facing each other at the table, which they always referred to as their thinking table. They discussed the events of the past few days and Meena shared her concerns over her decision to send her people with the injured airman on another perilous journey to the border. She also agonised over the deaths of Lal's family and the deteriorating political situation that was threatening to overwhelm them. Sister Gertrude thought for a moment before replying.

"You, more than anyone, know that any answer I give you will be based firstly on my perceived wisdom as an old woman, but secondly, and more importantly, on my life experiences. We can do nothing about what will happen in the future and instead only influence future events and hope for an agreeable outcome. The jeep has departed, so we have no control over what may happen to them. You took all reasonable precautions and your decision to send Prem Das with them was inspired, thereby giving the venture a high probability of success. Now, that's enough Teutonic logic, so let us address the political situation and how I think it will affect us here.

"The Indian Army will certainly invade, and this will hopefully stabilise the situation in urban areas, but it may take some time for rural areas to catch up – unless, of course, we are lucky enough to have your Indian friends descend on this area because of your involvement with them and the insurgents." Sister Gertrude held up her hand to prevent Meena from interrupting. "Don't worry, my dear, I am not criticizing your actions in any way. In fact, it was the only course of action open to you. However, your dramatic arrival on the aircraft did not go unnoticed by the Pakistani military, so expect a visit from them and make sure you have all your answers ready for their aggressive questioning. They may eventually be defeated but they still pose a great danger to people who they feel opposed them and who collaborated with the insurgents. Your name will be on top of their list, I'm sure of it, and that is why you must now leave here and seek refuge in one of the remote jungle villages until the danger passes."

Meena thought for a moment before responding. "You are correct as usual, Sister. I should have gone in the jeep, but I needed to be here for the villagers, to support them after the death of Lal's family, and we have so many people waiting for treatment in our clinic. I promise to leave with Esther early tomorrow morning. Her village is a day's walk from here. We should be safe there until we hear from you. You have spoken of the war in Europe and your experiences there many times. I did listen and I understand that nobody is safe when soldiers go on the rampage through the civilian population."

"Very good. I knew you would see sense. It would be wiser for you and Esther to depart now, but tomorrow should be fine. With regard to my experiences in the war in Europe…well, can I tell you something I never shared in the past, just to reinforce how dangerous it is for you as an influential woman in what is becoming a war zone?" Meena simply nodded; she knew that Sister Gertrude's stories were always instructive.

"You will remember me telling you that I was serving as a nurse in our hospital in Freiburg when the war was ending in 1945. We were treating wounded soldiers who returned from the Russian front. Many died in our care due to horrific wounds from battle, and also from severe frostbite. Limb amputations were an everyday occurrence, so you would have been in your element." They smiled as Meena lowered her eyes and blushed, acknowledging her reputation for dealing with traumatic limb injuries. "We started to receive civilian patients with horrific burn injuries from the bombing and fire-storming of Dresden. It took about one month for us to stabilise the situation, having worked twenty-hour shifts helping people to have a pain-free death because, quite honestly, the extent of the burns on most of those men, women and children did not allow for the possibility of survival. I then turned my attention to finding out about my youngest sister Elsa and her twin daughters, Freida and Petra. Elsa was thirty-five years old, and I knew she was very sick. They lived to the south of Dresden, and I was confident, based on what our patients were telling me, that they would have escaped the bombing and catastrophic fires. No phones were working so I asked our superior if I could take a trip north to check on my only remaining family. She agreed because she knew that my two brothers and Elsa's husband had all been killed in Russia, serving with the German Army.

"Some of the soldiers we were treating were incensed at the

stories they were hearing from Dresden, and those who were fit enough decided to go north to help fight the Russians and their Polish allies as they were advancing into Germany. Most of them were veterans from the war on the Russian front, which seemed to drain our country of all its young men. These soldiers commandeered an army truck and an assortment of weapons and prepared for their journey. They were being led by an army captain who had also served on the Russian front for three years. He was a very experienced officer, and the other older men deferred to him as a dependable leader. Hauptmann Maier had more shrapnel in his body than most of the other soldiers combined, causing him to move with great difficulty.

"I approached him and asked to accompany them in the direction of Dresden. He readily agreed and his men helped me up into the rear of the truck. I knew all of the fifteen men as I had treated their injuries, mental and physical, in the previous months. None was fit for combat; all of them were suffering from mental and physical decay. But they all possessed that one quality in a soldier that makes them a very dangerous and formidable enemy: absolutely no fear of death. I was fifty years old then, but they very kindly referred to me as their angel.

"I remembered the atrocities they had admitted to in Russia, and they saw no possibility of recovering from the constant nightmares and visions of the faces of the innocent people they had brutalized." Sister Getrude remembered Maier's own experiences as he had reluctantly related them to her, in the hope of relieving himself of his memories and the demons that were a constant presence in each of their lives.

"He was a young officer when they captured the city of Kyiv in Ukraine. His commanders had been ordered to kill all the Jewish people in the city. Over thirty thousand of them had been assembled with all their belongings and convinced that they were being deported. With the aid of local collaborators, the people were herded to a place called Babi Yar, where they were all relieved of their valuables and other belongings, stripped, and marched to a ravine where they were shot. Maier had watched from behind a line of soldiers who were directing the people towards the place of execution. An elderly lady stopped and asked him in perfect German where they were taking them. She introduced herself as Frau Horowitz and she was surrounded by ten very young women. She was their music teacher, and their families had asked them to go to Frau Horowitz to find out what was happening because she was a figure of authority in their Jewish community. Maier simply said, 'Frau Horowitz, please follow all the other people. Don't be concerned; please tell your young ladies not to be worried.' Maier revealed that the spirit of Frau Horowitz was his constant companion ever since and he would prefer death to having her with him for the rest of his life. He and the other soldiers all suffered this mental torment. They were ready to die.

"We broke our journey for the night, and we slept in a farmhouse where the farmer gave us bread and cheese and a bottle of wine each. Yes, I was a middle-aged woman then, but I slept with Maier that night and saw the wounds and burns on most of his body. Don't look so shocked, Doctor, they were very unusual times and none among us was sure of being alive the next day. So, I do not have any regrets whatsoever. The soldiers dropped me about five kilometres from my sister's house the next day. Before leaving me, Maier gave me his Luger service pistol and taught me how to use it. He warned me that Russian and Polish troops were advancing on Dresden and that I needed to be very careful.

"Rape and murder of women were common with conquering armies, he confided, as all his men nodded in agreement. The look of childish innocence on the faces of those perpetrators of heinous crimes while agreeing with Maier gave me pause for thought. I fired several rounds from the Luger into a nearby ditch before they departed. They all laughed at my efforts from the back of the truck. Maier reloaded the pistol and told me that there were eight rounds available and not to waste any more by firing them into the ditch.

"I knew they were all determined to die in defense of their country and in the hope that death would release them from the torment of the demons haunting them. So, there I was, a nun in black, armed with a Luger and a bag full of bread, cheese and a bottle of Riesling, on a road packed with refugees heading west towards the advancing American Army, with me heading in the opposite direction towards our Russian enemy, a beautiful night with Maier firmly dominating my thoughts – evidence, if evidence were needed, that women have the ability to prioritise thoughts, even in times of great stress and trauma."

Meena was smiling and crying at the same time as she listened to this extraordinary story unfolding.

"So, I walked against the flow of pedestrian traffic with very kind people offering me food and advising me to accompany them to avoid the advancing Russians. I thanked them each time and proceeded, eventually reaching my sister's house, and was so relieved to find her and her fourteen-year-old daughters all packed and ready to take to the road. I was shocked when Elsa whispered to me that her cancer was very advanced and that her only mission now was to get her two girls to safety. She had planned to walk all the way to Freiburg and ask me to take care of the twins. All I could do was hold each of them tightly and reassure them that we would get through this crisis together.

"It was early afternoon and as we were locking the front door of the house, Freida shouted, 'Mama!' We turned around to find two Russian soldiers in an open-topped vehicle looking at us. The road had cleared of people, and I could see why as the soldiers got down from their vehicle and turned their attention to us. We retreated into the house and attempted to lock the door, but it was too late; they forced their way inside. I handed them the bottle of wine in an attempt to get them to leave and I was horrified when they turned their attention to the two girls.

Their intentions were clear, and Elsa bravely stood in their way and surprised me when she begged them with words in Russian, hoping that her familiarity with their language would distract them from what they were after. They stalled for just a moment before laughing and pushing my sister aside. Her daughters were screaming in terror, and this resulted in Elsa attacking them with a kitchen knife. One of the soldiers withdrew his sidearm from its holster and shot Elsa three times. She was dead before she fell. The soldiers were so preoccupied with events that they never noticed the Luger in my hand pointed at their backs. I fired two shots into each of them and when they fell to the floor, I shot them both once more in the head."

Meena couldn't believe what she was hearing. Her hands covered her mouth as Sister Gertrude continued.

"The twins had to grow up very quickly during the following hours. I instructed them to go to their garden shed and find anything that we could use to paint over the red star and hammer and sickle insignia on the soldiers' vehicle. We had to escape from there quickly. I listened for other vehicles approaching in the early evening. There was no electricity to provide light, so the road was getting dark, and no more refugees were fleeing from the advancing Russian and Polish troops. The girls returned with whitewash paint, and this was adequate to do the job on the vehicle. We did not want to get shot by our own people, who were in a heightened state of anxiety about all things Russian.

"We then faced the traumatic process of wrapping Elsa in a blanket and placing her in the vehicle. However, when we were making room for her, we came across two bags belonging to the Russians, which contained quite a lot of valuables stolen from people during their advance. The spoils of war for them became the spoils of war for us and all I could think of at that stage was the girls' education and future security. I was not even ashamed of my effortless transition into an animal of war. We dragged the dead soldiers out of the house and placed them at the side of the road, to be found by their comrades. I took their wristwatches and went through their pockets as the twins looked on in silence. From that day onwards, their attitude towards me changed forever. How could it not? No more affectionate hugs or smiles for their loving aunt. Our relationship was simply another casualty of war. What surprised me was the ease with which I had made the transition from comforter of the sick and dying to an instrument of death.

"We drove all the way to Freiburg during the night. We were stopped a few times by German police at roadblocks; seeing a nun driving a captured Russian vehicle was a source of some amusement to them. They relieved us of the Russian weapons I had taken but I kept my Luger with its two remaining bullets concealed in my clothing. We reached our convent without further incident and our sisters organised a beautiful funeral for Elsa the following day. The girls became permanent students in our boarding school, and both later trained as nurses. They are now married with children and living in Freiburg. The French subsequently invaded and took over our town without incident and our Russian vehicle attracted a lot of attention. We eventually sold it to a French colonel who drove it to his home in Paris. He identified it as a 'Gaz' jeep, and I took his word for it. I was sorry to see it go because it definitely saved our lives. I later went to Basle and sold all the valuables to a jeweler for a substantial sum. It was tainted money so I gave it to my superior, who diverted it to aid the many displaced refugees who had come to our city. Ten years later, I was asked to come to East Pakistan to set up this missionary hospital. I agreed but insisted on first doing my midwifery training. This I did in Basle and after a year there I boarded a boat bound for Bombay and went onwards by train across India to Dhaka in the east. Fifteen hard years followed in a remote jungle mission where we eventually built a smaller forerunner of this hospital. Then I went to the United States on a fundraising mission, where I met the most wonderful young lady doctor, whom I persuaded to join our order and eventually join us here."

Meena's eyes were filled with tears as she struggled to find words and respond to all that she had just heard. "It must have been really awful for you to have to shoot those soldiers after they shot Elsa," said Meena as she wiped her eyes.

Sister Gertrude thought for a moment before replying. "Oh yes, it was traumatic seeing Elsa falling dead in front of her children. However, she had a terminal form of cancer and did not have long to live... but the circumstances of her death were horrific. I did not have any problem shooting the soldiers for what they had done and protecting my nieces. But I join Maier and all his soldiers in being visited by demons who plague our thoughts and dreams with visions of the cruelties we have inflicted on others.

"I now understand exactly how veterans of war feel, and this has helped me many times in counselling victims of trauma. My constant nightmare, however, is not of my first shots into the soldiers' backs, but of the subsequent shots to their heads. This was callous and unnecessary. The only way I can rationalise it is by putting it in the context of revenge for all the women through the ages who have been subjected to rape, torture and murder at the hands of violent men. I say rationalise for a reason, because no justification can be made for such feral behavior."

After a while sitting in silence, Meena stood and went behind the seated elderly nun and embraced her for a full minute before walking from the dining room without saying a word. She thought of their many conversations about the Second World War and the times Sister Gertrude had felt guilty while remembering her euphoria, shared with all the German people, when her country's military was conquering all of Europe, and their delight at receiving postcards their young soldiers sent from so many countries that had surrendered to them – and then the recrimination and guilt when their atrocities were discovered. She fully accepted their responsibility and subsequent punishment but would always point to the misdeeds of others, such as Stalin in Russia and Mao in China, who had each perpetrated worse crimes against their own people without being punished by the international community. Meena never had an answer for her friend because they both knew that similar atrocities would undoubtedly happen in the future. She also agonised over the killings happening all around them now and prayed for restraint among all those intent on using violence to resolve their differences.

Chapter 21

Major Ali Khan relaxed in the armoured personnel carrier as the convoy left the garrison at Balashi. He instructed his driver to advance towards the main road in the direction of Gaibandha town. His first stop would be the hospital run by that wayward nun. He knew she had something to do with the terrorists in the area. He had tolerated this in order to await a legitimate opportunity to attack the place. He also knew that they may meet stiff resistance in the event of an attack. The prize of finding the occupants of the downed Indian spotter plane was too great and worth the risk. He really should have waited for reinforcements, but the presence of the helicopter gave him a distinct advantage. He was determined to bring these Indian spies back to the capital and parade them before the international media. This would surely secure him a transfer back to West Pakistan as a hero and secure legitimacy among fellow officers who routinely excluded him because he had been born in Bihar in India.

Biharis were usually treated with scorn in both East and West Pakistan, and being from India certainly didn't help, so the sooner he got out of this place the better. He did not wish to be here in the event of a war with India. The East was too vulnerable, and the supply chain could not be guaranteed because of the thousand miles of hostile Indian territory between East and West Pakistan. He remembered the trauma of captivity experienced by his unit in the last war with India. The fear was still there, and he did not wish to be subjected to such intense fighting, followed by the humiliation of captivity yet again.

Damn those Indians, he thought. They always seemed to be better equipped and were so self-righteous. He turned his attention to the road ahead and radioed the helicopter to keep pace with his convoy and report anything suspicious on the road. His worst fear was mines though, and he chided himself for not commandeering the supply truck that had visited his garrison earlier. He could have placed the truck at the head of the convoy to explode any mines or booby traps laid by the insurgents. The armoured vehicles provided some protection for them, but he did not relish the thought of putting the armour to the test. That is why his was the third vehicle in line; there was no point in exposing himself to risks.

The hospital was fifteen miles away and one mile off the main road. It should be taken by surprise; the helicopter would position itself to cover all the approaches to the target. He would have destroyed this facility earlier but a terse message from his commander in the capital, Dhaka, had precluded him from doing so. He did not understand the reason but there was a rumour that the lady doctor in charge was the daughter of some high official in his army. Nun, doctor, lady – he didn't care about her status; if she were sheltering terrorists or Indian spies, he would deal with her in his own way. He was well used to being castigated for making decisions without consulting his superiors, so he didn't feel the need to change the habit of a lifetime. He felt the tension mount as he mentally prepared for the encounter.

Chapter 22

Before departing for Esther's village, Meena made her way towards Lal's village to organise the people and ensure they were coping with recent events. She froze, horrified at the noise she heard in the distance, which was unmistakable and coming this way. Having spent time in Vietnam, she was acutely aware of the sound of helicopters and of the death and destruction they could bring. She could make out that there was only one and she wondered whether it could be Indian on its way to evacuate Keeler. She ran to the only open space adjacent to the village well where the children usually played, but today they were being kept at home due to the deaths of their friends.

Meena noticed that the bloodstains had been cleaned and fresh soil covered the patch of ground where the mother and children had been so callously gunned down. Standing beside the well, she looked skyward and could see the tiny speck in the distance. It was headed this way for certain and she could make out that it was a Russian design. That could mean anything because both Indian and Pakistani forces used them. There were other sounds also and she strained to listen. They seemed to be coming from the direction of the main road. Some of the men from the village came running and informed her that an army convoy had just left the main road and was heading their way. Several of them ran as fast as they could into the jungle and she assumed that they were probably Hossain's men, fearful of capture. Also, atrocities where whole villages and their inhabitants had been wiped out by the military were not uncommon these days. Meena panicked when she considered that Hossain's men could emerge from the jungle to confront the army in a firefight. Her alarm grew as she considered the consequences of such a violent encounter. She couldn't countenance fleeing to the jungle herself. These must be the army vehicles they had been expecting and there was no way she could abandon her hospital workers to face this menace without her.

Sister Gertrude had been correct, and she regretted not leaving for Esther's village earlier. She probably would have decided to stay anyway so there was no point agonising over what may have been. It was appropriate that she should be here; otherwise, her sisters could have been exposed to danger because of her actions and she would never forgive herself for not confronting trouble together. Had the army already been informed about Keeler's presence here? Surely Lal couldn't have informed them so soon. She wondered if Lal had heard about the massacre of his family. She knew that the insurgents were guarding the roads and watching out for him.

Just then, the lead vehicle came into view and the helicopter could be heard circling overhead. She felt very fearful, both for herself and for the local people, and wondered what the purpose of this display of force by the army was. She stood her ground and waited as the rolling dust from the lead vehicle enveloped her.

The helicopter noise came closer and although it hovered out of sight, she knew its occupants could see everything below. It would maintain a height safe from small-arms fire while adjusting its position all the time. It reminded her of Vietnam so much, but that war favored the use of many helicopters descending on unsuspecting villagers very early in the morning. The heat and dust mixed with the smell of jet fuel from those American Huey helicopters filled her with dread during those times. Now she held her ears and waited for the discharge of weapons. The lead vehicle came to a stop close by and she strained to view its occupants to gauge the threat posed by them. The outline of a soldier on top of the vehicle was clear and the machine gun he controlled was pointed straight at her.

Chapter 23

Abdullah tried to count the soldiers left in the compound now that about thirty of them had departed in the convoy. He was relieved to see the major departing, for he knew they would have a better chance of success in the absence of their senior officer. He was relieved also that the helicopter was gone. They'd shared a few anxious moments as it flew low overhead. He viewed the young lieutenant through binoculars and felt sure that he would not be an effective leader during a coordinated assault, while keeping in mind all the young men who had lost their lives during previous attempts to overrun the garrison. There was no room for complacency. He set about organising the attack.

Reinforcements had materialised from the jungle as soon as he had sent out word requesting help, and he marveled at the courage of the numbers who had answered the call. They were simple people: farmers, and factory workers who had been wronged and whose relatives lay dead in the fields nearby. He did not doubt that they would attack and fight without fear for their safety. They had tremendous faith in his ability to lead them and he hoped he could come up with a plan to overcome the remaining seventy or so well-armed soldiers left to guard the garrison. This must be accomplished before the major and his convoy returned, and he searched the sky for any evidence of the dreaded helicopter returning, and also the river for the gunboats. He motioned for the section leaders to take up positions at the agreed points of assault and they gathered up the men under their command. He extracted the field radio from his rucksack and after switching it on, he checked the set frequency and volume. Having satisfied himself that it was in working order, he carefully keyed the microphone three times and hoped Ali Hassan could hear the transmission. It was far too dangerous to use voice communication for fear of being heard by the soldiers in the garrison. He waited and hoped his man on the inside was safe, not only because the success of the mission depended on him but because Abdullah knew his family very well and felt responsible for the safety of the young man.

Ali Hassan sat on top of the sacks of rice and strained to see the front gate of the compound through the small window that he would knock out with the stock of his rifle as soon as the assault began. He felt relieved that the major had departed. That man had a wicked heart for sure and would not hesitate in having him shot should he be discovered. The young lieutenant could be seen reading his mail over and over again and seemed uninterested in anything else. *Who could blame him?* Ali Hassan thought. But then he remembered his comrades who had been killed by these men. These soldiers should not be here; their homes were thousands of miles away in West Pakistan and what right had they to come here and murder his people? They made the Bengalis in East Pakistan feel inferior and made no effort to give them their rightful place in government. He would see his country gain independence or die in the effort. Just then his radio burst to life with three loud clicks and he jumped with fright and banged his head on the window shutter.

When he regained composure, he hurriedly reduced the volume and scanned the compound from the window to see if anyone had heard the transmission. Thankfully, the lieutenant was still absorbed in his reading. He waited a few moments and took time to check the radio's settings before keying the microphone three times in response to Abdullah's signal. Abdullah keyed one more time to acknowledge and Ali Hassan commenced the countdown. They would wait exactly fifteen minutes before commencing the assault, so he eagerly went to check the dynamite placed in several positions around the warehouse. Apart from the two sticks he had placed on the rear wall, nine sticks were remaining, and he had divided them into three. Doubting his previous actions, he followed the wiring to each detonator, ensuring they were properly inserted into the explosives. He nervously checked once more that each bundle was properly placed strategically around the warehouse among both weapons and ammunition. He thought about repeating the checks once more but instead forced himself to relax and try to focus.

He tried to take his mind off the explosives by checking his rifle and the ammunition visible in each of the spare magazines. He then prepared two loaded revolvers for use in case he didn't have time to replace a fresh magazine in his rifle during a possible assault on his position. That would be a bad development. Shrugging off these negative thoughts, he succumbed to other nagging doubts and once more checked the detonators in each of the explosives, and the wires from the detonators that ran back to his ready-made bunker behind several sacks of rice. They should absorb most of the energy from the smaller blast at the rear wall. The wires from the detonators on the main explosives were connected to a separate plunger with enough length in the wire to reach far enough out through the hole that he would blow in the rear wall to enable him to detonate the main charges from a safe distance near the river flowing behind the garrison.

He prayed he would not need to use this option as it would mean that the assault had failed and destroying the weapons and munitions would be necessary to deprive the army of critical resupply. Even if he detonated the main explosives after escaping through the hole in the wall, he knew the explosion would demolish most of the garrison buildings, and him with them. More negative thoughts, so he checked the watch, which had been a present from his father, and this brought thoughts of his family to distract him further. Twelve minutes had elapsed from the time he received the signal from Abdullah. Three more minutes. He was sweating profusely. There was nothing to do now except wait and pray. He prayed for his family and asked Allah to protect them and protect his comrades from harm. The time was upon him so soon and he pulled the sacks around him and retreated into a fetal position as he held the switch for the rear wall explosives up close to his sweating face. He wondered if there was time to check the explosives one more time.

Chapter 24

Meena straightened up and raised her chin in a gesture of defiance. She was really fearful but determined not to show it. Nobody alighted from any of the vehicles for several minutes, but she could hear the soldiers through an open rear door in the lead-armoured car speaking in Pashtun and laughing as they commented on her body and who would be first to sample the goods on offer. Her mind was dwelling on the danger she faced, and she wondered whether or not she could reach the safety of the jungle without being shot. Maybe being shot would be the best option. She was distracted when the door on the third vehicle in line opened and two highly polished brown shoes could be seen settling on the dusty playground. An officer!

Thank goodness for that, she thought to herself. At least she could rely on this being a civilized encounter. Maybe she was fooling herself, but she must try to convey the notion that she was not afraid, in an attempt to take control of the situation. The officer came into view and was immediately surrounded by his men as he adjusted his tunic and placed a swagger stick under his arm while surveying the scene before him. He advanced towards her, having detailed his men to secure their position.

He walked slowly as the men took up positions at the edge of the jungle. The machine gun was, however, still pointed directly at her.

"Good day, madam," he said, and saluted. "Major Ali Khan at your service." He recognised her from the photo in the folder he had been given by army intelligence. The photo did not do her justice, however, and he was momentarily caught off balance by her beauty, but he regained his composure and immediately decided that her defiant look would need to be confronted. She did not seem impressed and made sure he knew it as she maintained a withering stare in his direction. He was too busy to notice as he tried to gauge the threat posed by this encounter and his eyes darted here and there in an effort to discover the most likely direction of an attack, should it come. She could see that he was relieved to reach where she was standing as if this afforded him some degree of protection. She said nothing and waited for him to continue the conversation. Then, suddenly, an old ally interceded just when she needed it. Her smile. It was an unconscious reaction, for she didn't feel like smiling. She was not in control of her actions and had no control of her hand as it shot out to invite a handshake.

"What can I do for you, Major?" she said in a stronger, more composed voice than she imagined possible.

"Well actually, madam, it should be what *I* can do for *you*. You see, there are reports of an Indian aircraft crashing in this area and my intelligence people seem to think that the occupants, having been injured, may have been treated in your hospital. Need I point out the serious consequences that such an action could pose to you and your people for failing to report such activity?"

He tried to maintain an air of authority while also trying to face down this beautiful woman. He had heard reports about her and her activities and knew all the barrack room banter concerning her. Now that he was face to face with her, he had to acknowledge the power that such a woman could have over lesser men than himself. He straightened up to his full height in an attempt to dominate this encounter but felt small and insignificant as she held his stare. He counselled himself to look at her chin in order to avoid her eyes. He remembered his worldly uncle telling him to try this whenever a woman was brazen enough to hold his stare. That way she would be unable to gain the advantage of regarding herself as his equal. This was sound advice, and it had worked for him in the past. But that was in the company of women in his family circle, where he was master. He could dominate them or, if he chose, allow them to dominate him. With the women in his family circle, there was an unwritten contract of mutual benefit and at least they knew the boundaries not to be crossed. Everything would be fine once the women in his family and those he encountered understood this.

He adjusted his cap to conceal his eyes from hers but, like the Medusa, her gaze magnetically pulled his face upwards until finally, his eyes rested in the full glory of her stare once again. They both knew the outcome. His face contorted into a look of fascination and wonder, and he was rendered speechless. He fought the urge to conclude that he could never see harm done to this woman and that he would endeavor to protect her regardless of her apparent misdeeds. He was shocked at how easily his resolve was crumbling.

He mentally readjusted and feigned anger but her reply shocked him to his core, for he expected blatant lies and subterfuge. "Major, please come and have some tea out of the sun in our hospital. You must be in need of sustenance. I will arrange for the people in our kitchen to bring lime juice for your men. Yes, you are quite correct, I did treat a boy in uniform yesterday. I am not an expert in these things, but it seemed like flying overalls he was wearing as there were pilot's wings on the breast of the garment. I honestly cannot say for sure where he came from. We spoke in English during the treatment. The men he was with took him away after the treatment, even though his injuries were serious. Those ruffians also took my jeep and promised to return it as soon as they accomplished their mission. I simply fulfilled my role as a doctor in treating the sick and wounded. I'm sure you understand."

Meena felt that half-truths were better than blatant lies, which could alter your whole demeanour in the presence of a skilled interrogator, especially one with a history of violence. The safety of her people was at stake here, so she tried to overcome her terror in the presence of this man.

Major Ali Khan was perplexed. Normally, in a situation like this, he would dispatch his men to the village, and they could dispense their form of justice as they saw fit. He knew this could mean rape and even murder. This did not concern him unduly for he needed to convey a message to the local population that defying the military authority could have devastating consequences for them. However, this situation was more delicate and needed a different approach. He desperately needed to capture the crew of the Indian aircraft, and this woman was the one who could provide him with the best chance of doing so. There had also been reports from informants that she too had arrived on the stricken aircraft, but he was also aware of how informants embellished their information to ingratiate themselves with the authorities and possibly earn more money, so he decided to resort to the formal approach as if he were attending a regimental dinner in the officers' mess. Polite and courteous.

He adjusted his tunic once more and accepted her invitation for tea. He tried to devise a strategy in his mind in the hope of coaxing more information from her. By volunteering some information, she had gained the upper hand. All he needed to do now was find out the destination of her erstwhile visitors and, more importantly, their time of departure. This would enable him to dispatch the helicopter to find them on their most likely route of travel towards the border with India. It should be a simple enough process. The doctor eyed his men with suspicion. Did he see a momentary look of fear in her gaze? His heart lifted. Of course! She would surely be aware of the deeds of his men in the past, and even must have treated the results of their previous excesses. A chink in her armour! *Softly, softly, though,* he thought. He must play on her fears in a more subtle way.

"Madam Doctor, I am aware of your good works in this area, and I must apologise for not making it my business to visit this remarkable establishment earlier. The ongoing political situation has curtailed our movements somewhat. We must rectify this in the future. Please do not hesitate to contact me at the garrison should you need any supplies or medicines. We would be only too glad to help the local people, for it is, after all, these people who we are here to protect and to serve."

Meena smiled in acknowledgment but inwardly suppressed a need to retch. She had treated victims of rape and torture, and as she eyed these men, she was overwhelmed by the sense that these same men may have been responsible for such acts in the past few months. She fought to maintain a neutral, friendly smile but she was frightened that this delicate façade could come tumbling down in an instant. Her words in the next few minutes could decide the fate of those in the jeep. They had not been gone long enough if the major used the helicopter to overtake them on their way to the border. She stole a glance at the sky and could not see the Russian-built machine, but she could hear it and knew that it was not far away. She wished her jeep were any colour but white, which was so visible from the air. "Yes, Major, we do feel safer with the military presence in the area, and I appreciate the offer of medical supplies. Come, let us have tea in the shade."

"Thank you, that would be nice. It will also give me a chance to see the facility and the work undertaken here. I suppose the Indian airman received the best of care in this very building. Of the four people on the Cessna, was he the only one injured?"

"Major, I don't know how many people were on the aircraft you speak of, and the nationality of the young man did not concern me as his injury required my full attention. To the best of my knowledge, he was the only one injured. I did not see anyone else requiring medical treatment."

"I see. I did hear a rumour of a foreigner, an American, being in the party, but this is pure speculation. My sources are not at all reliable, you know, so I do have to be careful in discerning truth from lies." This may not have been too subtle, but he needed to see her reaction when he implied that she may be lying. He laughed off this last statement in the hope that she would not feel threatened by its implications.

"I understand, Major. It is easy to be confused; I treat so many people during the day. This young man could have been any victim of the conflict. I will treat anybody in need, for that is my vocation in life."

Just then a soldier appeared, and her heart sank when she saw what he laid on the table. A blood-stained field dressing and empty morphine ampoules had been retrieved from the clinical waste bin, items she thought would have been burned by now. Her driver Lal usually performed this task, and she suddenly longed for things to be as they were before this madness of war and hate.

"Yes Major, these are dressings removed from the wounds of the young man and he had in his tunic some ampoules of morphine, which we gladly used, for he was in a lot of pain, and our supplies are short." She unconsciously fingered the cross hanging from her neck, only to suddenly drop it when she considered the futility of expecting any respect for her religious status from this hardened military interrogator.

The major eyed the gesture and dismissed it while

considering the information. "They are, of course, dressings used by military personnel but certainly not from our soldiers. They look like foreign items – Indian, to be precise," he said as he poked the items on the table with his swagger stick. "It would have been of great help to us had you informed us that personnel from our neighbor's military had been wounded on the sovereign soil of Pakistan. This may have involved a direct threat to our national security. This is the sort of information that enables us to protect and defend our interests and people from the acts of hostile foreigners." He was beginning to lose his temper and in his quest for information, he found it hard to remain civil and courteous. "So please, good doctor, can you not see it in your heart to furnish us with more detailed information concerning the movements of these individuals."

Meena felt trapped. The major knew that Keeler would be heading for the border, but he did not know the exact make-up of the party. He also knew of the presence of at least one foreigner. She was aware of the soldiers searching the compound and was glad Shane had departed in the jeep. She had bought all the time she could. All she could do now was maintain her professional detachment, yield some information, and plead ignorance about the rest.

"Major, you are being most persistent. I do not concern myself with the activities of my patients. Yes, the wounded man was in a military tunic, he was possibly an airman, and he was badly wounded by a high calibre projectile in the thigh of his right leg. He was in urgent need of expert care from an orthopedic surgeon. Even if he does reach a hospital within the next twenty-four hours, he is still in great danger. Frankly, I don't expect him to survive. If they are going to the border with India, as you seem to be suggesting, then they must take the most direct route. I pray that he remains unconscious because their morphine supplies were inadequate for a long journey. So please, Major, let the boy go home if he actually is from India;

it is his best chance of survival. Were you to capture him then surely it would be a death sentence. He could never receive the urgent care he needs in time. Does a military code of honour not demand this of you?"

His back was towards her as he looked out the window and she noticed him stiffen. She feared the worst and felt sure her pleading would be in vain. He slowly turned and she noticed the change in his face. The pretense was over now, and any hint of kindness had vanished. The unmistakable sound of the helicopter could be heard in the distance. The sound brought a crooked smile to his face as he listened to it approach and land as if it were the solution to all his problems.

The dreaded sound, so vividly evocative of the war in Vietnam, was returning to haunt Meena and there was no escape. The major did not miss the slight change in her demeanour as she realised the helicopter was landing. That look revealed a multitude to him, but mostly fear. For whatever reason, the sound of the helicopter caused her extreme discomfort and provided the breach in her defenses that he so desperately needed. *Now,* he thought, *in for the kill.*

Meena recoiled in horror as the major lunged at her while smashing his stick on the table, and before she knew it, his face was inches from hers and his eyes portrayed nothing but hatred as his immense physical presence forced her back in her chair. She knew instantly that he could be capable of anything, and she feared for her hospital workers and villagers, should he let his men loose to do as they pleased. Her inner strength did, however, prepare her for the inevitable onslaught. "Madam don't try my patience," he spat. "I am in no mood for chivalry towards you, or towards an enemy of our country who has been caught red-handed spying from the air. So, please explain to me the logic of your proposal that I should show leniency to this spy. I have fought these people before, and I know what they are capable of. His government has notions of subsuming East

Pakistan into India as some form of vassal state, and I have no intention of sitting idly by and letting that happen. Delivering this airman to Dhaka will convince the world of the intentions of the Indian Government. It will also secure me a promotion out of this backwater and a transfer to civilization in West Pakistan. I will be a hero in the eyes of my people and retire on a substantial pension. And you wish to deprive me of all this?"

He backed off and straightened his tunic again, trying to regain some composure, having said more than he wished to in the heat of the moment. He had looked into her eyes and did not see the fear he'd expected, and her demeanour suggested that his aggressive ploy had not worked. He reasoned that this doctor had witnessed more fearful situations than this in the past. He reverted to being reasonable in an attempt to coax more information from the woman. He was, however, conscious that he had betrayed his true colours and now he had to try to retrieve the situation.

"Now look here, my dear, you know how precarious your situation is. I am a reasonable man, after all. I even have a daughter your own age."

He observed her as unobtrusively as he could, but she caught his fleeting glance as her eyes never left his and followed his every move. His self-confidence was dwindling by the minute, and he made as if to be deep in thought to give himself time to formulate his next sentence and devise a new strategy to gain an advantage. He faced her once more as she seemed to be holding her breath in anticipation of his next onslaught.

"It will be necessary, of course, for you to accompany me in our search for these people."

A reaction at last! He tried not to telegraph his elation as she jumped to her feet and, finally, her neutral features were suffused with fear and alarm. Whatever she said from now on would be irrelevant to him. If it caused her such concern then surely it could only be of an advantage to him, even though he did not yet know why he should have her along on the journey. If his statement that she should accompany him caused her extreme discomfort, then that was the strategy that was most likely to produce results. As he headed for the door, beckoning for two soldiers to guard her while she prepared for the journey, he ignored her protestations. He congratulated himself and conceded that old age and treachery had once again triumphed over youthful exuberance and even beauty. He commanded his sergeant to round up his men and be ready to depart in fifteen minutes. The sound of crying came from the direction of the village, and he knew that the men had been a little too forceful in their demands for food from the people, as he convinced himself that food was all they were after.

"No, Major, please. I cannot leave this place. You don't understand; my work is here, and it is essential that I remain. What possible use could I be to you?" Meena tried to control the level of panic in her voice but could not. The two soldiers restrained her from following the major as he strode towards the vehicles. This was a sinister development and she was fearful for her safety, should she be forced to make this journey. Her pleading was ignored as she watched the major leaving the building with his sergeant, his decision made.

The hopelessness of the situation was made clear to her as the soldiers appeared at her side. They leered at her in such a suggestive way that it became clear to her the extent of suffering that these men could be capable of inflicting when left unsupervised among vulnerable people. Any power that she had was diminished by this turn of events and she knew her future was now in the hands of the major. She turned to leave but the soldiers made a point of blocking her path no matter which way she turned.

Robbing a person of their dignity would be the first step in controlling a prisoner. Meena knew this from the experiences related to her by former prisoners in Vietnam. It would be an ongoing process to break her spirit and all she could do for the present would be to frustrate their efforts as best she could and buy time for her friends in the jeep. She changed to the Urdu language to catch them off guard. This was, after all, the language of her youth in West Pakistan.

"Well, gentlemen, I suppose you two were sent to fight this war by your mothers, because your sisters were needed as the real breadwinners in your families?" They got the message. They stared at each other in disbelief, surprised at her speaking their language but shocked and incensed at this extreme insult coming from a woman.

Things suddenly became black, with flashes of light of every colour permeating her consciousness. Then pain. Meena's cheek was throbbing as though her head would explode. *And why could she not see?* She groped around her and her hand collided with furniture, and she realised that she was on the floor. She prayed for the pain in her cheek to go away as her sight returned and she could make out an army boot inches from her face. As she tried to make sense of what was happening, her hair was pulled so hard that she felt sure a giant crane had caught it and was lifting her off the ground. As she raised her hands to try and fend off the source of the pain, they were slapped down so hard that she collapsed again, to be left hanging by her hair. Her eyes finally focused, and she recoiled from the stench of breath and the eyes filled with hatred on the face of one of the soldiers, which was just inches from hers.

She was against the wall and her feet were off the floor as they held her suspended by her hair, their hands under her breasts. The other man was fumbling with her saree and at the same time loosening his combat webbing and belt. She froze in horror as she realised what was happening. Her scream was drowned as her mouth was enveloped by the mouth of the man closest to her. The other man was clawing at her waist, trying to release the folds of the saree from her petticoat underneath. She tried to thrash her legs but the extreme pain in her cheek made her whole body feel like lead. How many times had she counselled young women not to resist while being raped because of the horrific injuries, or even death, that could result from antagonizing the perpetrator?

Now she realised how foolish that advice had been; she was prepared to die struggling rather than succumb to this torture and violation without resisting. The saree and petticoat eventually gave way, and she felt her lower body exposed and her legs being pulled apart. Her mouth was still covered, and she was too weak to force her face away from the stench of the man's breath as he followed her to the floor, his hands savagely pulling at her breasts. Her undergarments were ripped away and she waited for the surge of pain that was to come. She struggled in vain for a release of adrenaline in her system to prepare her body for further attack and the inevitable violation that would follow.

The adrenaline rush did not come so she prayed for survival instead. *Would they kill her? Or would the fact that the major wanted her on the journey save her?* Her heart sank as she thought for a moment that the men hadn't understood that the major wanted her to accompany them. She fought to explain this to them, but they were now intent on only one thing and nothing could deflect them from finishing what they had started. Finally, the hopelessness of her predicament caused her to relax, and the fight went out of her. She thought that this was the reason the level of aggression had subsided from her attackers. She dared to open her eyes and noticed the soldier's face turned away in the direction of the doorway that led to the bedrooms. A look of horror had replaced one of domineering hostility. His savage grip suddenly relaxed and her hands mercifully became free, and she instinctively fought to cover her exposed body.

Out of the corner of her eye, she became aware of a white image in the doorway. She tried to focus properly but her mind would not let her be distracted from her predicament. A flash and a loud bang came from the centre of the white figure, and she could not make any sense of it. A dead weight fell across her legs. She could only follow the soldier's dead stare to the doorway as blood poured from his shattered head.

His companion stepped away from Meena, raised his hands, and started to plead in broken English towards the figure who stood in the doorway. "Madam, please, please, no, no..."

Meena was horrified as she eventually made out the figure of Sister Gertrude holding a pistol in her two hands and aiming it at the man who was now on his knees, begging for his life. Meena struggled to react, but words would not come out and her body could not move as she lay trapped under the weight of the dead soldier. In her mind, she knew what she wanted to do, but her body simply could not respond and allow her to shout, so all that emanated from her dry throat was a feeble "No, Sister!"

Another blast and Meena looked on in horror as the man's chest took the full impact of the bullet from the weapon that Sister Gertrude now slowly lowered, its job done. She looked at Meena and smiled as she knelt beside her. "Let's sort you out now, darling, and tidy you up." She patted the gun and started to extract the magazine from the handle of the weapon. "This is the old friend from during the war I told you about earlier. Do you remember the story about my ordeal during the war as the Russians advanced towards my village in 1945? I somehow knew it would come in useful again someday."

Her German accent was so self-assured and Meena longed to be in her embrace, but all she could do was stare in horror at her blood-stained saree enveloping the dead soldier draped across her legs. She held up her arms like a baby to be comforted and as the white figure leant towards her, she knew that her horrific ordeal was now over. The dream world took over again and she felt relief from the pain as the adrenaline finally coursed through her body.

Sister Gertrude dragged the soldier off her legs and adjusted Meena's saree. Meena felt like an infant in her embrace. The nightmare seemed to be ending as she found the strength to attempt to rise to her feet. Suddenly there were more angry flashes, and her savior was suddenly falling towards her; more gunfire and her white angel now rained blood; then everything turned red as she started to see the beautiful stars once more as her overloaded brain released her from this overwhelming horror into unconsciousness.

Chapter 25

Ali Hassan felt the floor shudder under him after he had gripped the switch tightly and turned it to deliver the electrical current to the detonator in the explosives at the rear wall. He was suddenly airborne, and he felt the tremendous heat of the blast. The change in pressure caused by the explosion caused terrible pain in his ears, even though his head had been jammed between two sacks of rice. He fell to the floor and was winded. He could not breathe properly because the air was thick with particles of dust, smelling of numerous things, but mainly of rice and burning sackcloth. He couldn't hear too well and strained to see through the cloud of dust towards the window he had knocked out just as the firing outside had commenced. The gunfire was now continuous, and he tried to coax his unwilling legs to carry him to the window to commence firing on the machine guns at the main gate, as he had planned.

The hole in the back wall was huge. *How was it possible for two sticks of dynamite to cause such damage?* he thought to himself through the fog that was enveloping his brain.

He eventually crawled clear of the debris and tried to make sense of the sight before him. He knew from training just how vulnerable a soldier could be while trying to recover from the effects of a nearby explosion. He needed to regain control of the situation while confronting the enemy, so he instinctively felt for his rifle and fired blindly in the direction of the compound. It was not long before live rounds started to tear apart the front wall around him, forcing him to retreat behind what was left of the sacks of rice. One round grazed him on his right hip, causing him to yelp in agony. This did not stop him from preparing several grenades and throwing one of them as far as he could from his place of refuge, through the shattered window. He was sure the soldiers would assault his position soon and he retained one grenade for that eventuality. He was determined to die fighting and take as many of the enemy as he could with him to give his comrades a greater chance of success. The grenade exploded harmlessly outside, bringing with it no cries of pain. He waited for the attack but figured out that maybe the garrison defenders would also be as afraid as he was.

His thoughts were with his family as he went in search of more ammunition among the scattered shelves of the store. A sudden breeze finally cleared the remainder of the cloud of dust from his position. When he looked in the direction of the main gate, the sight that confronted him made his insides recoil in fear. His attacking comrades were being cut down by fire from the compound as they assaulted the main gate. Feeling certain that the assault was about to fail, he continued to search through the rubble on the floor for the plunger to set off the main explosives. Suddenly, he heard angry shouts and fully expected an assault from the doorway, only to be overwhelmed by his own men pouring through the hole he had just blown in the back wall, where they had been attempting an assault from the river. They knocked out the door and immediately started firing at the soldiers manning the machine guns on either side of the main gate. Ali Hassan simply stared and fell to the floor, exhausted. His mission accomplished, he finally found enough energy to remove the detonators from the remaining explosives as his friends cursed him for trying to blow up the whole garrison and them with it.

* * *

When the explosion did come, it made Abdullah jump. Even though he was expecting it, it seemed excessive. He waited for the flashes of gunfire from the window of the storeroom to confirm that Ali Hassan was still alive. He knew that the explosion was the signal for each of his commanders to start the assault on the fortified compound. They only had twelve mortar rounds and the first of these was launched soon after the explosion. His mortar platoon would need to adjust the trajectory as the first round fell short of its target – the garrison soldiers on either side of the main gate. It would unnerve the defenders though, for no attacking force up to now had used mortars.

Through his binoculars, Abdullah could see the soldiers turn their attention from the storeroom explosion to prepare for a frontal assault at the main gate. Timing would be critical. He launched the next phase of the attack. This involved fifty men attacking from the direction of the river, the side with the best natural defense, comprising a steep mud bank bordering the rear wall of the compound. His men, having reached the bank, would be afforded some shelter from gunfire. Abdullah hoped it would divert the attention of some of the defenders. The ideal thing would be for them to gain control of the wall and direct fire on the machin-gun positions from the rear of the compound, thereby reducing some of the murderous crossfire directed at his men involved in the frontal assault on the main gate. This would get underway shortly when he assessed how the enemy was responding to the explosion in the store. Before that though, the local villagers insisted on contributing to the attack. He never doubted their bravery but when they informed him of their plan, he had grave misgivings. He was persuaded to go along with it simply because he had few options; his carefully devised plan was in tatters after only the first few shots had been fired.

The mortars were still falling short, and he ordered that they should cease firing. They would need to get closer, maybe by fifty metres to be effective. This meant they would need to leave cover and venture onto open ground, drawing a lot of fire. He did not want his mortar unit destroyed so early in the assault. He nodded in the direction of the villagers and they in turn signaled in the direction of the jungle. A loud roar went up from all the men and it caused the fighters on both sides to cease firing for a short time. Part of the jungle seemed to come to life as tree branches suddenly detached themselves from the surrounding vegetation. At least six carts, normally pulled by bullocks, were wheeled from cover towards the incline that led to the garrison along the road. Mounted on the front of the carts were horizontal rows of thick branches and a dozen or so men pushed their heavily laden cargoes on each cart in the direction of the gate. The carts picked up speed as they were guided down the slight incline in an arrowhead formation.

Abdullah's men fell in behind and cowered for shelter from the fire directed at the primitive makeshift weapons of war. Amazingly, the fire was being absorbed by the tree trunks, but occasionally some of the villagers would bear the brunt of the machine-gun fire and fall, only to be replaced by willing comrades running behind. It was suicidal but they were making headway, and the mortar crew availed of the diversion to position themselves nearer the compound, and immediately launched their first round, which now fell just behind one of the machine guns, taking out several soldiers as it exploded. Other soldiers went to their aid and Abdullah noticed a few retreating towards the buildings.

It was a critical time in the attack but he needed to act

now; otherwise they would lose the initiative. The main assault party was dispatched and as they left cover, he looked on in horror as some of the men nearest him received a blast of fire and fell, either dead or wounded. He recovered from the shock quickly and motioned for his reserve troops to follow him. They responded immediately to the call and set off in the wake of a second group of bullock carts, some men even overtaking the carts in their enthusiasm. It was all or nothing now and Abdullah's heart lifted as he noticed some of his men from the river contingent gaining control of the top of the wall. They then started firing on the defenders below who now showed signs of wavering as they retreated in increasing numbers from the perimeter. He also noticed many flashes from weapons in the storeroom and wondered how Ali Hassan could have so much firepower. That question was answered as several of his men poured out of Ali Hassan's refuge. Of course! They had availed themselves of the breach in the rear wall made by the explosives. It gave truth to the old war axiom that no plan survives first contact with the enemy; they simply needed to avail of any luck that came their way.

The first bullock carts reached the main gate and crashed into it but failed to dislodge the sturdy posts holding it, exposing Abdullah's men to withering fire from the machine guns at close range. Abdullah's heart sank as his men were slaughtered, but his prayers were answered when a mortar round fell beside the machine gun doing most of the damage. The cloud of dust thrown up gave them vital cover, and before the machine gun could be brought back into action, several men had clambered up the tree trunks on the carts and scaled the fence and were involved in hand-to-hand combat with the Pakistani soldiers, some of whom now dropped their weapons and raised their arms in surrender. The momentum was now overwhelming, and more attackers poured into the compound over the gate, which was now buckled and near collapse. When the defenders became outnumbered, they soon capitulated and the skirmishes in various parts of the garrison soon became silent, and a victory roar filled the air as Abdullah's ragged force took complete control of the defeated regular army, whose soldiers now knelt and begged for mercy.

Abdullah would not tolerate revenge in any form, regardless of the deeds committed by these soldiers in the past. His men knew this and set about rounding up the soldiers and putting them in the centre of the parade ground, sitting with their hands on their heads. Medics from both sides were permitted to attend to the wounded. Two of his men suddenly appeared from the officers' quarters with an officer in tow. Abdullah hadn't noticed him during the fighting and assumed that he had sought refuge during the assault and let his men do the defending without him. His insignia identified him as a lieutenant. As he got closer, Abdullah recognised him from his earlier visit and instructed his men to shoulder their arms.

The lieutenant straightened up and addressed him in English, his hands trembling. "This is treason, and you and your men will be severely punished for this crime against the legitimate forces of the state. I warn you now to surrender and have your men lay down their arms."

A laugh went up from those who understood English. Abdullah motioned for the lieutenant to accompany him to the shade of a verandah beside the officers' mess.

"Lieutenant, it is with a heavy heart that I survey the death and destruction around us here today. I am a tolerant man, but make no mistake, my men are not in such a merciful mood. I earnestly request you to accept defeat and let us move on from there. I must tell you that the Indian Army is poised to assist us in establishing our new state of Bangladesh…"

With that, the lieutenant had to be restrained by troops standing guard. "You traitor! You will be hanged by Major Ali Khan this very day, when he returns…"

He stopped abruptly and Abdullah knew that the lieutenant had given away vital information about the return of the rest of the troops sometime later that day. "Thank you, Lieutenant!"

He motioned for the lieutenant to be taken away. He could hear cheering from the direction of the storeroom and noticed his men carrying a stretcher out of the rubble. The prone figure of Ali Hassan could be seen with bandages on his head and arms. He was smiling, however, and Abdullah relaxed. Sending a brave man home wounded was a source of pride to his family and village. He looked around him and his heart sank. Dead men from both sides were being laid out in the shade of trees to the side of the compound. Each one of these brave soldiers had a family, and Abdullah prayed to Allah for all of them.

Soon, the reality of the situation shocked him back to the events around him. He ordered his men to lock the prisoners in the barracks, all except the lieutenant and their sergeant major. He had plans for them. The men were instructed to gather as many uniforms as they could from the thirty or so remaining unwounded Pakistani soldiers and this they did with relish. He checked his watch and wondered when the helicopter would return. As he formulated a plan in his mind, he noticed the two journalists photographing the dead fighters and some of his men were even posing for the cameras. It was distasteful, but he was too busy to take any action. Some men were lowering the Pakistani flag, and he angrily shouted at them to raise it again. They noticed the edge in his voice as his orders became more urgent as the men rushed to carry them out. He wanted the bullock carts to be taken away and the main gate repaired.

The sandbags around the machine-gun positions had to be rebuilt. He hoped the hole in the rear wall could be repaired well enough to stand scrutiny from the crew of the helicopter as it approached.

DaSilva stood looking forlornly at the line of dead soldiers, and at Abdullah's dead comrades being loaded onto the carts to be transported to their villages. With agreement from the Pakistani lieutenant, Abdullah instructed his men to remove the bodies of the garrison soldiers to the storeroom as soon as it was cleared of debris. Once Abdullah's men knew that the purpose of all this work was to deceive the returning patrol, they worked feverishly to return the garrison to its original condition.

"Mr. DaSilva, forgive me for ignoring you but we really must prepare for the next phase of our operation. I am determined to prevent more bloodshed. I can only imagine how you must feel, but please understand that we only wish to bring about a situation where these soldiers can go home to West Pakistan and leave us to manage our own affairs in an independent Bangladesh."

"Mr. Abdullah, I know you are an honourable man, and I can understand your motivation. I had hoped to be able to reverse the policies of our army here and attempt to reinforce the positive aspects of the relationship between West and East Pakistan. But the situation is out of our control and all my efforts must now be directed towards limiting the scale of death and destruction, and whatever further damage limitation is needed to stabilise the situation."

"Sir, I must inform you that the Indian Army will cross the border soon and our forces will act as pathfinders for their forward units. The momentum is now unstoppable, and hopefully, our government-in-exile will be installed in Dhaka in the near future. The Pakistani military in East Pakistan is in a precarious situation. Their supply lines from the West are now compromised. They are unable to overfly India and their journey by sea is pointless since we will eventually have control of all the ports. I urge you to contact the Martial Law Administrator and persuade him to intensify negotiations with us for a peaceful resolution to the conflict. My men can help you establish communications. I'm certain the phone line and radios here in the garrison are still intact."

"Mr. Abdullah, the army is very proud and unlikely to listen to me. As soon as they discover the intentions of the Indian Government, they will surely feel that they must fight to the bitter end. We are, after all, historical enemies and each side would view as a weakness any request to negotiate."

"Pride is a terrible thing, Mr. DaSilva. What happens now is in the hands of Allah."

Abdullah walked away, leaving DaSilva to survey the scene of the recent battle. Abdullah's men were now busy repairing the damaged walls and main gate and restoring the compound to its original state. DaSilva viewed with suspicion the men donning Pakistani uniforms and taking up positions around the perimeter. Abdullah's plan was daring. He intended to capture Major Ali Khan and his forces when they returned. He presumed that the helicopter would arrive first, and the major would be on board. It was a question of whether or not he would be fooled by all the cosmetic repairs being carried out by Abdullah's men. He retreated to the officers' mess, which was their new command centre. The garrison radio operator was seated at the field radio with two of Abdullah's men guarding him. When any message came from the helicopter, he had instructions on what to say to assure the pilot that nothing out of the ordinary had happened on the ground. If he deviated in any way, then he would be shot. He didn't look like a hero and seemed eager to please. Now, all they could do was settle back and wait for the major's return.

Chapter 26

Meena knew the smell of blood intimately and its presence caused her to sit up abruptly. The saree's original colour had been replaced by the colour of the blood that soaked it. She noticed the folds of the garment draped in an unusual way around her body, as if hastily fitted by someone else. She immediately started searching for the source of the blood and in doing so, discovered no underwear or petticoat. She felt fine but her cheek was still on fire. The memories started to flood back now, and she rose in panic from the bed and immediately collapsed on the floor in a fit of dizziness. She recovered somewhat and stumbled to the door, which was locked. Her feeling that it had been a nightmare during sleep didn't last long as she felt her cheek and remembered the lifeless form of Sister Gertrude falling on top of her. So much blood and none of it was hers. Tears welled up in her eyes as she went to the window to try to assess the situation.

Orders were shouted and suddenly the door burst open. A medic entered as she hastily covered her nakedness. He was in a hurry but found time to reassure her that she had no injuries, and he said this in such a way that indicated that she had not been raped. This now was the least of her worries as she asked about Sister Gertrude.

The major entered and threw a clean saree and underclothes on the bed. "We took these from your laundry earlier. Put them on and be quick about it. You can take a bath if you wish. Consider yourself lucky to be alive. The actions of that stupid foreign woman made it hard for me to control the anger of my men. They took it out on your precious villagers as a result, but you people have only yourselves to blame. Now, hurry along. We leave in fifteen minutes, and we don't want any more trouble from you." Meena felt her stomach turn as she wondered about the people in the village and the image of Sister Gertrude falling as shots rang out. This, coupled with fear for her own safety, overwhelmed her and she sank back onto the bed.

"Major, what barbarity have your men perpetrated against us? How are you letting this happen?"

He cut her off. "We are going to the border in pursuit of your Indian spy friends. You will be there to witness their capture, and we will persuade them, by whatever means, to reveal your involvement in this saga. Make no mistake, you will all be held accountable for your treasonous activities. Now, come along, my dear, or I will have my men dress you. Remember, it was their comrades who were murdered in cold blood by your foreign accomplice. Needless to say, my men do not have your comfort and wellbeing foremost in their minds, so I don't expect any more of your delaying tactics."

He barked an order to the medic to keep an eye on her. As soon as she was ready, he was to deliver her to the helicopter. When the major left, Meena asked the medic to please find one of the nuns called Sister Anna and bring her here. When he left, only then did she notice the broken picture frame on her bedside table. The treasured picture of her parents with her at her graduation was missing. Meena could not dwell on this as she retreated to the shower room adjoining the bedroom and stripped away the blood-soaked clothes. As she showered, she could do nothing else but cry as the blood from several bodies was washed from her body down the drain. Her memories ended when the lifeless body of Sister Gertrude fell on her, so she had obviously blacked out.

She was horrified to think of events after that, when other men had obviously roughly covered her with her blood-stained clothes, which had been ripped away during the assault, and then carried her to her bedroom. Her hand instinctively moved between her legs, but she could discern no pain or bruising there, and apart from the stinging pains in her cheek and breasts, she observed no other injuries other than bruises all over her body. Still, the need to scrub her body vigorously with soap and hot water was overwhelming. She felt ashamed that her own predicament had eclipsed the fact that she had lost her dear friend and mentor, and that the thing that preoccupied her most was the residual taste of the soldier's mouth, despite several carbolic soap and hot water mouthwashes. When she left the shower room wrapped in a towel, she straightened and assumed a professional demeanour, determined to present an air of authority and defiance, but mostly to reassure her workers, who must be devastated at the violence visited on their otherwise secure and caring environment.

Sister Anna arrived, and Meena asked her to dispose of the blood-stained saree. She also gave her the clothes the major had thrown at her; there was no way she could bring herself to wear anything touched by him. "Anna, please bring me clean clothes from the laundry. I know all this is frightening for all of you but remember the love that binds us all together. I am being forced to go with them in search of the young pilot, so the soldiers will be gone very soon. Look after Sister Gertrude and arrange her funeral service with Father Anthony. I'm praying that the villagers have survived this ordeal. I'm leaving you with so much pain and anguish to deal with, but I promise you that I will do everything in my power to return as soon as possible and that we will come through this."

Sister Anna was from Bangalore in the south of India and was very experienced in the administration of the hospital and all the programs they ran. "Meena, I'm really concerned about letting you go with that man. I want you to promise to be very careful and not antagonise him or give him a reason to harm you further. I recognise evil when I see it and I can tell that he will do anything to get what he wants. Now, take some medication for the pain of the frightening ordeal you have just come through. The soldiers locked all of us in the kitchen and we heard your screams and gunshots, and we thought you were dead." She could not hold back the floods of tears that came suddenly.

Meena held her tightly and let her cry. "Please, get me the clothes, Anna, and I will get those evil men away from here as quickly as I can. I feel awful for being the cause of them arriving here and I apologise for that. But please don't worry. I will be extremely careful, I promise."

Sister Anna left to fetch the clean clothes and returned with them and some medication, which Meena gladly took to try to relieve the pain in her cheek. As she dressed, she surveyed the bruising, which seemed extensive. Anna simply observed with her hands covering her mouth and tears streaming from her eyes as she watched Meena attempt to cover the horrific bruising all over her body. Meena tried to make light of the situation in an effort to console Anna.

"Well, if wrestling with men produces results such as this, then are we not lucky to have chosen a life of celibacy?" Anna could only try to control her distress and help Meena form the saree in a protective cocoon around her damaged body. Sister Gertrude, the one they would all turn to for counselling in times like this, was no longer with them, and they both realised the void in their lives that her tragic death had created.

Chapter 27

The major set about readying his troops for the journey towards the border. He knew the dangers involved and considered the fact that he would be dangerously exposed and far from help should he get into difficulty. His superiors would never sanction such a journey, but he was sure they would appreciate the capture of Indian Army personnel. He was determined that the gamble would pay off so it would be worth the risk. The key to success centered on his ability to use the helicopter to the best advantage. He surveyed the improvised mount for the heavy machine gun and ensured that enough ammunition was on board. He briefed his sergeant, who was checking the weapon in anticipation of the possible combat scenarios which lay ahead. The sergeant seemed eager to leave on the mission and the major assured him that all he needed to do was brief the pilots, who had already complained at having to land such a big machine in the restricted clearing around the hospital.

He found them huddled together in the shade of a nearby tree. He realised that the recent activities of his troops had not met with their approval and that they were not pleased to be exposed to combat when their main function was VIP transport. They indicated that their commanding officer would get a full report of the major's activities. The major didn't wish to antagonise them at this late stage and so he tried to cajole them once more into appreciating the importance of their contribution. They didn't seem all that eager and eyed the door-mounted machine gun with suspicion. They had never been involved in combat before and feared the worst with this mad major conducting operations. Reluctantly, they boarded the aircraft and surveyed the cabin. They cautioned the sergeant who was loading the fifty-calibre machine gun to ensure that the arc of fire from his machine gun should be directed downwards at all times, to avoid shooting away their main rotor blades. The man smiled mischievously and assured the pilots that he would be careful. The pilots looked at each other in dismay as they continued their preparations.

Taking their seats up-front in the cramped cockpit, which was accessed up a small ladder from the main cabin of the aircraft, they signaled to the major through the cockpit window that they were ready. He acknowledged this and gave final instructions to the convoy commander and insisted that they do a radio check to ensure adequate air-to-ground communications. This would be vital to the success of the mission. He ordered two men to fetch the doctor, whether she was ready or not. The helicopter would lift off as the convoy departed and immediately do a reconnaissance of the road they were to travel. He asked the sergeant in the helicopter to check his machine gun, and the sudden volley made even the major jump. He looked in the direction of their fire and hoped nobody was walking in that particular part of the jungle during the shooting. He could never know that Hossain and his men were watching the major's every move from the jungle and felt sure their whereabouts had been discovered when the shots penetrated the jungle so close to them that they had to dive for cover.

Meena jumped when she heard the gunfire and immediately

ran to the window. The major was standing beside the helicopter, and she noticed the military vehicles getting ready for departure as they started their engines in a cloud of exhaust fumes. She desperately wanted to go to the village to survey the destruction she knew had taken place.

The door suddenly opened, and two men motioned with their rifles for her to accompany them. She shouldered her medical bag, which they checked for weapons. Luckily, she had decided to place two surgical scalpels in their protective wrappers securely in the folds of her saree at her waist. The soldiers were eager to be on their way and the look of hostility on their faces made her realise that they would have no hesitation in shooting her if she were to deviate from their orders in any way. They were obviously aware of the circumstances of the deaths of their two comrades but refused to believe that this woman was not directly responsible, regardless of the rumours of their comrades' actions.

The staff at her hospital waited and conveyed their worry to her with anxious looks as soon as she reached them. What could she say to them? They were all from the nearby villages and they too were eager to find out what had happened to their families.

One of the soldiers stepped forward and informed them all in Bengali that all was well in the village, and that the soldiers only wanted supplies of water and food. With two of his comrades lying dead nearby, he assured them that they were lucky the other soldiers had not been in a more vengeful mood. As they escorted Meena to the helicopter and out of earshot of Meena's workers, the same man admitted to having plundered the village but said that they were not rapists, and from his tone she realised that he did not approve of the actions of the men who had assaulted her earlier. Having made that clear, he assumed an air of aggression once more and guided her firmly towards the helicopter.

Esther, who was one of Meena's best surgical nurses, forced

herself between Meena and her escort and assured her that they would all help Sister Anna look after Sister Gertrude's burial, and that they would be praying for Meena's safe return. Meena hugged her briefly before the soldiers forced them apart.

"Make yourself comfortable, madam and secure your seatbelt; we will be flying with the door open because of the machine gun," one of the young pilots said in English as he gently fastened the seat harness around her and pulled the straps tight. "The major will be with us on board and the sergeant here will man the machine gun. My friend, Flight Lieutenant Khan, will be flying. He is an excellent pilot so there is no need to worry. I am Flight Lieutenant Das, and we are normally involved with VIP transport in Dhaka. Our services have been commandeered by the major for this mission, but we don't expect much trouble, and the mission should be completed before nightfall."

The pilots looked a little guilty in her presence and she concluded that they were all aware of the assault that had taken place and were ashamed of the actions of their comrades.

"Thank you, Lieutenant, I think I have flown in this helicopter once before, during a medical evacuation about two years ago. There had been a bus crash nearby and several of the victims were transported to Dhaka for emergency surgery. So please relax, I've recovered from my ordeal earlier and now I only wish to grieve for my sister, who died so violently trying to protect me. She saved my life. May she rest in peace."

He nodded awkwardly, said 'Inshallah', and turned towards the flight compartment. 'Inshallah' was repeated by the sergeant. Meena looked through the trees towards the village and made out some people standing around the well, looking in her direction. She waved and they all waved back. They seemed all right; if anything, they looked more concerned about her predicament than their own. The major was waving the convoy away and the dust enveloped the whole area as they turned along the jungle path towards the road to the border. He jumped aboard and studied a map with the pilots. The pilots explained that if needed, there was a helicopter landing area at an artillery garrison near the border and this would take them away from the convoy for less than an hour if they needed to refuel. They reassured the major that they would still be in constant radio contact with the convoy should they need to avail of this option. He briefed them on what he expected of them and the need to maintain an altitude of two thousand feet to minimize the risk from small-arms fire from the ground. There were too many trigger-happy people on the ground, from many factions, and flying too low was only asking for trouble. The pilots needed no reminder of the need to steer clear of situations that would threaten their safety. They knew how vulnerable their machine would be to gunfire and avoiding such situations would be high on their agenda, even though the major had other ideas.

They had thought about deserting this madman but, perversely, they also craved glory and saw a successful conclusion to this mission as a passport home to their families, as well as to certain promotion. Like all combat situations, it was a gamble where the victor gained everything. Now that they were committed, it would be essential to apply themselves wholeheartedly to the mission, thereby increasing their chances of success. Also, a history of actual combat experience would enhance their reputation among comrades with whom they would legitimately be able to relate credible war stories.

When the briefing was complete, the major asked the pilots to radio their headquarters once airborne to arrange for a military ambulance to come and collect the bodies of the two dead soldiers. He then came back and sat beside Meena and strapped himself in. He knew that she had heard him make arrangements for the ambulance. He wanted her to be aware of his displeasure at their deaths. But at the same time, he could not condone the actions that led to their killing at the hands of the foreign nun. He had seen the Luger pistol and assumed that the elderly nun must have obtained it during the Second World War. He could only guess at the circumstances that led to her having a German army officer's sidearm.

The sergeant sat at the doorway, ready for action. The major put on his headset and signaled the pilots to get underway. They initiated the start sequence and soon the engine came to life. The main rotor blades then began to turn, and the dust swirled around them with the downdraft as they lifted off and at first hovered before the aircraft turned towards a clearing in the jungle and climbed away from the hospital compound. Meena looked down towards the village where the people were looking skyward and waving. She convinced herself that they must be safe, and she prayed for this to be the case. They searched for the convoy on the road as they climbed, and radio contact was established. Very soon she could make out the vehicles in the convoy as it snaked its way through the jungle and, to her relief, away from her hospital and villages.

As she looked closer at the lead armoured vehicle, she noticed some men sitting on the engine compartment as the vehicle moved through the jungle. The major caught her quizzical look and informed her that they were villagers put there by his men to discourage ambush and mines being remotely detonated on the road. "This is simply a precaution, Doctor. The realities of war are becoming apparent to you more and more, I can see."

She noticed the smugness of his tone. "Major, I am already well aware of the consequences of war, I can assure you. I am also aware that it is the activities of men like you that contribute to the slaughter and maiming of innocent people, particularly children. My experiences in Vietnam were no different from my experiences here. I sometimes wonder what your daughter 'the same age as me' would think, were she to see the activities of the men in your command."

He slowly removed his headset, released his seat harness, and turned to face Meena directly. "You are so self-righteous, madam. It is typical for a woman to make lofty assumptions concerning the activities of men during war, while at the same time enjoying the lifestyle and freedoms made possible through the sacrifices of men like me in previous wars. To their credit, my family is proud of my contribution and recognises the realities of war and the hard choices that must be made during conflict. You are like an armchair general, making lofty pronouncements from the comfort of the home front. Well, let us see how you cope with this mission, during which I ask you to kindly keep your opinions to yourself. Remember also that in Vietnam, a typical way of dealing with uncooperative captives was to throw them out of a helicopter at altitude."

He retreated to a seat opposite her in order to intimidate her with his stare. He replaced his headset and immediately asked for a report from the convoy below. Meena gripped the handrail tightly and visibly recoiled from the menace of the man opposite her. Maybe he was right; most soldiers never did have a choice when it came to fighting for their country and they were at the mercy of the whims of generals and died in their thousands doing their bidding. Atrocities committed on civilians were simply seen as collateral damage or the casualities of war, no mention being given to their rights or their needs.

Maybe she should review her opinions of conflict and war. Respect for the rights of others only came from notions of self-preservation, after all. We safeguard the rights of others in the hope that they will observe our rights. We clear a path for an ambulance and expect others to do the same in the event of us being the casualty on board. Her work saving lives was simply a part of this pact of mutual self-preservation.

She was shaken from her thoughts when the helicopter suddenly plunged towards the ground at an alarming rate of descent. The pilots had seen another aircraft, maybe a helicopter, and dived towards the trees to observe its movements without being seen against the skyline. Meena scanned the sky and eventually did see another helicopter in the distance. It appeared to be travelling away from them so they simply followed to enable them to duck down to cover should the other aircraft land. The shouting on board was frightening and on the major's orders, the sergeant primed the machine gun for action. He instructed the pilots to position themselves in such a way so as to keep the machine gun's sights constantly on the other helicopter until they determined whether it was friend or foe. From their lower vantage point, they could easily make out the other aircraft silhouetted against the sky, and they followed at a safe distance.

The treetops were a hundred feet below them. Providing cover for the convoy now seemed forgotten. One of the pilots was searching the sky for the other aircraft with binoculars and eventually turned around to the major and informed him that it was indeed a helicopter with the insignia of the Indian Air Force, and that it seemed to be alone. The major's eyes opened in surprise, or expectation; she could not tell which. He looked in her direction and she could see fear and apprehension etched on his face as he considered the situation. The sergeant also looked at him anxiously, waiting for orders.

"We'll surprise this fellow, that's for sure. We will follow him and I'm certain he will lead us to your Indian pilot and the other spies. It is a foreign war machine flying over our sovereign territory without permission and that constitutes an act of war."

He took the binoculars from the pilot and scanned the airspace around the Indian helicopter to make doubly sure they were alone. He didn't want to be surprised by the enemy while he was figuring out a strategy to capitalise on the fact that they had the advantage of surprise. They would simply follow the other aircraft until they set down and then he would attack. They would need to get in fast once the other machine was on the ground with its engine still running; that way the noise would disguise their approach. He ensured that the sergeant had his sights trained on the Indian helicopter at all times. He radioed the convoy and as he studied the map, he guided them to a road that would take them in the same general direction. He could make out the road leading to the border and calculated the distance at around fifty miles.

He felt sure that the doctor's jeep must be close and looked for signs that the other helicopter was beginning its descent. He felt sure it was descending towards an agreed rendezvous point to rescue their pilot. Everything was ready and he removed his sidearm from its holster and checked the ammunition. The sweat rolled down his brow and as Meena was reflecting on his state of mind, a shout came from the flight compartment.

"Major, they have turned and are now facing us. I think they are looking for a landing site. I don't think we are visible to them because the sun is behind us and the crew will be concentrating on searching the ground for obstacles."

Their pilot slowed and hovered above a clearing at treetop height and Meena looked in the direction of the other helicopter and wondered if her jeep was just below it. She thought of Shane, Monica and Keeler and knew that Prem Das had done his job well and delivered them to this rendezvous point. She assumed that Keeler must have been able to contact his people to organise a rescue mission, rather than proceeding to the border by road with all the dangers that entailed.

Meena wished she could warn them. She thought of leaning over and simply pressing the trigger of the machine gun, but the sergeant had it covered and surely the major would instinctively shoot her dead in an instant were she to interfere with his plan. All she could do was wait and pray. Suddenly the major shouted an order to the pilots.

"Advance towards the target immediately. Get ready to fire on my command," he instructed his sergeant, who was ready on the deadly machine gun, which Meena knew could deliver death and destruction to her friends while she sat helplessly watching as a spectator.

It was evident that the major had taken into account the information about the sun being behind them and he calculated that the enemy was now at their most vulnerable while in their landing configuration. The advantage of surprise would be total, and it would be foolish not to attack now. If he could destroy the Indian helicopter, then he would be free to apprehend his prey unopposed. The Indian helicopter was obviously descending towards an agreed rescue point, a logical geographical feature at the junction of road and river he was now observing on the map.

He had visions of being in the headlines of all the newspapers back home, pictured with his men in front of the wreckage of an enemy helicopter, downed in combat by his decisive actions. The subsequent capture of an Indian Air Force pilot would prove to the world that India was indeed violating their airspace in an act of war. The international media would have a field day and India would have a lot of explaining to do at the United Nations. His promotion would be assured. He just needed to ensure a successful outcome to this encounter. He looked at Meena and knew from her expression that she was indeed fearful for her friends, and this confirmed to him that they actually were in the area. He made a radio call to the convoy, directing them to their location, and took one last look through the binoculars as he leant forward and calmly laid his hand on the shoulder of his sergeant. The Indian helicopter descended through a gap in the jungle, oblivious to the danger stalking them from above. Meena sat rigidly, overcome by fear and anxiety, unable to comprehend the devastation about to unfold.

Chapter 28

The reflection he had seen in the sky was no longer visible, but Shane was certain that it had been a helicopter. He looked at the map on his knees and felt sure they were lost, but nevertheless, he guided the jeep in the direction Prem Das suggested. He figured that they were running parallel to the main road leading to the border. As they neared the border, they would be sure to encounter more soldiers and so the track through the jungle, while slower, would still provide them with cover. Prem Das directed him off the track and they drove through the jungle for about ten miles before he requested Shane to stop just short of a clearing in the trees. The area was deserted but some old, rusting machinery became visible, protruding from the undergrowth. Prem Das said that it was an old depot used for grading the materials for building the road many years ago and that the adjacent clearing would be suitable to take a helicopter. The area corresponded to one of the rendezvous points on the map.

They both turned to Keeler, who didn't look so good. Monica looked concerned as she held up the three remaining ampoules of morphine from her bag. The transmitter was working, and Keeler said that it would not be long now. Keeler had transmitted their position for ten minutes every hour and he assured them that the signal would be picked up by Indian aircraft in the air on the other side of the border. As far as he knew, the Pakistani Army had no aircraft in the area, and the Indian forces were gathering in ever-increasing numbers just fifty miles away. They listened for any sign of approaching aircraft but all they could hear was the occasional truck on the main road in the distance. They concentrated on making Keeler comfortable in the shade of a tree. Shane moved the jeep away and parked it in tall grass beside a larger tree that would provide some cover should military traffic approach through the jungle from the direction of the main road. The possibility of enemy aircraft being in this vicinity never occurred to him as his thoughts were solely focused on the arrival of an Indian Army helicopter. Their white Land Rover jeep shimmered with light from the sun shining through the leaves in the overhead canopy.

They settled down in the shade and listened for the sound of the helicopter Shane had seen. They knew that any flight over East Pakistan would be extremely dangerous. The helicopter would need to undertake the mission to evacuate them in as short a time as possible. They would certainly show up on radar, so it would be imperative to be back across the border before the Pakistani Air Force had time to send fighters to investigate. Shane wondered about Meena and whether he would ever see her again. He had toyed with the idea of sending Keeler on the rescue helicopter with Monica and returning to the dispensary with Prem Das, but his situation was precarious, and he was fearful of being caught by the army. He should not be in East Pakistan, which was the simple truth, and anyone found with him could be in serious trouble. Monica would wish to return to the hospital too and he knew he would have a hard time convincing her to leave with Keeler.

Prem Das assured them that he would drive the jeep back to the hospital alone. The journey by air to the border would take less than half an hour. If Prem Das could get them all safely across the border and avoid interception by soldiers, then this would be the best option. Prem Das assured them that this was indeed possible by using old jungle routes known only to locals. Having safely delivered Keeler to an Indian Army hospital, they would then need to retrace their steps. Even Prem Das admitted that this would be dangerous and ill-advised.

"We can translate these words into as many languages as you like," he reasoned. "But 'don't push your luck' describes it very well. The chances of avoiding Pakistani military patrols indefinitely would be slim. My advice to you all is to evacuate with the injured lieutenant to India and permit me to return to the hospital with the jeep."

They all knew this was the sensible option, but Shane decided to stay and approached Keeler to inform him of his decision. Monica looked up as he approached and by the look on her face, she seemed to know what was on his mind.

"No, I will be returning to the hospital with the jeep, Shane. Lieutenant Keeler will get medical attention as soon as they reach India. He will be transferred to a military hospital for the best treatment for his leg. The surgery carried out by Dr Meena is not the problem; it is the possibility of infection in the main wound and the wounds where the support wires pierce the skin that is the concern. There is no need for me to go with him. I will be needed here with Dr Meena. Please don't ask me to go because I will never be able to return. There will be a war very soon and the border will be closed."

"Okay, Monica, I understand, so please don't worry. I'll return with you once the lieutenant is safely on the rescue helicopter and on his way home. We must be very careful though. Prem Das is correct; I don't think we'll be able to avoid the military for long. I hope to convince Dr Meena to leave with us and go to India until the political situation stabilises. I must admit that things don't look good at present. Remember when we left

Hili on our recent journey here, when we encountered Indian troops massing on the border? You are correct; it's only a matter of time before fighting erupts between India and Pakistan. Unfortunately, East Pakistan will be on the frontline so I think it will be extremely dangerous to stay here. We would all be safer in India. Lieutenant Keeler, what do you think?"

Keeler seemed more comfortable as he lay in the shade, propped up against a fallen tree trunk. The journey in the jeep must have been really challenging for him. Monica tended to his every need and the true nature of nursing seemed evident in the way he was responding to treatment. He seemed to have grown in wisdom also, in a way so often seen in those who have had a close encounter with death. There was, however, never a hint that he had even considered anything other than a full recovery. He adjusted himself into a comfortable position on the stretcher and considered the question seriously.

"As you all know, I have no doubts about what will happen to me should the Pakistani forces capture me. Technically, we are not at war with them but the history of relations between our two countries makes for unpleasant reading in any textbook. We are born into a society with deep distrust of foreigners, particularly those from Pakistan. This is not the time to discuss the root causes of our animosity, so I will simply venture an opinion based on my observations over the past few days.

"Both of you have intense feelings for the doctor, and so I presume that both of you will be staying here to re-join her at the hospital."

He held up his hand as Monica made to speak and as tears welled up in her eyes. Shane simply glanced at Prem Das in the distance, squatting on a rocky outcrop, observing the jungle towards the road.

"Shane, you know what will happen to you if you are found in my company. There is no need for me to remind you as I imagine you have already given it some thought. As you can tell from my name, I'm a Christian and I have prayed every day for the doctor because she has surely saved my life. I'm glad that she has devoted friends like you and I hope you will both be safe and successful in persuading the doctor and her workers to evacuate to the safety of India. I can assure you that there will be a war very soon, and the only question is how long the war will last. I have every confidence that the military forces of India will prevail, but I'm uncertain about what will happen after that.

"The talk among the officers in our army seems to reflect the wishes of our government – that a new country will emerge, a Bengali nation, independent from Pakistan and hopefully at peace with India. It will be impossible for Pakistan to sustain a fighting army for long, given the fact that India lies between East and West Pakistan, making their supply lines impossible to maintain. The plans we delivered to our friends in the insurgency contain the blueprints for invasion all along the border so you must move quickly since this may be only days away. Now, please don't be angry with me for saying so, but Prem Das is correct – you and Monica should evacuate with me and allow him to return and try to persuade the doctor to seek refuge in India."

Shane knew he was right. Looking at Monica, he knew where she wanted to be and that there was no way of convincing her to go on the Indian helicopter when it arrived.

"Lieutenant, you are quite right. At least now we each know what we want. It hasn't been easy for you and I'm sure you will recover well once you reach India. We will make our way back to the hospital, against your advice, and who knows what will happen after that? We don't wish to be caught up in a war so I will try to convince Dr Meena to do as you suggest, and hopefully, we will all meet again in India soon."

If Keeler was disappointed at what they had decided, he didn't show it. He was, however, still vigilant and alert. Prem Das stood up and suddenly all eyes were on him as they listened to the unmistakable sound of a helicopter approaching. He held up two fingers as he listened. "Two machines, sir," he said. Shane ran and climbed up on the rock beside him and both of them turned in the direction of the sound.

Keeler spoke into the radio and seemed happy from the short reply from the helicopter that it was coming from the border. He grinned and raised his fist in salute at the prospect of rescue being close at hand. The effort was too much for him and he needed to lie back as Monica readied the stretcher for loading onto the helicopter. She helped him sit up and then he suddenly held her hand and didn't need to say anything; he just simply transmitted a non-verbal signal of deep gratitude. Language had no place in this intense form of communication and Monica acknowledged this with a tearful smile.

They both waited for the arrival of the Indian rescue helicopter and looked to the sky in anticipation. Keeler suddenly gripped her two hands more tightly and his alarm was transmitted forcefully to her by the intensity of his grip. His eyes told her that something was not quite right, and she thought he was having a seizure and readied herself to intervene.

"Something is wrong, Monica. Prem Das is correct; I can hear two machines and only one of them is an Indian helicopter. We must leave now and find cover. Shane, bring the jeep quickly and get us away from here," said Keeler assertively.

Shane needed no further persuasion and ran as fast as he could to get to the jeep, while shouting at Prem Das and Monica to lift Keeler's stretcher ready to load into the jeep. The sound of the helicopter came nearer; he could only hear one but he knew Keeler's hearing would be more attuned to listening to the various sounds made by aircraft in flight, so he did as he was told, started the jeep and drove as quickly as he could to the others, who were in the process of lifting Keeler. He skidded to a halt beside them while eyeing the sky anxiously. He left the engine running and jumped out to open the rear door.

The rotor noise grew louder and as he reached the stretcher to help with the lift, they all froze as the aircraft suddenly made an appearance over the clearing. It hovered at about fifty feet above the ground and the pilot seemed to be negotiating the safest approach to land as close to the jeep as possible, avoiding the trees. The side door was open, and two crewmen were visible. One of them was issuing instructions to the pilot by radio headset in his helmet, guiding the big machine safely down through the trees. As it came closer, the rotor blades created a downdraft as it slowly sank to the ground, causing debris to fly through the air.

The concentration of those on the ground focused on the spectacle unfolding before them so much that they didn't notice Keeler scanning the sky anxiously and untying the sheet that was holding him on the stretcher. Had they noticed the look of fear on his face they may have had time to prepare for the unthinkable.

Chapter 29

Abdullah knew exactly what he needed to do and became increasingly animated as he shouted instructions to his men. DaSilva became aware of the leadership qualities of the man as he cajoled the men into preparing the compound for the return of the helicopter. It was clear now what he intended. The Pakistani flag flew once again, and the men were frantically clearing away the signs of the recent furious battle from the main gate, and others were working to rebuild the wall of the storeroom to the rear of the compound. DaSilva was impressed at the transformation of the place in such a short time. He was surprised also when two armed guards suddenly appeared beside him, the look on their faces suggesting that they had serious intentions.

Abdullah came towards him with an apologetic shrug. "My apologies, sir, but I really must insist that you accompany these men back to your observation point in the jungle. To be frank, we are about to undertake an extremely delicate operation, and I cannot trust you not to intervene and do something foolish to disrupt our plan. You are, after all, an officer of the Pakistani military, are you not? Please forgive my bad manners, but I will allow you to return here should we be successful. In fact, should my plan succeed, I hope to avail myself of your negotiating skills. If it is the will of Allah, there will be no more bloodshed. Your cooperation will be greatly appreciated."

"Mr. Abdullah, you are a good judge of character, and I understand exactly what you are trying to do. It is a brave plan, and I too hope for a peaceful resolution to this situation. But please, allow me to stay in the compound and I will give you my word not to intervene in any way. I feel that the situation may require my presence, so I implore you to reconsider your decision. I know what motivates the major in charge of the convoy, and it is likely that my intervention will be essential to your plan. Based on what I am hearing from Lieutenant Shah, it seems that the major and I are acquainted. We served together in Burma against the Japanese during the war."

"Very well, sir, please go with these men and remain in the radio room until I feel it is necessary to call you. I must warn you, though, that these men will follow my orders to…"

"That will not be necessary, Mr. Abdullah. I can assure you of my full cooperation."

DaSilva knew that Abdullah was finding it difficult to threaten him with harm. He warmly shook his hand and retreated with the guards to the radio room. On the way, he observed the storeroom, where the men had miraculously repaired most of the rear wall; soon it was as if no explosion had taken place, apart from the smell of burning still in the air. He turned his attention to the other buildings, where the garrison soldiers were held captive, and wondered if Abdullah could pull off such a bold plan and whether the major would fall into the trap so readily. He doubted it but settled down to wait and see. Meanwhile, he viewed the two journalists taking photographs of the remaining bodies being loaded onto the bullock carts to be transported away to the jungle. Abdullah's men were dressing in uniforms taken from the captive soldiers and soon the place was transformed to such an extent that from a distance, nobody could tell that a bloody battle had recently taken place there.

In the radio room, the radio operator sat sweating while listening out for a transmission that would signal the return of the major. Abdullah didn't believe in torture but had consented, in this instance, to his men demonstrating to the radio operator the appendages that would be hacked from his body should he stray from the exact script they required him to transmit when clearing the helicopter to land, as if everything were normal. The men took delight in the man's discomfort as they sharpened a bayonet in front of him to reinforce their intentions. They were certain he would cooperate fully with their instructions.

Abdullah surveyed his men's handiwork and declared himself reasonably satisfied. His men had even spread wet mud on the exposed brickwork on the outside of the repair on the storeroom wall. He had overlooked nothing. He finally dispatched the journalists away to the jungle and ordered them to follow the instructions of his men for their own safety. He told his men to permit them to take photographs with their telephoto lenses. He also instructed that their truck should be well camouflaged in the jungle, as it was imperative that it should not be visible from the air; otherwise, their operation would be compromised.

He then checked the flag and ensured there was no debris or obstructions on the helicopter landing zone. He worried about how the garrison would look from the air in the eyes of the major, who undoubtedly possessed the shrewd mind of an experienced combatant. The only thing that concerned Abdullah was the repair of the damaged storeroom wall on the side of the river. It would surely be visible from the air, and the wet mud at the repair site may seem suspicious. And what if the gunboats returned? So many things could go wrong. He looked in the direction of DaSilva, who stood at the entrance to the storeroom with his hands in his pockets. He would dearly love to know the man's thoughts. As they eyed each other, one critical thought was shared by the men. What if the convoy returned before the helicopter? This would be catastrophic, and so Abdullah blotted it from his mind. He noticed DaSilva looking to the sky as if confirming that they both shared the same thoughts.

Abdullah subscribed to the school of thought that declared that the harder you practice at an activity, the luckier you become when taking part in that activity. He understood that they had indeed been lucky so far, but then he realised that their perceived luck was solidly based on the long hours of training he demanded of his men. He had purposely enticed many Bengali non-commissioned officers, corporals and sergeants to desert the Pakistani military in the preceding months. This ensured the best possible training could be imparted to his mostly civilian fighters. He was proud of his men and knew that they would form the backbone of any security force in their fledgling nation. It pained him to admit that they would also need to avail of the services of officers who had served with the Pakistani military. He'd had this discussion many times with Sheik Mujib, who would undoubtedly become the first prime minister of their new nation.

Abdullah scanned the sky once more and prayed for the helicopter to return soon. There was nothing more to do now but wait.

Chapter 30

It was Monica who first noticed the look of horror on Keeler's face, just before he shouted a warning to run for cover. She followed his gaze towards one end of the clearing and thought that lightning bolts were hitting the ground, but the light was intermittent and, incredibly, it was weaving over and back as it worked its way towards the Indian helicopter. Keeler knew exactly what it was and searched the sky for the source of the firing while forcing himself to stand, and at the same time, wildly gesticulating a frantic signal to the pilot of the Indian helicopter to wave him away to safety. At the last second, the pilot noticed his fellow airman standing beside the stretcher. He recognised the signal immediately and started to configure his controls for a rapid exit from the danger zone.

Shane and Monica had dropped the stretcher and held each other tightly as the nature of Keeler's alarm became evident. Prem Das was already cowering behind the nearest tree, his old age and restricted movement no impediment to his hasty exit from the danger overtaking them, belying the notion that motor reflexes deteriorated with age. Shane and Monica, on the other hand, were frozen to the spot and eyed the Indian helicopter that now seemed to react in slow motion as it moved forward and started its climb.

The crewmen at the side door fell forward with the violent change in attitude. On the ground, they all watched helplessly as the ground erupted around the tail of their aircraft. Suddenly, Keeler was between Shane and Monica and the horrible spectacle and was practically lifting both of them to cover behind the fallen tree trunk, displaying superhuman strength to remove them from the danger area. Keeler's shouts of agony didn't distract them from rolling over in time to see the lightning bolts slamming into the tail rotor and working their way along the body of the helicopter, causing it to lurch violently until finally the inevitable happened and a fuel tank was hit. The fuel ignited into a tremendous fireball at fifty feet and the debris plummeted to the ground all around them. Another fireball erupted nearby as the main wreckage hit the ground and a wave of intense heat burned the scrub and trees in a huge area around where they lay. Remarkably, their jeep avoided the falling debris and sheltered them from the worst of the blast and the flames from the stricken machine.

Monica recovered first and had the presence of mind to locate her medical bag and set about preparing a morphine injection for Keeler, who was writhing in agony as he collapsed on the stretcher. Shane felt his eyebrows and hair singed slightly and leant over to extinguish a flame on Monica's salwar kameez at her ankles. She was oblivious to the burning and calmly filled the syringe.

Keeler was in pain but suddenly became quiet and pointed in the direction of another helicopter making its way towards the clearing and eventually settling down just fifty metres away. A soldier in the doorway was holding the still-smoking heavy machine gun that had inflicted the devastating damage. He quickly dismounted, carrying a lighter weapon, and immediately came running towards the group huddled together around the shelter of the fallen tree. The jeep marked their whereabouts and Shane cursed himself. Keeler observed the star and crescent on the green and white flag on the side of the helicopter and yielded to the inevitable. He lost consciousness as Monica calmly injected the morphine into the cannula attached to the back of his hand. The last thing he saw was an officer adjusting his tunic after stepping out onto the scrub and raising his hand in mock chivalry to help a lady in a saree climb down from the cabin. She refused and instead gripped the stock of the machine gun for support, dismounting from the doorway without help.

Shane looked on in amazement as a sergeant trained his weapon on them. But his heart lifted as he saw Meena walking towards them. He gazed in her direction, unable to figure out how she could possibly be here. As their eyes met, he could see the pain and sorrow etched on her face. He lowered his face into his hands in a gesture of hopelessness and eventually tried to raise himself up from a kneeling position only to be forced back down by the boot of the sergeant guarding them.

***

Earlier, as their helicopter descended Meena was horrified when the sergeant started firing at the helpless target slowly ascending from the ground. She pleaded with the major to stop. But the sergeant on the machine gun was an expert as he 'walked' the machine gun fire along the ground towards the stricken Indian helicopter. She scanned the area for signs of her jeep and her movement caused the major to jam his pistol into her side to keep her quiet while he encouraged his man to annihilate the enemy intruder. She cried out loudly as the bullets tore into the tail of the Indian helicopter and all along the fuselage as it tried to escape. She imagined the rounds tearing into flesh as they found the cabin and recoiled in shock as the aircraft suddenly exploded in a fireball. She retched but nothing came up from her empty stomach, and she held her hand to her mouth in disgust as every crewman cheered their victory. One of the pilots looked back with a big grin on his face, but when he caught her horrified expression, he sheepishly looked away in shame and realised the horror of the deed that they had just inflicted on men similar to them in every way.

When they landed, Meena was in no mood to tolerate the jubilant behavior of these men and recoiled in disgust as the major offered her his hand as she jumped from the helicopter. She had toyed with the idea of turning the machine gun on them but the thought of the time it would take to figure out how it worked restrained her. Besides, the major's promise to shoot her dead was no idle threat. Instead, she looked towards the trees where her jeep was located and saw Monica administering an injection. She quickly reverted to doctor mode and noticed Shane looking in her direction with a blackened face. Prem Das peeped out from behind a tree and the sergeant ordered him out. They all seemed to be free from injury and she turned her attention to Keeler. The major saw her look of concern and roughly grabbed her arm.

"Madam, this man is my ticket to glory and out of this troubled country. If he dies before I have the chance to present him to our military command, then you will suffer, I can assure you. So, get to work on him and prepare him for the flight to Dhaka and our appointment with destiny. We can land at our garrison to refuel on the way and restock the necessary medical supplies while there. As for the other foreigner – well, it looks like we have discovered a nest of spies here. And please, madam, save the tears for later. The situation in which you are implicated will be dealt with harshly by the military court, which will be set up to deal with all of you."

He ordered the pilots to radio the convoy, guide them to their location, and instruct them to dispatch one vehicle to the nearest town to locate a camera and spare films. He needed to record this event. He looked towards the burning helicopter, already picturing himself in international newspapers with the doomed enemy helicopter in the background. He then searched Keeler for weapons and any incriminating documents and found the radio. "More evidence of espionage activities," he exclaimed. His man searched Shane and then the jeep. They didn't seem concerned about Prem Das and ignored him. Meena had a sinking feeling that he may be employed by the military. As she watched him, though, he displayed just as much fear as the others. She noticed the look of defiance on Monica's face and cautioned her against resisting the search. The sergeant was very thorough when it was her turn, and she kept her eyes on Meena as he probed her clothing. They communicated on a higher level, where beauty and tranquility reigned, and this enabled her to blot out the humiliation. Shane looked to be in shock as they dragged him to his feet, and Meena was prevented from going near him as he stumbled. It seemed that he had taken the force of the blast on his face, which showed signs of minor burns. She hoped his hearing was not damaged and decided to find some medication for him to settle his nerves and take away the pain of his injuries.

She was relieved when he looked at her and smiled with a shrug. This confirmed to her that he would be fine and that he was shocked more from being captured than from the trauma of the recent battle. He had been exposed to so much in the past week and she admired his resilience. He probably measured this encounter against those he experienced at the death of his wife and child, she thought. So, in his mind, nothing could match such horrific past events, and this had the effect of insulating him from even the most traumatic experiences. The sergeant pulled Keeler's map from under a blanket where Shane had been lying. He passed it to the major, who walked to where Shane stood and asked him whether he was employed by the Americans or British as he observed the contents of the map.

"Sorry to disappoint you, General, but I'm Irish. Might I request you to provide us with safe passage to the Indian border, like a good man? We may then be prepared to overlook your assault on a legitimate Red Cross medical evacuation."

The major was caught off guard and struggled to find an appropriate answer to this impertinence. He knew about the Irish and their colonial history and didn't quite know how to categorize Shane. Why would an Irishman be spying in this region, after all? He had to think of something.

"Irish maybe, but in the pay of the Americans or British, no doubt. They insist on having their grubby fingers in every pie. Pity about the luck of the Irish on this occasion, I suppose. Now, you can save your distorted reasoning and eloquent speeches for the military court," the major said, waiting for a reaction. He laughed heartily as his humour was met with hostile stares, and he ordered them all to be put in the helicopter. If recent events had not been so serious, they might all have laughed at the audacity of Shane's remark and the major's reaction.

The convoy arrived and suddenly there were soldiers everywhere. Some of them were detailed to search the wreckage of the Indian helicopter for bodies and especially for identification discs of the military personnel who were on board. The major was informed that his men would soon arrive with a camera as instructed.

The major recovered his composure and seemed determined to load up every scrap of wreckage from the downed helicopter, particularly the Indian Air Force roundels insignia, Indian flag, and the military registration number. The bodies of the airmen would be returned to India after examination for burial. He was a military man, after all, and some traditions could never be compromised.

Meena looked at the major strutting around like the victor in a cock fight and thought about the families of the Indian airmen who would soon be receiving the terrible news of the deaths of their loved ones. She examined Keeler and was astonished to notice strong vital signs. His wounds showed no signs of infection, even though there were signs of further minor injuries. Monica described how he had saved their lives in an extraordinary act of bravery just before the crash. Meena could not even imagine the pain the young man went through with his actions and concluded that his body must have been working on pure adrenaline. Now he was paying the price, and his body had shut down. She was, however, optimistic about his chances of survival now that infection had been prevented, mainly through the intensive nursing care provided by Monica.

Meena would have liked to see an X-ray of Keeler's leg, but that would have to wait. It would not be her problem when they reached Dhaka anyway, because Keeler would be taken to a military hospital, where medical experts would prepare him for the encounter with the world press and military tribunal promised by the major. She feared for his safety since she knew his cooperation would be assured by the threat of some form of torture. As for Shane, she would insist that he was simply a victim of circumstances and caught in the wrong place at the wrong time. As a last resort, she would request the intervention of her father, but this would be difficult for her because she didn't wish for him to know her business, and she felt sure of her ability to extricate herself and the others from this dilemma.

She would have to think very carefully before declaring her actions as a Red Cross intervention, thereby compromising the integrity of that organisation. The channel she might have to choose for help may be through her mother. She had never asked, but she had concluded long ago that her mother was a very senior official in the intelligence community. Meena had vowed never to use this emergency fallback strategy but now felt the need to give it serious consideration. She observed the major and wondered how he would react to the revelation of her ties with such important diplomats and dealings with Indian Army Intelligence. Concealing her family ties with her father and his role in the government intelligence services was her main concern.

Chapter 31

The soldiers from the convoy remained to gather up as much of the wreckage as they could and prepare for the return journey to their garrison. Meena noticed Prem Das slipping quietly and unnoticed into the jungle, confirming her frequent assertion that elderly people on this sub-continent seemed to be absorbed into the terrain surrounding them, increasingly so as they got older. She had no fear for his safety and wished that they had taken the jeep all the way to the border. Obviously, Keeler had other plans that he did not divulge, plans that seemed more sensible at the time. Evacuation by helicopter would certainly have been the safest option, so she chided herself for thinking otherwise. They were all alive, that was the main thing, and now they must simply confront this new development as best they could. She tried not to think of the horrors that had just taken place aboard the Indian helicopter and concentrated on the fact that they were all alive and together.

Shane sat opposite her in the helicopter and Monica clung to Meena, with Keeler strapped to the stretcher on the floor between them, where both women could monitor his condition. While the pilots went through their pre-flight checklist once again, she felt obliged to say something to the major, even though she knew she risked being on the receiving end of yet another tirade of verbal abuse from him. She eyed him cautiously as he issued instructions to the soldiers, as they set about collecting the wreckage from the Indian helicopter. A military vehicle arrived with the camera and he immediately went into propaganda mode as he and his men posed for photos, not only with the wreckage of the Indian helicopter in the background but with burnt remains of crewmen who had tried to escape the crash and subsequent inferno. The two Pakistani pilots interrupted their pre-flight checks and eagerly ran to be included in the photos.

Meena thought about escaping now that they were unguarded but decided against it when she observed an unconscious Keeler and Shane's scorched and bewildered face. She also considered Monica's total dependence on her for constant reassurance that they would all remain safe. She considered the unguarded machine gun once more but knew she couldn't gun down the soldiers as they were totally focused on recording their victory. She could only view them as people, regardless of their hostility and total disregard for her and her friends' welfare.

The pilots finally returned and hurried about their business, while trying to ignore the looks of disgust from Meena. The major stood outside and gestured through the cockpit window for the pilots to start their engine as he and his sergeant climbed aboard. Some soldiers opened the doors at the rear of the helicopter and loaded the parts from the Indian helicopter, which contained the Indian flag, the military registration number and the roundel insignia that identified it as an Indian military aircraft. The sergeant squatted on the floor at the opposite side of the cabin cradling a submachine gun in his arms. The major sat beside Shane with a satisfied, smug look on his face. Meena overcame her fear and decided to attempt to intrude on the major's obvious triumphalism. "Major, your man seems to be an expert on that machine gun."

"Oh yes, these men are well trained, and I picked Sergeant Hamad for this duty because of his expertise with this weapon," he said. He placed a hand on the unmanned machine gun and seemed to regard the weapon with a degree of fondness that sickened Meena.

"Your man handled the weapon skillfully, that's for sure, Major. What a pity you let him proceed to fire rounds into the occupied cabin of the Indian helicopter, when you could so easily have ordered him to cease firing when it was evident that once the tail rotor was destroyed, the helicopter would have been forced to land anyway. It would have given the occupants a chance of survival. They never even had a chance to surrender. Once they were on the ground, they would have been foolish to open fire on an armed helicopter hovering above them. And besides, you are not at war with them, so as things stand at present, you are the perpetrator of a heinous crime and shall be tried for murder, in all likelihood." She noticed Shane's eyes widen and Monica's grip on her arm tighten.

The major had not yet come down from the high he was experiencing as a result of the battle. Shane noticed the veins in his temple gyrating as he ground his teeth and stared at Meena in a way that suggested at first that he was incapable of comprehending the significance of what she had just said. Enlightenment then preceded a tortuous process of formulating a response that would verbally equate in intensity to physical violence on this insane, infuriating woman, who had usurped his every thought and action since the start of the day. He knew his response would need to be calm, so the final expression of his inner turmoil produced a measured response, without seeming to justify or make excuses for his actions, but at the same time conveying his utter contempt for her distorted and deranged reasoning. He removed his hat and, not for the first time, Meena saw his sweat-soaked grey hair. As he rubbed his hand through it, she caught a brief glimpse of the man as seen only by his family and close friends and relatives. The hat went back on his head and his military persona was once again on display. He calmly removed his service revolver from the holster at his side and examined the chamber for ammunition. Meena recoiled in horror; she and Monica clung tightly to each other and shrunk into their seats.

Shane reached out a hand and implored the major to put the weapon away. "Please, Major," he said in a nervous voice, totally unsure of the man's intentions.

One of the pilots sensed the tension and was horrified when he looked back and saw the major holding his sidearm in both hands and pointing it in such a way that he was certain he intended to use it. In an attempt at distracting the major, he loudly requested permission from him to lift off now that their checks were complete, and the helicopter was ready for departure. The major blinked several times, wiping sweat from his eyes, and suddenly realised his predicament. He slowly lowered the weapon. He seemed unable to comprehend the request from the pilot and so they lifted off anyway, turning the aircraft towards the east and taking up a heading that would take them back to the Balashi garrison. The pilot nervously eyed the major once more and was relieved to see him slowly replace the weapon into its holster. The major rubbed one hand over his face and settled back in his seat, staring out of the door at the wreckage of the Indian helicopter below and his men swarming over it.

Meena and Monica still held each other, unsure whether this episode was over. They all lapsed into an uncomfortable silence and each was oblivious to the roar of the engine as they gained altitude. When they had reached about two thousand feet, the engine noise reduced, and eventually the major leant forward to speak. He had regained his composure and the tension that had existed in the cabin now seemed to have abated somewhat. He gestured with a move of his chin towards Keeler, who lay unconscious on the stretcher.

"You know, my family once lived in India. We only moved to Pakistan after the British disastrously divided our country. We have a proud tradition of service in the army, and we have fought and died in many campaigns, from Gallipoli to the Somme in the Great War. In the Second World War, I was a junior officer in North Africa and also fought in vicious battles up through Italy with our British friends, before being transferred to fight the Japanese in Burma. I actually trained at Sandhurst Military Academy.

"When we returned to India after the war, there was a terrible tension in our country between Hindus and Muslims, and as you know, this eventually led to partition from India, during which Pakistan became an independent country. It was a dream of all Muslims to have a land of their own, free from Hindu tyranny and oppression. We had to leave our family home and friends in India and travel to Peshawar, where I continued service in our new army in Pakistan, eventually being transferred to East Pakistan because of the prejudices of the ruling elite in the west towards those considered outsiders, like me. Then I had to endure similar treatment from Bengali officers, because I am from Bihar in India. Nevertheless, those were exciting times, and we soon forgot our fellow officers who had remained in India because they were Hindu. The British had a grand plan to allocate a fair proportion of all the equipment and armaments of their original army and move it to Pakistan. We signed up to this deal, trusting that the British would see through the division of armaments and material fairly and equitably.

"Well, my friends, I must educate you in the ways of our erstwhile colleagues in the Indian Army. There has not been a moment since partition that they have not denied us our share in some devious way or another. They have consistently undermined our efforts to secure our legitimate borders and have frequently infiltrated our country with spies and saboteurs. Our last conflict a few years ago resulted in us inflicting a crushing defeat on this aggressive enemy, and we showed the world our willingness to resolve our differences by negotiation when we had the upper hand. They grudgingly agreed to a ceasefire and this uneasy stand-off still exists today, simply because we have, on numerous occasions, refused to be provoked by their incessant border incursions. Well, today our patience finally reached its limit. You, sir, are a witness to this violation of our territory," he said while looking at Shane.

"Tomorrow, the world press will be carrying images of this great victory by our army, and it will make India think carefully before sending their troops across our borders in the future. Don't be surprised if world opinion forces them to withdraw their forces from the border area and cease their intimidation of our nation. Oh, and yes, madam, our young pilot friend here features prominently in my plan to display to the world that Indian forces are on active service on foreign soil, in flagrant disregard for international law." He pulled from the pocket of his tunic the charred identification tags removed from the bodies of the dead Indian airmen, and also held up Keeler's unburned tags for them to see.

Meena could only think of the Indian airmen who had just lost their lives, and her look of contempt was not lost on the major. Internal panic welled up inside her as she realised that he was on the verge of a decision, and fear gripped her further as she had a premonition of doom. She could see that this man had reached the limits of his mental capacity to evaluate their situation, and his demeanour suggested that he was about to embark on a course of action that she knew would compromise their welfare, especially hers. He turned to the pilots and ordered them to contact the convoy, which should have left the scene of the recent battle, and arrange a rendezvous at a location where they could land. The best she could hope for was that the convoy would have medicines they needed for treating Keeler. She asked the major if this was his intention to distract him, and possibly modify whatever he was planning.

"Don't worry, madam, I have a special plan in mind for you. That is, for you personally."

Shane looked at her in disbelief and observed her fingers digging deeply into the flesh of Monica's arm. He could see her inner strength crumbling and the cascade of fear overtook all of them as they awaited their fate, over which they seemed to have no control. Shane looked at Sergeant Hamad, but the man showed no inclination to help them; he resolutely waited for instructions from the major, ready to carry out any order. The fact that he had just been responsible for several deaths did not seem to bother him, and Shane could only conclude that killing was a regular feature in the life of this soldier.

The helicopter circled, looking for a place to land, and they caught sight of the convoy emerging from the tree-lined road into a clearing capable of handling the approaching helicopter. Meena observed that there was no possibility of escape; they would be gunned down if they attempted to run for the trees. Besides, they could not leave Keeler and so she waited to see what the major's next move would be.

A great cloud of dust rose as the rotor downwash neared the ground. It took a while to settle as the roar of the engine subsided to idle power after touchdown. The major disembarked and ran through the downwash from the slowing rotors to meet the commander of the convoy, and they huddled in animated discussion, occasionally glancing in the direction of the helicopter. The pilots looked around at Meena and she instinctively knew that something horrible was about to happen, and that both pilots perceived the worst for her. Her eyes pleaded with them to take off and escape but once again they averted their gaze, depriving them all of one final chance of rescue. Meena saw the futility of this plan as the sergeant stood observing them from the open door, his hostile eyes portraying his willingness to carry out, without question, any order the major may issue.

Suddenly the convoy commander broke away and ordered two men from Meena's jeep to accompany him to the open door of the helicopter. The major followed, while gesticulating to the pilots that they should once more prepare for departure, with a raised finger above his head in a circular motion. As they configured the controls for lift off, Meena looked wildly about her in sheer terror as the two men entered the cabin and dragged her away from the safety of Shane and Monica's arms, restraining her, and exited the door with her suspended roughly between them. Her screams and the screams of her companions were drowned out by the increasing pitch of the engine noise. The sergeant stood in the doorway, blocking Shane and Monica as they looked on helplessly. The major took a folded and creased photograph from his breast pocket and thrust it into Meena's hands before she was led away.

"I know exactly who you are, madam, and I am not surprised that this man would produce such deviant offspring." He spat the words at her and commanded his sergeant to climb aboard and take Meena's seat. Through the dust, all Meena could see was the major sneer at her from the open door as the helicopter ascended. She viewed the photograph of her, taken with her smiling, proud parents at her graduation. He had obviously taken it from her room at the hospital after her ordeal with his men. She tried not to think of the aftermath of Sister Gertrude's death. She had no recollection of being carried to her bedroom in a state of undress and dumped on her bed with men fumbling to rearrange her clothing. It was then that the major must have taken the picture from the frame on her bedside table, after he had recognised her father. She was left wondering how this man could possibly know her father before reality asserted itself. Terror engulfed her as she was roughly thrown into the back of her jeep and her captors settled in each side of her so that she could barely move. She cried like a baby as she realised her dire predicament. All the terrifying possibilities ran through her mind, and none excluded her slow, agonising death, preceded by events that she could only think about momentarily before blotting the thoughts from her mind.

The men told her in Urdu to stop crying and said that they would take good care of her. One of them seemed concerned that she did not understand, so he said in broken English, "Not be afraid lady, not be afraid." The driver sat alone in the front, but she knew he was fully aware of what was being planned for her. In vulnerable situations such as this, the weaker party will try to forge links with potential allies, but there were none among these men. She placed one hand on the seat of the jeep and tried to concentrate on all the previous good works done by loving people who sat on this seat. While doing so, she looked at the photo of her with her smiling parents and tried to immerse herself in the overwhelming love she'd experienced on that day of her graduation in an effort to sustain herself. One of the soldiers deduced that she was desperately gleaning comfort from the photograph, so he roughly snatched it from her, tore it into pieces, and threw it out of the window, plunging her further into despair while they all laughed at her predicament. She was, after all, directly responsible for the deaths of their two comrades. The vehicles headed in convoy towards the road, and she presumed that they were heading to their garrison. She prayed and considered the best-case scenario, while trying to suppress the involuntary keening she could not control. Maybe they were keeping her separate for a reason. That was wishful thinking, she concluded, and her worst fears surfaced once more, only this time their intensity made her shake so much that her two captors clamped her into a tighter grip between them. Her panic was compounded as she observed the other vehicles pulling further and further away. Soon, they were left alone on the road, trailing far behind the convoy. Her hopes that passersby would realise her predicament and intervene to save her were futile. The few people they passed were too caught up in their own problems as they headed towards the Indian border. Their driver shouted that he was leaving the road soon. They conversed in Punjabi also and were unaware that Meena understood what they were saying. She wanted to hold her hands over her ears because of the lewdness of their conversation but her arms were rigidly held between the two soldiers. Them saying such things in the company of a woman appalled her, but she was helpless and forced to listen.

They eventually turned onto a side road that had not been maintained and, after driving for ten minutes on the uneven surface, they stopped near what appeared to be a disused factory. She was roughly pulled from the vehicle and thrown to the ground.

"What is the meaning of this?" she said in Punjabi. She was shocked that she could find the courage to express indignation at being treated like this. Her revealing that she had been privy to their conversation enraged them further. They didn't seem at all concerned about her welfare. One thought did surface in her mind through all the fear and panic she was experiencing. The only times she had wrestled with a man had been when her father had taught her self-defense. She was sixteen and about to depart for medical school, having skipped her penultimate year in high school on a scholarship for gifted students.

Her thoughts were interrupted by searing pain as she was suddenly kicked on her hip while lying on the ground, and it was only then that her worst fears were confirmed. Mentally, and without realising it, she shifted into survival mode.

Meena tried to concentrate through the wall of pain that descended over her, and she opened her eyes and could just about make out the forms of her captors standing over her with broad, uncaring smiles on their faces. The driver sat in the driver's seat of her jeep with his legs hanging out of the vehicle as he observed events while smoking. She pleaded with him for help, but he returned a leering smile, and she knew that no help would be forthcoming from him. Part of the self-defense training her father had taught her was how to feign helplessness when overwhelmed by a superior force. This would have the effect of disarming the attacker, who would relax and adopt a domineering stance with their guard down. Then strike – a painful disabling kick to the shin or, if they were standing over you, a quick fist into the groin area. If they were close to your face, then a finger in the attacker's eye. Whatever you decided to do, the next step must be to run away from the encounter as fast as your legs can carry you while screaming as loud as you can, in the hope of rescue from someone nearby.

Meena's options were very limited as she was wearing a saree, which was not the best garment for combat and a running escape. Her sandals were robust, however, and securely fastened. She cried again in pain as she was lifted by her hair to her feet and pushed ahead by the men as she stumbled forward in the direction of the deserted buildings. *Why is the first point of attack always a woman's hair?* she thought to herself. *Is it an essential feature of a woman which defines her, so must be the first thing to be compromised?* As she righted herself, she lifted her saree as far as her knees, drawing further lewd comments from the two soldiers as they pushed her once more to the ground in front of them, near a large opening that led to the dark interior of the abandoned factory. With her saree still raised above her knees, she glanced at the men from under her arm and noticed that they felt in total control of her to such an extent that their rifles were slung over their shoulders.

Their defenses were down. She knew that once they had her inside the building, she was finished and would never emerge alive. She thought of her mother's smiling face.

The gravel was easy to gather unnoticed in her hand as she recovered, and in one motion, as she rose to her feet, she swung her arm towards the men and forcefully unleashed the gravel at their faces, while continuing her graceful pivot fully until she was facing the entrance to the factory. She then sprinted as fast as she could without looking back, ignoring the startled cries of the men at this totally unexpected turn of events. She heard the driver laughing at their predicament and imagined the men recovering and retrieving their weapons. They could only stare in disbelief as the form of the woman disappeared into the darkness while holding the folds of her saree above her thighs.

Meena ran as fast as she could and tried to figure out the best direction to take to somewhere she could find cover and possibly hide from her pursuers. It took a while for her eyes to adjust to the darkness as she ran. The floor was rough under her sandals as she frantically scanned the area in front of her, hoping to avoid unseen obstacles. She tried to remember the weapons the men were carrying and thought they were Lee Enfield rifles, similar to one in her father's collection at home. She had accompanied him to his army firing range on occasion and had observed him operating the bolt action between shots. She was straining to hear this very distinctive sound behind her, with the intention of taking cover on hearing it.

The round took her completely by surprise. She heard no shot, just the shocking displacement of a huge amount of air as the bullet passed to the right of her head. She stopped dead, held her hands over her ears and tried to recover. She staggered to her left and managed to move forward and found refuge behind a partition adjacent to a slightly open steel door. She wanted to try pushing the door to see if it would open more but stopped and remained rigid as she heard one soldier running towards her location. The other man must have circled around to try to cut off her escape. The footsteps slowed and suddenly all she could hear were the cautious steps of army boots advancing in the direction of her dimly lit hiding place. She worked really hard to control her breathing and struggled to overcome the temptation to run.

The interior of the factory was dark, but not so dark that she would not be discovered within the next few seconds. She was resigned to her fate when she remembered the scalpels from her hospital, which she had hidden beneath the folds of her saree at her waist. With one hand she deftly removed the plastic cover from one of the blades, then held the scalpel as a surgeon would while performing a primary incision during an operation.

One of the men suddenly appeared around the partition and was surprised to see her hand shoot out and gently tap him on the neck. The look of shock on his face was replaced by a total absence of understanding as to why he was looking at this beautiful woman while at the same time being totally powerless to command his body to do his bidding. His hand clamped on the left side of his neck as the strangely warm fluid gushed through his fingers, and he fell to the floor, his rifle clattering down beside him.

Chapter 32

Meena was totally shocked and horrified at what she had just done. She immediately reverted to her role as medic and attempted to stop the bleeding with pressure using her saree pallu material as the man rapidly faded into unconsciousness. She knew the futility of her actions and realised that even in a fully equipped operating theatre, saving this man's life would be a real challenge. The pressure she was applying to the wound was useless as she tried to stem the flow of blood from the severed blood vessel. Her distress was interrupted by the deafening explosion of another bullet hitting the partition beside her. The other soldier was visible at the other end of the corridor along which she had run, and coming at her from the rear of the factory. She was lucky not to have continued in that direction. She observed him dropping to one knee and once again taking aim at her. She instinctively jumped aside, leaving her fatally wounded patient and heading for the steel door as another shot landed close by. She prayed that the door would open enough as she pushed hard at the rusty structure. It creaked and groaned and opened just enough for her to squeeze her slim frame through. On the other side, she struggled to shut it again as she noticed a rusty bolt that could seal the door and save her from the other pursuer.

It was not possible to close the rusty door, so she abandoned the effort and ran as fast as she could across the factory floor to an open window, through which she could see trees. Her only hope was to reach the cover of the trees and disappear into the jungle. Being captured now would invite instant death at the hands of a very angry soldier, who had just witnessed the death of his friend. As she climbed through the window, she could see her jeep and driver in the distance. The driver looked at her distractedly but did not seem too interested in her plight as he casually smoked his cigarette. He did, however, raise his sidearm and release a few half-hearted shots in her direction. They slammed harmlessly into a tree ahead of her. He may have been more animated had he known the fate of his comrade and her gruesome part in it.

More importantly, there was no sound of the steel door being forced open behind her as she jumped to the ground and ran into the nearby jungle, resolving to put as much space as possible between her and her captors. She ran until she was tired and needed to stop and double over while gulping vast breaths of air. While recovering, she settled beside a tree and made herself as inconspicuous as possible, listening intently for the sounds of human pursuit behind her.

Meena didn't really like being alone in the jungle. It was not a tropical jungle; instead, the sunshine could penetrate to the earth below well-spaced trees. She needed to move from her refuge soon; she didn't want to be alone in the jungle, especially as the light faded. She listened once more and felt sure she was totally alone, while never underestimating the ability of trained soldiers to creep up on her position unnoticed, so she cautiously left her hiding place and worked her way to her left. She was sure that was the direction she must take to intercept the main road they had left earlier. If she judged it correctly, then she would end up some distance from the road junction that led to the abandoned factory. Then it would be only a matter of hiding in the cover of the jungle at the side of the road. From her hiding place, she could assess passing traffic with a view to waving down a non-military vehicle that would take her to safety in the nearest town. In the meantime, the only thing she feared was wild animals. Snakes she hated, but in her previous encounters with them she found that they were keener to avoid her than she was to avoid them. There were tigers in this jungle, but they were rare.

There were also bears. Bears. Of course, bears! She suddenly realised that she was close to Jagdish's village. The man who had been mauled by a bear and whose life she had saved was from this area. She felt sure that she could find the village once she reached the main road. This put a spring in her step and she picked up her pace, until very soon she was sure that she could hear voices ahead. She paused and listened. Straining to make out the source, she determined that it didn't sound like the military with powerful truck engines and men barking orders, but instead it sounded like large numbers of people talking, and this included the voices of women and the reassuring sound of crying babies.

She eagerly hurried forward and as she broke cover from the jungle, the sight that greeted her took her breath away. There was a constant stream of refugees in a long unbroken column, making its way along the road towards the border with India. She had seen this before and immediately knew that they were fleeing to safety from the fighting. She fell in beside a family with a bullock cart drawn by two oxen. The cart was heavily laden with their possessions, on top of which were perched an elderly lady and two small children. The men informed her that their village had been burned by the military in reprisal for attacks by insurgents. She asked about Jagdish's village, Ghoraghat, and they pointed in the direction from where they had just come. The village could be reached in about two hours, they said, if she left the main road and followed the small stream three miles back. This would lead her directly to the village. The people said that Ghoraghat was a mixed Muslim and Hindu village and seemed to have been immune from the attentions of the military for some reason, possibly because the actions of the army were now more cautious in this area due to the constant threat of ambush.

She thanked them and set out against the unending stream of refugees, many of whom shouted warnings to her about the dangers she would face, but her only worry was encountering army vehicles. On seeing them approach, she hurriedly absorbed herself into the mass of people, paying particular attention while looking out for her hospital jeep appearing on the road she had just travelled.

Soon, Meena reached the stream and reluctantly left the safety of the crowd of people on the road, once again heading into the jungle on a dirt road, which ran parallel to the stream to guide her. It was getting dark, and she hoped she didn't find a deserted village, abandoned or burned. After one hour on the trail, she could see the outlines of village houses that were intact and the smoke from cooking fires, which was a welcome sight as it hung over the canopy of trees. As usual, she was greeted by barking dogs and small children, and this sense of normalcy relieved her to such an extent that she needed to collapse, exhausted, onto a fallen tree trunk beside the stream. She immersed her feet in the cool water of the stream while the children ran to inform their parents of the arrival of a strange lady. Several women came running, trailed by every child and dog in the village as she soaked her feet in the cool stream.

Meena's heart lifted and she started to cry as she was enveloped by women she knew very well and whose children either she or Monica had delivered. Prominent among them was Jagdish's wife, Sujata, who took charge and led an exhausted Meena to her house. The emotion of it all and the sudden release from the imminent threat to her life was overwhelming, so much so that Meena collapsed onto the cushions of the raised platform in the room that made up the main living area of the beautiful mud house. She drank water and washed her hands, which were still stained with blood, before eating freshly cooked rice with vegetables. She never realised how she must look, clad in a blood-and-mud-stained saree, as she was devouring the food and talking non-stop about her horrible experiences over the past few days.

Very soon, every woman from the village filled the living area in Sujata's house, listening as the lady doctor held them spellbound with extraordinary tales while speaking in broken Bengali. Such events did not happen too often in their village, and they were determined not to miss a word. During this process, she noticed Jagdish enter quietly at the rear of the room, supported on his crutches and showing no discomfort due to his disability. She instantly jumped up and forced her way through the women seated on the floor and threw her arms around him, confirming that she was finally safe. At first, there was silence at the inappropriate gesture but then all the women laughed and clapped. This would be a long evening of celebration and singing. Whatever respite they could find to distract them from the trauma of the fighting was welcome. Meena was sleepwalking when the celebrations finally wound down and hardly noticed Sujata as she helped her remove her sandals. She had declined the opportunity to bathe, availing herself of the option to succumb to the sleep she craved so much.

Chapter 33

Meena couldn't remember falling asleep, but she awoke to the sound of a cock crowing and the early dawn light seeping in under the door. Sujata was preparing chapatis for breakfast over the early morning fire and Meena's heart lifted when she saw Jagdish, minus one lower limb, sitting on the floor and drinking tea. The smell of village tea was wonderful. She didn't think they had realised she was awake until Jagdish leisurely poured an extra cup of tea and handed it to her. Nobody said one word while she immersed herself in the pleasures of this universal beverage, which revived her but eventually left all of them talking incessantly once more.

Jagdish was especially interested in her revelations about the helicopter and her ordeal with the major. She was surprised to hear that many of the young men from the surrounding villages had left to fight against the military. The insurgents had set up a makeshift field hospital in the jungle to look after their wounded. Jagdish was leading the efforts, and all his time was taken up with this venture. However, he promised to have men accompany Meena to her hospital, but first he requested her to accompany him and his men to their jungle hospital near the town of Baona, near the border with India. He said they must go on foot through the jungle due to the danger of being intercepted by units from the army on the main roads. When Meena asked about the final destination of the helicopter, Jagdish was less sure, but he did know that an assault had taken place on a garrison near Balashi, where a helicopter was seen operating. This threw Meena into confusion and anxiety about the welfare of Monica, Shane and Keeler. The women had all been shocked when she told them that Monica was also on the helicopter. Monica had spent long hours with several of the women in this village during childbirth. All Meena could do was wait on word about the assault and news of her friends, if they were found, hopefully safe and well. Jagdish promised to contact their commander in the area near Balashi by their radio, which was located at their makeshift field hospital in the jungle. Meena exchanged her saree for one given by Sujata and, having bathed in the river, they were all set for the long walk. Jagdish reminded Meena that this was the same journey made by him on a stretcher when he had been attacked by the bear.

Their jungle hospital was located on higher ground near the border, and very well hidden from aircraft patrolling the area. Jagdish was surprisingly agile on his crutches and led the way at a blistering pace. He asked her to assess their efforts as they were lacking the medical skills needed to deal with some combat injuries. He reminded her of the good job she had done on his 'no leg', as he called it with a smile. He had certainly healed mentally from the traumatic injury and the sense of purpose he now showed was due to his playing the role of leader in this resistance movement. She was concerned that this journey was taking them in the opposite direction to her own hospital but went along simply because she felt really safe with these people. All the others in their party were armed, including a group of determined-looking young people, which included women. They were students from the university in Dhaka, which had been attacked earlier in the year by the army, during which many students and their professors had been indiscriminately slaughtered. These young people all spoke perfect English and had been trained in the use of all the weapons at their disposal. Their enthusiasm and fearless determination were a testament to their commitment to right the wrongs of the previous months. Meena was left in no doubt as to their capabilities in pursuing any objective set for them.

They finally reached the area in the jungle where the hospital was located, but Meena only realised this as she noticed camouflaged guard posts protecting the approaches to the secure area of the hospital. The activity increased as they neared a well-concealed entrance to a line of tents covered in foliage. In front of the entrance, three young men pedaled stationary bicycles, which were attached to belt drives operating generators, which in turn charged huge banks of truck batteries via battery chargers. This provided enough electricity for lighting and power for their radio communications equipment. The smoke emanating from the encampment was minimal during the day, enabling the whole area to blend in with the surrounding jungle. This ensured safety from air strikes and aerial surveillance.

Jagdish informed Meena that all their cooking was done at night. This included the fires that heated the sterilizers for the hospital. He felt the need to relocate their medical facility due to the activity of spies in the area, but moving the wounded presented major challenges, so instead they relied on an early warning network of fighters strategically located on the perimeter. An attack by infantry could be dealt with, he felt, but what he feared most was an artillery bombardment or an assault by tanks.

Meena was immediately confronted by a group of young medical students who had been informed of her imminent arrival. They overwhelmed her with questions relating to the many injuries they were treating. It seemed that she was now the only experienced doctor and surgeon among them, so she took charge and set out to reassure them, while also being conscious that this was not where she wanted to be. She needed to get to her hospital and also try to determine the destination of the helicopter with Monica, Shane and Keeler on board.

Jagdish made further enquiries and returned with news that several of their patients had been wounded during a siege at a military garrison at Balashi before being transferred to this hospital. A helicopter had been seen taking off from the garrison before the assault. There was no news of foreigners or injured Indian forces personnel. It was a relief to get any news at all and Meena convinced herself that her friends would be safe. All she could do was ask to be kept informed of developments connected with the Balashi garrison, in the hope that it actually was the helicopter commanded by the major. It would be a relief to know if that man had been captured, resulting in freedom for Shane, Monica and Keeler. She silently prayed for this outcome while also remaining aware of just how unlikely it would be for the major to fall into the hands of his enemies.

Meena was glad to have Jagdish with her as she set about prioritising treatment for the seriously wounded. As usual in war, she first assessed those with the least chance of survival and detailed a medical student to concentrate on making each one of them as comfortable as possible. Next were those with obvious internal injuries, who would need immediate surgery. Jagdish made sure her instructions were carried out as he accompanied her, and he ordered the young fighters to set up a separate shelter that would serve as a makeshift surgical area. They walked towards the radio tent to attempt to contact the commander who had carried out the assault on the Balashi garrison, in the hope that her friends ended up there.

Meena was wondering about the possibility of anesthesia and blood supplies while walking with Jagdish close behind her when the first two explosions happened. She felt two strong arms envelop her shoulders from behind as Jagdish dived on top of her. Her last memory was of intense light and heat on either side as they fell to the ground, and a burning sensation on the side of her right arm and right foot as her face was driven by Jagdish's weight into the soil as they were blown together by the force of the blast. She registered shock and alarm just as the trauma-induced darkness overtook her once more.

Chapter 34

Abdullah's heart skipped a beat when he heard the helicopter. Then the sound faded, and he cursed himself for allowing wishful thinking to influence him. Then he noticed all the young men running to take up the positions they had decided upon while planning for the return of the helicopter, their youthful hearing apparently more acute than his. He was thankful that the convoy didn't return first because that would have resulted in another fierce firefight, and quite honestly, he had witnessed enough killing for one day. He checked that the ground marshaller prisoner for the helicopter was in position and that his men had their weapons trained on him from cover in the buildings just in case he suddenly waved off the helicopter with some emergency signal known only to pilots and ground crew.

The big helicopter eventually came into view between a clearing in the trees on one side of the base and began its cautious descent towards the parade ground at the centre of the base. Abdullah's men had been very creative in repairing the damage they had inflicted during their attack. Everything looked normal and he hoped the pilots would be fooled. If the helicopter suddenly deviated from its approach path, then his men had been instructed to shoot it down using their fifty-calibre machine gun positioned discreetly behind one of the buildings. DaSilva had cautioned against this as he needed to interrogate the crew and suggested to Abdullah that they could possibly retain the use of the helicopter for future missions of their own. Abdullah reluctantly agreed and checked to make sure DaSilva was out of sight as agreed and also that a nervous-looking Lieutenant Shah was covered as he stood to attention beside the repaired flagpole flying the Pakistani flag. Abdullah had reservations about allowing the helicopter to escape as it had the potential to inflict serious damage from the air if their deception was discovered. He wanted to close his eyes and pray but couldn't tear his eyes away from the spectacle of the helicopter as it slowly descended towards the compound.

***

On board the helicopter, the major crouched beside the door of the Russian-built machine and rested his hand on the shoulder of his sergeant, who primed his weapon once more and rotated it towards the few people standing near the flagpole. All the radio communications had assured them that the base was ready to receive them, but the ever-cautious major was not easily persuaded, and on this occasion, his suspicions were aroused for no reason that he could fathom. He scanned the garrison from an altitude of two hundred feet and everything seemed in order, with the young lieutenant standing beside the flagpole, so he instructed the pilots to land and put his suspicions to the back of his mind, while still readying his sidearm to help calm his nerves.

The helicopter entered into the flare and was enveloped in a cloud of dust, forcing them to cover their faces. Shane sheltered Keeler from the dust and anxiously awaited as the engine noise faded on shutdown. Monica simply buried her face in Shane's shoulder as she realised that she had just descended into a hostile army barracks where she would be the only woman.

Before the dust settled, the major and his man were readying themselves at the open door to greet the welcoming party when suddenly four men appeared from the tail area, each carrying a rifle pointed directly at the major. As he and the sergeant swung around to face this threat, another group of armed men came into view as the dust settled, and one of them immediately pulled the barrel of the fifty-calibre machine gun towards the ground, rendering it useless and leaving the sergeant immobilized by the sight of numerous weapons trained on his chest. The major thought better of trying to confront the armed men and eventually lowered his sidearm. The noise of the machine faded, and the major was confronted by Abdullah and DaSilva. He jumped from the cabin of the helicopter and surveyed the camp and the armed men pouring out of each building. His gaze finally came to rest on DaSilva.

"I might have known that a traitor would be behind this violent coup. Treachery was always in your nature, and it was only a matter of time before you would betray your country in a spectacular fashion such as this. For many years I have been saying this to anyone who would listen. But no, they were only interested in including you in their exalted circles, to the detriment of other more loyal and dedicated officers."

Abdullah introduced himself as the commander of the local Mukti Bahini and informed the major that he had taken control of this base on behalf of the Provisional Government of Bangladesh. He requested the major to holster his weapon.

The major turned his attention to Abdullah. "Bangladesh? Bangladesh? I can assure you that this is very much the sovereign territory of the Islamic Republic of Pakistan, and I would advise you now to surrender yourselves to me this instant. I can possibly put in a word for you with the Martial Law Administrator to prevent you all being shot."

Few of the armed men understood what he had just said, but as usual, those who understood English translated for them, and soon a ripple of laughter started, that eventually turned into chants of victory.

"Major, I have no time to debate the issue with you. I would be grateful if you could help us avoid further bloodshed by advising the soldiers in your convoy by radio to stand down when they arrive."

The major considered this and noted the demeanour of this commander, who looked like a shopkeeper. He was surprised at the respect being shown to him and the fact that he had not been relieved of his weapon. His situation was hopeless so he decided to retreat and bide his time to see how this situation would develop. He now remembered this man visiting the garrison earlier and berated himself for not recognising that visit as a reconnaissance mission. He had to admire the audacity of the man, and the fact that violence was not his first instinct.

"The convoy commander will deal with you and your rabble when they arrive, so try to exercise good judgement and surrender to me now, while you still have the chance to extricate yourselves from this criminal venture you have undertaken, obviously without consideration for the safety of your families."

Abdullah ordered his men to escort the major to the commanding officer's quarters and his sergeant to the barracks, where they would remain under guard. Abdullah then made sure his men prepared the base to receive the convoy, which, as yet, had not made radio contact. Shane introduced himself and made sure Keeler was handed over to medics. As the major and his sergeant were being led away, DaSilva stepped forward and took a serious interest in what Shane had to say. He was about to question Shane when the major broke away from his guards and angrily confronted Abdullah.

"You, sir, are making a big mistake," he said, pointing at DaSilva. "Do not trust that man, for he will surely stab you in the back. He is a general staff officer in our military intelligence, and he is noted for aligning himself with the highest bidder. Don't fool yourselves, he is almost certainly in the pay of the Indian Government under the guise of their so-called 'back-channel group', who are noted for lining their pockets at the expense of their own countrymen. I served with him in Burma, fighting the Japanese along with General Niazi, who is now the Martial Law Administrator. Our commander at the time, General Slim, gave all of us junior officers strict instructions to capture Japanese soldiers for interrogation. His was the only platoon to return every time with no prisoners and no casualties among his men. We lost many men because, I can assure you, capturing Japanese soldiers was far more dangerous than shooting them all in cold blood as he did, including those willing to surrender."

DaSilva bowed his head, and Abdullah was forced to request an explanation for these allegations. "Those were different times and the major neglected to say how close we all were, fighting a ruthless enemy," DaSilva replied.

The major spat at DaSilva's feet before walking away in disgust. "I caution you all again to watch your backs with that man," he said with a backwards wave of his hand as he departed.

Abdullah called Lieutenant Shah over and requested him to continue looking after his dead and wounded, and to use as many of his own men as he needed. The man was relieved to be kept away from the major, who would surely have had strong words with him for relinquishing control of the garrison to this rabble. Abdullah then walked towards the radio office while eyeing DaSilva in a manner that communicated to him that this conversation was not over. DaSilva acknowledged the fact with a nod and turned his attention to Shane. After brief introductions, Shane related all the events of the past few days while DaSilva listened without interrupting. He became very animated when Shane first mentioned a lady doctor and the vital role she had played in saving the Indian airman's life.

"This lady doctor, did you happen to get her name?" DaSilva asked with an increasing look of apprehension on his face.

"Oh, yeah," said Shane. "Her name is Dr Meena."

DaSilva staggered back and needed to sit in the helicopter doorway to steady himself. The pilots were still on board, securing the machine and doing their shut-down checks. An armed guard covered each pilot from either side of the helicopter and when the pilots were finished, they exited past DaSilva and proceeded to walk towards the barracks with the armed men covering them. DaSilva asked them to wait and requested them to fill him in on the events that had taken place to see if they could add more details to what Shane had just told him. He was hoping they would then have a better understanding of the major's intentions. Neither was keen to say anything until DaSilva produced his Pakistan Army identification card proclaiming his status as a general in military intelligence. They both examined the credentials and then came to attention and saluted in unison.

"At ease, gentlemen. This is a very complex situation and I'm sure everything will be resolved soon. But in the meantime, can you both please tell me exactly what happened during the encounter with the Indian helicopter and what happened subsequently to the lady doctor you had on board."

Their heads hung in shame as they related how the doctor had been treated by the major and her subsequent handing over by the major to the soldiers in the convoy. Their last sighting of her was as she was being placed in a white ambulance jeep before the convoy's departure through the jungle to the main road as their helicopter was lifting off. DaSilva dismissed the pilots and promised he would visit them soon and keep them informed of events. He asked the armed guards to allow them to get something to eat and drink from the cookhouse and place them in a separate room, away from the major.

"Mr. Shane, Dr Meena is my daughter," he said with a look of deep concern on his face. "The major will not deal with me, so I really need you to go and talk to him and ask him what his plan was when he decided to give Meena into the charge of those soldiers in the convoy."

Shane promised he would do his best and went in search of tea and water to bring to the major. But first, Shane took Monica in his arms and assured her that they would all do their best to rescue Meena. Monica, who had been sitting in the shade of the nose of the aircraft, went with him and sat on the verandah beside the cookhouse. Shane brought her water and held her hand as they talked for a while before he left to confront the major. The army cook assured him that he would take care of Monica and she visibly relaxed. She watched Shane as he left to speak with the man who had caused them so much trauma, and who was responsible for taking Meena from them and putting her in grave danger. He was unsure of DaSilva's intentions and conscious of the major's revelations concerning the man, so he proceeded to meet the major, while keeping an open mind. His primary concern was for Meena's welfare and to gather any information he could to ensure this.

DaSilva berated himself mentally for letting his agents lose Meena so easily, assuming that she had simply intended to return to the safety of her mission hospital. He feared the worst and watched the young Irishman fill a bottle of water at the cookhouse in the compound. A kitchen orderly gave him tea and he walked towards the barracks where the major was being held having first looked after the young woman who had arrived with them. DaSilva would never have thought of bringing tea to that man. He found himself praying that Shane's strategy would work. The young man did seem to be very concerned about Meena, and DaSilva simply assumed that he too, like so many others, had fallen under her spell. He needed to talk to Abdullah and make clear that the consequences of any firefight with the returning convoy would endanger the life of an innocent young lady doctor.

On learning of the predicament of DaSilva's daughter, Abdullah immediately radioed local commanders to be on the lookout for the doctor. He cautioned DaSilva about expecting too much, given the volatile situation and the actions of men in a society where all conventional rules had broken down. After an hour, Shane returned from his interview with the major and informed them that the major had simply sent the lady with the convoy to elicit her help in medical emergencies. Shane was not keen on sharing the other information revealed by the major, mainly relating to DaSilva. Nobody believed what the major had said, so Abdullah prepared to interview the major more robustly.

They were interrupted by the radio operator with the welcome news that the convoy had diverted to the capital, Dhaka. The convoy commander had obviously received information that the Balashi base had been overrun by insurgents. Abdullah's medics also reported that several of their wounded, including Keeler, would need to be evacuated to a hospital as soon as possible due to the seriousness of their injuries and the shortage of surgical equipment and medicines to provide adequate treatment.

Abdullah had so few vehicles at his disposal that he considered using the helicopter to evacuate more wounded. He mentioned a jungle hospital near the border at Baona, which had been set up by the insurgents to treat their more serious cases. The only problem was that the hospital was heavily defended by heavy machine guns that would certainly shoot down any approaching helicopter. He had dispatched their truck to this jungle hospital earlier with the most seriously wounded. They had recently lost radio contact with the hospital. Contact by radio had also been restricted to prevent radio signals revealing the hospital location to the Pakistani military. His only option was to get a message to his Indian military contacts across the border to arrange the evacuation of the wounded. Those forces were massing on the border, and he was one of the few people who knew when they would invade.

He went to make the radio call to request the Indian military to expect a helicopter medical evacuation and instructed his men to paint a red cross on a white background over the Pakistan flag on the helicopter. Their efforts were comical as the only white paint available was lime-based, used for painting the garrison walls. The red paint was the same whitewash mixed with turmeric given to the men by the cook, and looked more orange than red. He asked DaSilva to talk with the pilots and ask for their help in the medical evacuation. He planned to arrange for Indian forces to meet the helicopter at a pre-arranged rendezvous point on the border and escort it safely to their main base of operations. Keeler and the other seriously wounded could then be transferred to a military hospital to receive better medical treatment.

They were all surprised by the sudden arrival of a single vehicle that had driven into the base, only to be surrounded by hostile fighters. Two shocked occupants were dragged out of the vehicle, and on inspection, they noticed the body of a third soldier, obviously dead and with wounds to his neck. Shane immediately identified the vehicle as belonging to Dr Meena's hospital, and the jeep's occupants as the ones who had taken Meena on the orders of the major. On interrogation, the new arrivals revealed that they had been treating the woman with respect and kindness and simply wished to deliver her to safety when she suddenly produced a scalpel and callously slit the throat of their comrade. Before they could react, the lady had escaped into the nearby jungle, leaving them to try to save their comrade's life. Everyone was skeptical and DaSilva was left in no doubt that his daughter stood little chance of being found alive. Abdullah promised that his men would get the truth from them one way or another, and the prisoners were taken away.

The helicopter pilots assured DaSilva that they would cooperate in the medical evacuation of the wounded. They were apprehensive when told of the proposed rendezvous on the border with India because they found it hard to trust their old enemy. Both were local Bengali flying officers and their families lived in the capital, Dhaka. They were aware that many of their Bengali officer friends had defected to the insurgency, but they were undecided, and DaSilva respected this. Finally, based on his assurances, they pre-flighted the helicopter for the trip to the border. One of their ground crew had been killed in the raid on the garrison and the one remaining was a qualified mechanic on their Mi-4 Russian-built helicopter.

Together they rolled out a drum of aviation fuel, refueled the helicopter and prepared it for the flight to the border. They dismounted the machine gun from the doorway and supervised the medics loading the wounded, after unloading the wreckage from the Indian helicopter. Monica arrived with Keeler to ensure that those on board were fully aware of his serious condition. DaSilva tried to entice her to travel to the safety of the border, but she resolutely refused and informed him that she would prefer to go to their own hospital, fully certain that Dr Meena would try her best to get to her home base. She anxiously looked towards the room where Meena's captors were being interrogated. DaSilva knew she was relying on those men revealing more truthful information concerning Meena's whereabouts. They had tried phoning Meena's hospital to see if she had somehow reached there but the phones were useless and only working intermittently. DaSilva was heartened by the faith this young woman had in Meena and her ability to survive. He assured her that he too would travel to the hospital in the hope that Monica was correct.

The pilots started their engine, aware of the presence of one of Abdullah's men sitting behind them. Abdullah had made it clear to the pilots that this man was instructed to shoot one pilot if they attempted to deviate from their flight plan. The helicopter took to the air in a flurry of dust and headed in the direction of the border. They were instructed to offload the wounded into the care of the Indian military and return to the garrison as soon as possible. After less than an hour flying, they encountered another Mi-4 helicopter, a replica of the one they had shot down, hovering directly over the land border, and they cautiously headed straight for it. Keeler was conscious and propped up beside a window from where he observed familiar landmarks on the Indian side of the border. The pilots listened to his shouted instructions, and they followed the other helicopter as it descended into a huge clearing beyond a deserted border post and his heart lifted as he saw an Indian flag flying over hundreds of military vehicles. He counted twenty tanks at the vanguard of an advance column with many infantry units assembled nearby. This was a military force primed and ready to march when the order came. The helicopter alighted beside other helicopters near a compound of tents with prominent red crosses on white backgrounds on their roofs.

They were immediately surrounded by curious onlookers and a crew who had been briefed on the arrival of the enemy machine. They ran forward and signaled to the pilots that it was safe to shut down their engine. The door slid open, and Keeler immediately requested to be taken to the commanding officer to brief him on the situation on the other side of the border. He intended to request that the forward units be on the lookout for Dr Meena after giving a briefing on the situation on the ground in the areas he had visited.

On reaching the command tent, the stretcher-bearers were instructed to place the stretcher on a cleared table adjacent to another, surrounded by senior officers consulting detailed maps of the area. The commander stepped forward and commended Keeler on the vital mission he had undertaken and informed him that they were aware of the doctor's contacts with the Indian military intelligence in the past. They were surprised to see Keeler, having presumed that he had been captured by the Pakistani military when his aircraft failed to return from his mission. Keeler was intent on overcoming any pain he was experiencing to give a full briefing and show the grid reference where the wreckage of the Indian helicopter could be found. He suggested that they use that location as their starting point as it was a strategic location with a major road junction and river bridge. He mentioned that Abdullah, the local Mukti Bahini commander, would soon have intelligence from the doctor's captors after their interrogation.

The Indian commanding officer promised to do his best to search for the doctor but advised Keeler that she was not a priority. The commander stated that he would dispatch a reconnaissance patrol immediately to link up with the local fighters in an area where a jungle field hospital was located. The fighters there would be instrumental in assisting the Indian Army in negotiating the many river crossings that would face the full invading force when the order to invade eventually came. The commander reassured Keeler that those fighters would be well informed and most likely know any information concerning the doctor.

He instructed a young Sikh captain present at the briefing to take three tanks and one hundred men in a reconnaissance convoy and proceed immediately to the insurgents' jungle hospital near the town of Baona, and to await further instructions from there. The commander was preempting the political decision to invade but he simply could not wait any longer; he was seizing the initiative, prepared to suffer the consequences later. He was anxious to maintain the element of surprise over his Pakistani counterpart and provoke a reaction. Historians could later debate over who fired the first shots. Maybe this incursion into enemy territory would also be the catalyst to galvanize the politicians in Delhi into action.

Captain Singh collected all the necessary maps and set about assembling his unit, which would be the first Indian Army unit to cross the border. He was aware of recent army artillery exchanges that had taken place in response to provocation from Pakistani units firing from their side of the border. They had also witnessed aerial combat between the two nations in the previous days, but war was not yet declared, so the captain was aware of the significance of his mission and the spark it may ignite in this volatile region. He mounted the third tank in line and ordered the convoy to move out. Four trucks and two jeeps followed. He warned the lead tank commander to disperse into the jungle at the first sign of trouble, particularly if unidentified aircraft were spotted.

Very soon they crossed the border with no resistance, but he knew that any sense of security would be premature as they followed the road that would lead to the area where the jungle hospital was located. He selected the radio frequency that had been agreed upon with the Mukti Bahini as he listened to the static in his headset. He also reviewed the daily codes and the radio frequencies to call for ground artillery or air support. He scanned the skies constantly for enemy aircraft. He knew how vulnerable his convoy was to attack from the air and the speed at which modern jets could suddenly descend on them and wreak havoc from above.

His lightly armoured, Soviet-built PT-76 tanks were built for speed and crossing rivers but could not survive a direct hit from artillery or an air attack. The Indian Army convoy proceeded cautiously but made good progress, and Captain Singh was surprised at the absence of resistance from units of the Pakistani military. Their intelligence reports had never mentioned that the artillery that had been causing so much trouble seemed to have been withdrawn. That was a relief for he knew that his column would otherwise have been easily obliterated by an accurate artillery barrage. He nevertheless continued his scan of the road ahead with his binoculars from the vantage point on top of his tank and noticed the commanders of the leading tanks doing the same. He looked rearwards and got a thumbs-up from the driver of the first truck. They were all primed for immediate action at the first sign of trouble.

Chapter 35

Pakistan Army cavalry officer Lieutenant Faisal Ahmad surveyed the road junction ahead from atop his American-built M24 Chaffee tank. It was not by any means a heavyweight among tanks, but it was certainly adequate in this terrain, with good maneuverability and speed that would hopefully keep him out of trouble. It offered good protection against attacks from anything other than a direct hit from heavy artillery. He also scanned the air for the aircraft that could bring instant death and destruction to any unwary tank crew. He checked their progress on his chart and calculated from the landmarks around and the nearby road junction that their target would be one mile ahead. His friend Afzal waved from the tank following to go right.

He could see the dust from the main column as it rose over the trees about two miles behind. His forward reconnaissance patrol was simply to locate the target and radio back to the commander that they were in position. One mile later, through his binoculars he could see the faint outline of smoke emanating from the jungle in the target area where army intelligence had reported enemy activity. Despite their best efforts, he knew how difficult it was for the enemy to obscure traces of its presence, and the faint residual smoke from campfires simply confirmed the accuracy of their intelligence.

Faisal instructed his driver to leave the road and very soon the two tanks were perfectly concealed in the jungle on either side of a small mound of earth covered in low-lying shrubs. Without engine noise, they all took time to adjust to the welcome sound of silence. Both tank commanders scanned the air once again and Faisal then trained his binoculars on the target area of the jungle for any sign of movement. The road to the border with India skirted the tree line in the distance and they set about calculating firing solutions for their 75mm main guns. He checked his Browning heavy machine gun, mounted on top, and was satisfied that all armaments on both tanks were ready for battle. He was confident that their engines were reliable and ready to start immediately when called upon, should they need to reposition in a hurry.

He scanned the target area once more and was surprised to see two armed men break cover and run into the jungle just below their target. He was annoyed but convinced himself that it was inevitable that the progress of their tanks would be monitored. He eventually made the radio call to his commander who ordered him to open fire immediately, while the column waited to reinforce Faisal if needed. Faisal couldn't believe what he was hearing. He was fully sure that the commander would have joined them with the main column once the target had been identified. To his dismay, his request for infantry units to join them was also refused. He hated operating without infantry support as the presence of ground troops protected a tank commander's perimeter. Afzal simply shrugged and set about preparing his crew to commence firing. Faisal had seven rounds for his main gun, and he knew Afzal had eight. They agreed to offload every round except two each, to be kept in reserve for when they needed to retreat to the main column.

They started their engines in a cloud of black smoke to

power their electrics and loaded their first rounds. He shouted the fire command and watched through his binoculars as the shells from both tanks found their targets in the jungle. They quickly reloaded and the second rounds were just as accurate. Debris could be seen flying through the air and Faisal knew that their intelligence reports had been correct. Some small-arms fire emanated from the jungle, where the smoke was rising from fires created by their accurate bombardment. He instructed his crew to commence firing with the Browning machine gun and watched as the lazy line of tracer ammunition found its target on the enemy positions at the edge of the jungle.

Some fighters appeared from the jungle and advanced on their position, and Faisal cursed his commander for not allocating infantry to support him, confirming just how vital foot soldiers were for successful tank operations, and with ammunition running low, Faisal knew that they would have to retreat soon. Had his commander been more courageous, their full force of ten tanks and infantry would now be advancing on the enemy, with victory assured. Just as he was considering using his last two rounds, he heard a frantic transmission in his headset over the noise of the firing from the Browning heavy machine gun where two of his crew had relocated. His driver remained inside, ready to reposition if needed.

Afzal shouting in his headset made Faisal look over at his friend as he sat on top of the other tank with a quizzical look on his face. He had never seen Afzal looking so frightened, and he followed the direction in which he was urgently pointing. Faisal's whole being drained out through his feet at the sight that confronted him through his binoculars. A column of tanks was advancing over a hill from the direction of the Indian border. He could not make sense of this and struggled to figure out in his mind which units these tanks came from. Afzal didn't need to figure out anything as he shouted at Faisal in his headset.

"They're Indian," he said in alarm and when Faisal recovered, his training finally took over and he followed Afzal's lead in shouting at his crew to reposition into the tank from where they could move their main gun and recalculate a firing solution to engage the new targets, while muttering to himself several times that war had not yet been declared with India. It was pointless informing his commander that they were engaging an Indian armoured convoy. He could hear the response he would get: *"Nonsense, Faisal, we are not yet at war, you are hallucinating."*

He heard Afzal's first shot and instinctively looked to see a direct hit on the lead tank in the column, which he recognised as a Russian-built PT-76 amphibious tank, which he knew to be very lightly armoured. Two tanks following peeled off to the left and right of the road and Faisal could see a Sikh commander on one of them gesticulating to the occupants of the following vehicles to disperse. Faisal gave the fire command once more and looked on in horror as his round scored a direct hit on the lead truck, the explosion throwing bodies and mangled wreckage high up in the air. He could not dwell on this horrifying spectacle as they were now taking fire from elements of the column that had dispersed into the cover of the jungle on either side of the road.

They were soon out of ammunition for their main guns and both he and Afzal were now firing their Brownings on top of the tanks as their crews clambered out to look for cover in the jungle. The enemy would now have their range, and they could expect heavy rounds to start falling in their area very soon. With no ammunition, the tanks would be deathtraps as the Indian tanks calculated the range. He realised the futility of making a run for it as it would expose their flanks to broadsides from the two remaining Indian tanks. He was not sure whether his tank could survive a direct hit from the main guns on the Indian tanks, but his crews had been in no doubt and decided to abandon their own tanks before the Indian commander could calculate their range.

Faisal was running low on ammunition for his Browning machine gun as he observed the Indian soldiers advancing on their position. Also pouring out of the jungle were heavily armed men he recognised as Mukti Bahini insurgents, fighting alongside the Indian soldiers. This was not a good development as he knew of the horror stories of Pakistani soldiers falling into the hands of these so-called freedom fighters. He crouched down behind the turret of his tank and made a radio call for help to his column commander.

He was informed that the column was making a strategic withdrawal to consider the real implications of this Indian incursion. The commander had obviously heard the intense firefight up ahead. Faisal stared across at Afzal in disbelief. As he was contemplating their options, an Indian high-explosive round hit the hill between their tanks, and in slow motion, Faisal and Afzal were suddenly airborne and tumbling in the air with a clear view of their tanks beneath and even the line of enemy soldiers as they advanced towards them. Faisal had the presence of mind to pray to Allah to look after his family in Peshawar as he fell, and then everything went blank as he impacted the ground.

***

Faisal eventually regained consciousness and struggled to make sense of his situation. He looked up at the trees and tried to focus. His hands appeared before his eyes, and he recognised them as his own even though they were red-raw and sore. Touching his face brought more pain and someone roughly pulled his hands away. He turned to see a medic with an angry look on his face.

"You are lucky to be alive. All your friends are dead. Unfortunately, your freedom-fighting countrymen got to them before I could stop them. I managed to save your life by convincing them that I need you as a prisoner for intelligence gathering."

Faisal refocused on the other figure standing above him and adjusted to conversing in English with the Sikh captain he had seen earlier on the enemy tank.

"I actually saw you and your friend in the air when my round struck your position. All the soil in the explosion seems to have miraculously sheltered you from the shrapnel. You are a lucky man to be alive and in one piece. I suppose I should be recommending you for a medal to your superiors for the damage you inflicted on my column, but unfortunately, you also fired several live rounds into a field hospital in the jungle being run by your freedom-fighting countrymen. I better get you packed off to India as soon as possible, because your countrymen want to lynch you, and I have to say, my men feel the same way. You also killed many of their friends when your shell hit our troop carrier."

Faisal thanked him and couldn't believe how hoarse he was. He seemed to have swallowed a ton of earth in the explosion. His ears also hurt badly, and this was not helped by the sudden arrival of a formation of jets overhead. "Those are our aircraft on a bombing run on your main armoured column, which has dispersed and is on the run. The Pakistani Air Force is putting up a good fight, according to reports we are receiving from other areas, but their position is impossible, and it's only a matter of time before the Indian Air Force gains air superiority. The war has kicked off and we have invaded on several fronts. The Indian Army is advancing rapidly with the help of local insurgents."

There was a commotion behind one of Faisal's tanks as a group of Indian soldiers, known as Jawans, dragged someone from underneath the other tank. Faisal's heart lifted as he recognised the prone figure of Afzal.

"Please, sir, save my friend, I beg you," he said weakly. Captain Singh barked an order and directed the medic to attend to Afzal, who gave Faisal the thumbs-up signal after being revived. If anything, Afzal was in worse condition than he was.

The captain left them, but not before supervising the loading of the two men on to stretchers and into one of his trucks and wishing them both good luck while squeezing Faisal's hand in the most welcome and painful handshake as he and Afzal began life as prisoners of war on the way to captivity in India, glad to be alive and on their way home.

Captain Singh had one final request before they departed. "You will be taken to our headquarters for processing. An officer will be assigned to interrogate you after you receive medical treatment. You know, of course, that you cannot be compelled to divulge sensitive information. However, it is only a matter of time before your forces are overwhelmed. It would, therefore, save a lot of lives if you were to offer us some strategic information to help bring this conflict to a conclusion as quickly as possible."

Faisal did not need to think about his response. "Sir, you have been more than fair with us, but I think your commanders have all the information they need about our lack of resources, due to the impossibility of resupply from our mother country."

The truck drove off towards the border as the captain observed his remaining tank crews and the dead from the battle being laid out in quite a long line. He looked to the sky as a flight of Indian Air Force Mig fighter aircraft circled, ensuring total air superiority in his sector of operations. Their squadron leader had informed him by radio earlier that they had destroyed several tanks in a column nearby. The captain was relieved that those Pakistani tanks from their main column had not joined in the battle. Their superior numbers would have annihilated his smaller force, with disastrous consequences for the jungle hospital and its lightly armed defenders. Relying on luck was never an advisable military strategy, but any victory was gratefully accepted, regardless of what influenced the outcome.

Commanding from the top of the third tank in the column had also been lucky for him but seemed callous as he observed the burnt-out wreckages of the lead tank and troop carrier in his convoy. This was, however, a prudent move based on experience from many encounters in the past, where commanders had been early casualties while insisting on leading from the front, thereby rendering their attacking force leaderless. Rather than dwelling on matters beyond his control, he instead moved on and concentrated on his next move, as he observed the smoke rising from the area in the jungle where the hospital was located.

His sergeant informed him that they had just received a radio message that their main force would arrive within the hour, which was a relief when he considered his many wounded. He could only guess as to the level of carnage that would confront him when he reached the insurgents' field hospital in the jungle.

Chapter 36

Captain Singh intercepted a jeep and commanded the driver to take him to the jungle clearing that had been targeted by the Pakistani tanks. He dreaded finding a similar scene of devastation to that found in his own column after his lead tank and infantry transport had been hit. The tank was totally burned out and the crew had died instantly. His PT-76 amphibious tanks were very maneuverable and had a decent main gun, but the armour could not sustain a direct hit from anything other than small-arms fire. The tank's very useful ability to cross rivers also necessitated a lightly armoured construction. He had observed the hole where the shell had entered, and he could only imagine the instant destruction visited on the three-man crew, who were well known to him.

He had to see the truckload of infantry that had been hit in order to realise the true extent of the carnage resulting from a high explosive detonation in the midst of twenty of his soldiers, tightly packed in the rear of the truck. There was only one survivor, remarkably screened from the full force of the blast by the compacted bodies of those between him and the explosion. He sent the man to the rear, bearing mental scars far less tolerable than the physical scars commonly received by foot soldiers in any battle. Witnessing the total annihilation of all his close friends would surely leave its mark on the man for years to come. The captain thought about his satchel full of burned and bloodied identification tags and he dreaded writing up his battle report for this particular engagement. He sincerely hoped for easier and less bloody encounters in the coming days. These thoughts remained with him as he made his way from the jeep through the trees to the chaos of the makeshift jungle hospital. Dead and wounded bodies were being extracted from the remains of exploded trees, and he was amazed at the industry of everyone who had survived and their ability to treat this catastrophe as just another chapter in a long line of tragedies inflicted on them in the previous months by the occupying power. He looked through the trees towards the main road and was relieved to see medical vehicles arriving. Thankfully, his commanding officer had understood from reports that getting medical assistance after the battle would be a priority.

As he stood taking it all in, scanning the ground around him, he observed a strange sight. A man lay face down, obviously dead from deep shrapnel wounds in his back. One of his legs was missing but the wound was not new, and he concluded that his limb must have been missing prior to the attack. That in itself was not hard to figure out, but beneath the man, the captain could make out two fair-skinned arms stretched out on either side of the dead combatant, in a grotesque parody of a multi-limbed Hindu goddess. He rushed to investigate and was shocked to see movement from one of these arms. He hurriedly turned the dead man over and discovered the muddy figure of a lady lying face-down in the soil. He called his medics and kneeled to gently turn her over and was astonished to discover the lady doctor he had met days earlier in the convoy while heading towards the border. He held her in his arms and used water from his bottle to gently wash the mud from her face and from her eyes, which suddenly opened and focused immediately on him in a look of shock and confusion.

"Welcome back from the dead, Doctor," he said with a big grin.

She was suddenly totally conscious and aware, but she lingered in the warm and comforting embrace of this handsome Sikh. Decorum won out in the end, and she jumped to her feet and surveyed the carnage around her, while feeling the painful scorch marks on her arm and ankle. A fit of dizziness forced her to fall once again into the waiting arms of the army officer. Her heart sank as she discovered Jagdish's dead figure at her feet.

"It seems that this man took the full impact of the explosion and saved your life in the process. You owe your survival to this brave man, Doctor."

Meena couldn't take in all the devastation around her without crying. It was hard to comprehend the fact that all these dead people had been living and talking with her just a short time ago.

"You are in shock, Doctor. Please come with me to see the doctor in our field hospital, which is being set up near the road by Dr Sarita, who was a medic in the Pakistani Army until recently and has been running a hospital just over the border in India for the past few months. She was a major before she deserted the Pakistani military, and now dedicates herself to the creation of a new country, Bangladesh. Nobody is brave enough to challenge her on that ambition. We can go to meet her now and get that burn on your arm treated."

Meena took all this information in and seemed to be recovering her composure. "Captain, I am well aware of Dr Sarita as we have worked together in the past. She regularly visited my hospital and because of her former position in the Pakistani Army, she was in a position to supply me with medical supplies, which saved so many lives. Oh, and Captain, I advise you not to let her hear you calling her a deserter as she will take great offense. She refers to her situation in life as a 'redeployment'. So kindly keep that in mind.

"Now, please take me to meet with her, and if you would be so kind as to detail your medics to look after the body of my friend Jagdish. It seems that he was a commander of this facility before its destruction. We need to arrange a Hindu funeral service for him, and I need to get word to his family of his tragic death. I cannot believe that this attack happened so suddenly and without warning. How can these people recover from such devastation?"

Captain Singh did as she asked. He marveled at the woman's resilience and was amazed at her recovery and ability to assume the degree of authority common to natural-born leaders. He led the way to the cluster of medical tents being erected nearby. They did not need to see Dr Sarita, but simply needed to listen to her commands in the distance. When eventually she saw Meena and the state she was in, she dropped everything and immediately ran to embrace her. All the tension and many tragedies of the past few days erupted once more in a cascade of emotions as Meena allowed her tough exterior to dissolve.

"Come Doctor, let's get you sorted and functioning again, and you can tell me all about what troubles you have encountered this time."

She called for assistance and soon Meena was surrounded by several nurses whom she knew and who took her to one of the tents, with Dr Sarita instructing them to treat the burn on Meena's arm. She quickly assessed the burn on her ankle and declared it superficial. Captain Singh was left staring after them until he suddenly noticed Dr Sarita watching him with her arms folded.

"Yes, Captain, don't be alarmed. You are not the first person to fall under that lady's spell. Now, please radio your headquarters and demand the delivery of our medical supplies. Your commanders promised me close support and I'm still waiting. Also, have your men clear a suitable helicopter landing zone and transmit its coordinates to headquarters. Things are going to get very busy around here and I need to ensure that our hospital is fully functioning as soon as possible. Thank you."

She briskly walked away and left Captain Singh scribbling the last of her instructions in his notebook. He recovered his composure and hurried to carry out her instructions, not entirely sure whether his encounter with this lady was not more frightening than his recent ferocious battle.

Meena was so glad to be among women friends, where she could let her guard down. Most of these nurses had been trained in her hospital. They had also completed their midwifery studies with her and Monica. Now they fussed over her, and she knew she was loved by each of them. While the senior nurse, Aleema, looked after her arm, the others brought fresh clothes.

"Don't worry, Doctor, at least the truck with our clothes and surgical gowns arrived with us. The ladies have a shower set up, but apologies for the cold water, and we have only carbolic soap, I'm afraid. I'm also worried about your arm. I think it will almost certainly need a skin graft and there is some debris, mostly soil, forced deep into the wound by the exploding shell. I will put a waterproof cover on the dressing so you can shower. Let the ladies wash your hair because I think half the Bangladeshi jungle is in there."

Meena certainly hadn't expected to be naked so quickly as they stripped away the earth and blood-stained clothing before they scrubbed her from head-to-toe. She had no time to be embarrassed as the carbolic soap suds covered her body and her scalp tingled as their strong fingers expertly massaged her scalp. Her soap-filled eyes opened wide in alarm as they tackled her nether regions without inhibition, as if she were an infant. Her constant protests that she could do that herself fell on deaf ears. "Dr Sarita's orders," they said repeatedly. She held her blushes in check as they dried her off with starched towels that surely removed the top layer of skin.

Meena felt like a baby in their care and soon she was gleaming in beautifully smelling fresh clothes, and she felt that there was nothing like the smell of carbolic soap to instill a sense of purity and cleanliness.

The youngest nurse, whom she didn't know, brushed coconut oil into Meena's hair before tying it up in a neat bun, after which she led her to Dr Sarita's tent, which was located in the surgical area. Meena was amazed at the efficiency of the operation and how the army medical corps had transformed the jungle site into a working hospital.

"Well, my dear, the ladies seem to have performed quite a transformation. I specifically instructed them to make sure any sources of infection were dealt with, not only for the burn on your arm but also for the surgical work I have planned for you."

Meena perfectly understood the need to maintain a sterile environment, especially in what was, essentially, a battleground. "Yes, Doctor, I gathered that was why they were being so... thorough."

Dr Sarita smiled, knowing full well that the ladies had scrubbed every inch of her young colleague's body. "I'm so glad you survived the experience. Now, let's take a look at that wound. We may not need a skin graft, my dear, but I simply need to extract as much of the debris as I can. We need to be very careful of infection because of the usual level of contamination in debris from explosions. Although, it looks like your arm was only exposed to extreme heat for a short time. You were so lucky to have been shielded by that brave man. I heard the story of your miraculous escape."

Meena felt tears welling up once more, but she was more in control now, even though foremost in her mind was Jagdish's family and the families of all the people losing their lives daily in this conflict. "Thank you, Doctor, I am so grateful to be among friends again. Please assign me to whatever work you have planned."

Dr Sarita finished the dressing and apologised to Meena for not being able to let her rest as she was desperately in need of her surgical skills. "We have three very urgent stomach wounds that need your attention. Nurse Aleema is organising our makeshift surgery and prepping for the first casualty. I understand that you need to return to your hospital, but I cannot allow that for the moment because of the fighting. Let us see how things develop and review your situation in a few days."

Meena saw the sense of this and readily agreed. She could not resist embracing Dr Sarita once more and the affection was returned ten-fold from the normally very stern, formal woman.

"Of course, we really need to discuss the bruising all over your body, Meena. Nurse Aleema tells me that, apart from the new bruises inflicted today, there are older bruises that are consistent with repeated assaults evident on your body. Now, don't be alarmed, we see this so often these days as increasing numbers of women seem to be exposed to sexual violence in this conflict. We don't need to talk about it now, but you really must set aside time for counselling in the near future. You are one of our most capable surgeons, and I need to be sure that you are mentally fit to cope with the challenges confronting us in this war."

"It is so hard for me to discuss, Doctor, but our friend Sister Gertrude was shot while saving me from an assault by soldiers in our hospital. Also, during a subsequent assault by soldiers, I managed to escape after fatally wounding one of them. I have had to suppress the feelings due to being involved in such hectic activity around me. But yes, Doctor, I agree that some counselling will be needed, and I promise to make myself available for this as soon as possible."

"I'm so sorry to hear about Gertrude. She has been a really good friend for many years and was instrumental in providing health care in our country. We will miss her. These past few days have indeed been traumatic for you. Hopefully, this war will not last long. I will write to my friend Samaya, who is a Buddhist nun near here, in Siliguri. I will ask her to expect you for counselling. It will involve a stay of at least a week.

"The sessions will not rid you of your demons, but Samaya certainly will help you focus on all the positive elements in your life, of which there are many. Also, we could possibly use Samaya's methods as a template to treat the many traumatised women survivors of this conflict. You are mentally very strong, Meena, but come and talk to me any time you need to. Now, please visit our surgical tent and let the ladies show you around."

As she made her way to the surgical tent, Meena encountered Captain Singh, who was mounting a tank in an armoured column, ready to move out. She ran to speak with him before they departed. "Captain, I am surprised you are leaving so soon."

He jumped down and asked his driver to shut down the engine so that they could talk without smoke and noise. "Yes, Doctor, we have been detailed to search for Pakistani units that have dispersed into the jungle. We are concerned that they may threaten the local villagers and discourage them from helping us as we advance."

Meena asked him if he had heard any word of a Flight Lieutenant Keeler, her nurse Monica, and the foreigner Shane, whom the captain had met with recently.

She was so relieved to hear from him that Keeler had safely reached his lines. "I was actually present when your lieutenant arrived by helicopter from a garrison in Balashi that had been overrun by the insurgents. It was a captured Pakistani helicopter, and the lieutenant briefed us on the tragedy surrounding the Indian rescue helicopter and his subsequent capture by a major, who was commanding the helicopter that inflicted the damage on our machine. There was no news about your foreign friend Shane and nurse Monica. I remember your companion Shane, but Lieutenant Keeler simply asked that we search for you and then my commander ordered medics to remove him for treatment. That was the last I saw of him, Doctor."

The Pakistani helicopter he described certainly sounded familiar to Meena, but Captain Singh had no further information. It was not the time to relate to him her recent experiences and the fact that she had been at the scene of the devastating attack on the Indian helicopter. There were simply too many thoughts surfacing at once and they threatened to overwhelm her. Silence was the best option for now. As he mounted his tank, he promised to relay any further relevant information to her as it became available. The convoy departed in a cloud of engine fumes and deafening noise, embarking on another mission, fraught with danger.

The young captain gave a cheerful wave, which Meena returned with a smile, while at the same time feeling far from confident and worrying about more bloodshed in the coming days.

On entering the surgical tent, Meena was greeted by Nurse Aleema, who briefed her on the first three surgical cases. There was one young boy whom she remembered from before the explosion. He was one of the boys pedaling the stationary bicycles generating electricity. He was seriously wounded, and she could tell straight away that their intervention would be hopeless as his injuries were far too severe. He returned her smile, and she asked the nurses to make him as comfortable as possible, and they simply knew what this meant. He did not have long to live, and she promised him that the nurses would look after him as she moved on to the next two patients, while at the same time holding back tears.

They were in much better shape and after a quick examination, she determined that they had superficial shrapnel wounds without internal organ damage. She informed them that they should have a full recovery after surgery to remove the metal fragments. She would have liked X-rays to confirm the diagnosis but knew this would not be possible in the short term.

As she was leaving to scrub up, she noticed a green uniform beside one of the men's stretchers. She held the blood-stained tunic and was surprised to see Pakistani Air Force insignia and the name 'Chatterjee' over the breast pocket. She recognised this as a Bengali name. Most Bengali officers in the Pakistani military had been stood down recently and disarmed by their Pakistani superiors. Their senior officers from West Pakistan simply didn't trust them as quite a few had deserted and now fought alongside the insurgents. Their more sympathetic commanders requested their Bengali officers to take leave and avoid deserting.

"Yes Doctor, I am Bengali," the young man said. "I was shot down earlier today and had to bail out as my aircraft exploded beneath me. My seat shielded me from the explosion, but one piece of shrapnel caught me on my side. Luckily, I landed adjacent to an advancing Indian Army convoy. Had I landed among the local population I would almost certainly have been executed. I understand this perfectly well, but I signed up with the Pakistani Air Force and that is where my allegiances lie, regardless of political developments in East Pakistan."

The man on the stretcher beside him shouted, 'Bangladesh!' and let the young Flight Lieutenant know in Bengali that he was a traitor to his country. Meena instructed the orderlies to have them separated before their injuries worsened due to the intensity of their animosity towards each other.

"Thank you, Doctor, and apologies for bringing conflict to your hospital. Earlier today I shot down an Indian Air Force Russian-built Mig fighter, and was relieved to see the pilot successfully eject from his stricken jet. I was so distracted watching the progress of his parachute towards the ground that I failed to see his wingman coming out of the sun and scoring a direct hit on my aircraft, causing it to explode. Thankfully, I had time to eject, and the process was so violent that I hardly noticed the shrapnel from the explosion striking me. I floated towards the ground, right on top of the waiting Indian troops. I could actually hear their officer ordering them not to shoot me. Their medics looked after me very well, even though I had earlier strafed them with a devastating attack from the air that surely killed and wounded some of their comrades. I am grateful to be alive and I appreciate your medical intervention. May I ask you to kindly relay my wish to be taken to India as a prisoner of war? It is the only place where a Bengali officer in the Pakistani military will be safe."

Meena promised him that she would speak to his Indian captors and relay his request. It was situations such as this that revealed the complexities of this conflict. "My home is here in East Pakistan, or Bangladesh, as our friend so forcefully pointed out," he said. "As you can imagine, I will no longer be welcome in my hometown. I'll eventually be repatriated to West Pakistan when this war is over, and as a Bengali, I will not be welcome there either. What will my fellow air force officers think about having a Bengali from East Pakistan in their midst? It may have been a simple decision for Bengali officers to desert from the Pakistan military, but I value the oath I took and intend to uphold all the promises I made, regardless of the political consequences for me and my family."

Meena left the young man with conflicting thoughts and made an effort to concentrate on her work. Her thoughts went to Monica and Shane as she tried to reassure herself that they were safe. She based this assumption on the fact that Keeler was safe. She was slightly annoyed that Keeler did not mention Shane and Monica during his debriefing. Her thoughts were interrupted by the arrival of more wounded from the jungle where she had mercifully been rescued earlier. She unconsciously rubbed the bandage protecting the wound on her arm and felt blessed to be alive as she set about treating those less-fortunate wounded. She was grateful also that a primitive jungle medical facility had now been transformed into an advanced trauma centre, with the first helicopter arriving to evacuate the most seriously wounded. Dr Sarita's assertiveness had certainly been a factor in ensuring survival for many of the young fighters from both sides of the conflict.

Chapter 37

Shane sat in the shade with Monica as they ate the samosas given to them by the cook, and he realised just how hungry they were. They had not eaten recently because of the constant tension they had experienced, and also, their welfare had not been one of the major's priorities. Shane observed Meena's jeep, which had recently arrived. Monica knew exactly what he was thinking.

"No Shane, you cannot leave this place, it is far too dangerous. Please wait until they have finished questioning those men who arrived in our jeep."

Shane considered this and looked to the quarters where the men were being questioned, knowing full well that the interrogation process would be merciless. Monica gave him hope as they discussed the options faced by Meena if there was any truth in what those men said about her escaping into the jungle.

"Dr Meena is very resourceful, Shane. I cannot even begin to believe that she is not alive."

Abdullah eventually appeared from the interrogation room. He stated that they did not need to use much persuasion to convince them to divulge the events surrounding the disappearance of the lady doctor. "We couldn't stop the driver from talking as he revealed the whole saga surrounding their dealings with the doctor. It's true that she certainly did fatally wound one soldier, but it happened when she broke away from them as they forced her to accompany them to a disused factory. He did not elaborate on what their plans for her were, but we all knew exactly what they intended, and that they would eventually emerge from the factory without her. But as they herded her to the factory, she outwitted them and threw gravel in their faces while making good her escape. I believed the driver when he said that after hearing shots and the soldiers shouting, he witnessed the lady emerging from the factory and running towards the jungle. He confirmed that she certainly didn't seem wounded. One soldier finally emerged from the factory carrying his comrade, who had died from a neck wound that, according to him, had been inflicted by the lady.

"Now, I am sorry, but we have no more time to spend on this. Your doctor friend probably linked up with refugees on the road to the Indian border. I suggest you both accompany my men in that captured vehicle and let them escort you to the safety of the border with India, where I'm sure you will find your friend. Mr. DaSilva will also accompany you as I'm unsure of his motivation for being here. My instinct tells me that he is a very dangerous man."

Abdullah walked away and proceeded to organise his men for their next mission, which seemed to involve linking up with the Indian Army as they crossed the border. It was obvious that they would soon invade and that an uncertain future lay ahead for this country. Shane and Monica readied themselves for the journey, but they both knew that Meena would not run to India. They figured that reuniting with them would be her priority and she would then try her best to return to her hospital. But as their eyes met, they also knew that nothing but intrigue would attach itself to their beautiful Dr Meena, and that she would automatically gravitate towards the most challenging events that would soon overwhelm the fledgling nation of Bangladesh.

Monica and Shane later sat dejectedly in their jeep, waiting for Abdullah's men to take them to the border. Monica retrieved a map from the sun visor and studied it for a while. She suddenly jumped from the vehicle and ran to the communications office to find Abdullah. Shane followed her and wondered what was so urgent. He arrived and saw them looking at the map. They spoke in Bengali and eventually, Abdullah pointed to a location on the map.

"Shane," Monica said excitedly, "this is the location where Dr Meena ran away from those soldiers. I know this area well. We regularly visited a village about ten miles from this factory and people came from all over to our clinic in this village. Do you remember Jagdish, the man who was mauled by a bear? Dr Meena needed to amputate his leg."

Shane didn't need to be reminded of his traumatic time in the operating theatre during that particular operation. "Yes, of course I do," he replied. "But I'm not sure what this has to do with finding Dr Meena."

Monica was way ahead of him, though. She studied the map on the table and tried to explain what she was thinking. They all gathered around to hear her explanation.

"Dr Meena ran into the jungle here," she said, pointing to the location of the disused factory. She then marked the location of the village where they held the clinic. "Jagdish is also from this village!" She waited for all the men to catch up. "This is obviously where Meena would go for help. All the villagers know her. We need to go there and find Jagdish. I'm certain he would have helped her."

DaSilva had been listening in the background and finally spoke up. "The lady has a point. She knows how Meena would think, and I feel we should at least travel there to find out if she is correct. It certainly seems plausible."

They all looked to Abdullah for a final decision.

"I understand your need to find this lady and I agree that she has served our people very well in the past, but I have other priorities. This war will soon escalate, and the next few days will be critical. I cannot divert resources to look for just one person who may or may not be in this village."

DaSilva pleaded with Abdullah to at least give them the vehicle for a few hours. "Mr. Abdullah, we need the vehicle for about four hours and promise to return here as soon as we find out what has happened to my daughter."

Abdullah relented but gave them three hours and detailed a driver and another armed man to take them to the village. "They will take you to this village and spend five minutes there while you make enquiries about the lady. I am instructing them to shoot you if you try to detain them any longer." His animosity towards DaSilva was obvious and it was also clear that his views were tempered by what Major Ali Khan had said earlier. He left the room and detailed two men to accompany them, with specific instructions to return within three hours. The men understood exactly what to do if they were delayed.

Abdullah sent for the two journalists while he went and asked Lieutenant Shah to give him a list of all the Pakistani prisoners. When the journalists finally reached the compound, Abdullah asked them to contact the Red Cross by telephone when the line worked and give them the names of the prisoners so that their families may be informed. Lieutenant Shah produced a list of seventy-three soldiers, listing also the thirty-three dead and eleven wounded. Two soldiers were missing. Everyone could see that this whole process was distressing for Abdullah, but he was mostly concerned for the families of soldiers who must be frantically waiting for news as they listened to news reports of the escalating violence in East Pakistan.

One of Abdullah's men, a student named Nauman from Dhaka University, had earlier revealed to Shane and Monica that Abdullah had also fought in the Second World War in North Africa and Sicily, but that all his nightmares centered around their fight against the paratroopers of the German Army at Monte Cassino in central Italy. He was wounded and sent home to India to recover in a military hospital in Calcutta. He related that Abdullah was always a very religious man and those experiences tempered his faith and instilled in him an extraordinary empathy for the suffering of others.

"He is our Imam, and all the students love him and rely on him for guidance. He was forced to take up arms a few months ago when the military started to abuse their power. The situation deteriorated rapidly until eventually, to avoid arrest, he had to flee to the jungle. Of course, hundreds of his followers joined him, including deserters from the military. They brought their weapons and expertise to an insurgency force that has been a major headache for the Pakistani military, which they now view as an army of occupation."

They all watched as Abdullah indicated that their conversation was over. "Now, I must go to prepare for the next phase of our operation. You can probably guess by now that we are scheduled to rendezvous with advance units of the Indian Army, whose invasion is imminent. We sincerely hope that they don't stay too long and simply replace one occupying army with another."

They loaded up their jeep and departed for Jagdish's village. Monica, Shane, and DaSilva sat in the back, glad to be doing something positive in their search for Meena. As they were leaving, they noticed Abdullah organising his men and the prisoners in lines. "They are gathering for prayer. Imam Abdullah insists on it every day," said their driver. Shane looked towards the barracks to see the major leaning against a pillar on the verandah, smoking a cigarette and drinking tea as two armed men kept a close eye on him. Shane could only wonder if the stories the major told him about DaSilva were true; his one-hour conversation with him had been very revealing. Shane's instincts told him that the major's recollections of the part he and DaSilva played in the war against the Japanese in Burma were accurate. As the major held up his cup of tea in salute to the departing vehicle, Shane watched DaSilva in the corner of his eye and tried to reconcile this distinguished-looking man with the sadistic young officer in Burma the major alluded to, and the atrocities perpetrated on the Japanese by the father of the object of Monica's affection and Shane's desire.

Chapter 38

Monica's world had fallen apart once more. She sat holding Sujata's hands as tears rolled down their cheeks. Sujata had just received the news of Jagdish's death from two young boys who had run away from the attack on the jungle hospital. As they ran from the carnage, they recounted every detail they could remember, and one detail that stood out in both their minds was the image of Jagdish's lacerated body being lifted from the ground, and underneath, the dead figure of the lady doctor lying face down in the dirt. Jagdish had taken the full blast of the nearest explosion while shielding the doctor, but the blast was not survivable. It had killed both of them and many other people.

The boys were too scared to remain near the carnage and had not stopped running until they had reached their village. When pressed, the only other detail they could remember was the sight of a Sikh soldier lifting the dead figure of the lady doctor who had been in their village, and who had accompanied them as they all marched with Jagdish to the jungle hospital. When the explosions happened, they had been waiting their turn at cycling the bicycle generators used to produce electricity and had managed to avoid the explosions that had happened without warning, the trunk of a nearby tree sheltering them from the worst effects.

Sujata informed Monica that Dr Meena had taken refuge with them after an ordeal in the jungle, where she had escaped captivity from the Pakistani military. It had been hard initially for Dr Meena to tell the full story, and they did not press her too much until, finally, she revealed all before sleeping for ten hours. The following morning, she had insisted on accompanying Jagdish to help at the hospital in the jungle before travelling on to her own hospital. The last Sujata had seen of them was as they left the village with supplies of food, accompanied by several of the local fighters and students from the university in Dhaka, who had been hiding from the military in their village.

It was heartbreaking to see Monica so deflated after her elation at figuring out – quite rightly, as it turned out – that Meena would seek refuge in the familiar surroundings of this village. Their armed escorts waited patiently and gave them all the time they needed. Both knew Jagdish and they assured Sujata that they would ask Imam Abdullah if they could return to retrieve Jagdish's body and deliver him to his village. DaSilva sat in the corner, numbed into silence, and eventually he went to sit in the vehicle. The others soon followed, and they set out on a sadness-filled return journey, during which none of them said a word, each absorbed in their own memories of Meena from totally different perspectives. Their request to visit the jungle hospital was refused by their driver, who was intent on carrying out the strict instructions given by Abdullah.

Later in the evening, as they sat on the verandah near the cookhouse, DaSilva assured them that he would use all his resources to find Meena's body, and have it returned to her hospital for burial. Monica couldn't think of Meena in terms of death and burial; that combination simply didn't add up in the thought processes that were threatening to overwhelm her.

DaSilva left them to request time on the base telephone to try to phone his wife in the United States and inform her of the death of their only child. Shane observed the retreating figure of a defeated man and pushed all the negative images he had of him to the back of his mind. He held Monica's hand and forced her to drink some tea. The evening was chilly, and the cook provided them with blankets. They soon fell into a fitful sleep, with Monica keening like a baby. What could Shane do to comfort her in her loss? He remembered well the futile attempts of his friends and family to console him after his family tragedy. Time eventually dulled the pain somewhat, but that terrible knot of grief in the centre of his chest was always present when he thought of his beautiful wife and child. All they could do now was return to their hospital and try to motivate people to continue to function in the vacuum of their great loss. Shane looked at Monica and felt sure he was observing a feisty, resilient woman who would build on the legacy of her dear friend. With that thought, the mental and physical exertions of the last few days finally overtook him, and he drifted into a deep, dreamless sleep.

They awoke the following morning to find a long line of Pakistani soldiers staring at them as the men awaited breakfast from the cookhouse. Several of them were preparing chapatis and the refreshing smell of tea competed with the aroma of spice-enriched potatoes and onions frying. Abdullah's orders had been clear, and the few remaining guards were fully aware of their duty of care to the prisoners. He had left in their truck, which had returned from the jungle hospital. Two captured military jeeps with the remainder of their small armed force left to meet the Indian Army as it invaded. He had reluctantly agreed to leave the hospital jeep with Shane. Visible at the edge of the jungle was a line of graves that had not been there when they had departed the day before. Abdullah had led the burial service for soldiers from both sides in the Muslim tradition.

Shane and Monica walked over to the freshly dug graves to pay their respects to all the young men.

"You know, Mr. Abdullah offered me a place in the army of their new State of Bangladesh." They both turned to see the major watching them from the shelter of one of the trees lining the compound, his two guards not far away. "Oh yes, he insisted that the new nation would need experienced officers for their fledgling army. I assumed from this that he is a good judge of character, and I promised I would give his offer serious consideration. I get the impression that he is more inclined to believe my version of events in the fight against the Japanese in Burma during the Second World War."

This was too much for Monica, who was normally extremely polite and rarely outspoken. She turned away from Shane and confronted the major head-on. "Sir, you are a disgrace to all decent people. You deliberately isolated our dear friend from us and placed her, against her wishes, into the care of soldiers you knew would deal with her in the way corrupt soldiers have been dealing with women for thousands of years. It pleases me greatly to let you know that she outwitted them and triumphed over their sickening plans for her and escaped to reveal to the world your plan to have her raped, tortured and murdered." Monica could no longer face his sickening grin and instead ran to the cookhouse.

"Collateral damage, my dear, casualty of war," said the major to the retreating figure.

Shane was disgusted and, like Monica, turned to leave, happy in the knowledge that the man was unaware of Meena's death. It felt good to leave him with the thoughts that his plans for Meena had been thwarted. Shane was astounded that Abdullah had offered him a position in the military of the emerging nation. It revealed Abdullah's seniority in the ranks of the Mukti Bahini in their fight for freedom.

There was, however, a certain logic to Abdullah's motivation.

He could obviously see the bigger picture and knew the new country would need skilled people to rebuild all sections of society, including the military, which would provide security during the dangerous early phase in the birth of this new nation.

Infuriatingly, the major seemed to be reading his thoughts. "I take your silence as affirmation. It seems that, as an Irishman, you are fully aware of the complexities of countries unburdening themselves from the shackles of an oppressor." The major, it seemed, was already a full participant in his potential senior military role in any new government that may be formed in the coming months. "It's true, you know," he continued. "I may finally become a big fish in a small pond after many years of struggling against a military elite who rejected me as an outsider. My only crime, it seems, was to have been born in India and not West Pakistan. Ironically, I may finally find acceptance among the Bengalis in the east."

After a pause, he struggled for words. "You know, I am glad the lady doctor escaped. I sincerely apologise for my actions. Yes, the fact that she was so confrontational motivated me to put manners on her," he admitted. "However, my main motivation was revenge against her father for his past actions. I told you of his crimes, for which he has never paid, instead gaining promotion, and moving in the inner circles of the military elite in the Pakistani Army while I floundered in the lower ranks. Hopefully, his role in failing to prevent the loss of East Pakistan will finally reveal his true allegiances and traitorous activities with Pakistan's enemies."

Shane thought for a moment before responding. "Yes, Major, I agree with everything you say. I am certain that you will carve out for yourself a prominent place in the new government of Bangladesh, the name of the country that, up until recently, you despised so much. However, as you observe senior politicians from Bangladesh and its neighboring countries, don't be surprised to see DaSilva hovering in the background, pulling those invisible diplomatic strings that will govern all your future movements. Both he and his beloved daughter have actually triumphed over you."

Shane walked away and left the man with these thoughts, concealing the fact that he simply wanted to crumble before the man in his desolation at the loss of Meena. He eventually found Monica and she handed him the ever-reliable hot cup of tea. Their eyes smiled at each other over the steaming cup. In the depths of her eyes, Shane could see a definite resolve making its way to the surface, through the obvious grief that had been threatening to overwhelm her.

Later, Abdullah's men gave them the use of a driver to escort them through the jungle and around military checkpoints on the journey to Meena's hospital, from where they may eventually be able to retrieve something of the lives they had been living before the tragedy of Meena's death. DaSilva accompanied them with one of the journalists Abdullah had left behind, possibly to ensure the safety of the Pakistani prisoners until the advancing Indian Army could process them as prisoners of war. He need not have worried, because his men were loyal to him and looking after the prisoners very well. This included Abdullah's insistence that they attend prayer daily.

They were glad to finally leave the garrison and wanted so much to go to the jungle hospital to retrieve Meena's body, but Abdullah had left strict orders preventing this. "That area is now a war zone, and your safety cannot be guaranteed," he said. Therefore, they embarked on another lonely journey. However, this time they were inundated with questions from Alicia, the journalist who accompanied them. She finally coaxed DaSilva to open up and give his thoughts on the conflict.

When he revealed his credentials as a senior officer in Pakistani military intelligence, she felt she had struck gold. He, however, immediately went into his media manipulation mode and Shane could not believe the slant he was putting on the narrative and the skillful way he projected the actions of the Pakistanis in such a favorable light. Shane smiled as she succumbed to the charms of a man well-versed in the art of political intrigue.

DaSilva managed to display a pleased look on his face as Alicia found a working phone in a small town on their journey to file copy to an editorial room somewhere, hungry for the inside story on this developing conflict. He had not managed to make an international call from the garrison and Alicia could only call her office in Dhaka and hope her story would be relayed to her news editor. This was a distraction for DaSilva that didn't last long before he reverted to a dignified silence, his jaw firmly set as he gazed out the window in a world of his own. He was immersed in memories of Meena's every interaction with her parents, and the blossoming of an intellect and beauty that had them follow compliantly in the wake of all her achievements.

It was certainly a shock when she joined the religious order, mentored by Sister Gertrude, whom she met at a conference exploring the role of voluntary doctors in conflict areas around the world. This influenced her to spend two years working in villages during the Vietnam War. The experience never dulled her passion but instead added an edge that marked her out as one of the leading war-trauma surgeons of that conflict. Her mental disposition on leaving that war-torn country was certainly compromised, but renewed contact with Sister Gertrude brought Meena to Switzerland for her religious formation and a time of relative calm in her life. The tranquil setting in the mountains healed the mental scars accumulated during the war.

A different type of conflict with her religious superiors ensued when Meena regularly went missing, only to be found working alongside an eminent surgeon and radiologist in the local hospital. Professor Dietrich delighted in passing on as much information as he could to this gifted young surgeon. The protestations of her religious superiors were always dulled by the professor's charms and finally, after two intense years, Meena was on her way to their missionary hospital in East Pakistan, under the watchful eye of her mentor and friend, Sister Gertrude. DaSilva could not have been happier as it brought her into his area of control. His position in military intelligence in the Pakistani Army enabled him to monitor her movements closely and attempt to keep her safe, reporting regularly to her mother in New York. Not an ideal situation, but one both parents could live with.

DaSilva was shaken out of his reverie by the sudden braking of the vehicle that announced the arrival of the jeep at Meena's hospital in what was his first visit. *This will not be easy,* he thought, as he dismounted and observed the somber mood of the others. The village was just recovering from the trauma of the violence perpetrated, first by the insurgents and then by the army, who had taken their doctor away. Monica went with the nurses, who greeted them to break the bad news. Shane instinctively knew that it would be a long night but still, both he and DaSilva were shown to separate rooms with shower facilities and beds with clean, starched sheets. Their driver insisted on leaving them to meet with other insurgents in the area while Alicia went in search of transport to Dhaka, feeling that the real action was now happening in the capital city.

Shane immediately thought of Hossain and hoped that they would never see him again. He heard crying coming from the quarters shared by the nurses and female hospital workers. He could only imagine the shock caused by the announcement of Meena's death. He couldn't figure out how they would manage without her. As he left DaSilva, he agreed to meet later and discuss their plans for the coming days. They would somehow have to retrieve Meena's body for burial and surely DaSilva would have his own family plans.

Shane showered, collapsed on the bed and fell into a deep sleep. He was surprised to dream of Amy and this simple interaction comforted and assured him that even this sad situation would resolve itself in the end. The self-assured smile on Amy's face was curious in the sense that this same smile had always preceded the fulfillment of her remarkable intuitions. Shane could only stare longingly at her retreating figure as it faded into the bright light that always accompanied her ethereal visitations. What was she trying to communicate to him?

Chapter 39

Dr Sarita should not be here in East Pakistan. She was a commissioned officer in the Pakistani Army. Her allegiances had changed in the past few months as the insurgency had taken hold and finally, she and her Bengali family were forced to leave her home and seek refuge in India. She found work immediately in a hospital in India and devoted herself to the care of the displaced citizens and refugees from her country, now referred to as Bangladesh. Nobody spoke of East Pakistan. Their hospital was the Bangladesh Hospital. When the opportunity came to form a medical corps to accompany the Indian Army as they invaded her former home, she set about the task enthusiastically. She was, after all, an army officer. In the recent past, a civilian doctor colleague had unwittingly referred to her as a 'deserter'. He woke up several hours later with a lump on his head and suffering from concussion. For days afterwards, the nurses wondered about the severe dent in one of their bedpans. No one ever referred to her as a deserter again.

It was a fact that if she were to be captured by the Pakistani Army, then they would probably have her shot as a deserter, so it may be prudent not to venture any further into Bangladesh.

She would establish her present location as their main medical facility inside the border and detail some of the doctors and nurses under her command to accompany the Indian Army as it ventured further into her troubled country. Her people had local knowledge, after all, and would hopefully be in the vanguard as they eventually entered the capital, Dhaka. Captain Singh assured her that when that time came, she would accompany them. He seemed confident that this would be a short war. All the signs were that the Pakistani Army was in retreat on several fronts.

After some initial success on the ground and in the air, they now seemed isolated and were surrendering in large numbers. Their supply lines from West Pakistan were severely compromised and the Martial Law Administrator was under pressure to start negotiations to end the conflict and prevent the loss of more lives. There was also tremendous pressure internationally to stem the tide of refugees fleeing across the border into India. Dr Sarita needed someone to lead her Bangladeshi medical team accompanying the Indian Army, which did have its own medical units. But it was important for her team to assert itself and make it clear to the Indian commanders that their soldiers were only temporary guests in Bangladesh. She went in search of Meena.

She was not at all surprised to find Meena performing surgery on combatants from all sides, with Captain Singh hovering in the background. He had just returned from the interior with several wounded soldiers from his unit after an encounter with a Pakistani armoured unit concealed in the jungle on the route his convoy was taking. He had to call in an air strike to deal with the Pakistani tanks and artillery. They were well dug in and very well trained.

Their fire was accurate, and his unit suffered several casualties. He was about to order a retreat when the Indian Hawker Hunter ground attack aircraft appeared and devastated the Pakistani positions. Before the Pakistanis could regroup, he ordered his tanks forward with infantry support and overran their positions. He only relaxed when survivors started to emerge through the smoke, their arms raised in surrender. He looked to the skies to once again salute his air force colleagues and realised just how lucky they were to enjoy air superiority over the battlefield. It certainly made a difference in this encounter. The outcome would have been very different had the battle been without intervention from the air. The tenacity of the Pakistani forces confronting them on this occasion had surprised him and he had a sense of foreboding about future engagements.

Dr Sarita observed a long line of stretchers and walking wounded with army medics from both sides tending to them. Her heart sank as she recognised some of the Pakistani medics who had been her colleagues up until recently. She could not afford to worry about their attitude to her. Instead, she concentrated on enhancing their field hospital's capabilities, even if that meant requesting the Indian commanders to retain the services of the opposing army's medics as their comrades were led away to captivity in India. It was also useful to have medics who could converse with wounded Pakistani soldiers.

She kept her opinions to herself, but she simply could not view her former Pakistani comrades as the enemy, while wholeheartedly supporting the establishment of her new nation. In her mind, she settled on the term 'opponents' for the moment, and this satisfied her mental processes as she tried to reconcile her present role with the distinguished career she'd enjoyed in the Pakistani Army.

Meena joined Dr Sarita for coffee at the army cookhouse during a short break. Working alongside Indian Army medics had its advantages, and receiving good coffee was one of them. She listened to Dr Sarita's proposals and readily agreed to her plan.

"Meena, I understand that technically you are a civilian and as such, you are free to avoid any danger. I will ask Captain Singh to accompany you to your hospital as soon as they have cleared that area and made it safe. The good captain seems to be very fortunate and has avoided becoming a casualty himself. It would be a great help to us if you could supervise the construction of a temporary extension to your hospital. This will simply be a replica of this facility with tents extending into the jungle adjacent to your buildings. I understand that the road near your hospital is full of fleeing refugees. If you could also extend medical care to those people, then that would assist the efforts of the local Mukti Bahini fighters to convince those people to return to their homes and villages. Hopefully, it will be safe for them to do so in the coming weeks. We have four of Captain Singh's trucks at our disposal to restock your hospital with medicines and surgical equipment. His soldiers will assist you and provide security from attack from any remaining Pakistani units in the area."

She lowered her voice before continuing. "I am aware of the way the Mukti Bahini has been treating certain groups and some of their activities are reprehensible. The Indian soldiers will prevent any retribution or killings of the Pakistani soldiers or civilian collaborators who have supported them. This security will continue until our new government establishes law and order in the cities and rural areas."

Dr Sarita asked Captain Singh to join them and reassure Meena that he would do his best to assist in this operation and provide security for Meena and her hospital. He seemed confident that the worst of the fighting in that area would soon be over. Meena hoped this was true as she longed to be reunited with her friends and colleagues at her hospital. She agonised over the fate of Monica and Shane and hoped they would have somehow made it to safety, and that the major hadn't inflicted the same trauma on them that he had planned for her. She desperately needed to contact her hospital, but the phones were so unreliable. She requested that she be allowed to deliver

Jagdish's body back to his family. The village was on the route to her hospital with only a short diversion through the jungle. Dr Sarita and Captain Singh readily agreed to this.

Meena resumed her work with thoughts about arriving at Jagdish's village and of how Sujata would react to the death of her husband. She fondly remembered their conversations after they had rescued her, and how Jagdish had remained so positive after suffering the trauma of losing a limb.

Chapter 40

Meena was astonished at the quantity of supplies destined for her hospital. The four trucks were full to capacity with all the equipment and medicines she had previously worked so hard to source. Even better news was that the logistics company of the Indian Army would ensure a steady supply as soon as the area near her hospital was secure. Meena rode at the end of the convoy in one of her trucks. Captain Singh chose to travel with her as she sat between him and the driver. He was commander of the convoy, but he had allocated command of the forward units, mainly comprising of tanks and armoured vehicles, to junior officers who were eager to prove themselves in battle. Most of the opposition had been defeated at this stage but some rogue units persisted in the fight and could strike from jungle positions at any time.

They continued unopposed for two hours until they reached the turn-off to the jungle track that led to Jagdish's village. Captain Singh ordered the convoy to halt by radio to the leading units and told them to set up defensive positions for the two hours it would take him to accompany Meena to the village. He took their truck and one armoured vehicle that had a heavy machine gun mounted on top as a precaution, to defend against possible attack.

This vehicle also contained Jagdish's body wrapped in cotton sheets. They soon reached the village, and the initial welcome was provided by the usual group of children running along beside the vehicles, reminding Meena of her recent journey on foot along this same road. Some of the older children ran ahead, and as they reached the first mud huts all the adults started to emerge. The older children had determined that there was no danger and were excitedly trying to tell the adults that the lady doctor had returned. The vehicles stopped in a clearing at the centre of the village, and the people watched as Captain Singh jumped down from the cab of the truck, soon followed by a lady in a saree who turned to face the villagers.

One of the ladies in the crowd fainted and the others chattered loudly as they pointed at Meena. It was hard to figure out the cause of their surprise as Meena went to assist Sujata, the lady who had just collapsed. Sujata finally awoke to someone patting her gently on the cheek. She eventually regained full consciousness as she surveyed the faces above her from the comforting arms of their lady doctor who had returned from the dead. Meena gently reassured her that she was very much alive but that they had very bad news about her husband. Sujata visibly tensed in Meena's arms as the tears rolled down her cheeks.

"Let's make some tea for our guests," said Sujata as she gently disengaged from Meena's comforting arms and rose to make her way to her house.

Meena detailed the men of the village to retrieve Jagdish's body from the armoured vehicle and they began a process that would start the very specific Hindu ritual leading to the cremation of Jagdish's remains. Meena knew that the men would immediately build a funeral pyre beside the stream and secure the services of their local Hindu priest to officiate at the ceremony. Together with their Muslim neighbours, the men went to the jungle to collect enough wood for the funeral pyre. It was obvious that Jagdish was held in very high regard by everyone.

Captain Singh ordered his men to unload two sacks of rice from the truck and present them to the village headman for distribution. They then sat in Sujata's house with her children, who were too young to appreciate what was happening; they simply stared at Captain Singh and at all the badges and coloured ribbons on his uniform. Sujata mentioned that she had known about Jagdish's death but that the villagers were unsure whether the boys who witnessed it were telling the truth, or at least that they were too shocked by the battle to be able to relate exactly what had happened. Her biggest shock was seeing Dr Meena, because the boys who reported Jagdish's death had been certain that they had seen the dead body of the lady doctor being lifted from the ground after the battle. Meena was happy to present flesh and blood for all to see and Sujata rejoiced that Meena was indeed alive. This somehow seemed to compensate in some small way for the death of her husband. Meena knew that Sujata was putting a brave face on things as she held her hand and that there would be lonely days of desolation ahead when the full impact of the death of her husband became clearer.

Captain Singh took time to inform Sujata about the exact circumstances of Jagdish's death and bravery, while Meena translated. He then gently informed them that they must return to their convoy soon and apologised that they could not stay for the cremation. Meena rose and hugged Sujata and promised that they would return as soon as the country returned to some form of normality. They left with heavy hearts and the only reason to smile was the sight of nearly every child in the village on top of the armoured vehicle, intent on pretending to try out the machine gun. They all scurried off as the engine started and soon they were on their way once more, with the children running alongside for as long as they could keep up.

Sujata ran from her house when she suddenly realised that she had forgotten to mention to Dr Meena that Nurse Monica and other people had been at their village looking for her. Her mind was so preoccupied with the thought of venturing to where her husband's body lay and all the procedures that must be followed leading up to the cremation. The men in the village would look after this strictly defined rite, as they always had. She could rely on support from all in the village, especially the women, and more importantly, she would not be left alone to grieve for her husband, whom she had also regarded as a dear friend during the eight years of their relationship. This tragedy had come just when they were recovering from the bear attack, which had resulted in the loss of his leg.

She remembered their constant heated discussions over whether he should embark on a fight as part of the insurgency, which would put him in danger and risk leaving her a widow, and their young children without a father. All her worst fears were realised. She also felt the extra worry of failing to tell Dr Meena that she had told her friends that she had been killed, based on the inaccurate account given by the two traumatised boys. It was pointless having one of the men run after the vehicles; they would surely be gone by the time they reached the main road. She sank into despair and looked towards the stream, where the funeral pyre was being constructed and the cotton-clad figure of her husband being tended to by the men of the village.

***

Meena sat back and retreated into a world of her own for a while. The only indication of what she was thinking of were the tears welling up in her eyes without actually falling. Captain Singh simply left her to grieve, not only for Jagdish and Sujata, but for all the deaths she had witnessed in her short life. For a soldier, death was fleeting and rare, and a consequence of war, but for a doctor, death and dying were constant companions, to be confronted every day without being overwhelmed.

Instinctively, he said without even thinking, "There is always rebirth and new life, Doctor."

After a few moments, she simply took his hand and held it tightly on the seat between them until they reached the convoy, and he once again radioed the lead units to move out. The captain didn't mind having his hand held but tried to look past the doctor to see if the driver had noticed this intimacy between them. He thought not and relaxed in the feeling of comfort offered by her touch.

Then, just when he was starting to feel comfortable, the image of his mother, aunts, and two sisters suddenly invaded his thoughts. He imagined the looks they would have exchanged with each other as they observed him holding hands with the lady doctor. Why was he suddenly feeling guilty under the imagined judgmental stare of these women? He convinced himself that he needed neither permission nor affirmation from them and jutted his bearded chin out in an unconvincing show of defiance. Encounters with the enemy on the battlefield seemed preferable as he tried in vain to dispel their image. It was not so easy in his patriarchal Sikh culture, the solid foundations of which were made up of women. He surreptitiously observed the hand of one of the strongest women he had ever met as it nestled delicately in his own.

Chapter 41

As they took their place in the convoy, Captain Singh's thoughts turned to home and to the most significant time in his life, when he had returned from the last war with Pakistan a few years previously. Just before that war, he had volunteered for the very demanding training that would lead to either acceptance or rejection into the ranks of the army's Special Forces. He left his cavalry regiment and, after the grueling training, he was finally successful and entered the elite ranks as a young second lieutenant.

He did not have much time to settle into his new role before the war started and he was suddenly dispatched on his first mission. His team was detailed to infiltrate their enemy's positions and destroy an artillery battery of three howitzers. Destroying these guns would be critical to safeguarding against an attack on an infantry advance planned for the following day. They easily evaded the sentries on duty and succeeded in disabling the guns. But during their retreat, they got into a firefight, resulting in the deaths of about ten ill-prepared Pakistani soldiers who were in the process of surrendering. They were obviously the gun crews who would not normally be involved in frontline combat.

He knew this but could not take prisoners without being discovered, compromising their mission. So, he ordered his men to open fire on these men before escaping back to their lines. His commander was very pleased by their success. Lieutenant Singh, however, was disgusted and traumatised by his callous actions. He requested to be transferred back to his own regiment, citing a preference to confront their enemy face to face and rejecting clandestine killing.

He had returned home on leave soon after with his mind in turmoil. Unthinkable for a Sikh, he had shaved his head and beard as an outward sign of the internal conflict he was feeling. The taxi dropped him outside his home in Jalandhar in Punjab. Nobody in the busy street recognised this clean-shaven, bare-headed soldier in uniform with the kit bag on his shoulder. Harveen and Jauna, his two younger sisters, were returning from college when they spotted this strange soldier on their doorstep. They both dropped the books they were carrying when the soldier turned to face them.

They immediately ran to embrace him, and the neighbours looked on in amazement as they too recognised him. The sisters shouted to their mother that Palvinder was home. Their mother, never easily flustered, managed to stay upright as he came to embrace her. Having observed his bare head, she nervously looked to their father's study, and noticing the women's concern, he straightened himself, looked at each of them in turn, joined his hands in reverence to their shrine to Guru Nanakji in the hallway, and then ventured into the room to meet his father. His father, a retired army colonel, who always conversed in English with his children, simply looked over *The Times of India* newspaper he was reading. "Ah! Good man. Welcome home!"

Palvinder immediately ran and knelt at his father's knee. "Father, I have dishonoured you and our family. I killed unarmed enemy soldiers while they were surrendering."

His father calmly folded his newspaper and placed his hand tenderly on his son's shaven head. "Son, I have every faith in you and the decision you took. I am certain that you had good reason to do what you did."

The three women stood silently outside the door, listening intently to what was being said. "Mother, we are going to the Gurudwara to pray," he said in a quiet voice, knowing full well that the ladies were outside.

"Palvinder, my son, it is so good to have you home safely. Come, let us go to pray and celebrate your homecoming. Jauna, phone the Gurudwara and inform them that we are coming," his father said, again in a very quiet voice.

"Yes, Papa," said Jauna. Their father smiled while saying, "My son, isn't the hearing capability of women amazing?" He extracted a saffron-coloured rumal cloth from his desk drawer and tied it on his son's head before leaving the room. "We will have a good chat about all your experiences later when we return home."

When his family exited the house, a crowd had gathered and started clapping in delight. Palvinder's closest friends had heard of his arrival and came to shake his hand and embrace him. None of them seemed worried about his head covering and bare face; they simply observed Palvinder's father, who proudly led the procession to the Gurudwara. On observing the well-respected figure, they simply deferred to the sanctity of their friend's family and proceeded towards the Gurudwara. Very soon, there was a crowd, with all the women of the neighborhood tripping over themselves so as to not miss out on this momentous event. Palvinder was adorned with garlands as the large crowd entered the Gurudwara, the doors of the Sikh temple always open, it seemed, to the spontaneous celebration and prayers of thanksgiving.

***

The captain was shaken out of his reverie as he stared out of the window of the truck with Meena's hand in his as he fondly remembered the celebrations of his homecoming that day and, more importantly, the overwhelming love of family and friends.

Meena noticed the tears in his eyes and wondered where his thoughts had taken him. She sensed contentment though and left him in peace as the truck made its way along the road, still crowded with refugees heading towards the safety of India. She understood their fear as she remembered her encounters with the Pakistani soldiers and was so grateful to finally be safe. She prayed that Monica, Shane, and all the people in her hospital would also have avoided the worst effects of this conflict. The solid, reassuring presence of the captain beside her gave her cause to hope for the best possible outcome for all of them in the days ahead.

Chapter 42

Shane observed DaSilva, who had retreated into a world of his own, staring at nothing in particular from an armchair on the verandah of the hospital. He had not been successful in phoning New York from the garrison. The phone in the hospital only worked intermittently, so he could not talk with Meena's mother. Even when the phone lines functioned, the Pakistani military in the capital Dhaka monitored all international calls, and the operators needed to report all requests to communicate with foreign countries. This was to control the flow of information from East Pakistan, which was still under martial law. DaSilva kept trying in the hope of getting a sympathetic operator who would risk connecting him with a New York number.

Declaring his rank in Pakistani military intelligence would only attract unnecessary attention to his clandestine activities. Shane could only imagine the turmoil the man was going through, not only because of his personal grieving process for Meena, but because of his inability to communicate with his family. The marital status of the couple was not clear, but Shane knew they would be united in grief, and that the inability to speak with Meena's mother would be hard to bear. Shane tried not to think about all the revelations about DaSilva's questionable military history.

He tried to see the human side of the man's vulnerable condition and recalled his own dark journey through mind-numbing grief. The grief was ever-present but somewhat diluted by the passage of time.

He then observed Monica and her total immersion in her work, and her refusal to countenance thoughts of rest or attempted sleep, during which she would be overwhelmed by feelings of guilt at their inability to protect Meena from the evil that had overtaken them. She had, nevertheless, taken great care of Shane and DaSilva, ensuring that she provided an outlet for them and others in the hospital to express their grief. To compound her emotional distress, Monica had also lost Sister Gertrude, who had been her mentor during nursing training, before she came to know Meena.

Monica had revealed in an unguarded moment how she had initially seen Meena as aloof and unfriendly when she first met her, until the day when Meena had embraced her warmly and thanked her for being so helpful during a particularly difficult delivery, during which they nearly lost both mother and baby. From that point on, they relied totally on each other, to such an extent that Meena had been giving serious consideration to sending Monica to the United States to study medicine, and hopefully, on completion of her training, retain her as a doctor in their hospital.

Shane made a pact with DaSilva to be supportive of Monica. They would try to encourage her in her work as she assumed the lead role in the hospital. They would reinforce her as someone who the workers could rely on for encouragement. In this regard, DaSilva was surprisingly helpful, and Shane assumed that his military background contributed to his ability to motivate the people supporting Monica. What confused Shane was this duality in the character of men like DaSilva and

Major Ali Khan. They were family men and interacted with society politely and courteously, but their belligerent nature manifested itself when the stability of society was threatened in any way. They would be the ones relied upon by society to confront those intent on destabilising the social order. Shane could not condone their excesses but acknowledged the necessity of deterrence in the shape of men like these, who were no strangers to enforcement tactics, by whatever means. He was trying to adapt to the complex nature of extreme events and the need for comprehensive evaluation before judging individuals. This objective reasoning was, however, severely tested when he remembered the actions of the major in his treatment of Meena and of DaSilva's treatment of Japanese prisoners in Burma.

During one of their meetings over their evening meal, Shane had delicately broached the subject of organising a memorial service for Meena. Both Monica and DaSilva simply stared at him for what seemed an age and just as he thought he had gone too far and with tears welling up in Monica's eyes, she suddenly took his hand and smiled. "That is a wonderful idea. I feel so ashamed; I had thought about it but I was afraid of how both of you would feel."

DaSilva adjusted himself in his seat and sat upright as he thought for a moment. Shane and Monica feared that he had taken offense, but they were relieved when he simply smiled. "That would be most appropriate. Meena seems to have regarded you two as family, so let us have a celebration of her life and give all the people the opportunity to gather in memory of someone they held in very high regard."

Everyone visibly relaxed, having made the decision to honour Meena. Monica agreed and Shane breathed a sigh of relief. Monica immediately took hold of the project and started voicing her proposals for the event. "Yes, we will have the gathering in the open area in front of the church. We don't want to offend the sensibilities of most of the people in the area, who are Muslim, by asking them to come into the church. I will have the hospital cooks organise food for everyone on the day. We can invite our priest, Father Anthony, to officiate and ask anyone who wishes to pay tribute to Dr Meena to say a few words if they wish."

She looked at DaSilva for agreement and they could tell from the sad smile on his face that he was more than happy with the plan. For once, they observed Monica relax and enter a new phase of grieving, an acceptance that she maybe could survive the trauma that seemed to have overwhelmed her in the past few days. DaSilva, for his part, was humouring them, having dug deep to feign enthusiasm, so that these wonderful young people should not slip into the realms of despair and absolute desolation he felt.

They planned the memorial service for the next day, late in the afternoon. All worries about Hossain and his men were dispelled soon after they arrived back at the hospital, when Sister Anna informed them that Hossain would no longer trouble them. "Yes," she said, "when the army departed with Sister Meena in the helicopter, the military ambulance arrived soon after. The two Pakistani medics loaded the two dead soldiers into their vehicle and were about to depart when Hossain and his men suddenly appeared from the jungle. He forced the two medics to kneel and ordered his men to shoot them. I ran forward and protested that medics are protected during war. He roughly shoved me aside and turned to his men, waiting for one of them to follow his orders.

"None of them would comply, and they simply pointed their weapons in the air. Hossain angrily grabbed a rifle from one of them and was just about to shoot when suddenly every weapon was turned on him. One of his men stepped forward and disarmed him, while telling him that they had had enough of his sadistic killing. They ordered the medics to drive away and assured them that they would be unharmed on their journey.

342

I thought they were going to shoot Hossain but instead, they escorted him to the main road, where they forced him onto a truck travelling to Dhaka. When they returned, they assured us that there would be no more trouble from them and they disappeared into the jungle, to the relief of everyone here. The man who had disarmed Hossain had apparently assumed leadership of the group. Before leaving, he briefly mentioned that the expected Indian Army invasion had begun and that the battle plans delivered to them by the lady doctor would prove vital in the military operations that would soon follow."

Shane and Monica had been delighted with this turn of events and felt safer now that the volatile and devious figure of Hossain was gone. Now, all they had to do was wait for the Indian Army to arrive and help provide security in this lawless country until order was restored. Meena's contribution to these momentous events was a sad comfort to them and was overshadowed by the huge void they felt in her absence.

Chapter 43

The convoy moved slowly along the jungle road. There was intermittent small-arms fire from small groups of Pakistani soldiers who had become detached from their battalion. When they saw the strength of the Indian force, they soon surrendered. Their officers explained just how precarious their situation was. It seemed that the local Mukti Bahini resistance fighters they encountered were not taking prisoners, so they were glad to be finally under the protection of the Indian Army. Captain Singh radioed headquarters to have reinforcements come and deal with the prisoners in order not to hinder his progress. This meant that they had to wait for at least three hours until the relief column arrived. He had to scatter the convoy's vehicles into the cover of the jungle when fighter jets appeared overhead. They witnessed a dogfight between Indian and Pakistani fighters, where one Indian jet exploded when hit, and the pilot ejected and landed close to their position. An armoured vehicle was sent to rescue him, and they returned with an Indian Air Force flight lieutenant. Both he and his wingman had just bombed the nearest Pakistani airfield, during which they were intercepted by four Pakistan Air Force Sabre jets. When he was shot down, his aircraft was low on fuel and out of ammunition and they had been returning to their airbase.

Apart from this setback, he felt that they were getting the upper hand in the air encounters. The overall situation, when viewed from the air, seemed to indicate that Indian Army units were advancing rapidly on several fronts. Intelligence reports suggested that senior officers from both sides were in talks, so it was only a matter of time until hostilities concluded, hopefully ending in victory for the Indian Army and their local allies. The Pakistani Army was in an impossible situation with all their supply lines from West Pakistan compromised on land, sea and air. Captain Singh requested headquarters to send a helicopter for the flight lieutenant, as he was eager to file his report and get back into the air as soon as possible. When the helicopter arrived, the captain asked the crew to do a brief reconnaissance of the road ahead of his convoy for any signs of Pakistani tanks or artillery. They obliged and later informed him by radio that their intended route was clear before returning across the border to India.

The relief column finally arrived to take charge of the hundred or so prisoners and escort them safely back across the border. These prisoners needed to be protected from attacks by locals who had suffered so badly at the hands of the Pakistani military in the past few months. Meena had treated their wounded while they waited and all she could see were ordinary, defeated men whose only wish was to return home safely to their families. They knew they would be out of danger in the care of the Indian Army, but their officers still insisted on leaving their names and family address details with Meena to be passed on to the Red Cross. The relief convoy had several journalists with them when they arrived, which meant that the Indian Army commanders were convinced the road was now safe and confident of eventual victory. They wanted to make sure their rapid victories were recorded and transmitted around the world.

It seemed to Meena that the war to control information was just as intense as the land war. She tried to avoid the cameras but was caught unawares on one occasion when exiting a field surgery tent that they had set up at the rear of the convoy. On removing her surgical mask, she turned directly into the camera flash of a lady reporter. Meena was too tired to be angry and was further disarmed when the young woman asked her permission to use the photo that would hopefully appear in her paper in two days. They talked for a while and without thinking, Meena let slip that she had been involved as a medic in the Vietnam War. This got the attention of the woman, who introduced herself as Vanessa. She begged Meena to be allowed to do a feature on her. Meena declined forcefully and retreated into the surgical tent to treat the remaining prisoners who had only superficial wounds.

Very soon, soldiers came to dismantle the tent and prepare for departure. It seemed that Captain Singh was anxious to advance at a quicker pace. The reports from the air force pilot and the crew of the helicopter made him fearful that they were missing all the action up ahead. He was now in the lead group of vehicles and Meena caught glimpses of him at the front of the column, ensconced once again in the turret of his tank. Her heart sank when she also discovered another female reporter with Vanessa in the back of one of the troop-transport trucks. She wondered why there were so many women war correspondents in this war. The reporters must have cajoled Captain Singh into allowing them to join the convoy. Maybe he too was conscious of the media war and eager to have his contribution recorded.

She could not blame a career soldier for attempting to enhance his reputation during the conflict, and press reports charting his achievements would do his promotional prospects no harm at all. Nevertheless, Meena vowed to have words with him during their next meeting.

They made two river crossings, and the local fighters proved invaluable with their detailed knowledge of shallow crossing points. They then encountered one bridge being held by several Pakistani tanks, much to the surprise and dismay of Captain Singh. He had been too reliant on reports of a clear road ahead from the helicopter crew. A brief skirmish knocked out one of the Indian tanks before the remaining Pakistani tanks disengaged and fled towards the capital Dhaka. Having seen the explosion at the front of the convoy, Meena borrowed binoculars from a young Indian Army officer and scanned the lead vehicles to see if she could see Captain Singh's tank leading the charge across the bridge. Her heart sank as she observed an Indian tank lying on its side in a ditch with smoke billowing from the turret.

She grabbed her medical bag, commandeered the nearest jeep and driver and demanded to be driven to the front of the convoy. She closed her eyes and prayed that the captain would be alive when she reached what seemed to be the lead tank in flames. She let out an involuntary scream as she recognised the familiar number on the side of the tank, and she got the unmistakable smell of death and burning flesh as she dismounted and ran towards a group of soldiers standing around a few of their dead comrades lying on the ground. She was also horrified to see the charred remains of two crew members from the tank. She burst through the group in a panic and nearly cried when she came across Captain Singh sitting on an ammunition box being treated by a medic. His shirt was removed from one arm to expose a bloody vest. The medic was cutting the vest with scissors to reveal several shrapnel wounds in his back. He turned to see the contorted, beautiful face of the lady doctor.

"Hello, Doctor. I suppose you could call this a million-dollar wound – serious enough to be sent home but not serious enough to cause lifelong incapacitation."

She visibly relaxed and even managed an agonised smile as a breathless Vanessa suddenly appeared to record the wounding of a hero. The medic removed one piece of shrapnel from the worst wound and declared the other wounds superficial. Meena agreed and prepared to anesthetise the wounds before cleaning and suturing.

"Thank you, Doctor. Please patch me up as quickly as you can. I have a battle to fight."

Meena looked skywards as Vanessa couldn't write fast enough to record his every word and take an occasional photo of the aftermath of the encounter at the same time. As she began to stitch, Meena vainly tried to convince the captain that he was going nowhere other than back across the border, by helicopter medevac if possible. "There is no way you can continue, due to a very real threat of infection, and we need to get you on a drip as soon as possible. One of those pieces of shrapnel came close to puncturing your lung, and I am worried about internal bleeding."

He was soon on his feet, buttoning his shirt and carrying the bloodied wound holes on his shirt as a badge of honour. "Seriously, Doctor, I will take it easy from now on, but I cannot leave the battlefield. Just before the attack, I received a radio call from my colonel to proceed to the area around your hospital and consolidate our position there until further orders. You can treat me further if needed when we reach there, hopefully in the late afternoon. I am confident that my junior officers will provide the leadership necessary to deal with any more encounters with the enemy. I think we may have seen the last of them. I am hearing from our local allies that we are massing on the outskirts of all the major towns and the capital Dhaka. It is only a matter of time before our generals negotiate a surrender. I will command from the rear of our convoy, so don't worry about these." He gestured with his head towards the wounds on his back. "I am sure we can find a seamstress to repair my shirt when we reach your hospital."

She turned away and suppressed a smile but when she turned back, the emotion of the moment overwhelmed her, and she placed his arm over her shoulder and helped him to her jeep.

It was difficult to know for sure who needed support most, but she silently prayed heartfelt thanks for his deliverance.

He seemed to have read her thoughts. "I am very lucky, Doctor. I had just jumped down from my tank to get closer to the bridge on foot to see the enemy positions with my binoculars when a round hit my tank behind me, killing all on board. I was knocked to the ground by the force of the explosion. I was fortunate that the shrapnel missed my head, and I was far enough away for it not to have penetrated more. Fortunate also to have the best doctor on the subcontinent to provide such prompt medical assistance."

He commanded the driver to take up a position at the rear of the convoy as, one by one, their vehicles crossed the bridge. Meena was glad to finally be going home, and she could not wait to hear news of Monica and Shane. Surely Major Ali Khan could not have been so callous as to have hurt them in any way, she thought, for the umpteenth time. If he carried out the threat he had made, then they would now be in Dhaka with him, safely awaiting the surrender to the Indian Army. She could not contemplate any other scenario.

Chapter 44

It was late afternoon when people started to arrive at the compound in front of the church. Each of them held a small earthenware lamp containing a folded piece of cotton in oil, which they lit as they gathered in the fading light. The setting sun was still visible through the trees and the area was soon alive with subdued conversation. It was the first time they had all come together in such numbers. It seemed to be not only the memory of their doctor they were marking, but the memory of everyone who had died in recent months. The smell of garlands and flowers mixed with the smell from the nearby kitchen, as children, oblivious to the significance of the event, ran through the groups of assembled adults.

The elderly priest, Father Anthony, chatted with those at the front. He interacted very well with everyone, and they all remembered his valuable service over many years. He and Sister Gertrude had been founding members of the hospital and school in the area and soon after they were built, the people started to build houses in the area, leading to the formation of several villages. Some people had taken to the road to India as refugees, fearful that the war would finally overwhelm them, but most had stayed and asserted themselves as a community, willing to confront groups threatening them in a countryside where the rule of law was absent. Thankfully, Hossain had been banished and his fighters did not appear as they all remembered the atrocity they had visited on the village nearest to the hospital. People were hopeful that the reports from Dhaka were correct and that the war would soon be over, and that they would all eventually be secure and safe under a new government.

Monica, DaSilva and Shane joined the people and Monica asked those who wished to speak to come to the front. The agreed format was informal and not particularly religious, although Muslim, Hindu and Christian prayers were welcome. Father Anthony started with a short multi-denominational prayer as he thanked the people for coming in such numbers to pay tribute to someone they all knew and loved so well. He mentioned Sister Gertrude and the tireless work she had done, which had resulted in the creation of this remarkable hospital. All of the people who had died during the war were not forgotten, particularly Lal's young family and all the other innocent children who had been sacrificed during the past year. He skillfully moved the conversation on from the pain of past events to an overwhelming investment in hope for the future. The noise of children running between the groups of adults seemed to reinforce what they all hoped would be a new beginning.

***

Meanwhile, Meena had asked Captain Singh to separate the four trucks destined for her hospital. She knew that the whole convoy could not descend on the area around the hospital; there was simply no room to contain so many large vehicles. He agreed and ordered the convoy to proceed and assemble on either side of the junction where the dirt track to the hospital met the main road. Meena was fearful that any vehicles approaching the hospital would cause panic among the villagers. So, she decided to go alone on foot along the same jungle shortcut they had taken with Keeler, which would take her out behind their church. The others agreed to continue with the convoy and her four trucks would wait for an hour to allow her time to prepare the people for their noisy arrival.

Captain Singh halted the convoy when Meena pointed to an area where smoke was visible over the jungle canopy about a kilometre away. She alighted and made her way to a pathway, barely visible in the undergrowth. She looked back and reassured him with a smile and beckoned for him to continue with the convoy. She proceeded through the jungle shortcut she knew well. After a while, she stopped suddenly and looked behind her and realised that she was being followed. She wasn't at all surprised when Captain Singh and Vanessa burst through the undergrowth, hot on her heels. Their innocent, childlike expressions made her laugh, and she gestured for them to join her as they made their way to her home.

Eventually, they reached the hospital compound. They entered the rear of the church through an open sacristy door. She led the way down the aisle to the front of the church, past the empty pews to the main doors which were slightly ajar, and through which faint candlelight could be seen and the soft murmur of people could be heard. Filled with curiosity, she swung the heavy doors fully open and emerged onto the front steps, only to be confronted by a large gathering of people holding votive lights as she came to an abrupt stop behind Father Anthony, who was addressing the crowd. The effect was electrifying as total silence descended on the gathering as everyone stared openmouthed at her.

"What's going on?" she said, and then nearly collapsed as she noticed Shane and Monica in the crowd.

Her sudden arrival set off a sequence of events that could only be described as surreal. The first thing that happened was that Monica dropped everything and rushed forward, nearly upending the elderly Father Anthony, threw herself into Meena's arms and squeezed the life out of her while emitting a joyful scream. Most of the votive lights fell to the ground as people held their hands to their mouths in disbelief at this apparition. DaSilva, at the rear of the crowd, fell to his knees and touched his forehead and outstretched hands to the ground. Shane's arms went on top of his head, and he simply stared wide-eyed at the two women embracing, eventually looking skyward at the few stars emerging in the twilight and saying a prayer of thanks for this totally unexpected deliverance. He felt sure that this was the event his wife Amy had been trying to convey to him in his recent dream. The women in the crowd finally started to sing a joyful song while clapping in unison; some of them started ululating, as was the local custom during a joyous occasion. Sister Anna and all the other nuns were on their knees, undecided whether to cry or pray.

Vanessa was on her second roll of film as she recorded this extraordinary event and Captain Singh simply looked on with his arms folded. He was sweating profusely and slightly nauseous. Meena could see this from where she was being mobbed and she suddenly broke away from the crowd and asked Monica to help her get the captain to the hospital. They checked the wounds on his back and discovered that the one from which they had extracted shrapnel was indeed infected.

While Monica cleaned and redressed the wound, Meena set up an intravenous line to a drip and administered a strong dose of antibiotics. They then wheeled Captain Singh's bed onto the verandah, where they could keep a close eye on him as they took part in the celebrations. DaSilva watched all this from a discreet distance as he meekly stepped forward onto the verandah. Meena suddenly turned to see what Monica and the captain were looking at.

When she saw her father, her hands went to her face, and

she doubled over, hardly believing what she was seeing. The few words he could muster portrayed guilt and resignation and apology for not looking out for his only child. He need not have worried as she stepped forward into his arms and wept uncontrollably. The tension of the past few days finally caught up with her and she offloaded all the pent-up emotions that she hadn't been able to properly share with anyone as her mind was suddenly overwhelmed by all the trauma she had recently suffered.

"Oh, Daddy, I can't... I can't..."

"Don't say a word, you don't need to say a word. It will all come out eventually, in good time. I'll be here with you, so don't worry about a thing. You will have my undivided attention. Now, can you please tell me where we can find a working telephone? We really need to talk to your mother as soon as possible."

Sister Anna mentioned that the hospital phone was only working intermittently for local calls and that international calls were still not possible; she had been trying to phone Germany to relate the tragic circumstances surrounding Sister Gertrude's and Sister Meena's deaths. Captain Singh and Monica had been silently observing this emotional family reunion. Meena looked at him expectantly.

"Sure, we can have a call relayed through our field telephone with our signals unit in the convoy." He made to get out of bed to organise this, but Monica and Meena restrained him. The arrival of the four supply trucks and a jeep with a young officer solved the problem. Captain Singh ordered the officer to take Meena and her father to the convoy and organise communications with Meena's mother in New York as a matter of urgency. "Doctor, Lieutenant Chopra will look after you and your father. It shouldn't take long for them to make the call. Return as soon as you can because I think your people are eager to celebrate your resurrection."

Meena and DaSilva departed in the jeep for what would

be an emotional phone call. The captain watched them depart with emotions coursing through his head that he had never experienced before. Once again, the images of his mother, aunts, and sisters materialised in his thoughts, each one again looking at him in expectation of an explanation for his fixation on this lady doctor. He was glad to have these images dispelled by the constant clicking of the shutter in Vanessa's camera as she continued to record the plight of her chosen hero in this war.

Thankfully, she had not heard him instructing his lieutenant to organise communications with New York. Sure, he would certainly facilitate her efforts at enhancing the reputation of the Indian Army in this conflict on the world stage. If that meant sacrificing himself to the whims of the media in this venture, then so be it. But it would be on his terms. When she asked him to sit forward in the bed to enable her to get a shot of a bloody bandage on his back and the drip attached to the back of his hand, he feigned pain as he complied. She constantly engaged the shutter release on her camera.

"Perfect," she said. Captain Singh suddenly felt a tiredness come over him as he lay back, exhausted. As sleep overcame him, he never noticed two nurses suddenly appear and wheel his bed back indoors.

Meena could not understand the wizardry being performed by the signals officer in the communications truck, but as she wore the headset and he flicked a switch, she could suddenly hear her mother's voice as if she were sitting beside her. A flick of another switch transmitted the voice from New York to a speaker. The officer left and Meena and her father were on their own. Meena had never heard her mother cry. The closest she came to crying was during Meena's graduation ceremony at Harvard. Now, however, she could tell that tears were coursing liberally down her mother's cheeks as she tried to express her absolute delight at hearing her daughter's voice.

"Mother, don't worry, everything is good here and Dad is

beside me. We can both hear you on the speaker. We are safe, and as soon as this country returns to normal, we will be on a flight for a reunion in New York. We have a lot of catching up to do." She looked at her father and he nodded in agreement. She knew that their relationship had been distant for the past few years, but they still communicated regularly, Meena's exploits being the common topic of conversation.

Antoinette DaSilva sat alone in her New York apartment, feeling guilty at the way she had tried to manipulate Meena in the past. She thought about her own college days and the academic successes that had attracted the attention of the United States Government's intelligence community. Her eventual seamless integration into these agencies ensured a life full of intrigue. When her relationship with DaSilva blossomed when they worked together in the United Nations for their respective countries in New York, her superiors were only too willing to exploit this relationship with a high-ranking Pakistani intelligence officer. The Pakistanis had felt the same; having their man in a relationship with a senior US intelligence operative seemed to guarantee a flow of sensitive classified information. Her eventual move to Abbottabad in Pakistan with DaSilva also presented her people with the possibility of regular intelligence reports from a very sensitive region of the world. Neither was clear as to who was providing the most valuable material as they both attempted to inveigle their respective nations' secrets.

They were both distracted when they realised that their marital union had produced an intellectual beauty who absorbed information at an astonishing rate and challenged their ability to engage in espionage while spending all their time feeding increasingly complex information to their child. Antoinette finally convinced DaSilva that the key to unlocking their daughter's full potential necessitated a return to the United States. She had been correct in her assessment of the situation. She thought of Meena's many qualifications and medical studies that guaranteed a meteoric rise in whatever branch of medicine she chose.

Just when everything seemed to be aligned and the plan for the future agreed upon, Meena came under the spell of Sister Gertrude, who seemed to motivate the young woman in a direction alien to her parents' plans for her. They were astute enough to recognise that frustrating her plans would only enhance her resistance to what they assumed to be the best career path for her. They felt certain that, given time, Meena would eventually revert to a line of employment more suitable to her obvious abilities and take up residence in her mother's palatial apartment in Manhattan. How wrong they had been. Meena knew that her mother expected only one thing from her father, and that was an uncompromising commitment to keep their daughter safe, and he solemnly agreed to do so. The past few days had severely compromised this undertaking.

"Mother, I know you have friends to call upon who can help you cope with the trauma of the past few days. We will call you again very soon. I love you both so much and I couldn't ask for better parents. Please get some sleep and rest assured, we will be with you in spirit." Her mother was a very strong woman, but she found it hard to find words to describe how she was feeling, so Meena ended the call and turned to her father. "What do you think, will she be able to cope?"

DaSilva too was stuck for words. He simply squeezed Meena's hand and then exited the communications vehicle and decided to walk alone back to the hospital. She could not have known of his shock that her mother had already received word of Meena's apparent death. If he had not told his wife, then who had? He finally accepted that her mother's intelligence sources in this country had been responsible. Antoinette had not been content to leave the welfare of her daughter to her husband alone and had put in place other resources.

On a professional level, DaSilva occupied himself trying

to come to terms with the fact that Antoinette's intelligence network consisted of a complex web of sources on the Indian subcontinent, which ensured her access to the most up-to-date information on unfolding events. She was responsible for advising her government on aid packages, so he understood her need to be aware of the most influential politicians emerging in this volatile region. He was saddened that Antoinette, whom he loved dearly, had been convinced that Meena had been killed.

Thankfully, the reports of Meena's death had been inaccurate, and this fact gave him further avenues to explore concerning the source of his wife's information. It was a sobering thought when he considered the extent to which her network reached into his organisation. He looked up at the stars and rejoiced at how good it felt to be back on familiar territory and worrying about normal espionage issues.

Meena didn't follow him, deciding instead to give him some time on his own. She went looking for the officers' mess tent. She knew that the officers would be uncomfortable admitting a woman, so she simply requested one of them to bring her tea, which she drank outside as she looked up at the star-filled sky while slowly walking home, totally absorbed in thoughts of recent events. In the darkness, she could see the figure of her father in the distance, no longer hunched over in defeat, but walking purposefully in the manner that she was used to seeing. She knew that he had mentally moved on from the trauma of the past few days and was now already immersed in devising a strategy to influence the developing political situation. She was so relieved that his normal scheming, devious personality had once more asserted itself.

On reaching her compound, the celebrations were over and most of the people had dispersed. She spent some time with hospital workers who lived in the nearby villages as they returned home. The shock of seeing Lal and his young daughter caused her to stop abruptly. There was no way she could bring herself to speak with him as she regarded the forlorn figure of the child with him. The trauma Lal had caused for everyone, and her in particular, was simply too raw. So, she skirted around them, agonising over the future of the little girl while consigning her thoughts to a possible future reconciliation with Lal. Not in the immediate future, she thought.

Meena then went to check on Captain Singh. He was asleep and looked comfortable; the medication she had given him seemed to be having an effect. She went in search of Shane or Monica and found both of them in the dining room of the hospital. Father Anthony and a few nurses who were on night duty were all about to leave. She hugged Father Anthony and thanked him for coming. She gratefully received his blessing before he departed.

Shane looked exhausted and Monica simply stared at Meena, still with a look of disbelief on her face. Meena sat between them and held their hands as if to reassure them that she had survived the horrible events of the past few days. She promised to catch up in the coming days and reveal all that had happened. She still hadn't come to terms with having killed a man and having nearly been killed herself on a couple of occasions.

"I really need to sleep in my own bed for a change. I am emotionally and physically exhausted. We can all have breakfast here tomorrow morning. There are a few very busy weeks ahead of us. We are to be the central medical facility for this district and will be responsible for all those wounded in battle. Hopefully, if the reports are true, the fighting will soon be over. We will also be responsible for returning refugees as their numbers grow. The Indian Army will set up their medical tents here tomorrow and provide security for us and the civilian population. It is still a very dangerous place, so we must be vigilant. Now, I need to lie down before I collapse! Goodnight."

She left and as she walked through the familiar corridors,

she was overwhelmed once more as she passed the area where the soldiers assaulted her and where Sister Gertrude had died saving her. Entering her bedroom was also an uncomfortable experience as she recalled Major Ali Khan shouting threats at her and rummaging through her belongings. The starched sheets on her bed looked very inviting but she could not stay here, at least not tonight. She quickly brushed her teeth and changed into pajamas before grabbing a blanket and making the short journey to the nurses' quarters and knocking on Monica's door. When Monica answered, Meena didn't need to say anything; she simply rolled the blanket out on the floor and collapsed into a deep sleep. Monica smiled and pulled another blanket over the prone figure and gently closed the door.

Shane had a lot of thinking to do. He could not travel because of the political situation so he resigned himself to staying here for as long as necessary. He wasn't so sure about returning to Europe just yet. He reviewed the past few days and concluded that he had been close to death more than once. Their safety had been uncertain while in captivity; anything could have happened in the presence of Major Ali Khan, who had been so unpredictable and volatile. He remembered Meena being offloaded by him during his fit of rage, and Shane knew that the major was fully aware that her life would be in danger when he handed her over to those soldiers. To think that Abdullah had enlisted the major's help was hard to comprehend but understandable when he considered that the new country certainly would need experienced officers, and the major had all the experience and ruthlessness needed to train the new military in the volatile environment of this fledgling nation.

On learning of this, Meena might not have been too pleased. War and conflict threw up all sorts of anomalies and alliances and Shane could only hope, for the sake of the people, that a stable, new country would emerge. In the meantime, he would try to contact his sister-in-law Maria, and hopefully persuade her to locate her aid agency in this area, ensuring a steady supply of medicines and food once the Indian Army had departed.

Maria would be relieved to hear from him. She was aware of the volatile political situation in East Pakistan and would be shocked to learn that he had crossed the border from India.

He thought it extraordinary that the three women constantly on his mind shared the same traits of feistiness and outstanding leadership qualities. Amy, Maria, and Meena could have been hewn from the same stone, and he dearly wished that Amy could have been here with Maria to meet Meena. He was certain they would have immediately bonded like triplets.

Shane was hopeful that Maria would at least consider locating her aid distribution centre in this area. He needed to discuss these options with Meena the next day. Her miraculous survival was the last thing he was thinking of before sleep overtook him.

Chapter 45

Meena awoke, simply because all the tiredness had been purged from her system. She had never felt Monica placing the pillow under her head as she slept. Monica sat cross-legged in her blurry waking vision holding a steaming cup of aromatic coffee, which Meena gratefully accepted while observing the time on Monica's watch, shocked that it was now the afternoon and that she had slept for so long.

"I brought clean clothes from your room and there's hot water ready for you to shower. Unfortunately, Captain Singh has discharged himself from the hospital and left word for you to commence medical operations immediately."

Meena arose and ventured barefooted outside wrapped in a blanket and into the early afternoon sunshine, to be confronted by a totally alien landscape. Her whole compound had been completely covered by army tents, some with red crosses on their roofs, and the bustle of soldierly activity indicated that this was now more than a medical outpost. "While you slept, it seems that Captain Singh informed his superiors that this would make an ideal command centre due to its strategic location. There was a lot of activity this morning, during which some general arrived for an important meeting. Just an hour ago, the general's entourage headed off towards the capital. "It would appear that a surrender has been negotiated and every Indian Army unit is now descending on the capital Dhaka, for the signing of the surrender papers by the Martial Law Administrator. Captain Singh seems to have ingratiated himself with the general because he rode in the general's jeep as they departed," said Monica.

Meena smiled as she sipped her coffee and said, "Was the American lady photographer with them when they left?" She imagined their dashing captain appearing in historic photos on the front pages of the New York papers.

"Oh yes, that foreign lady, Vanessa, accompanied them in a vehicle provided by the army for journalists."

Meena went to shower, feeling elated that finally the conflict seemed to be ending, and she prayed that the retribution that usually followed every conflict would be short-lived, and that the generosity of these people would overcome their recent divisions. She thanked and hugged Monica for looking after her before entering the welcome relief of a hot shower. The bruises on her body had now turned yellow and less painful. On removing the bandage from her arm, the wound from the burns seemed less angry and healing was progressing well. She forced her mind elsewhere to repress the traumatic memories, and mentally prepared herself for the new challenges facing them.

Meena was so grateful to have people like Monica to work with. She looked forward to long discussions of their ordeals during cold winter nights. Having dressed and welcomed Monica's offer to sort out her hair and dress her wounded arm, she ventured out to meet her hospital workers and the army medical team occupying the adjacent tented village. The first person to greet her was Esther, who had a really broad smile, only some of which was reserved for Meena. The reason became clear when two handsome army medics appeared beside her requesting her advice on setting up a special section for treating the increasing number of refugee children.

Meena returned the smile but asked Esther to include a monitoring program to detect nutritional levels in the children, knowing from experience that hunger, malnutrition and dehydration would be a feature in the treatment of refugees caught up in war. This also reminded her to find out the number of aid agencies in her area and from the Red Cross and United Nations, the quantities of rice and flour available to them.

While Meena slept, Shane had awoken very early and showered. He was eager to observe all the activity taking place around the hospital. When he went to the dining room, he greeted the night nurses, who were just finishing. He joined DaSilva, who was sitting alone at a corner table. DaSilva knew exactly what questions Shane had on his mind as they sat facing each other over the breakfast table.

"What do you want me to tell you, Mr. Shane? That everything the major told you is a lie?"

DaSilva was a changed man, full of the self-assurance of a senior officer in the Pakistani Army, his whole demeanour transformed by the miraculous appearance of his daughter. Shane still could not comprehend the fact that an enemy general officer was sitting unhindered right in the heart of what had turned into the regional headquarters of the invading Indian Army. He could only conclude that the 'back-channels' manipulator alluded to by Major Ali Khan must be true and that the man seated opposite him was active in all the behind-the-scenes negotiations taking place around them.

Earlier, he had seen DaSilva talking briefly with the Indian general who had arrived that morning and he was scheduled to attend a meeting of other high-ranking officers later in the day. DaSilva had also spent a lot of time being shuttled back and forth to the Indian Army communications truck. Shane guessed that he was probably formulating strategies with his political superiors back in West Pakistan now that a surrender seemed inevitable.

Shane had accompanied him with his Indian Army military police escort on one of his trips and managed to get a five-minute conversation by phone with Maria, who had been so surprised and relieved to hear from him. She promised to locate her aid operation as near to the hospital as possible and was glad to have a location with a formal structure in place.

Before the brief conversation ended, he assured her that he would have the hospital director, Dr Meena, contact her directly. They both agreed that this would be soon now that hostilities had more or less ceased. He was so relieved to finally have a conversation with Maria and they both looked forward to meeting again in the coming days. He acknowledged to Maria that she was his essential anchor who sustained him during his grieving process.

DaSilva asked, "Do you want me to admit to mistreating all my Japanese prisoners in Burma during the war, as the major suggested? Please understand that our orders were to capture them so that our intelligence people could interrogate them. Do you have any idea how hard it would have been to first capture and then transport so many prisoners through hostile jungle terrain with their army still trying to ambush us, and even targeting the prisoners for dishonouring their Emperor by surrendering in the first place? They were also starving, and we had no food ourselves for the three-day journey back to our base. And remember, their officers had absolutely no respect for the Geneva Convention. You only need to consider their treatment of the prisoners they took after the fall of Singapore. We all had friends among those who died of starvation in the inhumane conditions they were subjected to during their captivity and the subsequent forced labour during the construction of the Burma railway.

"So, please don't ask me to be more explicit about the difficult choices we had to make during the horrific events of that war. Both the major and I were twenty-two years old then. What were you and your friends doing at that age? So yes, Major Ali Khan and I go way back. We were junior officers together during that time and quite frankly, we never liked each other. But I can tell you this in all honesty: there is no one I would rather have covering my back in battle than that man. He never told you that during Pakistan's last war with India a few years ago in '65, he was captured by the Indian Army. While he and his fellow officers were being transported by train to a prisoner-of-war camp near Delhi, he managed to escape in a rural area during one of the many stops. Because he is from Bihar in India, he was able to blend into his surroundings very well and passed himself off as a farm manager returning to his hometown in Bihar. This was plausible enough during that time because it is common for such men to follow the work as contractors all over north India.

"He was a lieutenant colonel of infantry, and he had his uniform secreted in his belongings. Through sheer resourcefulness, he managed to not only obtain civilian clothes but also enough money and food for his journey to relatives in Bihar. Trying to return to West Pakistan was out of the question due to the heightened security at the border during that war. His relatives in Bihar were shocked to see him when he eventually arrived at their door. They knew he was a high-ranking officer in the Pakistani Army, so they needed to hide him for a few weeks and formulate a plan.

"They finally agreed that two of his cousins would accompany him to a town close to the border with East Pakistan and seek out some tribal people who had villages on both sides of the Border. They knew all the jungle paths between the two countries. Both governments tended to leave the people from these tribes alone due to their violent tendencies focused on governing themselves. The plan worked perfectly and the major bid farewell to his cousins and set off to the border with his tribal guides. After walking in the darkness for what seemed like ages, he finally asked them how much longer it would take to reach the border. The oldest man in the group made a comment and all the other men laughed. Eventually, a young man who could speak some English informed him that they had crossed the border two hours earlier, and not only that, but very soon they would part company at a main road adjacent to a military training school. Still in a state of shock, he bid farewell to them and offered them what money he had, which they had refused to take as they continued in great spirits on their journey. He would always remember with fondness those men from the Khasi tribe who had helped him gain his freedom.

"Within sight of the military camp and in the cover of the jungle he extracted his army uniform from his backpack and straightened his battered army cap as best he could, and, with as much authority as he could muster, marched towards the sentries at the main gate of the army training school. Due to the ongoing war, all the soldiers he encountered were in full battle dress. While the sentries came to rigid attention at the unexpected arrival of a lieutenant colonel, the officer on duty merely saluted half-heartedly and immediately phoned his superior.

"A military-police vehicle soon arrived, and the major was escorted to a room, where he was left alone with a bottle of water for six hours. It was late afternoon when the camp superintendent arrived with four military police, and promptly stripped him of all insignia and arrested him for desertion in the face of the enemy. Despite his protestations, he was then transported to a military prison, where he spent the next six weeks. All appeals were futile and the hostility he experienced from his fellow officers took its toll on his mental health. Just as he was about to face a court martial with a predictable outcome, he was finally offered a lifeline from an unexpected source.

"The major's file crossed my desk over a thousand miles

away in West Pakistan. I could not believe what he had been through and all the charges he was facing. All such files passed through my section in army intelligence so that we could evaluate the implications of each case and ascertain whether aspects of the case could be exploited by us in any way. It put me in a position of power over a man for whom I had no feelings, one way or another, but I can tell you now, I was determined to help this fine soldier in whatever way I could. I immediately set about compiling all the battle reports from the engagement with the Indian Army, during which he had been captured. His headquarters had been overrun during the battle, but he had personally taken command of a mortar platoon, and through inspired leadership they had inflicted significant losses on the enemy. These reports had been difficult to find, and I suspected that officers from West Pakistan had buried them because he was an outsider from Bihar in India and his surrender had humiliated their army – which was all nonsense, of course.

"I dug deeper and, through clandestine contacts with my sources in Delhi, I found out that the Indian Army battle reports for that encounter mentioned the capture of several officers who did not put up any resistance when their headquarters had been overrun. However, the actions of one senior officer commanding infantry and three heavy mortars had put up stiff resistance for several hours, resulting in two Indian Army tanks being destroyed and the deaths of twelve Indian soldiers. Lieutenant Colonel Ali Khan had been forced to surrender only because they had run out of ammunition.

"With great difficulty, because of the ongoing war, we managed to get word to the officer in charge of his defense on the day of his court martial. The proceedings were adjourned until all the facts could be verified. The poor man had to spend two more weeks under arrest while all the reports were cross-checked by the officer prosecuting. The man was finally exonerated, and a verbal apology was given. But the strange thing was that all traces of paperwork relating to the court martial disappeared. His status and rank were eventually restored, and he was freed. However, the hostility continued and after the war between India and Pakistan had ended in an uneasy truce, he was refused leave to return to his family in West Pakistan. Instead, he was put in charge of reorganizing border security in East Pakistan, at a time when the Indian Army was still making its presence felt along its extensive frontier with East Pakistan. He was subsequently demoted to major for insubordination but that's another story. As you can see, the major has had a checkered career. I am not privy to Mr. Abdullah's thinking when he selected the major for a leadership role in their new government. It would, however, be naïve of me to think that Abdullah was not in full possession of all these facts before he considered the major for inclusion in the command structure of the new Bangladesh security services."

Shane had been listening, wide-eyed, to the exploits of the man who had caused such trauma to himself, Meena and Monica. He mentally tried to rationalise the man's actions in callously shooting down a defenseless Indian helicopter. Nobody could argue that both Keeler and the crew of the helicopter were enemy combatants operating on the sovereign territory of East Pakistan when no declaration of war had been issued.

What could not be forgotten was the terror he had inflicted on an innocent woman by orchestrating Meena's abduction, knowing full well that she would not survive the encounter. It was this action that made his mind up about how he felt about the fate of Major Ali Khan. It would be up to Meena to pursue the issue with Abdullah if she should ever meet that honourable gentleman in the future. He thought about discussing options concerning the major with DaSilva but finally decided against it. Instead, he stood and shook hands with DaSilva.

"That's a fascinating story, sir. Doctor Meena has so much to discuss with you. I can't relate to you just how relieved we all are to have her safely back with us. I'm sure you and your family will be shocked when you hear what she has been through in the past few days. Don't be surprised if she refuses to discuss her horrific ordeals with you. I get the impression that she lives for the present and plans meticulously for the future. I don't think she dwells on past events; she simply seems intent on learning from them and moving on."

He watched DaSilva leaving to continue his subversive role as a shadow man. It was the most accurate description he could apply to him. His shadows of intrigue reached deep into the corridors of power in many countries. No matter the level of hostilities among nations there would always be DaSilva-type characters infiltrating, corrupting and intimidating powerful figures to seek negotiating advantage for their governments in world politics. How could anyone judge men like the major and DaSilva, when their ethical foundation was forged during the unbelievable horrors of war in the Burmese jungle as officers barely into their twenties? Shane found it troubling that he could so easily fall into the trap of rationalising war crimes committed by both men. Dejectedly, he went looking for Monica to offer help in the hospital.

The number of wounded soldiers had decreased significantly but refugees were showing up in increasing numbers. Representatives from the Red Cross and the United Nations were establishing bases nearby. He would attempt to contact Maria again later to update her on the situation. She had hinted at retaining his services as a ground coordinator for distributing the twenty tons of foreign supplies already in transit to Calcutta Airport. She would arrive soon and the plan was for them to secure transport and the necessary permits for crossing the border with the consignment into the new state of Bangladesh. Shane knew Meena would have expertise in this area and they could discuss options in the evening. He presumed she was still sleeping and smiled to himself at his irritability at not seeing her.

Chapter 46

Captain Singh arrived just before sundown in a flurry of activity. Meena and Shane observed his arrival as they sat on the verandah of the hospital. He immediately sought out Meena and mounted the steps of the verandah two at a time. If his wounds were bothering him, then the pain was disguised by his euphoria and his almost childlike excitement while trying to contain his news. Before he could utter a word, Meena deflated his ego straight away with a curt reprimand.

"I don't remember discharging you from the hospital."

He slumped, deflated, but pressed on, nonetheless. "Oh, that… yes, I decided to discharge myself due to pressing military matters and…"

"Where's your girlfriend?" said Meena, before he could continue. Shane could recognise what she was doing and noticed her struggling to contain a smile.

"My girlfriend? Who…?" said the captain.

"Your personal journalist from New York," said Meena.

"Oh yes, that lady. She stayed with the general during the surrender ceremony," he said uncomfortably. He dismissed such trivia and proclaimed his good news. "Yes, it's official, the

Pakistani forces have surrendered," he said triumphantly. "The war is over, and this paves the way for the formal process leading to the formation of Bangladesh as a country in the community of nations. It is really exciting to be involved in this extraordinary event."

Shane stood and warmly congratulated the captain and complimented him on the part he had played in achieving the victory.

The captain continued, "I have also been promoted to the rank of major. It seems that my actions in the past week have not gone unnoticed by my superiors." Meena could contain her haughty, disinterested demeanour no longer. She stood and warmly embraced him, then invited him to sit and have a celebratory cup of tea.

"We are so proud of you, Captain – sorry, Major! – and so glad that there will be no more fighting. Although, I fear that there will be a lot of local revenge and retribution before the country can return to normality. There have been many local groups supporting the Pakistani Army who willingly took part in atrocities committed against defenseless civilians. I hope they will be brought to justice by the new government."

Major Singh thought about this as he sipped his tea. "I am sure there will be a period of transition, and I presume we will assist in maintaining security during this process. However, we cannot stay indefinitely due to world opinion and the scrutiny of the major powers. They will be keenly observing the actions of India and our timetable for withdrawal. My orders for the moment are to enhance the security in this area and supervise the transition of power to elements of the new police force. Strange though it may seem, the new government of Bangladesh has appointed a former major in the Pakistani Army as interim commander of the new Bangladeshi forces responsible for security in the border areas."

Meena looked at Shane in shock at this revelation, refusing

to consider that the major referred to could possibly be Major Ali Khan. Shane said nothing.

Major Singh did not appreciate the significance of the words he had just spoken as he took his leave and went to confer with his junior officers.

Shane noticed the worried look on Meena's face, so he hesitated before telling her about his conversation with the major. He reluctantly related to her what Major Ali Khan had told him, including the half-hearted apology he expressed over his dealings with Meena. The colour drained from her face and she lost her composure, but only for a short time before recovering.

"Well, that makes sense. Although I have never met him, I can see that your Mr. Abdullah is a very astute commander, and will no doubt have an important role in any future government. You see, Major Ali Khan is a Bihari. The state of Bihar in India is just inland from where we are here. When the British left in 1947, the Muslims and Hindus formed their own countries, the Hindus in India, and the Muslims in West and East Pakistan. There was a huge movement of Hindus into India from the areas designated as West and East Pakistan. They wished to avoid living in a country that would have Islam as its preferred religion. Likewise, some, though not all, Muslims decided to move from Hindu-dominated India.

"The process involved much slaughter of both groups as they encountered each other while travelling by road and train. Muslims from Bihar moved to East Pakistan, now Bangladesh, and those Bihari Muslims have been persecuted by the local population since they arrived. Mr. Abdullah knows that these Biharis will have to be accommodated in the new Bangladesh, so he may have plans to have that man given a visible role to try to appease these people.

"It may be nauseating for me to consider, but realistically, there will be many compromises in the future before this new country matures into the secular democracy they are hoping for. Oh dear, sorry for the lecture. Do I see your eyes glazing over again, Shane? Now, please excuse me, I must get back to prepare the operating rooms for tomorrow. I hope you have a better understanding of the complex politics of the region and the challenges that lie ahead. And please, don't worry about my recent traumatic experiences, I have really good friends around me who will help me cope with any eventuality. Hopefully, we will never encounter Major Ali Khan again in the future."

The smile she gave over her shoulder as she left caused Shane's heart to flutter momentarily.

Earlier, Shane had mentioned that his sister-in-law Maria would soon arrive in Calcutta. Her aid agency had been active in East Pakistan since the previous year, after the destruction caused by the cyclone that had devastated the area. Meena had, of course, dealt with Maria when trying to source the new component for her X-ray machine, so she was delighted that Maria would be interested in setting up a base near their hospital. She promised to talk with Major Singh to see if he could spare two army trucks to collect Maria's consignment from Calcutta Airport.

"If Major Singh can have a general sign the release paperwork, then the material could be released without too much red tape from customs at Calcutta Airport. The military can be incredibly powerful during times of conflict, and we can take advantage of this. I will need to discuss with Maria the plans she has to distribute her aid, but I hope she is open to releasing at least some of the medicines to our hospital. Many refugees are presenting themselves with complicated medical needs, mostly related to hunger. Intervention, especially for malnourished children, will be vital."

Shane couldn't imagine their newly promoted Major Singh refusing Meena anything she asked.

Maria arrived two days later. Her entourage included two

doctors and several nurses. Their two jeeps had a military escort, including two trucks laden with the consignment from Calcutta Airport. Maria was greeted by Shane, and she couldn't stop talking about the ease with which they had cleared their consignment through Calcutta Airport. Shane simply smiled when he considered the influence Meena had over Major Singh. The major had apparently dispatched Lieutenant Chopra to Calcutta with military jeeps and trucks and the necessary paperwork signed by their general to ease the progress of the consignment through customs.

Maria and Meena eventually met and were absorbed in each other's company straight away. Shane felt that he was observing sisters interacting, as Amy and Maria once had. The aid agency's operation was seamlessly absorbed into the hospital's busy schedule. The medics fitted into the routine and soon they were also providing services to outlying areas as the country slowly started to feel the effects of a stable government.

One of the medics, Doctor Cosmina, was an eye surgeon from Romania. Meena was delighted to have a surgeon who could deal with the constant stream of people with operable eye conditions, especially cataracts. Maria announced that she had sourced the most modern equipment to help Cosmina establish an advanced eye treatment centre.

The other medic, Doctor Kamila, was an experienced pediatrician who easily fitted into Meena's plans for a separate children's unit in the hospital. They regularly assisted each other in the operating theatres. Doctor Kamila had spent several years training and working in London before deciding to volunteer as a doctor in the emerging new country of Bangladesh, where her family now resided. Meena was hoping to have these wonderful young doctors stay for the foreseeable future, to help build the hospital into a world-standard medical facility. Both Kamila and Cosmina promised to give it serious consideration. Because Kamila's family lived nearby, she suggested that Meena might like to meet her parents, and that she would involve them in her decision to stay with Meena in Bangladesh. Meena readily agreed and arrangements were made for Kamila's parents to visit the following day.

After lunch the following day, they all waited at the hospital entrance for Kamila's parents to arrive. Meena was curious on hearing several vehicles approaching from the main road, assuming that an Indian Army convoy was arriving. When several jeeps finally appeared from the jungle trail with the new Bangladeshi flag flying on their front fenders, she was intrigued and could not figure out what was happening.

The dust settled and a driver jumped from the lead vehicle and opened the rear door, and a senior officer emerged. "Come and meet my dad, Meena. He is the Director General of the Border Guards."

Shane had to step forward and support Meena as she was near collapse. Kamila was smiling as she excitedly escorted her father forward to meet her new friends. The man came to attention and saluted.

"Good afternoon, Doctor. It is a great pleasure to be here and finally meet the people about whom my daughter speaks so fondly."

Meena tried to maintain decorum for Kamila's sake as she shook the hand of the man who had nearly caused her death.

"General Ali Khan at your service," he said without the slightest hint of irony. "Maybe you would be good enough to show me around this wonderful establishment."

Kamila could not have been prouder as she linked arms with her father, totally oblivious to events of the past and the traumatic interactions of the people around her. Meena, Monica and Shane, for Kamila's sake, dug deep in an effort not to shatter the illusion created by this extraordinary turn of events.

It was Monica who stepped forward and said, "Welcome to our hospital, sir. It is such a pleasure to be involved in the struggle we are all having in overcoming the animosities of past events, as we endeavour to participate in the creation of a stable and prosperous new Bangladesh."

"Well spoken, madam," said General Ali Khan as he turned to introduce the subdued figure of Kamila's mother as she emerged from the vehicle in the wake of her husband.

Later in the evening when they were alone, Meena, Monica and Shane met at the grave of Sister Gertrude. Meena insisted on involving her mentor as they all joined hands over the flower-laden grave. "Let us all move on from the traumatic events of the past and not let them capture and corrupt our hearts and minds into the future," she said as their grips tightened. "Now, let's go and have dinner."

Politics did intrude occasionally as different groups fought for control of the local government. The Indian Army set a date for withdrawal as the area became more secure under the protection of the new local police force and Border Guards. They rejoiced with Kamila as she proudly recounted the frequent interventions her father made in this process. Certainly, the local population did fear the police, but crucially, so far they also seemed to respect them. It was hard for Meena to attribute these improvements to Kamila's father but instead, she adopted a neutral stance when discussing law enforcement in their new country. Objective reasoning and pious platitudes were ideals that deserted her when she remembered her traumatic ordeals in the recent past and the selfless bravery displayed by Sister Gertrude to save her.

Chapter 47

"Doctor, one of our girls in the kitchen reminded me that we are due to visit her village for the birth of Adiba's baby, which is due around now."

Meena stared at Monica for a moment before understanding exactly what she was referring to. She was shocked that they had forgotten all about Adiba but she still had the presence of mind to formulate a plan as she calmly locked the medicine room where she had been doing an inventory. "Monica, please assemble all we need for a section. Do you remember us deciding on a caesarean when we last visited six weeks ago? Also, we can take the two girls in the kitchen who are from that village. We can set up our operating theatre in a classroom in the school. Please ask Shane to get the jeep ready."

Meena remembered Adiba very well due to her disability. It would be impossible to transport her to the hospital due to the pain it would cause in her severely deformed limbs. Adiba was, however, in a very happy marriage and taught in the local school. It would be a two-hour journey and, with this event, Meena realised that her hospital was slowly getting back to the routine they enjoyed in the days before the war. They now had plenty of medical supplies, thanks to Maria and the continued presence of the Indian Army.

Dr Sarita's influence was also evident in the supply chain and Meena knew she could rely on her for emergency blood supplies when needed. Meena was hoping Dr Sarita would secure a top job in the new government, ensuring the presence of an influential advocate on health strategies in the future. She finished the tasks she had been doing and met with the duty doctors in the hospital to inform them that she would be away until tomorrow evening. Monica had already assembled their mobile surgical kits, ready for loading into the jeep. Shane appeared just as she was inspecting the equipment.

"Sorry, Shane, for giving you such short notice, but we need to visit a patient in Harinbari village, which is about a two-hour drive south of here, one hour on the main road and one hour on a jungle track that should be in good condition as we have had no rain recently. There will be four of us travelling with you and quite a lot of equipment, as you can see. They are quite heavy due to the batteries needed for lights in our temporary operating theatre." She smiled at him as they both remembered his last experience holding a torch in an operating theatre. "Oh, and we must also take a new bicycle we bought for the headman in the village, one of the diplomatic necessities in maintaining good relations with the village elders. You will also need your toothbrush and a change of clothes."

Shane didn't need to say a word as he gathered all the equipment to be taken to the jeep. Meena left to pack an overnight bag. She was happy to be going to a remote village where she knew the people would be untouched by the war. It would be a great distraction for all of them and the two kitchen girls Amira and Amal would be delighted to be visiting Harinbari, their home village. When Meena arrived at the jeep, she found everyone ready and all the equipment loaded. Some of the bags and the bicycle were on the roof rack and securely fastened. Shane was aware of the dangers of losing unsecured equipment on the uneven jungle tracks. Meena insisted on a prayer before departing. Monica and Shane were conscious of the negative, traumatic memories she had of previous journeys in their jeep and her need to displace that negative with positive, loving energy in the form of a prayer. Meena assured them that her jeep was capable of absorbing this positive energy. Shane simply smiled as he started the engine.

The jeep departed and negotiated the new track between the army tents where Captain – now Major – Singh acknowledged their wave as he consulted with a group of senior officers. It was early afternoon when they left the main road, and the jungle track slowed their progress significantly. They crossed riverbeds with only a trickle of water flowing and Meena revealed how the monsoon transformed these same rivers into raging torrents. Their new country of Bangladesh was mostly just a few feet above sea level and prone to devastating floods. They eventually reached the final river crossing which had a more substantial flow, with the water covering most of the wheels on their vehicle. Halfway across they encountered an island and Shane felt it necessary to engage the four-wheel drive due to a substantial climb on the opposite bank.

They reached the middle of the island when a grinding, scraping noise came from underneath the jeep as it shuddered to a stop. Shane got out and went down on his knees to find out the source of the trouble. His heart sank as he discovered the propeller shaft to the rear wheels sheared and resting on the stony ground. The cover that shields the turning shaft from dust and debris was also missing. Meena and Monica were soon beside him and he didn't need to tell them that this damage was not possible to repair themselves and that they would need help.

"If the shaft was broken at a joint then we may have been able to do a temporary repair, but because the shaft is sheared off, it will not be possible to fix it," Shane said, with a worried look on his face. He was wondering how they were going to deal with this emergency.

The ladies didn't need convincing and soon Amira and Amal were fully loaded with huge bundles on their heads. Amal informed them that their village was less than a half hour away, and she and Amira set off through the water to the opposite bank, with Meena and Monica following with bags over their shoulders. Shane was shocked at the pace of events and quickly secured the jeep and followed with only the bicycle to carry on his shoulder across the water. On reaching the jungle he demanded that the ladies offload some of the equipment for him to carry. They did not even answer and continued at a brisk pace. He trotted alongside Meena and pleaded with her to ask the girls to give him some items from the huge bundles they were carrying.

"Shane, they are village girls who have been used to carrying such loads from when they were very young. Please run ahead of them; we will all need help climbing down a bank into one more dried riverbed before we reach the jungle near their village." Shane ran with the bicycle and overtook the girls, and eventually reached the dry river. He climbed down the bank, where he rested the bicycle while waiting for the women to arrive.

The two girls arrived but waited to allow Meena and Monica to climb down first. Meena laughed as she reached down to take Shane's hand. "They are too shy to take your hand," she said.

Her hand tightened in his as he looked at her face while grimacing at the sudden pain of her vice-like grip. He followed her stare upriver to his right to see what had caught her attention. Her grip never relented one little bit as he froze completely, and all his senses dissolved through his feet into the riverbed at the sight of a fully grown tiger staring directly at him.

"I think he has eaten," said Meena.

Shane could in no way comprehend the logic of this

statement as his fight-or-flight instincts battled with each other to dominate his next move.

"His whiskers are red with blood, so he has just eaten. They usually avoid humans, unless they are very hungry or wounded," she said in a remarkably calm voice.

The tiger sniffed the air in their direction and then turned to spray the trees, revealing his gender as he marked his territory. He then turned and leapt into the jungle, disappearing from sight. With the noise of the jump, Shane got an idea of the weight of the tiger and all he could remember was the ripple of powerful muscles in his shoulders as the tiger squatted before jumping. Meena calmly urged the others to climb down the bank as quickly as possible, without revealing the nature of their recent confrontation.

"Monica, take my bags. Girls, move as quickly as possible towards the village." The girls did exactly as they were told. "Monica, drop the bags when you reach the far bank and run as fast as you can, and tell the villagers to come and rescue us. We just saw a tiger and he may not have left the area."

Monica did not ask any questions and took off in the direction of the far bank, hardly struggling under the weight of all the bags. She and the girls reached the far bank and disappeared into the jungle towards the village.

"Shane, we need to hold the bicycle between us and back away from this bank without taking our eyes off the jungle. We cannot turn our backs on him; he may be trying to circle around behind us. The bicycle will give us some protection if he attacks. Hopefully, the villagers will come to our rescue soon."

They must have presented an unusual sight, reversing arm in arm, while holding a bicycle between them. Mercifully, they reached the far bank and quickened their pace while still remaining vigilant, carefully scanning the jungle behind them. Soon, they heard a tremendous commotion from the direction of the village.

"Thank God, that's the villagers coming. They bang pots and pans together when they want to frighten off wild animals. It's usually herds of elephants, intent on eating their crops."

Very soon they were surrounded by about fifty people. One man detached himself from the crowd, relieved them of the bicycle and cycled around them twice before departing in the direction of the village with a big smile on his face; obviously, he was the headman of the village, totally oblivious to anything other than his newly acquired treasure. Shane knelt with his forehead touching the ground, with all the village children surrounding him. He looked up at their smiling faces as Meena detailed about ten of the men to go and collect the bags that Monica had abandoned at the river and the batteries from the top of the jeep. "They are all armed with thick staves and will be safe in a big group. The villagers tell me that our tiger took two young goats earlier this morning and that he has been hunting in this area for the past week. Come, Shane, let's get you to the village and see if we can find some alcohol to settle your nerves." Shane stared after Meena as she walked towards the village with all the children following her.

How can she simply brush off our encounter with death as if nothing happened? he thought as he dragged himself to his feet. He suddenly thought of the tiger and hurried after the crowd. He nervously checked behind him every few seconds as he observed the ten carefree men armed with bamboo staves heading in the opposite direction to retrieve their equipment. They were laughing and joking among themselves and didn't seem concerned about the tiger or any other wild animal they might encounter. Shane could only assume that these men were everyday hunters in this wild environment.

The reason why a caesarean section was necessary became clear as Shane was introduced to their patient, Adiba, as she sat on a bed outside her house. Her limbs were badly deformed, and her swollen abdomen formed the greater part of her torso. She greeted him in English, and he remembered being told that she was the village schoolteacher. They instantly became friends and he kept her company as the ladies set up the operating theatre in preparation for the delivery.

"It's hard to believe I will be a mother within the next few hours," she said, as Monica took her blood pressure and gave her some tablets.

"We'll need to keep you conscious during the delivery, Adiba, so Dr Meena will be giving you an epidural, so you will be aware of all that is happening. Your husband will be with you, of course. Now, ask your husband to carry you into the classroom in the school so that we can prepare you for the procedure. The doctor will talk with you constantly and let you know what's happening at every stage. All the signs are that the baby is doing very well." Monica's tone was so reassuring as she accompanied Adiba, as her husband carefully transported her to their temporary operating theatre and placed her gently on a covered table in what had been transformed into a sterile space cordoned off from the rest of the room.

Shane was left to wander around the village until Amal came to bring him to her family home, where he met her parents. Thankfully, Amal could speak enough English to keep their conversation going. She and Amira were fifteen years old and both of them hoped to train as nurses at their hospital. He ate rice and vegetables, and her father produced a small glass of clear liquid for him to drink. It was very strong, but it warmed his whole chest inside as he drank the full glass. It was a mistake. His host insisted on a refill. Less than an hour had passed when Monica arrived to invite them all to see Adiba's new baby boy.

The whole village descended on the school building, where Meena stood outside holding the newborn baby boy. She declared mother and baby to be in good health. Adiba would simply need some time to recover before Meena would let the villagers see her. Meena herself looked exhausted and asked Monica to find somewhere for her to change. Monica had already organised a place with a bucket of hot water and soap. Meena handed the baby over to his grandparents and she walked with Shane and Monica to the village well, where they relaxed in the shade of a tree.

"I will write a note for the headman to take to the mission in the nearest town, which is about a four-hour cycle from here. The note will ask the sisters in the school there to phone our hospital and ask Captain – sorry, Major – Singh to come and rescue us. He can possibly bring a mechanic to look at our jeep. We will be spending the night here anyway, and hopefully we should be home tomorrow afternoon." She took the bucket of hot water and soap and retreated to the house where she and Monica were staying.

The villagers carried Adiba's bed into the shade of the tree at the well, where she could meet with everyone. She was still hooked up to a drip but otherwise in great spirits as she held her little boy, whom she'd decided to call Naman. There would be a communal celebration that evening and already food was being prepared in large pots on a fire near the well.

As night fell, an air of peace and tranquility fell over the village. People were contented to sit quietly and eat their food around the fire. Adiba had been taken with her baby to her mother's house and soon Meena, Monica and Shane were left on their own, sitting cross-legged on the ground beside the fire.

"Shane, we will sleep in Adiba's house, where we can monitor her condition. You have a bed in the headman's house. He will be leaving for the town at first light with several others. It will give him a chance to enjoy his new bicycle. So, if everything goes according to plan, Major Singh should have our message before lunchtime."

For the first time, Shane had a chance to ask them about the work they did in the villages. Meena sat back against the tree and thought for a few moments. "Work in the rural areas is a sensitive issue, both in this country and in India. Because we are Christian, there is a suspicion that we are trying to convert villages from the more established religions of Islam and Hinduism. This is not the case. We do have a religious input in the mainly tribal villages, which are already mostly Christian. You saw in our hospital that we have Hindu and Muslim nurses, both qualified and in training, and they all partake in our village programs, whether the villages are Hindu or Muslim. Mostly we deal with health and hygiene, particularly among women and children, to try to remedy the horrific instances of child mortality. Also, we involve ourselves in vaccination programs, in cooperation with government agencies.

"Controversially, I have instigated a natural family planning program. It is controversial simply because other medical professionals doubt the ability of uneducated people to base their family planning on monitoring the menstrual cycle of the woman, rather than on contraception by artificial means. Surprisingly, our efforts are, so far, quite successful, and because the men are involved so intimately in the process, it seems to inspire an overall improvement in the welfare of the whole village. An interesting side effect seems to be reduced alcohol consumption by husbands involved in the process. The men also seem more likely to involve themselves in the welfare of the whole village by ensuring access to cleaner water, and by building schools and medical clinics. When the government sees such progress taking place, they are more likely to invest in these success stories and claim all the credit, which is fine, once the overall objective of better healthcare is achieved. However, we are not so naïve as to think that artificial contraception will not still be the dominant form of family planning for the foreseeable future."

"My wife, Amy, was so enthusiastic about natural family planning. Thankfully, her cycle was regular as clockwork, so she knew exactly where she wanted to be in relation to coordinating her hectic work schedule with having children. I'd like to say that I was a keen participant in the process, but quite honestly, I was simply an observer. She meticulously recorded temperatures, symptoms and cycles in her bedside journal. I think she loved studying the biological science involved and could not understand why couples resorted to artificial means of contraception when nature provided all the tools needed for effective family planning and birth control. Needless to say, she had quite a few sceptics in her circle of friends. If our strong and abiding love was a side effect of the process, then your theory of harmony between spouses using this method is correct."

A mischievous grin appeared on Meena's face as she said, "So, your wife did all the hard work figuring out the complex biological science involved in this process, and you simply waited for her to declare that the optimum time for reproduction had arrived, before dragging you kicking and screaming into the bedroom?"

Monica blushed and averted her gaze to study the blades of grass on the ground in front of her while thinking to herself, *How can this brazen lady ask such a bold, personal question of this poor man?* Shane simply said, "Exactly!" and they all laughed.

Shane then observed Meena for a while before asking a question that had been on his mind since the discussion began. "What about unwanted pregnancies? Do you carry out abortions?" He regretted asking the question straight away, as he noticed Meena's features darken and Monica once again looking away. He felt that he had entered into controversial territory. Meena turned to face him, and he could not prevent his eyes from settling on hers.

"Shane, let me tell you a story that will help give you an indication of how I feel about terminations. About two years ago, in Hili, where you visited, on the Indian side of the border, Monica and I were attending Mass when a little girl rushed into the chapel and insisted on me accompanying her to her house, where her mother was very sick. We knew her mother well and indeed, I had been wondering about her absence as she and her daughter attended Mass with us on most days, even though they were a Hindu family. I think she got comfort from it – not from the religious aspect of our gathering but simply from sharing prayer with so many other women in a tranquil environment. Also, she was a beautiful singer and knew all our hymns. The priest told us to go with the little girl, so Monica and I went to the nearby village where they lived. The little girl was her only child, and her husband worked in the border security force and was stationed near the Chinese border with India. He had not been home in two years and the suspicion was that he had another family in the remote area where he was working.

"We opened the door to the house and straight away, the terrible smell alerted us to the presence of severe infection. We found Preethi, the mother, lying on the bed in extreme pain and in a state of delirium, and in an advanced stage of sepsis. We were too late to save her and all we could do was administer medication to manage the pain and let her die comfortably. By then the villagers had arrived and stated that they had been unaware of what was happening. Monica waited with a stern look on her face, which left the neighbours in no doubt that she wasn't accepting this. Further questioning of some of the women revealed that Preethi had been pregnant and fearful of her husband returning home after being away for two years and discovering her condition. She had therefore procured an abortion with a woman in their village. Monica knew of this lady and had tried, without success, to have her prevented from carrying out abortions, due to the total absence of even the most basic hygiene during the procedure."

Meena looked at Monica before continuing. Monica simply nodded and Meena took a deep breath. "Preethi died that evening, and the villagers arranged for her to be cremated in the Hindu tradition over the following days. Immediately after

Preethi died, Monica left the house in a hurry, and I had to run to keep up with her as she headed to the house in the village where the woman who had performed the abortion lived. She burst into the house and confronted the woman in Bengali. I was not too knowledgeable of that language at that stage and could only guess what was being said. Monica was so angry that the woman's husband retreated to another room and eventually, after a lot of angry words, the woman produced a canvas roll from under a bed. Monica untied the string holding it and rolled it out to reveal a line of implements. I honestly thought they were tools that could be used for repairing shoes and I was genuinely shocked when I realised that these same implements were used to perform abortions. They were filthy with rust and dried blood was showing on some of them. I tried not to think of what Preethi must have gone through during the procedure. It was shocking for me, even as an experienced surgeon.

"Monica gathered the items together and took them with her as we returned to the Hili dispensary, and on the way, when we reached the river, she threw the implements in, one at a time. Almost certainly, one of these implements had pierced the wall of the womb, and possibly the intestines. This is common when the procedure is performed by such people. They don't realise that the wall of the womb is very fragile. It was late at night before I could eventually calm Monica down. So, to answer your question, since that day I have reviewed how I treat women experiencing an unwanted pregnancy. I do not perform terminations myself, but I will refer the woman to a reputable medical practitioner who will do the procedure in a safe and sterile environment.

"If a woman decides to continue with the pregnancy, then we will advise them of the many options open to them and support them in any decision they make. For example, Sister Gertrude had a list of hundreds of couples willing to adopt babies born to women who feel they cannot provide for the child. It is a complex issue, Shane, and one we struggle with constantly. No solution fits every crisis pregnancy. All we can do is provide compassionate counselling to ensure the best possible outcome for the mother and child and support the women in whatever decision they make. Our jeep is at the disposal of any woman or girl who decides to proceed with a termination, and we will also provide aftercare if needed, both psychological and physical. We are trying to improve healthcare for very poor women in crisis pregnancies who do not have access to free treatment. Allowing them to die as Preethi did is simply not an option for us, and we will do all we can to prevent similar deaths from happening.

"Everyone has a different perspective on this," said Shane, "but I would give anything to have my beautiful wife and son back. The desolation of life without them is intolerable. Both of you have done so much to ease my burden, and for this, I am really grateful."

Chapter 48

Meena and Monica left Shane alone to ponder what he had just heard while he sat staring at the dying embers of the fire near the well. The headman of the village came to escort him to a bed in a very cozy room in his house, where Shane relaxed and listened to the night sounds of the jungle surrounding the village. The women had explained to him the protocols for using the bathroom while working in remote villages–the bathroom, in this case, being the surrounding jungle. So, when the morning came, Shane procured the requisite jug of water and headed into the jungle to perform his ablutions. He was feeling very self-conscious as he observed the men lighting fires in the early morning light to cook breakfast before undertaking their journey by bicycle to town. He nervously squatted behind a tree while listening to the reassuring sounds from the village as he scanned the surrounding jungle for signs of an approaching tiger. He doubted whether he would even be aware of the approach of the master hunter as he stealthily overwhelmed his victim. Shane could only think of the indignity of such a death, while squatting half-naked during a bathroom break in this remote jungle far from his home.

Shane survived his early morning experience in the jungle and had a shower with freezing water behind the house while the headman's wife cooked a breakfast of chapatis and what appeared to be sautéed potatoes, cooked in the usual wonderfully aromatic spices. Both he and the headman's wife spoke for a half hour during breakfast in a contented conversation that needed no translation. The gestures and facial expressions were universal forms of communication.

Shane then went to help at the clinic, where there were a large number of people from nearby villages waiting for treatment. Monica was looking after vaccinations of babies with some of the local women they had trained in childcare and hygiene. Meena stood at the head of a long line of people wishing to see a doctor. Most of the ailments were treatable but a few cases needed to be referred onwards to various hospitals in nearby towns. She promised to send transport to bring the more serious cases to her hospital. The status of the hospitals in the capital city, Dhaka, was unclear due to the war. It was mid-afternoon when they finished, and Shane marveled at the energy of the ladies after such a hectic day. The villagers were so happy to be the centre of attention in the locality and eagerly helped assemble the equipment for their return journey to the hospital.

Just as they were discussing whether Major Singh would be with them before nightfall, they heard the sound of a helicopter in the distance. The sound receded after a short while, so they continued with their work, only to be surprised by Major Singh and five of his men appearing from the jungle. Meena instinctively went and embraced him warmly as he self-consciously scowled at his men, who were looking on with grins on their faces.

"We have taken your jeep back to our maintenance base in a sling under our helicopter. The helicopter will return to pick us up in about two hours. The pilot will radio us in advance so that we can assemble at the river where we found your jeep, ready to board for the journey home. My men will help carry your equipment. What's this I hear about you all being attacked by a tiger?"

Meena gave them the full story as they drank tea.

"Well," said Major Singh, "I suppose it presents some new, unforeseen defense capabilities of the humble bicycle." There was a sudden silence from everyone before laughter broke out all around.

He then revealed that the Indian Army had been given a definite date for withdrawal now that the new army and police force were established. The Bangladeshi government-in-exile and its leader, Sheik Mujib, would soon be returning in triumph, and the fledgling country could embark on the extensive rebuilding process needed to help the new nation take its place in the world community.

The radio call came to the portable field radio on the back of one of the soldiers as they heard the now-familiar sound of the helicopter, and soon there was a procession of villagers heading towards the landing site. Meena, Monica and Shane were nervous about boarding the big Mi-4 helicopter, which evoked painful memories of recent events for all of them. It had Indian markings on the side, and they were forced to remember the deaths of the Indian airmen in their recent traumatic encounter. They were glad when the helicopter landed on the main road near the hospital and an army truck picked them up for the short journey home. The efficiency of the military assistance shocked them all and Meena suggested to Major Singh that she could make great use of this helicopter, should the army choose to donate it to her hospital.

"Sadly, Doctor, our days are numbered here. We will be handing over the security of your new country to the new police force. Out tented city around your hospital will soon be dismantled. I am sure Dr Sarita will manage to retain as much material as she can, to ensure the best care for her traumatised fellow Bangladeshis. As you know, she is a very persuasive lady."

Meena was shocked to see Dr Sarita waiting for them as they alighted from the military truck. They hugged and Meena once again collapsed in another release of emotion. Monica supported her as they all retreated to the hospital for another much-needed shower and night's sleep. Before Dr Sarita departed, she promised to meet with them at a later date to discuss plans for healthcare in their area. Meena told her that she eagerly awaited this meeting as she had lots of issues to discuss with the doctor. She could not have been more positive for the future when she thought of all the benefits of having such an influential doctor in high office in the new government. For her part, Dr Sarita felt certain that the necessary resources would be made available for healthcare and that the international community would invest in the new country now that the killing had stopped. However, she was not so naïve as to be blind to the fact that powerful personalities may emerge with a different agenda, and that the welfare of the people may not be a priority for them. She felt hope in her ability to control the excesses of those people and prevent the country from descending into chaos once more.

Dr Sarita had, of course, reminded Meena of her counselling appointment with Samaya. Meena knew that this would be unavoidable, while accepting the need to exorcise the ever-present mental anguish that visited her every night. What was it about recalling traumatic stress that forced past events into her psyche in the quiet of the night? How was it possible for the tastes and smells to become physically present? In her case, the taste in her mouth of the soldier who had assaulted her manifested itself intensely each time she relived the events of that day. Maybe she could arrange for Monica to accompany her when she visited Samaya in the coming weeks. Meena knew that acceptance was a critical part of the healing process. She simply needed to prepare herself, both mentally and physically, for the journey.

In the distance, she could see her father talking with senior Indian Army officers. The behind-the-scenes diplomacy would, no doubt, continue as all the countries on this subcontinent sought to assert themselves in uneasy future alliances.

Meena unconsciously glanced towards the church and knew her mother's local informant would ensure her agency received an accurate account of all the political intrigue unfolding in this region. She felt the comfort of the security blanket provided by her father's presence. Her mother's presence, however, felt like an overwhelming embrace – always present, always watching.

Chapter 49

Meena knelt beside the grave of Sister Gertrude, arranging flowers she had gathered from their garden, which was full of newly blossoming spring vegetation.

"Thank you, Sister, for saving my life. Yes, for the time recently when you gave your life to save me, but also for all the times in the past when you were always there to support me, both mentally and physically. I don't think I could have survived without you. I suppose you had an idea that I was in the process of leaving the order and that I have chosen to embark on a new life as a doctor away from religious life. You know that I cannot leave this place, and I hope to work with the sisters here in the future. I will visit my mother in New York and catch up on some surgical training while there. My mother will want me to stay there, of course, but my heart is here in a way that only you can understand. And yes, I have an overwhelming urge to have children of my own. The feeling is so strong and has seemed to become stronger after my close encounters with death in the recent past. Do I have someone in mind to accompany me on this journey towards parenthood? Well, nobody yet, but I do have a few candidates, I suppose…"

Meena looked towards the sun setting over the hospital verandah, where Shane and Major Singh were laughing at something amusing in their conversation. She looked at each of them in turn and felt her heart beat faster when she considered the possibilities of a future with each one.

And Monica.

She said goodnight to Sister Gertrude as she touched the soil of the new grave and went to join her friends as they turned to her invitingly.

Chapter 50

Samaya
February 1972, Darjeeling, Northern India.

Breathing was not easy at this altitude. Two of the three ladies trod laboriously in single file for the last few metres as the mountain dwelling came into view. Prayer flags of every colour blew energetically in the stiff breeze all around them, providing a tangible link for the ethereal souls to interact with their worldly relatives and friends. Their elderly Sherpa hosts sensed their arrival and waited patiently for their guests. They returned the smile and wave of Samaya, who showed no signs of fatigue or shortness of breath. Finally, they all huddled in greeting and the visitors offloaded the gifts of bread and cheese for their hosts – and a bottle of whiskey, which caused the smiles to broaden considerably. The prohibition on the consumption of mind-altering substances had a flexible interpretation at these altitudes and in these sub-zero temperatures.

Samaya set about preparing their meal and the hosts relented and took their seats at the rustic table beside their guests with the open fire in the background casting comforting shadows on the bare brick walls of the dwelling. No names were exchanged. Names were a fleeting convention of little use here and best left to interactions among those who dwelled at lower altitudes. Samaya introduced the ladies by their occupation: doctor and nurse. On hearing this, the old man lifted a leathery, weather-beaten foot onto the table in front of them. Monica was not fazed by this in the slightest and extracted from her bag all the items needed to treat frostbite on his big toe.

Meena sat back and nearly smiled. Monica rejoiced. The hint of a smile may have been forced but it was a smile nonetheless, and the first she had seen since they had set out on this pilgrimage from their hospital in Gaibandha, at sea level, thousands of feet below. Certainly, all her trauma of the past few months played on her mind nightly, but the most recent tragedy threatened to overwhelm her. Not for the first time, Monica had been her savior. She had packed their bags, forced the reluctant doctor into their jeep, and had Shane drive them to meet with Samaya in Siliguri. Despite all the protests, Meena knew this journey was overdue and she tried to empty her mind of all the administrative and medical tasks that would remain undone in her absence. The death of her captain was a cloud that hovered over her entire existence.

She had not adjusted to his new rank of major, so the urgent call for her to report to the surgical tent to attend to a wounded major had not injected a sense of panic as she had calmly made her way there. A nurse met her with a surgical gown after she scrubbed up and ventured into the inner surgical area as she usually did, fully expecting to apply herself fully to whatever surgical trauma awaited her. The sight that met her caused her to freeze as she established eye contact with two very experienced army surgeons. Their arms were raised in a gesture commonly adopted by surgeons as they stepped back from their casualty when all their efforts were in vain. Despite all their surgical skills, their intervention had been futile as the terminal nature of the injuries overwhelmed them. Meena had been here before, many times. In the past, she had stepped into the breech and saved the day.

This time was different though. She looked down at the prone figure of the army officer on the table before her. His bearded, bloody face with long hair cascading over the edge of the table confused her as she sought to make sense of what lay before her. Realisation dawned on her with the intensity of a freight train hitting her head-on. Nurses supported her as she collapsed while her eyes were riveted to the eyes of the patient. She recovered and went to kneel before the figure of her captain as his eyes transmitted a non-verbalised message of regret and apology. How could she possibly respond with a message of reproach? All she could do was elevate her intense feelings so that all he could see was love and compassion. He could only whisper 'mother' as life drained from his face. She held back the scream. Instead, she stood and surveyed the horrific abdominal injuries that allowed no possibility of survival. She calmly exited the trauma-filled surroundings and wandered aimlessly until Monica was at her side, supporting her and leading her to the sanctuary of their living quarters. Two days of numbness followed, when water was the only substance that passed her lips. No words, no crying, no sleeping. Just blank incomprehension and inconsolable grief.

He had answered the call to lead a platoon of sappers to clear a minefield around a village where two children had been killed by an exploding landmine. As he had been surveying the area with his binoculars, his sergeant had stepped on an unexploded mine beside them, killing the sergeant instantly. Major Palvinder Singh Arora survived the blast, but the medics knew the extent of his injuries didn't allow for survival. One more day and he would have been on his way home.

His family came from Jalandhar to accompany him home for a military funeral. Meena hosted them at her hospital prior to their sad journey. His mother shared one of his letters. She needed to sit down as she read of his plans to ask Meena to travel with him to meet his parents. Tears flowed freely once again as she thought of the implications. Having met his parents and sisters, she was in no doubt that a life within this family would be most appropriate and in keeping with her fervent wish to start a family of her own. She loved the interactions she had with his father and felt that they would have been such good friends. They had departed, leaving a void into which negative feelings could have flowed, had it not been for the insistence of each family member that she should honour his memory by applying herself to enhancing the life of service she was so used to. She complied and shelved her grief, but it sat uneasily in the background of daily life, interrupted by frequent descents into despair and floods of tears.

Before the tragedy, everyone, including Major Singh, had been annoying her to advise Shane to ask Maria to marry him, since they had become inseparable during the previous weeks. Finally, she relented and did as they asked. Shane said he would. Maria said she would. And that was that. Meena then retreated from the situation, unfazed, muttering that he could marry whoever he liked, and that it was none of her business. Monica comforted her once again as conflicting feelings overwhelmed her friend. Major Singh seemed happy with the turn of events.

Monica finished the treatment on the frostbitten toe and sought a smile from Meena at the humorous incident. Meena's lips contorted into the semblance of a smile before returning to the neutral expression of those experiencing grief. Earlier that day, another event that elicited laughter was when Samaya had insisted that they both wear long johns and woolly socks prior to their three-hour trek from the Buddhist monastery in Ghoom near Darjeeling. Monica's playful teasing as they observed each other in the unusual garments nearly forced a smile from Meena. Nearly. Later, before they settled for the night, they had eaten the food they had carried with them, Samaya not wishing to deplete the meagre food supplies of their hosts, who shared their really tasty potato stew and refreshingly hot tea.

Samaya explained to their hosts that she needed to converse with their lady guests in English. He retreated to the fire and lit his pipe, and his wife contented herself with needlework as she repaired clothing. Samaya joined Meena and Monica at the small table. Samaya, in her maroon Buddhist robes, seemed impervious to the cold, but they were glad of the sensible additions to their undergarments. Their shawls and sheepskin hats enveloped them in a cocoon of warmth as the draughts of freezing mountain air entered by the leaky doorway and exited through equally porous window frames.

"Tomorrow, we have a final two-hour hike to Samatha Monastery. Don't worry, we will be skipping around a hill and remaining at the same level, so no more climbing, you will be glad to hear. Samatha is where students, mostly male and two female students, reside for six months in the final stages of their formation, before being transferred as teachers to monasteries around the world. You will meet four lamas who are their teachers, and who have been chosen because of their intellectual expertise in many subjects, and for their advanced state of spiritual awareness. Every religious person seeks signs and wonders to bolster their beliefs, and we are no different. The medium of meditation is, however, common to us all and central to our way of life at Samatha Monastery. Don't feel threatened by this, instead; use it as a tool to enrich yourselves.

"You are both aware of the term 'Rinpoche'. It mostly refers to an enlightened individual of high learning and wisdom, who has chosen to interact with us to help us on the road to enlightenment. Their exalted status among us is not to be taken for granted. The spiritual leader and head of our monastery is our Rinpoche. His formal title is quite long, but please understand that he is extremely holy and exalted amongst us. During the final stages of his formation twenty years ago, his teachers recognised his special status and undertook to return him to society to enhance his appreciation of all aspects of human nature. He worked for four years as a taxi driver and six years as an ambulance medic in New York city. This ensured maximum exposure to the most extreme aspects of human nature. So, he can recognise subterfuge and duplicity in individuals, even before their conversation begins. He also recognizes holiness and selflessness in people. He decides on the suitability of each student to progress to the exalted role of lama.

"You will both meet our Rinpoche when we arrive at Samatha Monastery. Meena, you will then have a week of sessions with me. Monica, you will join our students in the classes that I have selected for you. You will both partake in our regular prayer and meditation, which will involve chanting to enhance your ability to absorb positive energy, which will promote inner healing and enhance your spiritual awareness.

"Now, I mentioned signs and wonders earlier. You will meet Lynette, a fourteen-year-old girl from Canada. She arrived a year ago with her mother Rachel, who teaches our students English and music. Rachel is an accomplished flautist and her early morning recitals are haunting and conducive to enriching people's moods for the day ahead. The echoes of the flute in the surrounding hills and valleys are truly magical. Lynette had terminal leukemia. She awoke one night in their home in Quebec, having dreamed about Samatha Monastery and our Rinpoche. Her descriptions were so vivid that her mother immediately carried out research, which eventually led them to our door. Lynette is an only child and her father visits occasionally. She assumed a seat close to the Rinpoche and interacted with him in an informal manner, which was both shocking and amusing for us at first. She calls him Exaltè. Nobody else calls him Exaltè. They can sometimes be seen conversing quietly for hours, but mostly she sits creating beautiful pencil drawings of each one of us, and of the monastery and mountains. Her practically lifelike images of the Rinpoche are astounding. The most wonderful thing is that her cancer is now in remission. Our Rinpoche is of the opinion that she is simply a medium through which his predecessors communicate with him as if it's the most natural thing in the world. The reason you are here, Meena, will be revealed when you meet Lynette. Now, let us sleep."

They reached Samatha Monastery at midday and were warmly greeted by students who placed garlands of white silk around the necks of the ladies. They were extremely deferential towards Samaya, confirming her exalted status. Meena and Monica were shown to their rooms in the area reserved for guests. Meena was relieved to be able to discard the long johns and woolly socks before showering in warm water, which was a pleasant surprise. She then met Monica, and they went to eat, and meet everybody. Lynette's mother Rachel showed them around and they finally passed through the kitchen, where students were preparing rice and vegetables. It was the first time they heard chanted prayer before eating. They each held out a wooden bowl as the students served food from large pots. Rachel then accompanied them to the Rinpoche's quarters, with Meena's curiosity building as they met Samaya before entering. Samaya had been with the Rinpoche for two hours, so Meena had an idea that he would be aware of who they were and why they were here.

The Rinpoche sat cross-legged on a raised platform as he read a book on a slanted table to his left, with reading glasses perched on the end of his nose. He looked up and a broad smile radiated warmth, and his open arms beckoned them forward to join him on comfortable rugs and cushions spread before him. When they were all comfortable, he turned to Samaya.

"Bhikkhuni Samaya, you honour me with such precious guests. Dr Meena, welcome. Nurse Monica, welcome. I have heard so much about your many challenges of the past few months. I have no doubt that the peace and tranquility of our home will wrap you in a blanket of healing and return you to your hospital restored in mind and body."

"Thank you for receiving us, Rinpoche. Monica and I are grateful for your hospitality and recognition of the trauma we have suffered during the war. May I say that our brief time with Samaya has already inspired healing."

A curtain parted to their left and a young girl dressed in black silk pajamas walked in and took her seat beside the Rinpoche. Meena collapsed into Monica as she observed the composed figure of Lynette, her hands at her mouth and her eyes wide in shock. Monica tried to comprehend what was happening as she too observed the young girl seated before them.

"What's going on, Rinpoche? Samaya?" Meena looked at both in turn while Lynette simply smiled as her eyes never left Meena's.

Meena stared and tried to make sense of what lay before her as she took in Lynette's features: the fair hair tied loosely in a ponytail, loose strands falling over her left eye, the slight inclination of her head and the familiar smile that Meena knew so well. And the green eyes.

The Rinpoche and Samaya looked on, fully understanding the significance of the moment, while Meena tried to compose herself and make sense of this extraordinary development. Meena leant forward to touch the hand of the girl who was an exact copy of herself as a fourteen-year-old schoolgirl so many years ago. As their hands touched, Meena could feel the child that she had been, the mannerisms, the personality, the physical presence.

Samaya stood and invited Monica to join her as she took Lynette's hand and led them both out of the room, leaving Meena and the Rinpoche alone.

"Okay, Doctor, let's suspend logic for the moment. You revert to being a cold, clinical medic, and I'll revert to being a New York cabbie to see if we can make sense of all this. My cabbie persona had a world of philosophy to call upon that could probably have as good a chance of explaining what's happening here as any Rinpoche. I suppose that's why my teachers sent me there. Yes, Lynette is special in many ways, not least because she is transmitting messages from some past Rinpoche, whose identity I have not yet determined. I need to consult with people in our worldwide community, who are much wiser than me. Oh, and Samaya – we may give the impression that I am her guru and exalted teacher, when in fact she is mine. She is destined for greatness. At least, that's what the holy man of the past is telling me through Lynette. So, there you have it. Signs and wonders, as your holy book says. Now, Doctor, what's your story?"

"I'm truly healed of all my ailments, Rinpoche. I could go home now – as soon as the shock wears off, that is. Rachel was so convincing, pretending not to be shocked at seeing a thirty-three-year-old version of her daughter. Yes indeed, signs and wonders. Well, I'll be leaving the mysticism to you, Rinpoche, but I'm asking your permission to take that young lady with her mother to Calcutta to see my friend, Dr Sengupta. He is a world-renowned oncologist and he will carry out tests to determine the progression – or regression, hopefully – of her disease. They can then return to Samatha, because, quite honestly, she is thriving here. I don't envy you the immense responsibility you have advising her parents on the best course of action in the future."

"I agree, Doctor. Seeing the two of you together confirms my feeling that something beyond our comprehension is taking place here. I'll leave you to figure out its meaning from your perspective and I'll try to make sense of it all from mine. Now, go and allow yourselves to be immersed in a world of healing under the tutelage of the most extraordinary counsellor. We are truly blessed in having Samaya to guide us all here at Samatha. Don't expect an easy road ahead, Doctor, when you return to your hospital. That is simply not possible for significant leaders such as yourself. Try to interpret the meaning of the spiritual forces that have orchestrated your encounter with Lynette. Samaya and I will do the same. Your journey with Rachel and Lynette will be the start of a lifelong relationship. They will return here, I'm sure, but who knows how events will unfold in the future. Please visit us again, Doctor, and invite Nurse Monica to join you; I doubt whether you two ladies have a future apart from each other, although I detect a strong sense of motherhood in you. Samaya informs me that Nurse Monica displays all the attributes present in our most advanced students. But I'm sure you are aware of this already."

Meena's interactions with Lynette during the following week were enchanting, as they both took in each other's personality traits. Lynette wanted to know what had happened to Meena during every minute from the age of fourteen to thirty-three. The therapy sessions and the daily routine of the monastery had magical effects on Monica and Meena. A tearful Lynette could not let go of the Rinpoche as they prepared for their journey. Samaya accompanied the four ladies to Ghoom monastery in Darjeeling where they once again shed their long johns and woolly socks. Before departing for the plains below, Meena and Monica bent to touch Samaya's feet in a time-honoured gesture of profound respect. Thus began the next chapter.

Acknowledgements

The National Archives (London); Imperial War Museum (London); Indian Defence Review; Pakistan Defence Forum; Bangladesh Defence Forum; 1971 Archive (Bangladesh); International Journal of Orthopedic Sciences; International Journal of Radiology; Libraries Ireland. The writings of Anthony Mascarenhas. The writings and broadcasts of Simon Dring. The writings and broadcasts of Professor Bina D'Costa. Special thanks to everyone in Troubador Publishing for their invaluable help especially Lauren Alexander, Jonathan White and Sam Thompson.

About the Author

Sean C Ward lives on the Irish Sea coast in County Meath in Ireland. Having spent many years working as a commercial aviation aircraft engineer, he now spends his time writing, reading, cycling and travelling. He has a pilot license and a degree in theology. He worked as a volunteer development worker in India in the 1980s, where he gained valuable insights into the politics and cultures of the Indian subcontinent. This contributed greatly to the creation of *Niramaya A Female Medic's War Journey,* his first novel.